I0764770

An Opening of Heart

An Opening of Heart

STEVEN SWERDFEGER

Star Cloud Press
Scottsdale, Arizona

An Opening of Heart

Cover design by Trisha Hadley

Published by

~ STAR CLOUD PRESS ~

6137 East Mescal Street
Scottsdale, Arizona 85254-5418

www.StarCloudPress.com

ISBN: 1-932842-09-8 — cloth — $ 29.95
ISBN: 1-932842-10-1 — soft cover — $ 21.95

Library of Congress Control Number: 2005908828

Printed in the United States of America

for
Madeleine L'Engle

The Megafauna

The Cenozoic Era, which began about 65 million years ago with the extinction of the non-aviary dinosaurs, has sometimes been described as the Age of Mammals, owing to the rise of the now vanishing megafauna ("large mammals") that abounded on this planet until very recently. The megafauna included giant ground sloths that towered to 20 feet in height, the well-known wooly mammoth, the saber-tooth tiger, among others, including *Indricotherium transsouralicum*, a giant rhino that was the largest mammal ever to walk the Earth, and estimated to have to have weighed between 11 to 20 tons.

Page *Chapters*

Chapter One
Settling In

"DAVID, BOBBY—IT'S TIME TO GET UP," called Aunt Lillian. The aroma of pancakes and sausage wafted through the house as warm air forced from the furnace dissipated the chill of night. Midville had not yet faced a major winter storm and, as Christmas approached, the likelihood of a large snowfall increased significantly, for Upstate New York has witnessed very few green Christmases.

Bobby Perkins stretched and yawned. The night had seemed strained and strange, partly owing to his having slept in a different bed. Lumbering out from under the snug covers, he found the toothbrush and towel Aunt Lillian had given him the evening before and went to the bathroom across from David's room to freshen up.

David Andrews emerged from his bedroom, still groggy and half awake, yawning. He met Bobby at the bathroom door, suddenly blinking as if remembering a dream.

"Funny. I almost forgot everything that happened this weekend. It seems like a bad dream or something."

"I know my dad didn't mean to kill Max," Bobby nodded. "I'm sure he's really sorry for it now, too, now that he's sober."

"I know," sighed David, his eyes beginning to water. "Part of me doesn't want to go downstairs. Max always waited for me in the kitchen next to my chair, hoping for some handouts."

Bobby shook his head sadly.

"*Now* I wish I had given Max more treats," lamented David. "He was such a good dog."

"Can't second guess fate," said Bobby stoically. "Can't know how long anyone or anything's gonna be around."

David nodded somberly in agreement, brushing his hair in the bathroom mirror. "You know, you were right a long time ago. I *do* look like Howdy Doody, freckles and all!"

"Nah. You look more like the fox in Disney's *The Fox and The Hound*, and *I'm* a dead ringer for Hound, pug nose and all."

"Boys, I've got a surprise for you," called Aunt Lillian from the bottom of the stairs, "and it's not just this marvelous breakfast that's getting cold. I hear you stirring; aren't you hungry?"

Bounding downstairs, David and Bobby sat at the kitchen table, looking with appreciation at Aunt Lillian.

"Thanks for springing us from school this week," said David.

"Yeah, for sure," agreed Bobby.

"When I called Mr. Ferlinghausen and told him about this weekend's tragedy, he agreed that our settling in together as a new family is much more important than a week of school. He sends his regrets to you, Bobby, about your dad being remanded to the rehabilitation facility and, of course, to you and me, David, for our loss of Max."

"Bobby was just saying how nobody ever knows how long we ever might have a family member or a pet or a loved one," said David.

"And you are so right, Bobby," agreed Aunt Lillian.

"Now I wish I had offered Max a lot more treats from the table," said David.

"Max loved the treats you gave him, David, and you were very generous. The treats wouldn't have been as special to Max if you had given them more often," Aunt Lillian smiled.

"Those big brown eyes could wheedle anything out of anybody," laughed David. "Max was *the* supreme expert at begging."

"More than receiving food, though, I think he just wanted to be a part of the meal," suggested Aunt Lillian.

"I don't know," David smiled, "he was pretty fond of lapping it up. I appreciate the hundred dollars your dad is giving me for a new dog, Bobby, but it's way too early to think of getting a replacement for Max. I need to mourn for him. I guess I'm getting pretty good at mourning."

"It's been almost a year since your parents' death, David," said Aunt Lillian, "and any new loss must compound that devastating pain, and I'm afraid it will always be there. Time does help, though. At least, that has been my experience."

"I know. I just wish we had had more time together, all of us. Now with Max gone, I think of all the things that we might have done, but never will. My parents will never even see me graduate from high school much less go to college."

Aunt Lillian shook her head sadly as David stared mournfully at his plate. Studying David and Bobby intently, Aunt Lillian suddenly brightened, announcing, "I've got an idea!"

"What?" asked David.

"I think we should have a party," said Aunt Lillian.

"A party?" questioned David. "I don't get it. Do you, Bobby?"

Bobby shook his head.

"What I'm trying to say is this: let's be grateful and celebrate our having known Max for as long as we did. And yes, Bobby," smiled Aunt Lillian, "that your dad loves you, even though he may have shown it in destructive ways."

"I still don't see your point," said David, perplexed.

"It's as if we were all sitting here saying, 'Ain't it awful, ain't it awful,' when it's really only as awful as we choose for it to be. Yes, let's mourn, but more to the point, let's be grateful. Many children lose their parents far sooner than you did, David. And Max gave his life protecting us, which might well be the ultimate in love."

"But they're gone," remonstrated David.

"Yes, but we *did* have them, we *did* know them, we *did* love them, and no one can take away that relationship *or* that love. I can't prove it, but I do know with all my heart that Love is stronger than death. David, your parents and Max made the world a better place, and us better people. Let's acknowledge what they did for us."

"But how?" asked David.

"By forgetting ourselves and focusing outward, by reaching out to others," replied Aunt Lillian.

David and Bobby sat silently, contemplating those words.

"That's why we should throw an Advent party," suggested Aunt Lillian.

"An Advent party? What's that?" asked David.

"Advent is the church's liturgical season during the four weeks prior to Christmas. It is traditionally a season of preparation in anticipation of the coming of the Lord."

"Why not just a Christmas party?" asked Bobby.

"Because Christmas doesn't come until Christmas Eve. Oh, I'm sure we'll cheat a little bit and sing some favorite carols. With any luck, my fingers will be supple enough to bang out a few hymns."

"When should we have the party?" asked David.

"I don't know. What do you think?" replied Aunt Lillian.

"I really like what you said about looking beyond our own loss and grief," said David, looking at Bobby who also nodded his approval, "so the sooner the better. Why not this Friday?"

"My! That is soon!" exclaimed Aunt Lillian. "It will also depend on how much we can get accomplished over at Bobby's dad's garage today. I've asked Mr. Dewey to meet us to help us clean up and to get the place ready for turning off the water and heat. Bobby, we'll have to pack your personal items and clothes in my car and probably make several trips back and forth until you have everything you want and need over here."

"I ain't got many clothes, Ma'am," said Bobby, his face flushing.

"Please, Bobby, call me Aunt Lillian, and if you don't have sufficient clothing, we'll buy some for you."

"I don't have any money," confessed Bobby. "Pop was always broke from gettin' so stone drunk. We never had two pennies to rub together. The garage and apartment is one holy mess of a wreck, ready to fall down on any innocent passerby who might stumble in. Maybe I should look for a barrel."

"A barrel!" laughed Aunt Lillian. "Now, Bobby, where did you ever see someone wear a barrel?"

"In one of them old-fashioned movies, somethin' like the Three Stooges or Charlie Chaplin. Funnier than all get out, when they went about wearin' barrels for clothes. Must've felt a wicked draft in the wintertime."

Aunt Lillian and David laughed heartily as Bobby's deadpan expression broke into a smile.

"David, pour me some more tea. I want to share something with both of you to ease your minds about my financial situation. Anyone for more jam or jelly? I see you both did justice to those pancakes. More juice?"

Both boys studied Aunt Lillian intently.

"Mom and Dad always said you inherited the Judge's old mansion, but then you gave it to the County Historical Society. Is that true?"

"Oh, yes, my dears. I would have looked pretty silly rumbling around in that old Victorian castle. It could have accommodated three families, but it seemed a shame not to preserve it for everyone's enjoyment. At that time our local historical society was looking for a place of its own for its meetings. They had accumulated lots of antiques and other paraphernalia, but had no place to show them, so I helped them out."

"It worked out, then?" asked David.

"Better than I had ever imagined. The historical society has also opened its doors to a number of community organizations, including *Pro Musica*. The Judge's old mansion is now a real treasure that belongs to the entire community. It has even been placed on the national historical register of important buildings."

"I think it was neat you wanted to share it," said David.

"Thank you, my dear. I'm glad I did. David Louis, our family attorney, managed to save me many thousands of dollars in taxes because of such a large gift to a non-profit organization. In fact, I did quite well. But I haven't even come to the best part."

The boys were all attention.

Aunt Lillian coughed gently and continued, "Judge Biggs was a wealthy man, even before he entered the legal profession. Upon doing so, he placed almost all of his assets in a blind trust and simply lived on the interest. Over the years, that money kept growing. When I inherited it, it was worth quite a bit, even after estate taxes."

"Is that when you gave up teaching piano?" asked David.

"Heavens, no! I didn't care about the money. I cared about music. Music and people and laughter and reading. So I asked Mr. Louis, our attorney, to set up an anonymous trust. Each year I receive a check that gives me the supplemental funds I need in order to live here. The remainder of the money is given quietly, anonymously to various charities and arts organizations. Every so often, through wise investment, we are able to offer a generous grant or scholarship. But, believe it or not, money has a way of accumulating, and I am now in the fortunate position of being able to draw out a considerable sum. This will permit me to help you, Bobby, with new clothes, furniture for your room, all of that, if you will allow me to do so."

Bobby looked a little embarrassed and stammered, "I have no way to pay ya back."

"No need to pay me back, Bobby. Just help someone else down the road, and not necessarily by giving them material things, either. I will withdraw whatever funds we need to establish our new household. All I require is your help, your preferences, your choices, your decisions. I am also earmarking some funds for a very special Christmas surprise that I will present to both of you in exactly two weeks."

"On Christmas?" asked David, with intense curiosity.

"What better time for a *Christmas* surprise?" retorted Aunt Lillian.

"Well, it won't be quite the surprise it would have been," said David.

"How so?"

"Well, you shouldn't have told us until Christmas Day. Now we'll go crazy trying to figure it out."

Aunt Lillian smiled.

"Well?" said David.

"Well, what?" smiled Aunt Lillian.

"Well, that's not fair."

"The anticipation of a joy is part of that joy—I wouldn't want to rob you of the pleasure," observed Aunt Lillian

"Bobby, don't you agree that she's being utterly unfair?" implored David.

"Well, seeing as I'm the newest member of this family, it ain't right to voice an opinion one way or—"

"You're just a cowardly turncoat!" shouted David.

"Am *not*. I'm not gonna take sides, at least not yet," Bobby defended.

"Bobby's right, David. You shouldn't be asking him to side with you against me."

"Well, phooey. We won't know the surprise until Christmas. I hope you're satisfied, Bobby."

"Makes no difference to me since I never had a surprise before. This *here* will be my very first, and I *aim* to enjoy it, with anticipation, too."

David rolled his eyes and sighed.

"By the way," announced Aunt Lillian, "When I called Mr. Ferlinghausen this morning, I asked him to please tell Lisa and the twins all that has happened to us this weekend. No doubt they'll wonder why both of you are not in school."

"They'll be wondering how our Slave For A Day went. Nothing like they imagined, I bet," said David. "I'm surprised they didn't call."

"They probably tried to," explained Aunt Lillian. "After our brunch with Wayne, I was so tired when we got back that I remember turning all of our telephones off before taking that extra long nap. Remember how tired we all were?"

"For sure. I was ready to fall down," said David.

"Me, too," said Bobby.

"I remember you each fell asleep in the living room watching television, or at least the movie had run out by the time I woke you both up."

"Yep," agreed Bobby, "we were goners, all right."

"I doubt if we saw more than fifteen minutes of that movie," laughed David.

"Well, we really did sleep the clock around," marveled David. "What time is it now?"

"About nine," smiled Aunt Lillian, "and how convenient it is that you are sitting with your back to the kitchen clock."

"Wow! Let's get moving. We need to be back here before the end of school," announced David.

"Why?" asked Aunt Lillian.

"Because I am sure that Lisa and the twins will come over as soon as Poor Old Thing can bring them. Sean will be devastated about Max. He played with him more than I did."

"Let's get the dishes done up and then we'll call Mr. Dewey. Do you have a key, Bobby?"

"We never had a key, as far as I can remember."

"Bobby's dad broke the glass in the front door of the garage, too, when he went looking for his second set of truck keys," explained David.

"Well, George Dewey will have to bring some padlocks so that we can secure the place," said Aunt Lillian.

"Can't imagine anyone wanting to get into a hole like that," reflected Bobby. "Ain't worth the trouble."

"You never know," cautioned Aunt Lillian. "Let's protect what little you do have in case you decide to sell it some day."

"My pa would never sell the place," said Bobby.

Aunt Lillian nodded in agreement, replying, "But *you* might, my dear. So let's be wise."

Dishes were done up quickly.

* * * *

They returned shortly before one o'clock that afternoon, exhausted but satisfied that they had gotten all of the personal items that Bobby needed, with the others safely secured in a small storage area that faced on to his former living area. The small residence, which had been added on to Bobby's dad's garage as an afterthought, received its first real cleaning and mopping since it had been built.

"You boys bring in those boxes and clothes while I make lunch," instructed Aunt Lillian. "How about tuna fish sandwiches?"

The boys were so hungry after their morning work that they would have eaten nearly anything. Their affirmative response to Aunt Lillian was hardly audible as they raced to get their work done so they could sate their hunger.

"Let's not do dishes now," suggested David, "but just go to bed and nap," knowing that his aunt looked forward to her afternoon naps.

"Fine by me," said Bobby.

"Well, I guess majority rules," Aunt Lillian smiled. "I must confess that I'm more than a little tired after our workout. It feels as if we did two days' work in half a day."

* * * *

David thought he heard church bells ringing, or at least that is what suddenly intruded into his dream. —But how, he thought, could church bells be ringing in the middle of the ocean? In his dream he had definitely been adrift on a large raft in the middle of a huge ocean with waves tossing the small vessel many feet upward, backward, and every which way. He vaguely remembered Aunt Lillian and Bobby as his raft mates but, as he awoke, the details of the dream receded from his consciousness.

A pounding now seemed to be following the bell sound.

Then the doorbell rang again.

Of course, someone was at the door, first ringing, then pounding. For how long, he wondered? Hadn't anyone else heard the bell? Then he remembered that Aunt Lillian and Bobby had taken naps, too. —I must be the lightest sleeper in the house, David thought, as he rose and shambled downstairs to the front door. —Or, maybe, just the least tired.

As David opened the door, a cold chill invaded the foyer. Lisa, Mary, and Sean stood next to each other, with Poor Old Thing standing behind them. POTS was an acronym Sean and Mary had invented for their very Irish housekeeper, whose real name was Muriel Mullarney. POTS was of average height and build. She was an experienced nanny, meaning that she had, in her amber years, traded her formerly auburn hair for straight gray, which became her. There would be no getting away with anything with POTS around and Sean, much to his regret, knew this better than anyone alive. No one was ever going to bully POTS or wheedle something out of her that she didn't intend to give away in the first place. David saw something more in her eyes today, however, and that was her deep regret and sadness.

Looking immediately to his Gang of Four comrades, he saw that Lisa, Mary, and Sean also had this inexplicable sadness, as if someone had died. —Stupid! David scolded himself, now waking up fully to himself and the history of the terrible weekend he and Bobby and Aunt Lillian had just endured. —You've had time to begin accepting Max's death, but they've just heard about it.

Silence had, until this point, held sway.

Lisa finally blurted, "Oh, David, we're *so* sorry about Max!"

David looked at Mary, who was nodding, and then at Sean, who had especially dark circles under bloodshot eyes, no doubt from crying. A tear began to trickle down Sean's left cheek. This, in turn, opened a wave of grief for David and he found himself suddenly on the verge of weeping.

The hallway light blazed on.

"Who's there?" called Aunt Lillian.

David could barely breathe, much less talk, as he attempted to choke back his tears.

"Oh, friends, hello," said Aunt Lillian, as if to answer her own question. "I'm so sorry we didn't call you last night, but we've been up against it, and I just turned the phones off when we crashed yesterday afternoon, not thinking to turn them on until this morning. I'm assuming Mr. Ferlinghausen let you know what had happened. David knew you'd come, and so did I."

"Mr. Ferlinghausen called us in at the beginning of school and told us about everything that happened," explained Lisa. "He didn't want us to worry about why David and Bobby weren't in school. He spent the whole period with us. He even said he would excuse us from classes if we wanted to be quiet somewhere. Sean went to the library for the whole morning. As soon as we were dismissed, the twins called Miss Mullarney to come bring us right over."

David nodded, accepting some tissues that Aunt Lillian was offering him.

"Please, come in," Aunt Lillian invited. "Do sit down. We are being very rude. Shall I put on a little tea?"

"I'll help," volunteered POTS, and the two elderly but very spry ladies left for the kitchen.

The Gang of Four sat in silence, facing its first loss.

"Max was such a wonderful dog," began Mary.

David nodded in agreement.

"He was always so playful," added Lisa.

"I'll always remember how he loved to romp with Sean when the rest of us were learning how to play canasta," said David, smiling at Sean, who sniffed and wiped his eyes with his shirt sleeve.

"Here, Sean, have some more tissues," offered Mary.

Shaking his head, Sean bolted for the bathroom.

David looked at Mary, as if to ask 'will he be all right?'

"He's been crying ever since he heard about Max," explained Mary. He didn't eat lunch and he spent the whole afternoon talking with Mr. Ferlinghausen. He was in no shape to go to any classes. I don't think any of us were, but Lisa and I managed, although we couldn't think about anything else all day. Sean's taking it really hard. He really had bonded with Max. I don't think I've ever seen him cry this much, at least not in a long time."

The clatter of dishes could be heard from the kitchen as Aunt Lillian's voice called, "Tea is served. Everyone please come."

David, Lisa, and Mary entered the kitchen and seated themselves at the table.

"Where's Sean?" asked Aunt Lillian.

"He needed to go the bathroom," explained Mary.

"Poor lad," said POTS, shaking her head. "He's quite beside himself about the death of your dog, as bad as if he had lost his own."

"I think he played with Max more than I did," said David.

"David," said Lisa, "Please tell us what happened."

Sean entered the kitchen and slipped quietly behind the table.

David explained how he had served as Bobby's 'Slave for a Day', since he had lost to Bobby in their canasta showdown. Expecting to be asked to perform lots of services, David had been completely surprised when Bobby treated him to lunch and a movie. The trouble started after the boys stopped at Bobby's, when Edward Perkins had unexpectedly returned, drunk and angry that his drinking money had been stolen, accusing Bobby of the theft and threatening to beat both of the boys. David and Bobby had then fled to Aunt Lillian's, but Perkins had followed them and forced his way in, demanding his son. When David's dog lunged at Perkins, the raging drunk had killed Max with one strong blow to the head, using Judge Biggs's old cane that was kept next to the front door. The police arrived and arrested Perkins. Through Aunt Lillian's influence, Bobby's father had been sent to a detoxification facility near Rochester the next day.

"I know he felt awful about Max when he got sober," explained David. "He's giving me one hundred dollars for a new dog, but it's too soon to think of replacing Max. We need to mourn him, but more importantly, we need to *remember him*, and all the love he gave us."

"Where's Bobby?" asked Mary.

"He's still asleep. This whole thing has really taken a toll on him, with his father being taken away and all," said David. "And he's embarrassed about what his father did, especially about Max."

"And *should be*," said Sean, glaring at the ceiling, as if he hoped Bobby would hear him.

"It's not *Bobby's* fault for what his father did, Sean," said Mary. "Give him a break. What's going to happen to Bobby now?"

"We've invited him to become part of our family," Aunt Lillian smiled, adding, "I never thought that I would have two boys to bring up, especially at my age. But they're good boys, most of the time."

David caught her wink and grinned, "Yeah. Except when we're teasing you, right?"

Aunt Lillian shrugged, announcing, "Who would like more tea?"

POTS and Lisa shoved their cups forward, inadvertently striking them together and causing a loud tinkle. Relieved that their china remained intact, each began to laugh, and soon laughter ensued around the table as Aunt Lillian refilled their cups. The new-found mirth eased the heaviness.

"Hey, what's so funny," inquired Bobby, ambling into the kitchen in his pajamas and bathrobe and stretching before sitting down at the table.

"A minor collision, but no damage," David smirked, looking at Lisa.

"Collision?" asked Bobby.

"Two china cups," explained Lisa.

"Oh," said Bobby. "Is there anything to eat? I'm starving."

"Here, dear," said Aunt Lillian. "Have some tea and cookies."

Bobby looked dubiously at the tea cup that was placed in front of him, but took heart in the cookies, taking a fistful.

"We decided this morning that we're going to have a party," announced David. "What kind was it, Aunt Lillian?"

"An Advent party," smiled Lillian.

"Yes. An Advent party this Friday and we hope you can all come."

"What are you having a party for?" asked Sean, frowning at the prospect.

"To celebrate Max's life with us and Bobby's coming to live with us," explained David.

"First rate idea," nodded POTS. "The Mrs. Doctor has to work but the rest of us will be able to come."

"Even Professor Potter?" inquired Aunt Lillian.

"Yes. He was scheduled to fly to Washington but they called today to say that his meeting had been canceled. So I know he'll be free, and I know that he'll want to come," explained POTS.

"Who else shall we invite?" asked Lillian, reaching for her pencil and memo pad, adding, "We must surely include the Norrises across the street. They have been such good neighbors."

"How many can we accommodate?" asked David.

"Oh, I should think we could manage a party of twenty people quite comfortably. That includes us, of course," replied Lillian.

"How about Mr. & Mrs. Ferlinghausen?" suggested Bobby. "Mr. F. is the closest friend I've got outside this here family."

Sean looked ruefully at Bobby, saying, "If we invite *anyone* from the school, it should be Mr. & Mrs. Pennythorpe. Mr. P. is the advisor to David's *Bare Fax* newspaper."

"Mr. Pennythorpe is sort of my 'father-confessor'," explained David. "I talk with him twice a week about what I'm doing, or at least what I'm trying to do. We could always invite both couples, couldn't we Aunt Lillian?"

"Certainly," nodded Lillian. "That would make fourteen. It's too bad that the Mrs. Doctor will be working at the emergency room that night."

"Well, it's all the same," observed POTS. "She's still gettin' a break, if you know what I mean."

Aunt Lillian look at POTS quizzically.

POTS threw her head toward Sean.

This gesture was not lost on the once and future little hoodlum, who sat stoically in his chair, frowning.

"Who else should we invite?" asked David.

"We must invite the Deweys. They have been so kind to us this last year," suggested Aunt Lillian. "Wait. I think they're out of town, or that they're going to be out of town. Yes. Now I remember. They are visiting one of their daughters who lives in Austin."

"We'll get what we get," sighed David.

"Well, on such short notice, it may well turn out to be a small party, but a party it will be, nevertheless," replied Aunt Lillian.

"Oh, dear!" exclaimed POTS. "We had better be going. I need to drop Lisa off at her folks' restaurant and then get home and make a stew for dinner."

Goodbyes and thanks were said all around.

David fell asleep that night still designing invitations in his mind's eye.

Chapter Two
A Party is Announced

TUESDAY MORNING BROUGHT MUCH EXCITEMENT during breakfast as Aunt Lillian, David, and Bobby began to plan for their Advent party.

"Bobby, you and I will go shopping to get some new duds for your wardrobe," announced Aunt Lillian.

"Okay by me, if you don't mind tellin' me what looks decent and what looks mortal ugly," agreed Bobby.

"I'll work on the invitations while you're gone," promised David. "Aunt Lillian, maybe you and Bobby could take them around this afternoon while I work on place settings?"

"Great idea," said Lillian. "Hand-delivered messages are a figment of the past that we will be restoring to what we've decided to call our *Old-Fashioned Advent Party.*"

"Will it really be old-fashioned?" asked Bobby.

"I don't know," wondered Lillian. "I'm not really sure what old-fashioned means anymore. I suppose it suggests a holiday time when people got together and played games and told stories."

"Yes! That's what we should do!" cheered David. "Let's invite everybody to tell a story or to sing a song or to play something on the piano or to share a joke. Wouldn't that be fun?"

"Do you think we should require it?" asked a skeptical Lillian.

"No, but make it so unthreatening that everybody will want to offer something unique. I can suggest that in my invitation. I'll work on it and run it by both of you when you get back for lunch."

*****

Shortly after the striking of noon, David heard the garage door opening. He was just finishing the touches on his invitation.

"David, this is absolutely beautiful!" exclaimed Aunt Lillian.

"Totally pro," admired Bobby.

David turned, his jaw dropping when he saw Bobby wearing a shorter and neater haircut over new black dress pants and a burgundy turtle neck sweater.

"Wow!" was all he could say, adding, "Really spiffy."

"Your aunt sure took the ruffian out of me?" grinned Bobby, sheepishly proud of his new attire and haircut.

"Bobby, you take those new shoes and clothes to your room. I'll be right along to help you organize them."

After Bobby left, David looked at his aunt, exclaiming, "How on earth did you ever get him to agree to wear sport clothes much less to get a haircut?"

Aunt Lillian smiled, "Well, he sort of played into my hands. I'm sure the Lord will forgive me."

"What happened?"

"Bobby asked me what I wanted for Christmas."

"You didn't," scolded David.

"I most certainly did, and just look at the great result!"

"His gang will disown him," said David, shaking his head.

"I don't think so. Bobby no longer needs to play the role of a bully, so he can stop dressing in the tattered roughness of that role. Perhaps he will even help them to tidy their appearances a little."

"It's a really fantastic improvement," said David.

"Poor Bobby. He looked at me on the way home and said he didn't know how he had gotten into all of it, but that if it was the best Christmas gift he could give me, he was glad he could give it, especially since he had nothing else to give," smiled Aunt Lillian.

"Probably never got much attention before this," speculated David. "We didn't bring many clothes from the garage."

"No," sighed Aunt Lillian. "And mostly because there weren't many clothes there, and the ones that we did bring I would just as soon have left behind."

"Bobby seems to be taking it in stride," smiled David.

"Well, I must tell you confidentially that there were a few tears in the car on the way home. After we left the store Bobby opened up and told me that nobody had ever been as good to him or had ever treated him so decently."

"Sometimes I forget how very lucky I am," David confided.

"May I please inspect the printed version of your Advent party invitation? It looks elegant on the screen."

"Sure thing. Here it is. Hope you like it. I consider it my personal triumph over the use of fonts. At first I was tempted to use too many. Then it dawned on me that more is not always better," David explained.

You are cordially invited to an old-fashioned
Advent Party,
chez Lillian Biggs on Friday, December 15th.
For old-time fun, please come prepared to share
a story, song, or any other intangible gift
that will enrich our hearts this holiday season.
R.S.V.P. by telephone: 393-4367

The party begins at 7:00 p.m.

"You have been most restrained . . . and successful, my dear. It is an absolutely gorgeous invitation, which Bobby and I will be proud to deliver. Can you print them up now while we have some lunch?"

"As good as done," said David, as his fingers nimbly struck the appropriate keys on his computer.

* * * * *

After lunch Aunt Lillian and Bobby left to deliver the invitations and to buy the necessary groceries for the party. A lengthy list had been compiled, for it was decided that in addition to luncheon meats, a number of complementary items would be offered including various dips, crackers, cookies, fruit cakes, punch, and hot cider.

David stayed to assemble the Christmas tree, an artificial spruce that had adorned his parents' home for many years. He had promised that he wouldn't decorate the tree alone and had instead done a general cleanup of the house.

When Aunt Lillian and Bobby returned, David helped them carry in the many bags of groceries.

"Let's leave the baking ingredients out because we'll be making Christmas cookies after my nap," said Aunt Lillian, adding, "Both of you look as if you could use a nap, too."

* * * * *

They were awakened by the telephone. The Ferlinghausens were calling to accept their invitation to the Advent party.

"Bobby, David, please come. I'm going to need your help,"Aunt Lillian called from the kitchen. When the boys arrived, Aunt Lillian thrust old aprons at them, saying, "This is going to be a trial run on making Christmas cookies. I haven't made this variety in at least twenty years and I need to get my touch back. We'll make the ones for the party on Thursday night or Friday morning. This is a small batch, which I'm sure both of you will enjoy."

After the dishes and pans and bowls were washed, dried, and put away, David looked at the clock and then at Aunt Lillian, saying, "It's almost nine o'clock. Let's see if there's something good to watch on television."

Aunt Lillian and Bobby deferred to David's suggestion and soon David was perusing the television guide.

"Hey, look here!" announced David. "Channel 46, the classic movie channel, is showing the old movie version of Charles Dickens' *A Christmas Carol* beginning at nine. If I turn the set on now, we'll just make it."

"Is there time to make popcorn?" asked Aunt Lillian.

Both boys looked at each other and then at the remaining Christmas cookies on the counter.

"Why don't we just finish the cookies?" suggested David.

"Why not, my dears?" Aunt Lillian smiled. "We will be making a much larger batch very soon. Let's enjoy the movie."

The movie turned out to be the fifties classic version serving up a definitive portrayal of Scrooge by English actor Alastair Sim. Throughout the movie David, Bobby, and Aunt Lillian had occasion to wipe a tear or two from their eyes, all for different reasons.

After the movie, the three sat together in silence for a few minutes, allowing the full impact of the story to settle in.

Aunt Lillian broke the silence first, announcing, "That movie always makes me a little weepy. It also has some funny moments as well."

"Yeah," agreed Bobby. "Like when that dippy maid threw her apron up over her eyes and started runnin' away from Scrooge after she thought he'd gone bloomin' nuts."

"And when she asked if old Scrooge was giving her a bribe to keep her mouth shut," David laughed.

"I noticed you boys were a little teary-eyed," observed Aunt Lillian.

"I'm not ashamed," announced David. "Scrooge got converted and started doing some really wonderful things for the very people he had been mean to."

Bobby gazed at the floor.

Looking up, he averted his eyes as he began, "I cried when Scrooge's sister died givin' birth to his nephew. It reminded me of how my own mom got run off early by my old man, who owin' to his drinkin' problem, was a lot meaner than even Scrooge."

"How about you, Aunt Lillian?" asked David.

"My tears came when Scrooge decided to spurn his fiancée in favor of money. It reminded me of a man named Frank who once two-timed me. I guess one never gets over major hurts. God knows I've tried."

"Well, it was a damn powerful flick, if ya ask me," concluded Bobby.

No one cared to argue with or to embellish Bobby's rating.

Soon all had retired to their respective beds, snuggling under warm and cozy covers for what was becoming a cold and windy winter night.

Chapter Three
Deepening Snow

THE TELEPHONE JANGLED.

David squinted his eyes and rubbed them. His room seemed colder than usual and he wondered what time it was. He had planned to sleep in. Looking at the clock, he was surprised to see that it was nine-thirty. —I really *have* slept in, he thought.

The wind was blowing fiercely outside, howling at the corners of the room. A flurry of snow buffeted the window. David lay there, contemplating the harsh elements as they struck the house. Finally deciding he must get up to see what was happening, he quickly put on his bathrobe and socks and went downstairs to see if Aunt Lillian had gotten up.

As he entered the kitchen, he rejoiced at the warmth and light he felt. Water was boiling on the stove. Aunt Lillian appeared from the basement door, holding two kerosene lanterns.

David stood there, mouth open, wondering what was going on.

"Good morning," Aunt Lillian greeted her grand nephew. "Did the telephone wake you? It woke me. The three of us were certainly sleeping in. Nothing like a cold winter night to encourage that kind of deep sleep."

"What have you got the lanterns for?" asked David.

"The blizzard! Just in case we lose our electricity."

"What blizzard?"

"We may even have to use the fireplace for heat. There is some wood in the basement if we need it," continued Aunt Lillian. "I'd call and reserve a room for us at the Village Inn in case we lose electricity, but then the question would be, 'How would we get there?' We would be snowbound."

"A blizzard?" said an incredulous David. "Why didn't we know it was coming?"

"You know how little we watch the news or read the newspaper. We were so busy making party preparations and cookies that we forgot all about the outside world. The telephone call was from Sean, and he was calling from school. Students are being sent home as we speak. He called to say that classes have been canceled for both Thursday and Friday. The brunt of the storm is expected to hit here around four o'clock tomorrow morning, but it's so bad now that school officials have released students to make sure they will get home safely. Sean said something about it being an old-fashioned 'Go Home Drill' or something like that. He said you'd understand."

David grinned, marveling at the little hoodlum's remarkable memory, explaining, "Oh, it's a reference to an old school protocol we found a few months ago when we were planning that air raid drill ruse. In the sixties, schools occasionally sent students home early as a rehearsal in case of the threat of nuclear attack."

"Oh, yes. Now I understand. Well, he seemed very pleased that he and Mary were going to miss a couple of days of classes. He hinted that he would be glad to walk over here and stay here until Friday to help with party preparations," said Aunt Lillian.

"What did you say?"

"I thanked him for his offer, and then found myself wondering aloud whether we would even have the party this Friday, especially if the blizzard lasts longer than expected."

"Gosh! I never even thought of that," said David.

"I'm afraid we'll have to play it by ear," suggested Aunt Lillian.

"What did Sean say at that?"

"He said he would be glad to come over anyway. I think he's missed you, David. You were seeing each other almost every day before all this trouble with Bobby's father."

"I know. Sean's dad told me that I've become sort of an older brother figure to him and that's just what Sean needs," said David. "Maybe we can get back to our old schedule in a couple of weeks. Bobby and I need to work out our relationship first."

"Try not to neglect Sean, my dear. He is enormously fond of you as well as very devoted to you," advised Aunt Lillian.

"We won't. We just need some adjustment time. What are you going to do right now, Aunt Lillian?"

"The most sensible thing in the world, in light of the blizzard. I'm going to make some hot tea and get a good book and go back to bed. There will be enough boiled water for hot chocolate for you and Bobby, if you'd like some."

"I don't think Bobby's even up yet. I'm sort of excited by the storm. I think I'll make some hot chocolate and tune in to the weather on television. Sure you don't want to join me?" coaxed David.

"Only if it's terribly newsworthy. I have a whole shelf of books waiting to get read. Call me only if you think it very urgent, my dear," announced a determined Aunt Lillian.

* * * * *

Bobby woke shortly before eleven and crept downstairs toward the sound of the television where David had become glued to the drama of the winter storm. As the wind outside increased and as the elements of winter raged, David's interest in this unusual weather phenomenon burgeoned.

"Any more hot chocolate?" asked Bobby, standing in the hallway wrapped in his boyhood tiger blanket.

"Hey! We're under a blizzard advisory," announced David. "Are you cold?"

Bobby pulled his blanket a little closer to his body and shivered, asking, "Aren't you?"

David was so transfixed with the unfolding drama of the winter storm that he had completely forgotten that he even might be cold. Suddenly he found himself shivering as well, and answered, "I guess the hot chocolate made me forget how cold the house was getting. Must be the wind chill. I'm going up and put a couple of sweaters on. Then we'll boil more water."

Racing upstairs the boys found new comfort in donning several layers of sweaters. Bobby still wrapped himself, however, in his tiger blanket, a little tattered around the edges but nevertheless his prized possession.

Returning to the kitchen, David started to boil a new kettle of water. Aunt Lillian entered and announced, "David! You read my mind. I was just hoping for a new cup of hot tea. A hot cup of tea will help take some of this chill away."

After hot chocolate and tea were prepared, the three of them sat and sipped their drinks as they listened to the most recent news of the storm. All community activities had been canceled. Residents were asked not to travel except in the event of an emergency. Telephone numbers of agencies providing help were listed on a moving banner at the bottom of the screen. Police and ambulance personnel were preparing a small fleet of snowmobiles to assist them in reaching and transporting people in need of their services.

When they had finished their drinks, David announced, "I'm getting tired of this. I think I may go back to bed."

"Me, too," said Bobby.

"And I, as well," said Aunt Lillian, picking up her book and heading toward her bedroom, adding, "Just leave the cups. We'll do them up later."

David had slept for two hours when he heard a knock at his door.

"Come in," he invited.

Bobby entered and walked over to David's bed, standing there as he formulated his message.

"Yes, Bobby," David prompted. "What is it?"

"I can't sleep," said Bobby. "And the wind's pickin' up somethin' fierce and I don't wanta stay by myself."

David thought a moment.

"Say, I've got it. Since this is the biggest of the upstairs bedrooms, why don't you move in here with me? We could make your room into a study area or something like that. All we have to do is move my computer over to your room and then your bed and dresser over here. From now on, we can share this room. Okay?"

"Way cool," Bobby nodded in vigorous approval.

Aunt Lillian had dozed off several times while reading her latest mystery when the sound of furniture on the move woke her. She listened intently to the rummaging above her head and a smile gradually appeared on her face when she realized what was transpiring. Donning her bathrobe, she walked to the foyer and called upstairs, "Need any help?"

Bobby could be heard whispering something to David who, in turn, came to the upstairs landing, saying, "Hello! Bobby's moving into my room and we're making his old room into a computer and study area. Sorry if we woke you."

"That's quite all right and what a capital idea! Do you need any help?"

"No, thanks. We have to decide where each thing will go and it's going to take a while longer. Why don't you come up and inspect the change when it's all done?"

"I'd be delighted to. Just let me know when."

"David and me are gonna put our beds across from each other so we can talk at night when we start gettin' the creeps or need to spill our guts," proclaimed Bobby proudly.

"What a great idea," encouraged Aunt Lillian. "Why don't I begin fixing us some dinner. We haven't had a real meal all day. Any requests? Maybe some spaghetti?"

"Spaghetti would be great!" said David.

"Yum, yum," added Bobby.

Soon the sound of Aunt Lillian's singing could be heard mid the clatter of kitchen pots and the howling of the mounting winter storm.

* * * * *

The television newscast that evening confirmed how wise school officials had been to send students home early in the day. Since those early morning hours, twelve inches of snow had fallen. Winds had also increased to forty miles an hour, with gusts reaching upwards of sixty. More snow was predicted, but no meteorologist could accurately say how much would fall before the blizzard subsided, and current best estimates ranged from three to four feet.

"So far, so good," said Aunt Lillian, "and I'll keep saying that as long as we don't lose our electricity."

The telephone rang. Aunt Lillian answered and visited briefly with George Dewey who had called to make sure everyone was well and everything at the house was still working.

* * * * *

David and Bobby were tired after moving most of their furniture, having completely reorganized their two rooms. Aunt Lillian praised their efficiency, observing, "This makes more sense, anyway. Each of you now has more room by sharing."

All retired to the larger rumblings of the clattering storm.

"David," asked Bobby, after each had said good night to the other, "are you scared?"

David reflected for a moment.

"A little," he said. "I don't know what we'd do if we lost our electricity."

"Someone would come help us, I bet," said Bobby, trying to be cheerful.

"Yes. With all the good people Aunt Lillian knows in this town, I bet someone would come, or maybe even a lot of folks. It's a good feeling to know that there are others out there who will help."

The strong winds outside continued to howl, their pitches increasing, ever buffeting the shutters and window panes.

David had not succeeded in falling asleep as he lay there wondering how severe the blizzard would get, and whether or not they would be able to throw their Advent Party on Friday.

Bobby also had insomnia. He tossed and turned in his bed, coughing now and again, finally looking over at David and whispering, "Psst, David. You still awake?"

"Yeah. I'm still awake."

"Have you been asleep?"

"No. How 'bout you?" asked David.

"Not a wink since we went to bed. It sure is a wicked storm."

"You can say that again," David agreed.

After a short interval, Bobby considered David's suggestion and announced, "It sure is a wicked storm."

David couldn't repress his mirth at Bobby's naive yet trusting repetition and he burst out in laughter.

"Hey? What did I say? What's so funny?"

"You are, you slyboots," explained David. "I said, 'You can say that again' only as a figure of speech, and then you actually did say it again. I guess I'm really nervous about the storm. Anyway, thanks for helping me to relax a little. It's good to relax the inner tension."

"Is that somethin' you get when you're all wrapped up in knots on the inside?" asked Bobby.

"Sort of, I guess," said David.

"Then I bet Dandy-Pandy is tied up as tight as one of them Gordian knots they talk about, or maybe even tighter," observed Bobby.

"If he uncoiled, he'd probably spin around really fast, just like a top," added David, building on the knot imagery.

"Until his damn wig flew off," concluded Bobby.

Both boys laughed for several minutes.

The storm outside now seemed less foreboding than before.

"David," asked Bobby, "What's a figure of speech?"

"It's kind of a poetic way of saying something, like saying this storm is a monster, instead of just a storm. Likening it to something else makes a comparison."

"Well, if it's a monster, it's a humdinger," concluded Bobby.

"Don't worry, Bobby. We'll be okay."

"You know, David," Bobby began, "You're a real brother to me. I never had a real brother before."

"And you're a real brother to me, too, Bobby," said David.

"Hey, what's the difference between being just a regular brother and a real brother?" wondered Bobby.

"What?" asked David.

"To be a real brother?" emphasized Bobby.

"I don't know. Maybe like in the movies, maybe we should become blood brothers," said David, thinking aloud.

"Awesome. But we ain't got no knife to cut our wrists with," said Bobby.

David paled when he considered what he had been suggesting, but he could hardly retreat now. An interlude of silence followed as each boy contemplated what it would mean to become a real brother, especially a real blood brother.

Finally David announced, "Bobby, we could use the point of a pin or a safety pin and mingle the blood from our right fingers. How about that?"

"Okay by me," said Bobby. "I ain't got no pin, though. Do you?"

"Yeah," said David, turning on the light. "I've got one of those travel sewing kits in my top dresser drawer. Let me get it."

As David procured the necessary pin for the bloodletting, Bobby got out of bed. Soon each stood facing the other on the cold carpet of the frigid room as the blizzard raged outside. In the shadowed light of the bed lamp, they each silently took turns pricking the index fingers of their right hands and then allowed their blood to mingle together.

"Never been a blood brother before," said Bobby, looking intently into David's eyes. "What do you think it means, anyway?"

Reflecting for a moment, David announced, "Mostly, I guess, that we don't have any secrets from each other."

Bobby smiled as he said, "Well, I ain't got none from you. Do you have any from me?"

David's first impulse was to say 'no', but something stayed his tongue. He closed his eyes as he sought to know what he must now confess to Bobby, what hidden knowledge had come round at last for revelation. Yes. Now he knew. Sighing and taking a deep breath, he looked Bobby directly in the eyes and said, "Well, there *is* one thing."

Bobby looked a little surprised but also very interested at the same time as he waited to find out what had been kept from him.

"Yes, brother?" prompted Bobby.

"Well," began David, "You remember the time when Sean and Mary escorted you into the library workroom last fall to read the petition I gave them?"

Bobby nodded, saying, "Yeah. Please don't remind me. That was the day my life passed before my very eyes. When that little hoodlum pulled out that .38 derringer and stuck it in my back, I thought I was gonna die."

"Bobby," announced David, as he closed his eyes and opened them again, looking his new blood brother directly in his eyes, "I need to tell you something now that I hope you won't hold against Sean . . ."

* * * * *

"A toy gun?" shouted an incredulous Bobby Perkins. "He scared the livin' tar out of me with a toy gun?" Bobby's eyes smouldered with anger as he began to calculate his revenge.

"Bobby, hold on now," urged David. "Sean was doing his best, considering the assignment he had. You were one tough cookie, or so we thought, and he wasn't taking any chances."

"That low-down little sneak," said Bobby to himself, his eyes narrowing.

"Bobby!" persisted David. "Listen to me. You can't hold that against Sean. Let bygones be bygones. Please! For my sake, since I'm the one who told you, now that we're blood brothers."

"Only for your sake," grumped Bobby. "But I still owe him. I owe him a BIG one."

"Just remember that Sean was only trying to do his best under rather strained circumstances," persisted David.

Bobby's eyes remained stubbornly fixed at the window, as if he wished he could fly out of it and over to Sean's house, where he would cheerfully strangle the little hoodlum.

"Let's get to bed," yawned David. "There's going to be a lot of work tomorrow to get ready for the party."

Bobby looked at David with surprise and then back at the window where the storm raged, asking, "Do you think we'll even be able to have the party?"

"I don't know," admitted David. "Let's hope so."

Chapter Four
The Sound of Voices

DAVID STRETCHED AND YAWNED, and quickly pulled the wool comforter up over himself. The bedroom was cold, and David did not want to venture out of bed. He looked over at his new blood-brother, who was still sleeping soundly. In fact, Bobby was snoring lightly.

—Maybe that's what woke me up, mused David, as he began to return to his blissful slumber. The room was not only cold; it was also filled with a heavy silence. This very lack of sound caught David's attention, and he suddenly remembered the blizzard from the previous day and night.

Bounding to the window, he looked out at a dazzling new world, composed mostly of snow. He could make out oval hills of snow where cars had once been parked. The road and driveways appeared to be buried at least three feet deep. The bedroom alarm clock was blinking, so obviously electrical power had also been lost sometime during the night.

David shivered from the chill in the room. Donning his wool bathrobe and slippers, he walked down the hallway to see if Aunt Lillian had gotten up. Her bedroom door was closed. David nudged it slightly.

"Come in, David," invited Aunt Lillian.

"How did you know it was me?" asked David as he entered.

"You and Bobby walk differently. You're lighter on your feet. You also tend to be the earliest riser in our family," explained Aunt Lillian.

"But you always get up and make me a great breakfast before I go to school," said David.

"Greater love hath no Aunt than that, my dear," teased Aunt Lillian.

"Have you looked out the window?" asked David.

"No. I was just waking up when I heard you padding along the hallway. Of course, a squeaky floorboard here and there helps," Aunt Lillian grinned. "I don't hear the wind anymore. Has the storm abated?"

David nodded, adding, "But you should see the mountains of snow it left all over the place. The road isn't even plowed and none of our neighbors have cleared their driveways."

"What time is it?" asked Aunt Lillian, looking at her blinking alarm clock.

David raced to the kitchen to get the correct time from the battery operated clock hanging above the sink, and ran back to announce, "It's almost nine-thirty."

"Then the blizzard did take its toll," pronounced Aunt Lillian. "I don't think we'll be having an Advent party tonight."

"Maybe they'll clear the roads by then," objected David, flopping on his aunt's bed.

"Yes. But the blizzard has set everyone back. It takes a couple of days to recover from a storm like this."

"What'll we do with all that food that we prepared yesterday!" urged David.

"Now, dear, I didn't say we wouldn't be ready. I merely observed that I doubt very much that anyone will come," added Aunt Lillian.

"We can call them," said David.

"And make them feel guilty if they don't bother to come?" retorted his Aunt disapprovingly. "I'll have none of that."

"I bet the neighbors will come," said David.

"Only if they can get into the house. There's a lot of shoveling waiting for you and Bobby out there."

"Do you think Mr. Murphy will come plow the driveway?" asked David hopefully.

"Not before tonight. He's probably snowbound himself. He lives way out in the country, you know," explained Aunt Lillian. "I should think he'll have all he can do to keep his cows warm and milking."

"What will we do?" asked David.

"We'll prepare for the party, and hope that everyone who can come will come. I think you're probably correct: only our closest neighbors will venture out. But that means you and Bobby should start shoveling now."

"How about a little breakfast first?" pleaded David.

"My dear," scolded Aunt Lillian, "It's getting on to ten o'clock in the morning. Nearly half the day is gone. Why don't you and Bobby go out and shovel for an hour and then come back in to shower and ready to devour a huge breakfast of pancakes, bacon, orange juice, and hot chocolate?"

"You're on!" shouted David, lifting himself off of his aunt's bed, readying himself to run down the hallway and wake up Bobby.

"Gently, my dear, gently," cautioned Aunt Lillian. "Be gentle as you wake your new brother."

"No problem," said David.

Striding back to his bedroom with new-found purpose, David threw the door open and walked up to Bobby's bed where he immediately flung the covers.

"What the—?" exclaimed Bobby, sitting up and clutching himself as he began to shiver from the cold. Poor Bobby was still not quite awake, trying as best he could to take in David's words and to comprehend their meaning.

"Your brawn is required for snow removal; so is mine," David continued. "Time is of the essence. We'll shower after we shovel. Aunt

Lillian is going to make one of her super breakfasts for us. Any questions?"

"Yes," said Bobby groggily. "What's *brawn*?"

"It's your muscle, your strength," sighed David.

"Well, at least one of us 'as got some," quipped Bobby.

"I bet I can clear my half of the driveway before you can," challenged David, as both boys sprinted toward the closet to get their coats and ski hats.

After forty-five minutes, both Bobby and David stumbled into the kitchen, red-faced and gasping, wilting to the floor in front of Aunt Lillian, who was stirring up the pancake batter.

"Shall I call 911?" she asked slyly.

David lifted his head and nodded in the affirmative, just as Bobby reached his right hand over and shoved David's head back on to the floor.

"Nearly an hour of all-out shovelin'," gasped Bobby, "and we ain't even put a dent in it. Davey and me think this blizzard driveway is a Mr. Mitchell snowplow job. We can't embarrass his four-wheel drive truck by competin' with it."

"Why don't you boys run up and shower?" suggested Aunt Lillian.

David shook his head, gasping, "No . . . strength . . . Can't . . . even . . . stand up."

"Well, then, go watch some television and I'll call you when breakfast is ready."

This last suggestion found new appeal and Bobby lifted himself up and hobbled toward the living room and looked behind at David, who began to crawl in the same direction.

Fifteen minutes later Aunt Lillian called the boys to breakfast. Having enjoyed a short respite from shoveling, they walked stiffly into the kitchen.

"Is there a path from the front door to the street?" asked Aunt Lillian.

David and Bobby looked at each other in embarrassment.

"Not exactly," said David.

Aunt Lillian raised her left eyebrow in wonder.

"We sort of had a contest," said Bobby.

"The driveway is shoveled from the garage door to about one third of the way down to the street," said David, "and I admit, Bobby shoveled farther than I did."

"Why don't you concentrate on making a small path from the front door to the street in case we have the party tonight?" suggested Aunt Lillian.

The boys agreed and began to devour their breakfasts.

The sound of a snow blower caught Aunt Lillian's attention as David and Bobby wolfed down their pancakes. Going to the dining room window, she exclaimed, "Why, Mr. Norris has his snow blower out and is clearing a path up our driveway."

"God bless the man," said Bobby as he poured more maple syrup on his pancakes.

"Good soul," agreed David, relieved that he probably wouldn't have to shovel any more snow that day.

When Mr. Norris reached the front door, he gave the familiar knock-knock, knock-knock-knock, knock-knock.

"Come in, come in," beamed Aunt Lillian, opening the door. "Bless your heart for thinking of us."

"There's got to be a way in for the partygoers," said Mr. Norris, a tall, thin man wearing a black overcoat and Russian fur hat.

"Would you like anything, Peter? Perhaps something warm to drink?" invited Aunt Lillian.

"No, thank you. But I will have some of your famous Christmas cookies tonight. Is there anything else that I can do to help you?"

"No. I think we'll be just fine, especially now that our guests will be able to get into the house—thanks to you," replied Aunt Lillian.

"Not at all, my friend. You are a good neighbor," replied Mr. Norris.

"And so are you, Peter. See you tonight," said Aunt Lillian.

When breakfast was over, Bobby and David put their dishes and utensils in the dishwasher, as Aunt Lillian set about to make her famous Christmas cookies. The boys watched and helped and begged to taste the cookie dough, which they heartily enjoyed.

* * * * *

Later that afternoon, as Aunt Lillian, David, and Bobby worked to set up the refreshments for their Advent Party, David again speculated on how many people might come, saying, "I suppose it doesn't matter. If only the Norrises come, we'll have a good time."

Aunt Lillian sat at the dining room table folding the dainty green napkins, which lent seasonal contrast to the bright red table cloth. She frowned for a moment, musing on David's words, then answered, "No. You're right. It's always nicer to have more, but two will do."

"Why is it always nicer to have more?" asked David.

"Because of the gifts they bring," answered Aunt Lillian.

"But they ain't gonna bring none," said Bobby, thinking of the invitations that he and Aunt Lillian had delivered.

"Only *intangible* gifts," Aunt Lillian agreed.

"When we first made up the invitations, I reckoned that word meant expensive," said Bobby.

David laughed.

"What's so funny?" asked Bobby.

"I just thought that was funny. But now you know that intangible means something that is not material, like singing a song," explained David.

"Yeah, and that'd ruin the party for sure, if the likes of me tried singin'," dead-panned Bobby. "It'd sure as heck clear the mob out."

"Bobby, are your worried about not having a gift to share?" asked Aunt Lillian.

"Damn straight," said Bobby.

"But you do, my dear," explained Aunt Lillian. "Everyone does. But don't worry. Sharing in a formal way is not required. You share by merely being there, because you share yourself."

"That's no bargain," said Bobby.

"Yes, it is," scolded Aunt Lillian. "Never let anyone tell you otherwise."

"Aunt Lillian is right," David agreed.

"So, what is my gift to share?" asked Bobby.

Aunt Lillian and David pondered for a moment.

"I've got it," announced David, "It's your sense of humor. You're a natural storyteller. Just tell them about something that happened to you."

"Nobody'll be interested in me," said Bobby.

"You'll see," predicted David. "Just do it."

Bobby frowned as he considered the impending trial of speaking to the guests who might gather; it now seemed to him that the fewer who came, the better.

"I think you boys should watch carefully when each of our guests arrives this evening," suggested Aunt Lillian. "Each will bring a certain tenor of character, a certain quality of personality to add to the larger ambience."

"I ain't a Frenchman," said Bobby. "Could you please say that in plain English?"

"Each person who joins a group brings special personal qualities. For example, Sean, if he is able to come, will bring exuberance, which means a certain, special kind of liveliness or enthusiasm."

"Not after I blacken both his ugly eyes for takin' a month, maybe even a half a year, off my life in that dang school library," countered Bobby.

"Bobby, dear, this is a party, and our guests are all due respect and cordiality, which means amiable good-natured hospitality," admonished Aunt Lillian. "Just be on the look-out to notice each person."

"Okay, okay," grumped Bobby, "I'll play like Sherlock Holmes, but I *still* owe Sean a BIG one."

"What kinds of things should we look for?" asked David, curious to know more about the subtle dynamics of human interaction.

"Someone might enter and give a beautiful smile," said Aunt Lillian, "while another might offer a hug. Some people say a great deal with their eyes, if one takes the time and trouble to notice. Others may stand at the door, merely happy to have arrived at the party."

"It's all pretty refined then?" asked David.

"At first, my dear, but only at the beginning, when you first begin to notice and look for such things. I suppose that we all do it unconsciously. Heavens knows there are probably a thousand books on what's called 'body language.' And, of course, it goes both ways. We want to make sure that everyone who comes tonight feels most welcome to be here."

"Even Sean?" asked Bobby.

"*Especially* Sean," answered Aunt Lillian. "Tonight is not the time for you two to be sparring at each other."

"Okay," grumped Bobby.

The punch bowl was put in the center of the table and the cups were stationed, some to each side of the bowl. Aunt Lillian also had set out her finest tea service, and that was set up on a separate, smaller server. Christmas cookies with dazzling colors of icing, caramel corn balls, cranberry bread, date bread, slices of fruit cake, and other treats adorned the large table. Plates and napkins sat waiting for use.

“Why are we having Christmas cookies at an Advent party?” asked David.

“I’ll eat the ones you don’t want,” offered Bobby.

“I wondered if you’d notice that, my dears,” said Aunt Lillian. “In truth, I suppose we’re cheating, but only a little. Many churches sing Christmas carols for weeks before Christmas Day. Let’s think of it as helping to ring in the Christmas season. We’ll have to remember to light the candles a few minutes before the party. All of our preparations are complete, and it’s only three-thirty. I think I’ll take a nap.”

“We’ll be quiet,” promised David.

“You’ll only hear the sound of Christmas cookies being munched,” predicted Bobby.

Aunt Lillian lifted her eyebrow, and all three laughed.

* * * * *

Rising from her nap at six, Aunt Lillian found David and Bobby busy playing canasta. Each had put on the matching holiday sweatshirts proclaiming “HO^3” Aunt Lillian had given them on Tuesday.

“Ho, Ho, Ho,” David greeted her, looking up from his cards.

“Don’t let me interrupt. It’s an hour before the party, and I just want to poke around to make sure everything is ready.”

The Norrises, the neighbors from across the street, rang the doorbell shortly before seven o’clock. David answered, and welcomed them in. Mr. Norris was wearing a red tie and green sweater and seemed taller than he had earlier in the morning when he came to forge a path through the snow. Mrs. Norris, of medium height and amply packed, wore a colorful green skirt and a red and green blouse. Together they made the perfect ‘Mutt & Jeff’ twosome. David, trying to notice what he could, was first impressed with the warmth of their smiles as well as the sparkle in their eyes.

“Are we the first to arrive?” inquired Mrs. Norris.

"Yes, Evelyn," answered Aunt Lillian, coming from the kitchen. "Welcome. And thank you again, Peter, for clearing a path for us."

"Not at all," replied Mr. Norris, bowing to acknowledge Aunt Lillian.

"Well, I just put the tea kettle on, and we also have hot punch," announced Aunt Lillian, pointing toward the dining room table. "Please help yourselves."

David took the Norrises' coats and hats and left to place them on Aunt Lillian's bed, which had been appointed to serve as an improvised cloakroom. Upon returning, David noticed that the Norrises had seated themselves on the sofa next to Aunt Lillian's easy chair, and she was formally introducing Bobby to them.

"Peter and I saw you and David shoveling this morning," announced Mrs. Norris.

"You did?" gulped Bobby.

"Yes. There was so much snow, so much to do. I'm glad Peter decided to lend a little help."

"It was real nice," admitted Bobby, adding, "Thank you."

The conversation then fell to the recent blizzard and it was compared to past snowstorms. The clock struck seven-thirty.

"Oh, dear," said Aunt Lillian. "I had hoped at least a few others would be able to brave the weather, but I can't really blame anyone for not venturing out after such a major storm."

"Many of the secondary roads are still difficult to travel," observed Peter Norris, nodding his head in agreement.

Suddenly voices, singing the Mendelssohn carol, "Hark! The Herald Angels Sing," could be heard outside.

"Carolers?" questioned Aunt Lillian, rising to go to the front door.

Opening the front door, she burst into a huge smile to see standing in front of her Mr. & Mrs. Ferlinghausen, Mr. & Mrs. Pennythorpe, Professor Potter, POTS, Sean and Mary, and especially Lisa Jones, who originally thought that she wouldn't be able to attend the party. The singing of the group filled the foyer and living room and David and Bobby and the Norrises joined Aunt Lillian at the door. The singers regaled their listeners in a second verse of their carol, after which welcomes were given all around, mid hearty laughter. David and Bobby promptly took their guests' coats and hats to Aunt Lillian's bedroom, as the newest arrivals were steered toward the refreshments.

"No use," remonstrated Bobby as he and David stacked coats, "I ain't seen nothin'. How 'bout you?"

David remembered Aunt Lillian's injunction to notice details about their guests' comportment and sighed, saying, "It happened too fast. I completely forgot. But wasn't it really awesome how they all came in?"

"A really friendly group," admitted Bobby.

"Let's try to notice when each person presents something to the group," said David.

"Hard to notice from the floor," retorted Bobby.

"The floor?" asked David.

"After I faint," Bobby explained. "Haven't got a clue 'bout what I'm gonna say."

"Don't worry. Somebody will lead the way," encouraged David.

* * * * *

Merriment and joviality filled the room, mirroring the warmth and light of the fire that blazed in Aunt Lillian's hearth. The Christmas cookies soon disappeared and Aunt Lillian set out a second batch she had kept in reserve.

A bright chord sounded on the piano. Everyone directed their attention to Aunt Lillian, who had seated herself at the keyboard.

—What a polite way to get everyone's attention, thought David.

"The time has come for us to share our intangible gifts. With your permission, I would like to go first by playing several Christmas carols, in way of affirming the marvelous Christmas spirit that our carolers brought to our door. David and Bobby will distribute these leaflets with the words and music."

As she played through several carols, Aunt Lillian's skill as former organist and choirmaster was evident. The singing was both hearty and joyful, concluding with "Silent Night."

"Who's next?" invited Aunt Lillian.

Peter Norris rose and walked over to the piano. Aunt Lillian began to stand up, until he said, "Please don't move. I'm no musician. But I do want to remark to everyone about those wonderful Christmas sweatshirts you recently gave to your boys."

"As a retired chemist, I am always looking for numbers and symbols. And I also want to say how happy we are to be here tonight, and we wish you all a Merry Christmas."

Warm applause filled the room.

As Peter Norris returned to his seat, his wife Evelyn rose and assumed his place by the piano, which was becoming the unofficial speaker's station. Smiling as she first looked at David and then Bobby, Evelyn announced, "My offering this evening is to tell you about something rather funny I saw this morning, and I hope that David and Bobby will forgive me, for it may be at their expense. Peter and I had just finished breakfast and were wondering whether Lillian would cancel this Advent party. We then heard the sound of shoveling and went to the window, where we saw David and Bobby scooping the snow out of Lillian's driveway for all they were worth.

"It was at that moment that we guessed that the party was still on. After about half an hour, I looked out the window again to see how far the boys had gotten. The taller boy, Bobby, had gotten farther, but David was working hard to catch up. Then I saw Bobby fill his shovel with snow and stand there, looking at David, who kept shoveling.

Finally, Bobby apparently called David's name, for David turned to him, only to receive a face full of snow."

"Yes!" affirmed Sean Potter, always eager for any form of fisticuffs.

"Well, David picked up snow with his shovel and lammed it at Bobby, who stumbled back but then lammed more snow back again. Before long one of the boys had shoved the other down into a snowbank, and they were squirming this way and that, trying to wash each other's faces with snow. Peter and I laughed at their antics. Peter has three brothers, so he well understood what was happening.

"'I guess those lads need a little machine help,' Peter told me as he went to get our snow blower ready. So after the boys went inside, Peter went out and cleared a path from the street to Lillian's front door. Even though the boys appeared to be fighting, it also seemed that they were having fun. That's my story, and I hope I didn't embarrass anyone."

Again, applause filled the room as Evelyn sat down.

Aunt Lillian smiled and looked at David and Bobby, wondering if either would offer a response. She had been unaware of the spat, but she also knew that boys often wrestled and knocked each other around.

Bobby rose and walked over to the piano. Looking at the group, he knew from the eager anticipation in their faces that everyone wanted to know more about what had happened. Clearing his throat, he began, "What Mrs. Norris has told you is true, although Davey and me never thought anybody saw it. I can explain, but bear with me. One thing you need to know is that I'm no morning person. I like to get up at civilized hours, like eleven or twelve. So, this morning, when Davey found out that we had to shovel the driveway for the party, he flew into our bedroom, where I was mindin' my own business and dreamin' about some far-off tropical island, and just ripped the blessed covers off me. It was mighty cold in our room, and suddenly I go from sittin' under a palm tree to sittin' in a deep freeze way up at the North Pole."

Everyone laughed heartily, which encouraged Bobby to continue.

"So I wake up, and as I come to, I hear all this guff 'bout needin' to shovel some snow. I mean, without even a decent shower. So I got up on the wrong side of the bed, and Davey is so cheerful, it makes me sick. I wake up slow, and that's under the best of circumstances. So I started to burn a little inside, and by the time we were out in the driveway, I was a regular five-alarm fire, 'cause all I can think about is how much I still wanted to be tucked under my warm covers. So I think to myself, —A lesson's got to be learned here and now. So I fill my shovel up full of snow and turn to let Davey have it, but he's just shovelin' for all he's worth, which at that time in my personal estimation wasn't very much. So I call to him, and say, "Davey, remember rippin' those warm covers off me this mornin'?" And he says, "Yeah, so what?" And I say, "Here's what." And then I let him have it. Nearly knocked him over, 'cause he wasn't expectin' it. Then one thing led to another until all we could do was crawl into the house, and I mean we *really* crawled, layin' there pantin' in the livin' room with our tongues huggin' the carpet, hopin' that we'd live long enough 'til breakfast was served. And a mighty fine breakfast it was."

Looking at Aunt Lillian, Bobby continued, "We didn't tell you, 'cause you had enough worries about this party. But no blood was shed, and a new understandin' about covers is now in the air. At least, that's my side of it; Davey 'll probably come up and tell you he saved my life, and he's got such a charmin' way with words so you'll all probably believe every word he says, but just 'member he came darn close to losin' his life this mornin' when he ripped them covers off me."

Enthusiastic applause acknowledged Bobby's recollection of events, and as he returned to his seat, David walked up to the piano.

David paused before speaking, looking intently at his audience, who would soon hang on his every word. What Bobby had shared had been the truth, and as he enjoyed the growing dramatic silence, David realized how he could best respond. Looking very solemnly at his audience, he proudly proclaimed, "This morning, I saved my brother's life."

The laughter and chortling was instantaneous, for it not only fulfilled Bobby's prediction, but lent new credibility to whatever each boy said. The challenge, too, was obvious, for how could David weave a justification for throwing off warm covers?

To play on his very successful beginning, David continued, "Although accused of ignominy, I did, in fact, save my brother's life this morning."

More laughter ensued, as Bobby leaned forward and whispered to Mrs. Norris, "What's 'ig-no-meany?"

"It means shamefulness," explained Mrs. Norris.

"Bobby was very nervous about what he would share with you tonight," continued David, "for he believed that there was nothing that he could offer. Sometimes we are lost in a dream until something out of the ordinary happens, such as a roommate pulling off the sheets and comforters on an especially cold morning. That was a wake-up call in more than one way. Bobby protested my prank and we had a little tussle. What's most important, however, is that Bobby found out that he really had something to say, to share, tonight; in fact, he has a lot to say and to share. So . . . *ipso facto* . . . I saved his life."

Everyone in the group admired how deftly David had turned the prank to his advantage. No applause came, however, for everyone was listening intently to hear more, something more, anything more. Although David had finished, he also realized he must continue. What was there to say? It was cruelly ironic, for David had fallen into the same position that Bobby had so fretted about, and the growing silence increasingly demanded him to come across with better goods than had already been proffered. In his mind, David searched for something seasonal. The movie he, Bobby, and Aunt Lillian had watched, *A*

Christmas Carol, flooded into his mind; the obvious tie was Scrooge's self-insight. —Yes, thought David, — That will work.

David continued, "Such self-insight is always helpful, and it reminds me in a very small way of the classic film that Aunt Lillian, Bobby, and I watched earlier this week, *A Christmas Carol.* Scrooge came to an insight that also saved his life by saving his immortal soul. This is perhaps the most enduring example of how love and the Christmas spirit can change a person. I guess that's it."

Applause acknowledged David's words as he took his seat. Looking back to where he had been standing, David was delighted to see that his mentor, Mr. Pennythorpe, had assumed the speaker's position next to the piano. The revered history teacher was clearing his throat and wiping his right eye.

"What David said about the story *A Christmas Carol* is very true. The 1950's film was very true to the celebrated Charles Dickens' novel, which became an immediate classic in its own day, a story which is thought to have brought many people to greater light. Since the novel's first printing, it has become an icon of our annual Christmas celebrations. However, I fear that its enduring message is today more obscure than ever. Fewer and fewer people seem to be reading these days, which marks a significant change for the society in which we live. By not reading the original, one loses the subtle force of Dickens' wit and satire, not to mention his astute social criticism. Instead, we honor it today, if at all, by merely viewing it as one of the season's obligatory customs, although I suppose that that is better than ignoring it altogether. I speak so passionately about the novel because I know the story intimately."

"He probably *knew* Scrooge," Sean whispered to David.

"Shhh. I'm listening," scolded David.

"I am blessed, cursed, with a rare affliction," confessed Mr. Pennythorpe. "It is something that I believe also haunts two other members of our gathering this evening, but I have not confirmed my theory with either of them. I speak of what is popularly referred to as a photographic memory, meaning a very resilient memory."

Professor Potter nodded in understanding and looked at Sean, who was now listening with new attention to the history teacher's words.

"As convenient as such a memory is, my friends, it can also be a curse, for aren't there things that we are only too glad that we can forget? But one has to take the worst with the best. My point in telling you all this is to say that, many years ago, I was invited to give a public reading of Mr. Dickens's celebrated work. The reading was so successful that I was invited to repeat it year after year. I am proud to say that I even became fairly good at the whole thing, gestures and all. In fact, it was something I dearly loved to do. But then, for some reason, it fell out of fashion. It's been twenty years since I've done it. But anything, anything at all that can evoke the deeper meaning of Christmas, that can bring honor to the Christ Child, who was but in a manger laid, that the animals should witness the birth of Deity, is a great and wondrous mystery. David's allusion to the 1951 classic rendering of Dickens' story has rekindled my memory, and this evening, for my small contribution to our party, I would like to recite the first chapter:

> *Marley was dead, to begin with. There is no doubt whatever about that. The register of his burial was signed by the clergyman, the clerk, the undertaker, and the chief mourner. Scrooge signed it. And Scrooge's name was good upon 'Change, for anything he chose to put his hand to. Old Marley was as dead as a door nail.*"

When Mr. Pennythorpe had finished reciting the chapter, an appreciative silence allowed the warmth and sincerity of his words to linger for a while in the living room. In fact, no one wanted him to stop, yet for him to recite the second chapter would merely have been a teaser for the third and so on, and the party couldn't continue into the early hours of the next morning, especially since others still had intangible gifts to share. And being both a gentleman and a scholar, wise-old Pennythorpe knew just when to stop.

Applause finally began, first a ripple and then an enthusiastic torrent of appreciation for Mr. Pennythorpe's recitation. Smiling as he raised his hands to acknowledge the applause, Mr. Pennythorpe gestured toward the other side of the room, and smiled as he announced, "Without further ado, I now give you Professor Potter."

Professor Potter solemnly rose to his feet, fixing a steady gaze on the elderly Pennythorpe, who was sitting down. Catching Pennythorpe's eye, Professor Potter intoned, in Latin, "*O magnum mysterium, et admirabile sacrementum, ut animalia viderent Dominum natum—*"

Thatcher Pennythorpe abruptly resumed standing, looking intently at Professor Potter, and responded, "*Et admirabile sacrementu, ut animalia viderent Dominum natum, jacentem in praesepio!*"

Professor Potter rejoined, "*Beata virgo, cujus viscera meruerent portare Dominum Christum. Alleluia!*"

"*Alleluia,*" intoned the frail Pennythorpe, "*Domine, audivi auditum tuum et timui; consideravi opera tua et expavi in medio duorum animalium.*"

"*Domine, audivi auditum tuum et timui,*" repeated Professor Potter, "*consideravi opera tua et expavi in medio duorum animalium.*"

Sean, by now, had become more than a little bored by all this mumbo-jumbo, but as he leaned over to whisper his displeasure to David, he noticed with surprise that David had become curiously attentive to the interchange between the two men.

Mr. Pennythorpe burst into an appreciative and huge smile, whispering to Professor Potter, "And in a manger laid."

"Yes," replied the professor, also smiling, "in a manger laid."

The contrast between the two speakers couldn't have been more pronounced. The wizened Pennythorpe could have passed anywhere as a benign gnome looking for treasure, his craggy hands, knitted brow and prominent bald head scouring the depths. Professor Potter, with his slender frame and long brown hair, might have been mistaken for an overworked graduate student, although a discerning examination of the little wrinkles around the Professor's eyes told a larger truth about his years. His eyes, in fact, were his most prominent feature. Their studied gaze grew from a latent curiosity the better to reveal a self-possessed clarity, betraying a seemingly ageless intelligence, one that held the secrets of the Pleiades and Orion's Sword. David marveled at the exchange the men had just shared, as if they had each recognized and acknowledged something in the other, and had raised it high, uttering in turn its common truth and glory, affirming in their words and silence a mystery and truth far deeper than knowledge itself.

Smiling at his listeners and carefully studying each person's eyes as he surveyed the room, Professor Potter announced, "I was most moved by Mr. Pennythorpe's impressive recitation, and now I would like to play the beginning movement from Johann Sebastian Bach's *Fifth French Suite*. My students and I listen a lot to Bach's music, for we believe that his fugues are so perfectly formed that they offer us a mirror into the very structure of the universe itself and its deepest secrets.

"There are many interesting parallels between math and music, and Bach was fascinated with numerology. In fact, there is a great deal of symbolism in his work. I sometimes wonder what our world would be like today had Bach been a mathematician. But before I say anything more, let me offer this short piece, written in the key of G."

The music which followed was glorious, carrying in its ebullience both clarity and joy, a purity and sprightliness that captured and held everyone's heart. The complexity of the piece, its astounding pace and rhythm, its utter beauty, caused everyone to hold their breath. Time itself seemed to stop as the glorious, interweaving harmonies thundered forth. After Professor Potter finished, his large, sad eyes contemplating other realities, his head still bowed in reverence over the keyboard, a fullness silence issued forth until he looked up, and then applause filled the room.

Acknowledging the enthusiastic response, he confided to his listeners, "Thank you, friends. For me, personally, listening to and playing the music of J. S. Bach is like looking into a separate universe, perhaps even glimpsing a small piece of the Mind of God. The depth, the life, the ineffable joy found in his work is, for me, an affirmation of the life and primordial energy that teems from every quantum particle in this and in every universe. We are surrounded by life, although we can scarcely comprehend its ubiquity. It might be easier to think of our cosmos as one gigantic organism or perhaps a gigantic thought, of which we are all a small but yet vitally important part.

"The more we discover, the less we know. It is a humbling time for us mathematicians and physicists as we endeavor to discover the nature of reality. The metaphors we have come up with seem to help us a little, giving us fleeting glimpses, but I feel sure that in the next twenty or thirty years we will see discoveries that will radically alter the prevailing notions of the universe which have colored our thinking for the past hundred years. For a physicist, this is a wonderful time to be alive.

"Perhaps, in the final analysis, music says it best of all. I would like to offer one more selection on the piano."

Everyone applauded, and the Professor turned to the keyboard and played J. S. Bach's "Jesu, Joy of Man's Desiring," after which everyone applauded again with fervent appreciation.

Then, one by one, guests continued to come forward to share from their hearts as laughter abounded throughout the evening.

Chapter Five
A Reading is Hatched

THE DISTANT CLATTER OF DISHES stirred David awake. Aunt Lillian was washing and putting away the dishes left over from the Advent party. Getting out of bed, donning his bathrobe and slippers, prowling downstairs like a leopard, David stealthily crept up behind Aunt Lillian, whispering "Gotcha" in her ear. She started and turned, sighing, "David, please don't do that to your old aunt, if you want her to stay around very long."

"Sorry. You should have rousted Bobby and me to help you with these dishes," scolded David.

"You heard what Bobby said last night about not being a morning person. Anyway, I wanted to rerun the party in my mind, dear. What a wonderful time we all had," explained Aunt Lillian.

David nodded, recollecting the evening.

"I think we captured the Christmas spirit early this year," observed Aunt Lillian.

"Yeah," agreed David, "And mostly because of Mr. Pennythorpe and his recitation. Wow. Can you imagine memorizing a whole book?"

"Some seem born to do it. I'm afraid I never could," replied Aunt Lillian.

"I sometimes wish I could," said David. "It must make life a lot easier."

"I should think there must be a downside to it, as well," sighed Aunt Lillian. "Remember what Thatcher said about being 'cursed and blessed' with it."

"Maybe I'll ask Sean about it. He seems to remember everything, but I sometimes wonder if he just doesn't get sick of all the clutter that must be up there in his head," observed David.

"Perhaps. But who knows?"

"I'll find out," said David.

David helped Aunt Lillian dry the china dishes and cups and returned them to the hutch. Both worked silently, yet each was pondering the aura of good will that had permeated the party.

"It's too bad that the whole village couldn't share what we enjoyed last night," David suggested.

"I think that lots of people would come to hear Mr. Pennythorpe give a reading of *A Christmas Carol*," said Aunt Lillian.

"Maybe we could coax him out of retirement," pondered David.

"It would be a tall order to make all the necessary arrangements in so short a time," said Aunt Lillian. "Perhaps next year."

"But Mr. Pennythorpe could brush up on the story," David persisted. "He probably knows it cold already. I'd bet on that just from the way he rattled off the first chapter last night."

"I do admit, David, that it was compelling," encouraged Aunt Lillian.

"And in keeping with the story's theme, we could ask everyone who came to donate a dollar, with all proceeds going to the community food bank," said David.

Aunt Lillian raised her left eyebrow, as she looked intently at David, "Sounds as if you're serious, dear. Are you sure you want to take on so much work?"

"I'll get Lisa and the twins to help me. And Bobby will, too," said David.

"Bobby will have to make up all the school work he's missed this week," observed Aunt Lillian. "And so will you."

David gave his Great Aunt an exasperated look, saying, "Bobby *never* does his homework. And I can get extensions if I need to."

"I thought Bobby was beginning to study," said Aunt Lillian.

"Oh, he gets the book out, but he mostly daydreams. I don't think anyone has ever taken the time to show him *how* to study. Maybe we can help him with that sometime during the holidays."

"Before you make any more plans, perhaps you should call Mr. Pennythorpe. After all, if he's unwilling, the whole thing won't work," cautioned Aunt Lillian.

"Just watch me," said David, going to the kitchen counter and picking up the telephone directory. Aunt Lillian, meanwhile, went to straighten up the living room.

A few minutes later, David gleefully shouted, "He'll do it! I knew he would."

"Shhh. You'll wake Bobby," scolded Aunt Lillian.

"About time, too," retorted David.

"What are you going to do now?" inquired Aunt Lillian.

"I'm going to call Mr. Ferlinghausen to see if we can use the middle school auditorium this coming Friday for the program," answered David.

"Do you think many people will come?"

"If we can really publicize it, yes," said David, adding, "And after I get permission from Mr. Ferlinghausen to use the auditorium, I'm going to call the Mayor."

"The Mayor!" exclaimed Aunt Lillian.

"Yes. The Mayor," said David.

"Why on earth the Mayor?"

"To invite his support," explained David. "If he endorses it and comes, so will a lot other people, besides just the kids and teachers."

Aunt Lillian nodded in admiration and approval at David's ingenious strategy.

"I hope it all works out, dear."

"It will. One way or the other. It will," said David confidently.

* * * * *

On Monday, Lisa, Mary and Sean were finishing their lunches when David plopped down at their table and took out his apple.

"Hey, Dude," greeted Sean. "What's this I hear about a public reading?"

David looked at each of them, announcing, "It's going to be a lot of work. It's also going to be a lot of fun. And I need your help, all of you."

"Count me in," said Sean. The girls nodded their willingness to commit.

"Well, here's what I've done so far. We've got to brainstorm from here, but I think we're off and running. As Lisa told you, Mr. Pennythorpe has kindly agreed to give a public reading this coming Friday. He especially liked the idea of asking everybody to donate a dollar and of giving that money to the community food bank"

"Lisa said you even called the Mayor," Sean admired. "Nothing like going to the top. Can he come?"

"Unfortunately, he'll be out of town," explained David. "But he did agree to tape several radio spots to encourage people to come, and he also pledged one hundred dollars to the proceeds."

"Did you meet him in person?" asked Mary, blowing her nose.

"No. I only talked to him on the telephone. He seems really nice, though. I really admire his wanting to support us even though he and his family will be visiting relatives over the holidays. And thanks to him, the radio station will air his spots beginning this afternoon. I think he planned to do four or five different fifteen-second announcements and the station will run them all week. That should bring in at least a couple of hundred people."

"Wow. That would be quite the crowd," exclaimed Sean.

"I want to see us fill the house," announced David. "That would be about five hundred people. Do you think we can do it?"

"If we used guns and threatened them, maybe," observed Sean.

"I'm serious," said David.

"And so am I," said Sean. "Seriously, who would come to a reading on a Friday night before the Christmas holidays? Everybody will just be glad to be out of school. Why come back?"

"Sean's got a point," agreed Mary, sniffing as she wiped her eye.

"We hadn't really thought of that, had we?" said Lisa.

"I don't care. Whatever it takes, we're going to fill that auditorium," proclaimed David, adding, "Hey, Mary, when did you get that cold?"

"It just started on Friday. I've been flirting with it for a week or more. I hate getting so stuffed up. It's really hard to sleep at night."

"You should hear her snore," chimed in Sean.

"No way," countered Mary.

"The house rumbles," teased Sean.

"Does not!" protested Mary.

"David," said Lisa, in an attempt to return to the former subject, "people in the community might come. I'm sure some will. But to expect students to show up at the beginning of the holidays — that's really asking a lot."

"I know. But if this is going down, it's got to really work. We need to pack that auditorium. Sean, how would you force kids to go?"

"I told you. With guns. My preference would be an Uzi."

"I mean if you couldn't use guns or knives," pleaded David.

Sean thought about it for a moment, then brightened, saying, "I'd get old Dandy-Pandy to go in and preach at them. That'd be worse than death itself."

"What good would that do?" asked Lisa.

"Easy. Get him to threaten them with lots of individual conferences if they don't show up. That'll kill 'em. Who wants to waste an hour staring at Dandy-Pandy and hearing all that psychobabble? I mean, it just fills you up 'til you're ready to vomit."

"Maybe Sean is on to something," agreed Mary

"Wait a minute," Sean implored. "If you're really going to ask him, don't let *anyone* know it was my idea. I mean, my life wouldn't be worth two cents."

Mary gave a bemused smile, and said, "We'll have him threaten the seventh-graders."

"No!" shouted Sean.

"Okay, okay," agreed David. "Make it the eighth graders. And if anyone noses around as to who thought it up, say I did. I don't care. It's about time my class got a little culture. And Mr. Pennythorpe will do an outstanding job."

"What kind of flowers do you want at your funeral?" asked Sean.

"I mean it. Kids will thank me after the program. I'm sure of it," said David with confidence.

"We probably had all better go down to the Guidance Office to see Mr. Dandy. Lunch is almost over," said Lisa.

As Lisa, Mary and Sean rose to return their trays, Sean asked David, "Hey. Why were you so late for lunch?"

"I had to sign up for my science project research presentation. Unfortunately, everyone else signed up when I was out last week, so I got what was left."

"What was that?" asked Mary.

"The megafauna," sighed David.

"The what?" asked Sean.

"I need to do research on some of the huge mammals that used to live on this planet. You know, like the famous Wooly Mammoth. Everyone else got a dinosaur."

"That's okay," encouraged Sean. "You'll make them forget all about the dinosaurs. Anyway, we're mammals, too."

"Good point," said David. "I'll have to remember that. I'll ask the cafeteria monitor for permission for all of us to go to the Guidance Office. I'll meet you where we turn our trays in."

The four proceeded to the Guidance Office, which was conveniently located adjacent to the cafeteria. As they entered, a startled Mrs. Fullerton, Mr. Dandy's secretary, became immediately alarmed, as if she were considering summoning the National Guard.

"Can I help you?" asked Mrs. Fullerton, eyeing the group with suspicion.

"Yes. We'd like to see Mr. Dandy," announced David.

Buzzing him on the intercom, Mrs. Fullerton announced, "Mr. Dandy, David Andrews and his friends would like to see you."

The twenty seconds of silence that followed was broken when the Counselor asked over the intercom, "Friends? What are their names?"

"You know, sir. The usual." prompted Mrs. Fullerton.

"Oh, well, it is the Christmas season, isn't it? Please have them come in."

The students entered the counselor's office and were shown to their respective seats, with Sean closest to the door.

"Now, what may I do for you?" inquired Melvin Dandy.

"We need your help, sir," began David.

"Ah, yes, the eternal plea. Couldn't you just surprise me once and come into this office and say, 'Mr. Dandy. We want to help *you*'? Now wouldn't that be a walapaloser? I'd probably have a heart attack or maybe even a stroke."

Sean lifted his eyes in question to David as if to say that he would be glad to exit the office and reenter so as to make such a specific offer, hoping indeed for this adumbrated result. David ignored him.

"No, sir, we wouldn't want that, would we?"said David.

"Okay, okay," said the counselor. "Let's cut to the chase. What d'ya want?"

"We want you, sir, to support a public reading of Charles Dickens' *A Christmas Carol* that will be given by Mr. Pennythorpe this coming Friday evening," announced David.

Melvin Dandy gave a smirk at his four guests, and said, "Surely you're jesting. On the Friday of a major school holiday?"

"We're not jesting, sir," said David.

The counselor surveyed the intent and resolve in David's eyes and protested, saying, "Come along."

"Sir, we want to raise money for the community food bank. The Mayor can't come, but is doing radio spots and has even pledged one hundred dollars to our cause."

Dandy's face turned red and he started to cough violently, sputtering, "One hundred dollars!"

Realizing that the Counselor had wrongly concluded that the Gang of Four had come to fleece him accordingly, David quickly announced, "Sir, we're not here for money."

The counselor stopped coughing and took out his handkerchief, wiping his brow, confiding, "You really do know how to give someone a start, don't you?"

"Sir, we need your help in encouraging students to attend," announced David. "Perhaps a target audience, say all of the eighth graders."

Sean winked at David, appreciating David's willingness to take the flack from his own class for the coming onslaught.

"But what can I possibly do? How do I figure into your equation? I doubt if the eighth graders would listen to me any more than to you. Ferlinghausen would carry more weight."

"Yes, sir. We thought of that. But you, sir, have a special way—quite unique—that sort of forces the issue, if you know what we mean."

"Forces the issue, you say?" inquired Dandy, trying to fathom the intent of the four students who had sought out his support.

Pondering the question for a moment, he looked directly at David, announcing, "Oh, you mean if I threaten them."

"To be precise, yes," agreed David.

"What could I threaten them with?" asked Dandy.

David began to say 'Yourself, sir' but bit his lip.

Pondering the best tact to take, David was relieved when Lisa interjected, "Sir, students value their time. You might consider threatening to meet with students who don't show up. Perhaps it could be in the form of special individual counseling sessions focused on the need to express school spirit and to support special school programs."

Dandy smiled, "Isn't that what used to be called . . . blackmail?"

"*This* is an educational institution," remonstrated David. "And, if anything, since our goals are not for our own personal gain, but rather for the community food bank, what we're asking you to do could be called nothing more than white mail. You'd just be sending them a little message."

"I like that," agreed Dandy. "Sending a little message. In fact, I'll do it. Beginning Wednesday morning. Mrs. O'Leary will be substituting for Mrs. Martin, whose uncle is going in for surgery. I will plan to go to visit all of the eighth grade English classes that day and lay it on the line. Give me the particulars and I'll guarantee you a ninety-five percent attendance rate out of the eighth graders."

"Thank you, sir," said David. "We'll even thank you in the program."

"The program?" asked the Counselor with sudden interest.

"Yes, sir. The one that will tell a little about Mr. Pennythorpe. It will also acknowledge the Mayor's generous pledge and thank a couple of businesses that are also giving money. We'll probably bill you as our Spirit Booster."

"Spirit Booster," considered the Counselor. "I like that. I may even take attendance that night, and woe to any eighth graders who don't show up. I'll make their lives a living hell."

The Gang of Four expressed their thanks and requested passes for their classes. Mrs. Fullerton obliged as Melvin Dandy began to make plans for his imminent browbeating of the eighth-grade.

* * * * *

When David arrived at the lunch table the next day, he saw Mary scowling at Sean, and wondered what had happened.

"Hello, everybody. What's up?"

Mary glowered at Sean, blurting, "I've never been so embarrassed in all my life."

David frowned at Sean as he asked Mary, "What did he do now?"

"I'm so mad I'm not even going to say," said Mary, picking up her tray and taking it over to another table where she sat down with some other friends.

"I guess you really did it this time, Ace," challenged David.

"It was just for a little fun," protested Sean. "I was bored."

David sat in silence, looking at Lisa, who averted her eyes from his gaze.

"Well?"

"We just had gym class. Right now we're studying dancing steps. So the guys and girls get put together. I mean, it's really boring," said Sean.

"So? It happens twice a year," said David. "Two weeks of dance."

"Well, I was just bored out my mind, and the guys were moving around the outside of the circle, changing partners every time we learned a couple of new steps. Mary was coming up and I was beginning to wonder what it would be like to dance with my own sister. I mean, that's gross, and we were about three or four partners away from the ordeal. Conrad Bowles, that little shrimpy seventh-grader, the one with those huge glasses, was standing next to me; so, I looked at him, because he was going to be dancing with Mary first, and I whispered, 'Conrad, be careful when you dance with my sister. She's got a wicked cold and is absolutely *full* of boogers.' And I swear, his eyes got almost as big as his glasses and he began to look a really pale. You would think I had just called down the plague. So the class does two more rotations and there's poor Conrad facing the bug monster, whose sniffing up a storm because of her post nasal drip. Then the coaches demonstrated the steps and we're told to dance them, but Conrad just stands there, refusing to dance. So our coach comes over and says, 'Hey, little boy. What's your problem?' And Conrad just stands there, saying nothing at all, but looking really desperate. And everybody's looking at Mary, Conrad, and the coach. So coach steps in real close to Conrad and put his hands under Conrad's chin and lifted him up, I mean, just lifted him up off the floor to eye level and whispered something, *really soft*, to Conrad. And then the miracle happened. He put Conrad down and hollered, 'Start the music', and man! that lad danced up a storm. I mean, it was like magic."

David was both appalled and fascinated by the story, and could only say, "I wonder what Coach said?"

"I asked Conrad on the way to lunch," brightened Sean, "and he said that Coach had whispered something like, 'Your troubles aren't gonna be with dancin' if you don't come around, little boy; they're going to be with walkin'. So down goes Conrad, dancing like a fiend."

"You're the fiend," scolded Lisa.

"Did the dance fit with the music?" asked David.

"Not really, but Conrad tried to make it fit. I mean, I think he was trying his best to sweep away all the boogers," said Sean.

"I think you two are perfectly beastly," concluded Lisa, rising and taking her tray over to sit with Mary.

"Perfectly beastly?" repeated Sean, looking at David. "I wonder where she gets that from?"

"From all those British mysteries she reads," sighed David. "And, you know something, Sean, she's right."

"Hey, it's just us now," Sean observed. "Do you want to take turns kicking each other under the table since Mary is gone?"

David considered taking his own tray over to join Mary and Lisa, but male bonding prevailed and he could only say, "Sean, you owe Mary a big apology, and you know it."

"Aw, she'll get over it," said Sean.

Wanting to strengthen his point, David decided that now was a good time to reveal to Sean that the little secret of his contretemps with Bobby was out of the bag. David hoped it would bring the little hoodlum down to earth.

"By the way, Sean, there's somebody else wh has decided he owes you a big one," said David blandly.

"And who might that be?" asked Sean with interest.

"Bobby."

"Why Bobby? I haven't done anything to Bobby."

"The night of the blizzard last week, Bobby and I were talking. We decided to become blood brothers."

"Hey, man, that's really cool. Seriously," said Sean, wondering how he might apply for membership.

"So Bobby said he wasn't holding any secrets back from me and then asked me if I was holding any back from him."

The implication of David's words suddenly stunned Sean, and all he could do was slowly shake his head and say, "David, you didn't?"

"I had to," David pleaded.

"What! No wonder he's been looking at me in that funny way, like he'd like to take a stiletto and twist it in and out of my back. Thanks a lot," lamented Sean.

"Look, it was going to come out sooner or later. You *know* that. Now it's out and you don't have to worry about it," said David.

"I'm not afraid of Bobby if it's a fair fight. I've proved that. But if he sneaks up behind me, I might not have any defense."

"He wouldn't do that," scolded David.

"When someone owes you a BIG one, he might do anything," objected Sean.

"So are you going to get up and go over and sit down with the girls?" David asked.

"In a pig's eye. This might get really ugly. I wish you had thought better of it, blood brother or no blood brother," said Sean, adding, "What's eating you, anyway?"

David sighed and stared down at the table.

"Well?" persisted Sean, who was very perceptive.

"It's Mallory Evans," said David.

"I've seen him. He's got a pretty big bump on himself. Probably the most arrogant eighth-grader there is—any where. Has he gotten on your case?" asked Sean.

"He's in my science class," explained David, "and I happen to be the top student, and for some reason it drives him nuts. He comes up to me and gives me a shove, not enough to start a fight, but just enough to be pushy. After shoving me he says stuff like, 'Hey, Andrews, just remember that I'm Alpha and you're Beta, and don't try to reverse it, or your ugly nose is going to be out of joint. Do ya get me?' But I haven't done anything. The way he talks you would think I had been trying to rub his nose in it. He's one of the top students in the class, but so far I'm three points ahead of him. This big report on extinct animals is going to be the clincher for the whole semester and he's really going way out."

"What's his report about?" asked Sean.

"Tyrannosaurus Rex," said David. "He's giving it Thursday."

"It figures," said Sean.

"What figures?" asked David.

"That he would pick the T. Rex. He considers himself an Alpha, and probably assumes the T. Rex was an Alpha, too," explained Sean.

"I just get sick of pushy people," said David.

"Do you want me to put him wise?" asked Sean. "I could make him an offer he couldn't refuse, that is, if he wants to live."

"A lot of good that would do. All he'd say was that I am afraid to fight my own battles. I mean, I don't want to fight him. I just wish he'd lay off," said David.

"I'll just tell him that in the domain of fighting, I am the *supreme* Alpha and I take on all challengers, including little sissies like him. Then I'll push him around a little. Can I *please* take him out for you, David?" begged Sean.

"You are fearless, my friend, and I appreciate what you're offering, but Mallory wouldn't be foolish enough to fight you. Your reputation has been rock solid ever since that number you did on Bobby. Nobody's going to call *you* out. I admire the fact that you don't throw your prowess around."

"I guess I'm a Beta," said Sean.

"Not in my book," corrected David.

"Well, don't forget. Brains count a lot more than brawn, so as long as you're an Alpha in brainy stuff, that's all that matters," encouraged Sean.

"But you're an Alpha in both," said David.

"I guess there's no accounting for taste," grinned Sean.

"Yeah, yeah, yeah," said David.

"Hey. Mallory's younger sister is a friend of Mary's. Let me see what I can find out. Maybe Mallory's pissed off at something we don't know about and is merely taking it out on you," offered Sean.

"Thanks. That might help to explain things."

"Do you think our strategy with Dandy-Pandy is going to work?" asked Sean.

"I don't know. He's going to start visiting the classes tomorrow morning. Mrs. O'Leary is substituting, so Mr. Dandy probably doesn't feel he's interrupting anything," said David.

"I wish I could be a little fly on the wall listening," said Sean.

"You could get in, I bet. Just go to library during your first period study hall and ask Mr. Lowery to give you pass into English 8. Tell him you're researching presentations. Mrs. O'Leary's pretty lenient."

"Maybe I'll do that. Great idea," said Sean. "I'll give you a full report at lunch tomorrow."

Chapter Six
Two Bantam Roosters

MELVIN DANDY PRIDED HIMSELF on his ability to lay down the law, especially to students, and he had been doing it for longer than anyone could remember. That he had excelled at this dubious art form had little to do with his credentials as a guidance counselor and everything to do with his Napoleanic stature.

Waiting until the passing bells had rung for first period, he adjusted his bow tie and rumpled suit and strode purposefully to Mrs. Martin's room, now under the care of substitute Norine O'Leary, a large, burley woman who enjoyed substituting because no one dared give her any guff. Sean Potter had just arrived and had presented a special observer's pass signed by Mr. Lowery, the librarian. Sean took care to seat himself at the rear of the room, lest the temporary presence of a seventh grader confuse Mr. Dandy.

Mr. Dandy had sent Mrs. O'Leary a memo the previous day, announcing the reason for his intended visit. As he entered the classroom, he noticed that she had just finished taking attendance and was beginning to announce that he would be coming.

"No need to keep them in suspense any longer. I'm here. And," the counselor continued, carefully looking at the class, "I'm here to tell you all that it would be absolutely smashing of you if you could please plan to attend a special presentation Mr. Pennythorpe is giving this Friday night."

"But that's the beginning of Christmas vacation," whined Melissa Drake. "Why should we have to come to school on vacation?"

The criticism caught the counselor point blank, and he backpedaled in order to find a reasonable answer. Clearing his throat, he responded, "For the sake of school spirit, my dear, as well as for the benefit of the indigent members of our larger Midville community."

"Indi what?" asked Billy Nottingham.

"Indigent," intoned the counselor. "It means poor. Do you understand? POOR!"

Billy merely shrugged and opened his arms, as if to say, 'So?'

This so infuriated the counselor that he suddenly turned on an innocent and unsuspecting Mrs. O'Leary, growling, "Doesn't even know the meaning of simple words! What kind of English class are you running here?"

Mrs. O'Leary, of course, immediately felt herself the victim — in fact, the royal goat — and bristled, "It isn't *my* class. I'm merely filling in."

"That's a lame excuse," scolded the counselor.

"Well," was all Mrs. O'Leary could utter, in way of passive protest to the counselor's tirade.

"Now listen up, everyone, and hear me plainly," continued Mr. Dandy, "I'm here to tell you that you are *all* going to attend Mr. Pennythorpe's presentation this coming Friday night, and that there'll be absolutely no exceptions or excuses. Have you all got it?"

Now, as one entity, the entire class bristled, partly because of the counselor's treatment of Mrs. O'Leary and partly because it did not appreciate anyone ordering it around, especially a shrimpy little counselor who put on airs and ridiculed people. A silent yet palpable bond began to form between members of the class and poor Mrs. O'Leary, the morning's scapegoat.

"That ain't fair," protested Jerry Matthews. "You ain't got no authority over us during a holiday."

"Maybe I do and maybe I don't," growled Dandy, glaring at the vociferous Matthews, "but just you remember that I've got a long memory. I'm serving up notice right now that anybody who doesn't show up this Friday is going to be put in a special guidance office plan called IMPROVING SCHOOL SPIRIT, and you and I are going to be seeing a lot of each other, and I mean a *real* lot. Now, if you don't understand that, we have a *failure* to communicate, one that might take us months to correct. I get paid whether I sit in my office by myself or with some ne'er-do-well upstart."

Jerry Matthews sat silent but looked daggers at Dandy.

Murmurs of dissent rumbled through the class, Dandy looked at his watch, wanting to insure that his visit to the class would not preclude his leisurely browsing in the morning newspaper, which he customarily picked up in the library right after the beginning of school.

"Now, I've just told you what you're *all* going to do. And I'm not going to take any guff about it. Are there any more questions?" intoned the counselor.

"Could we please write down our questions?" asked Sylvia Morin.

Convinced that he finally was making a little progress, Dandy said, "Yes, of course. Write 'em up, and Mrs. O'Leary can read 'em out loud to me. I will be glad to answer them, just to make sure you all see the big picture."

As students took out their paper and pencils, the counselor reflected on how this method of communication might offer new and improved ways of laying down the law. Dandy relished his current role and had been looking forward to fulfilling it ever since the Gang of Four had bamboozled him into agreeing to push the Pennythorpe program during their Monday visit to his office.

As students' questions were passed forward, Mrs. O'Leary sat solemnly at her desk and put on her reading glasses. Impassively she read the first question, "How will you read your precious morning newspaper if there's a rowdy bunch of students hanging around in your office?"

Dandy's face turned a deep shade of crimson, as if he had been caught red-handed doing something he shouldn't. But to put a brave face on it, he shouted, "Never you mind how I'm going to read the newspaper. Maybe I'll just decide to read it to the students who are with me. And I promise you that any students who are with me are not going to be rowdy."

This first question, which amounted to a knock and a challenge combined, was not the most auspicious way for the question and answer period to begin. To emphasize his authority, Dandy glowered at the class in general, smugly intoning to Mrs. O'Leary, "Next question."

Slipping the first sheet to the bottom of the pile, Mrs. O'Leary read, "Who burned the Constitution and left you boss?"

"That question is beneath my dignity and I *refuse* to answer it. If the student who wrote that little ditty had any pluck, he'd stand up and face me like a man, and I guarantee you that he'd have his ears pinned back so quick he'd think a tornado just blew through. Next question."

"What if your family is planning a trip out of town?" read Mrs. O'Leary.

"If that is true, and the family is leaving on Friday, I will accept a written excuse from the parent. But if the trip begins on Saturday, I want you here. You might even consider bringing your parents. I'm told it's going to be an excellent program."

"Who told you?" asked Jerry Matthews.

"Never you mind who told me," growled Dandy. "Just be sure you get your little duff in there, or I promise you you'll be seeing a lot of me. As you implied earlier, I can't force you or anyone else to come.

That's very true. But just remember this: I have a long memory, and I know where your homeroom is. If I don't see you at this Christmas program, let's just say that you will have cooked your own goose. Next question."

"How will you know if we come or not?" read Mrs. O'Leary.

"I already have all of your names on my clipboard, and I will be checking each of you off that night. So don't think you can escape that way. Next question."

"Is Mr. Pennythorpe paying you to force us to come?"

"Certainly not," growled Dandy, leering at the class. "I haven't even spoken to Pennythorpe about this. And we all know that I can't *force* any of you to come."

Here the counselor gave an odious smile, as if contemplating some future malicious action against his uncooperative wards. And everyone sitting in the room knew how very capable Melvin Dandy was at stretching a minute until it seemed like an hour, and making a mere fifteen minutes into what seemed an eternity. Students shuffled in their seats and bristled against the short-statured tyrant who now stood before them. Rebellion smouldered in their ranks, their intent silently affirming their need to assert their individual freedoms and to object to this rude and uninvited intrusion.

"So if you know what's good for you," blustered the counselor, "you'll jolly well show up and you'll all be wearing a real big Christmas smile on your faces. Next question, and I hope it's a whopper, just so that I can lam into any confusion about what's coming down."

As if to reaffirm the point he has just made, Dandy looked over at Mrs. O'Leary, raising his eyebrow as if to say, 'You fool. Can't you read?'

Mrs. O'Leary quickly placed the question lying on top of the pile on the bottom and scanned the next question.

"Just a minute," scolded Mr. Dandy. "Don't go editing those questions. I want to hear the one you just put at the bottom of the pile."

"Believe me," explained Mrs. O'Leary, "it wasn't worth it— "

"Listen to me," demanded the counselor. "I'm ordering you to read that question. We're not going to pull any punches around here, at least not as long as I'm in charge."

A bemused smile traversed Mrs. O'Leary's lips as she took the sheet of paper from the bottom of the pile and then read in a clear, strong voice, "When did that damn flying squirrel land on your head, and how often do you feed the poor brute?"

A shocked silence descended upon the classroom, for no one had expected to hear such a devastating insult. Dandy stood there, flabbergasted as well, finally throwing up his hands, shouting, "That's it! That's the end! I come in here to help you and all I get is sarcasm. Well, let me just tell you, I've got my ways of dealing with the likes of you, and I'm going to jolly well answer each of your questions, INDIVIDUALLY, because I'm going to find out who wrote each of these questions."

"But there aren't any names on these papers," protested Mrs. O'Leary.

"I want a writing sample from every student sitting in this room, and I want it now. Mrs. O'Leary, give me those questions."

The students of English 8 — Period 1 sat dumbfounded by this most recent development, especially the ones who had assumed they would be getting away with something called murder. Sweat began to form on several brows, but no one acceded to the counselor's demand.

"Mrs. O'Leary," prompted Dandy. "I said 'Now' and I mean 'NOW!'"

"No," came the unexpected response. "I will *not.*"

"What?" sniped the counselor, turning to look at his betrayer.

"I said, 'NO,'" repeated Mrs. O'Leary, with greater conviction.

"Are you deaf? Do I need to repeat what I said?" asked the stunned counselor.

"No, and NO," came the substitute's firm answer.

"Give me those questions immediately," ordered the red-faced counselor, advancing on Mrs. O'Leary's desk.

"No. I will not," insisted the burly Mrs. O'Leary.

"Give 'em to me," threatened Melvin Dandy, "or I'll see that you never substitute in this town again."

"I will *not,*" replied an increasingly stubborn Mrs. O'Leary. "You didn't require their names, and I will not betray their identities."

"Give 'em to me now," ordered the counselor, storming her desk.

Mrs. O'Leary stood, and although she was imposing enough when seated, she was even more spectacular after she arose. Towering a full ten inches over the counselor, she looked down into his eyes and said, with growing ire, "I will NOT give you these questions."

As Dandy thrust his arm out to grab them, Mrs. O'Leary's firm hands began to tear the sheets of papers in small pieces, crumpling them into a ball, and finally throwing the ball into the basket next to her desk.

"Don't you *dare,*" whispered the substitute in *sotto voce* as the counselor began to bend down to extract the crumpled questions from the basket.

Applause and cheers thundered from the students as Dandy, his wattles shaking beneath his crimson face, growled, "I'll be back. Just you wait and see. I'll be back."

The counselor then exited the room, slamming the door as he left, ignoring the cheers, whoops and applause that echoed throughout the classroom in appreciation for a substitute teacher who had protected her students from reprisal and sanction and who had refused to be bullied.

* * * * *

When David reached the lunch table later that morning, he realized that something had gone wrong, owing to the concern he read on the faces of Lisa, Mary, and Sean.

"Hey, guys. What's wrong?" was all he could ask.

"Dandy-Pandy blew it," announced Sean.

"What? Didn't he go in to the eighth-grade English classes?"

"Only to period one," Sean reported. "He's been sending Mrs. Fullerton in to all of the other classes to read a prepared statement. But what he did during period one really touched off a firestorm. A lot of eighth-graders are saying that they're not going to go to the reading just because Dandy tried to force them to. And Mrs. O'Leary vowed she would never let him in her classroom again. She went right to Mr. Ferlinghausen."

"We were so intent on making sure we packed the auditorium, we forgot the human factor," began Lisa.

"Human factor?" asked David.

"The Dandy factor," Mary sighed.

"Yeah. Most students hate Dandy's guts," explained Sean. "If he orders them to do something, they'll do anything but obey him. You know the little Bantam rooster routine. Mary's almost right in calling it the 'Dandy factor.' I would call it the 'Dandy-Pandy' factor. That man has some serious issues."

"I should have seen this coming," David groaned. "How bad was it?"

"Not good," said Mary. "Sean just told us about how he was able to visit the first period class and witness the entire disaster."

"Yeah, David, your idea of how I could go in to observe the class worked like a charm. I don't think Dandy-Pandy even knew I was there. I was careful to keep a low profile," explained Sean.

"That would be a first," retorted Mary.

"What happened?" asked David.

"Well, old Dandy strode in shortly after the period began, and he started in by saying that he had been asked to boost school morale and spirit and that he was going to do it by making sure all the eighth-graders attended the reading of Charles Dickens' *A Christmas Carol* that will be given by Mr. Pennythorpe on Friday. If he had just made the announcement and walked out, that probably would have been okay; but, no, he had to make a Federal case out of it."

Sean then recounted all of the horrendous details of the spectacle.

"Sounds as if Mr. Dandy had a rough morning," observed David.

"Not to mention our eighth grade classmates," said Lisa. "David, we owe them a major apology. They didn't deserve any of that. If we had only thought about what we were doing."

"Well, we didn't. And I think you're right. We do owe them a huge apology. Why don't you and I plan to visit each of the classes tomorrow. We'll explain everything, and hopefully we can win back their goodwill."

"What has Mrs. Fullerton been telling the classes?" asked Lisa.

Sean grinned, confessing, "I went back to second period, hoping old Dandy-Pandy would pop in and make a fool out of himself again, but in flounces Mrs. Fullerton to read a statement. I quote, from memory: 'Eighth-graders, this is a message from Mr. Dandy, your counselor: I am much too busy to come to speak to you myself, but I want you all to know that it will be very important for you to attend Mr. Pennythorpe's reading of *A Christmas Carol* this Friday evening, beginning at eight o'clock. I know that the holidays will have started, but I also know that you will want to support your very own history teacher. You should also be advised that I will be taking attendance to ensure that total class support is realized. Those not in attendance should plan to meet with me during their study halls and after school throughout the months of January through March of next year so that a new understanding about the need and value of school spirit can be found in our deliberations. Thank you for listening. See you this Friday evening.'"

"That's no better than his going in by himself, except that he probably irritated fewer kids," lamented David, cradling his head in his hands. "We've badly misjudged our peers. There's a real rebellion in the air."

"You would think that if Mr. Dandy knew *anything* about psychology and adolescents that he would know better than to tell them they 'had' to do something," said Lisa.

"He only knows the cheap psychology," grinned Sean, adding, "And I mean *really* cheap."

"Oh, shut up," said Mary. "A big help you are."

"David, you look really depressed," said Lisa.

"I am. We've got to figure out how to apologize to all of our classmates and smooth things out so most of them will come, and we've also got do it in a way so Mr. Dandy doesn't lose any more face."

"How could he lose any *more*?" retorted Sean. "I mean — is there any left?"

"He can't help it if he goes about it ass backwards," concluded David. "*We* are the ones who should have seen it coming. And now that it's here, we're going to have to eat a lot of humble pie, since it's *mostly* our fault."

"Like, be real, David," said Sean. "Dandy's nothing but a — "

"Watch it, underling," warned Mary, "or I'll tell POTS the words you've been using."

"Well, aren't you're quite the open-book?" said Sean sarcastically.

"Twins, please stop squabbling," said David.

Lisa stroked her hand through David's hair, asking, "Is there more, David? This seems like a lot about a little."

"I'm also being bugged by Mallory," sighed David. "He's out for blood with all this T-Rex Alpha and Beta business."

"Hey, man," said Sean. "Mary got the real scoop on Mallory. His youngest sister happens to be one of her friends."

"Sean's right, David," explained Mary. "I asked Kendra what was up. What she told me puts everything into perspective."

"So," challenged David, "I'm ready for clearer vision."

"Mallory has five sisters, four older and Kendra who is in my grade," explained Mary. "As it works out, his four older sisters have proven themselves to be Miss Smiley's best students. I know some kids think that she favors girls, and that may be true, but Mallory's sisters all worked really hard to earn the highest averages in their science classes. And their prize for getting the highest grade on these presentations, which means the highest grade for the first semester, has always been a trip up to see the Natural Science Museum in Ottawa, Canada, which has real dinosaur bones, as well as to a place near the St. Lawrence River where life-size concrete sculptures of dinosaurs are on display. All of Mallory's sisters have loved their field trips with Miss Smiley. She let them each bring along three friends."

"So Mallory really wants to go on that trip?" concluded David.

"He can taste it. And now he's become paranoid about the possibility of being bested by his four older sisters," agreed Mary. "Even Kendra admits that he's nuts. Absolutely nuts."

"Most sisters say that about their brothers, but they don't really mean it," chimed Sean, to which he received Mary's appraising raised eyebrow.

"So Mallory's nuts. That's not news to me," retorted David blithely.

"Yes. And he's nuts about the T-Rex and about Alphas and Betas," said Mary.

"You have a point," David admitted.

"You're not the only one who has to live with it," said Mary. "Kendra says that Mallory's always pushing her around saying that she's Beta and he's Alpha."

"What an inferiority complex!" Lisa laughed.

"I can fix that for him," said Sean.

"How?" asked David.

"I'll rent a T-Rex costume and walk up to him and give him a good kick in his shins. That way he'll know that he's *not* an Alpha, and that he'll never *be* an Alpha," offered Sean.

"Sean, you're sick," said Mary.

"I may be sick, but it's Mallory who's crazy," retorted Sean.

"Don't you see?" asked Mary. "Mallory is petrified that he won't be Miss Smiley's top student. And, David, your high average is standing in his way. He's afraid he won't be able to measure up to what his four older sisters did. If he fails, he's not as tough as they are and, because he's a boy, he's expected to be tougher."

"He shouldn't even be competing with them," said Sean.

"I know," said Mary, "but that trip has sort of become a family expectation. He's under a lot of pressure. That's probably where all this alpha and beta stuff began."

"That's a bunch of cheap psychology, if there ever was any," said Lisa. "I mean, inside we all have alpha and beta tendencies. No one is ever completely one or the other. What nonsense."

"Try telling that to Mallory," said Mary. "He's just gone bonkers with it."

"Maybe Sean's idea was the best," said Lisa.

"I'll rent the costume tomorrow," said Sean.

"You know, I wonder if alphas are only betas with inferiority complexes, trying to compensate for their feelings of inadequacy?" asked Lisa.

"You should become a psychologist," said Sean. "Your first client could be Mallory, followed by old Dandy-Pandy."

"I can think of a better second," quipped Mary.

"Well, crazy or not, I'm not going to cave in to Mallory," announced David. "And I'm also not going to let him upstage me in these science reports. I mean, he came up behind me this morning and shoved me, saying, 'Andrews, just wait until you see my big display tomorrow in the lobby. I've got a T-Rex so big, you're gonna crap in your pants. You'd better bring a second pair of briefs to school."

"Gosh," said Sean, "What did you say?"

"I just told him to bug off," said David. "I'll just do a better report than he does. Mine isn't until the middle of January, and I'm going to do a lot of research over the vacation. He'll crap in his pants before I'm done."

"That's the spirit," cheered Lisa.

"Don't forget our chess games," Sean reminded.

"Only if I have time. So give me a break. I need to upstage Mallory and to show him what a real class presentation is all about. In fact, I'm going to ask Miss Smiley to schedule me for a *two*-day presentation."

"Hey, David, you're sounding like an alpha," teased Lisa.

David frowned at her.

"Let's face it, David," said Sean. "We're both betas."

"Yeah, yeah, yeah," was all David could say as the passing bell sounded.

Chapter Seven
A Public Reading

On Friday morning before school David walked into Mr. Pennythorpe's room, took his gloves and coat off, and began rubbing his hands, grateful to be inside out of the freezing cold.

"Thanks, Mr. Pennythorpe," said David, "for meeting with me before school begins."

"Not at all, David, it's always good to see you."

"How are things working out for tonight?" asked David.

"Actually, better than I thought. The story came back to me quite quickly, with only two read-throughs. I've also practiced my gestures. My so-called book will serve merely as a prop. I just hope that I'm not too rusty."

"You'll be just fine, I'm sure," David encouraged. "I'm really sorry about the stink that Mr. Dandy caused; in all fairness, he *was* trying to help us with our request. We wanted to pack the auditorium tonight, and so we thought that if we could get him to cajole the eight-graders to come, we might have a full house."

Mr. Pennythorpe looked down at his desk in mild embarrassment, and then looked up at David with a broad smile. "Thank you for your interest in making tonight a success, but I think it won't really matter how few or many we get. The important thing is that those who come *feel* the truth and power of Mr. Dickens' story. And I believe that will happen. So, how can we fail?"

"Lisa and I went in and apologized to all of the eighth graders yesterday," said David. "Will you be speaking to your history classes today?"

"Yes. I plan to tell them that many silly things seem to happen around the holidays, including public readings. I will also tell them that I do not expect them to come, especially out of any fear of reprisal or because they have been bullied. In fact, I will add that I know them for the upstanding students that they are, and any that I see tonight I will know in my heart came solely to hear Mr. Dickens' fine story, no matter what others may think or say."

"Wow!" said David. "That'll get 'em to forget Mr. Dandy and come."

"But I will not say that to get them to come, David."

"I know. And *that's* why they'll come. That, and because of their affection for you."

"That's very kind of you. I hardly deserve it."

"No other teacher in this building has ever learned the names of all the students, at least not as quickly as you do," explained David. "It means something when somebody remembers your name."

"I can hardly take credit for a good memory, but I am pleased you feel that way," said the ancient teacher.

"Are you sure you don't want us to make a videotape record or a recording of your reading tonight?"

"Yes, I have given it real thought, and I am very sure. It seems to me that, although it might offer a sort of record of tonight's gathering, it could never catch the spirit of what I hope will transpire tonight."

"What do you want to happen?" asked David.

"I want the truth and power of Mr. Dickens' story to take root in the heart of each member of the audience, in a way that will bring lasting transformation."

"Isn't that a pretty tall order?" wondered David.

"The story has been doing just that for generations. I am but another poor vessel for its passage."

"Speaking of transformation, Mr. Pennythorpe, do you have any suggestions for how I can relate in a constructive way to Mallory?"

Mr. Pennythorpe, suppressing a grin, closed his eyes in thought.

Smiling, he said, "I like Mallory, David. Eventually you may, too. Certainly he has his comical and dramatic moments, but don't we all? He wears his heart on his sleeve, and one cannot help but feel sympathy for his need to be, or at least to *appear* to be, what he so fiercely calls an Alpha."

David couldn't help but grin at the generous but accurate description.

"I suppose one could say that Mallory is really searching for his own sense of self-worth and self-identity?" continued Mr. Pennythorpe.

David nodded.

"Perhaps the attributes that Mallory sees in the T-Rex remind him of some of the qualities he would like to see in himself," suggested the elderly teacher.

David pondered the idea.

"Mallory is *very* competitive. He always wants to be Number One," said David.

"With you, in particular, in science class, or in general?"

"Definitely with me; but more probably with everyone everywhere," responded David.

"Unrelenting?"

"Yes, sir."

"Can you imagine him having fun?"

"Not in an easy-going sort of way," said David.

"Laughing?"

"Only if someone he was trying to defeat stumbled," said David.

"Poor Mallory. He doesn't seem to be enjoying life very much, does he?"

"No, Mr. Pennythorpe," said David.

"He really seems fixated on this whole Alpha/Beta business?"

"Yes, sir, he does," admitted David.

"Perhaps we can help Mallory better understand that his own potential is best served when he competes only against himself, as opposed to his constant opposition with others."

"How does one do that, sir?" asked David.

"By beating him," said Mr. Pennythorpe. "Has he given his T-Rex presentation yet?"

"Yes, sir. He gave it yesterday."

"How did he do?"

"Actually, I thought it was quite good, on the whole," said David.

"What did it have going for it?"

"Well, I think the main thing is that Mallory has been devouring information about T-Rexes for years and that his science report gave him the opportunity to put all that accumulated knowledge into a cohesive whole," reflected David.

"That's a lot of reading," nodded Pennythorpe. "Did his presentation have anything against it?"

"I'm not sure, sir," said David. "Perhaps one thing: he was, in my opinion, a little too intense about it."

"How so?"

"Well, he stood up and started rattling off how superior the T-Rex was to not only all other dinosaurs, but also to all other creatures as well. T-Rex was, he said, the greatest and most perfect example of an alpha ever to walk the earth. I mean, you'd think the T-Rex was a god or something. Mallory really swaggered on and on about it."

"Obviously, Mallory must think that the T-Rex is the Grandest of all Alphas," Mr. Pennythorpe smiled.

"Yeah, and *nobody* in the class, including Miss Smiley, was going to risk suggesting otherwise," David frowned.

"Why not?"

"Because Mallory has such issues about it. I mean, you get the feeling he'd come back and cut your throat if you suggested the T-Rex wasn't the greatest Alpha that ever walked," said David, grimacing.

"Why does that bother you?"

David reflected for a moment, then said, "Because it's not a balanced view. It's just not true. At least, I don't believe it. Yes, it may be accurate on *one* level, but there are many levels to consider. I just think it's overblown. And Mallory is trying to get all of the mileage he can out of it."

"It sounds a bit as if he's also trying to get that trip out of it, as well," Mr. Pennythorpe laughed.

"No doubt because his sisters have done so before him," agreed David.

"Will it be hard to upstage him?"

"I'm not sure. I admit that I have my work cut out for me. Mallory brought in over eighty slides. He did a really professional job that way, although I suspect his father probably helped him. Mallory even created that papier-mâché T-Rex that was in the lobby this morning"

"Is *that* what that thing was?" exclaimed Mr. Pennythorpe, whose bemused smile broadened into an enormous and contagious laugh. "I thought it was a dog begging for food."

Mentor and student laughed heartily, David wiping tears from his eyes.

David felt better merely from laughing so hard and was beginning to thank Mr. Pennythorpe for his appraisal when the latter added, "Mallory certainly will never be an alpha in sculpture."

Mr. Pennythorpe's pithy pairing of Mallory's ridiculous papier-mâché T-Rex, with painted blood dripping from its lips, with Mallory's overly intense drive to be alpha in everything, brought a new round of laughter.

"David, these quizzical personalities do open themselves as vehicles of our gentle ridicule. And it's probably better to laugh than to cry. I'll see you tonight. I'm taking the afternoon off to go home and rest before tonight's reading. I hope you will be pleased with my performance. In any case, the community food bank will be happier."

"Mr. Pennythorpe, thank you, more than words can say," said David.

"Oh, David. I *do* have a suggestion of how to get one up on Mallory in January."

By the time Mr. Pennythorpe had finished giving his suggestion, David was smiling and nodding, saying, "That is absolutely brilliant. And I'll do it. Thanks."

* * * * *

That evening, Friday, December 22, many citizens of Midville journeyed to the village's middle school to hear an extraordinary member of their community recite a 19th century Christmas novel.

Seasonal carols played on a CD player sitting near the front of the auditorium as people entered. Members of the eighth grade were in particularly good attendance, most especially because of Mr. Pennythorpe's words to his students. The publicity, although hastily planned, seemed to have been effective. The Director of the Community Food Bank welcomed cash donations, for it would allow his agency to ensure that a balanced pantry would become available for the indigent throughout the holiday season. As people entered, they stood in queue waiting to deposit their dollar bills into large cans marked COMMUNITY FOOD BANK. As people milled about, many laughed and joked. Melvin Dandy stood at the rear of the auditorium, assiduously recording names of eight-graders present. At eight o'clock, he ascended to the third level to record the attendance of students who had elected to sit in the balcony.

At five minutes past eight o'clock, David Andrews walked to the front of the auditorium and turned off the music. Returning to his seat, he whispered to Aunt Lillian and Bobby, "Mr. Pennythorpe will come out on the stage in about three minutes." As expectations grew, the murmur of whispers grew louder, until a wave of soft voices coursed through the auditorium.

Suddenly the audience noticed a slight, almost frail, gnome-like figure entering from stage left. Applause greeted the advancing figure, fully bedecked in a formal period costume, including top hat, frock coat, and silk tie, which could just be seen under a bright blue scarf. Tipping his top hat to acknowledge the audience, Mr. Pennythorpe removed his coat with a great flourish and put them both on a small table next to the reader's chair. The costume lent itself to the imminent reading, and looked absolutely exquisite on the diminutive yet dapper Thatcher T. Pennythorpe.

Acknowledging the audience's continued warm applause with a dignified bow, Mr. Pennythorpe smiled as he looked out, saying, "I cannot thank you all enough for taking the time and trouble to come tonight. For, in doing so, you have demonstrated a genuine concern for others. This time of year, more than any other, brings rich opportunity for the renewal of friendship as well as the strengthening of family ties. The story you are about to hear is about a man whose life, whose very heart, grew to look selfishly at the accumulation of wealth, with his heart eventually growing cold to the world. Unfortunately, it is not an isolated instance in the history of humanity, although the permutations are not always for the sake of money; sometimes they involve power, fame, glamour and all of such enviable things, which at a particular moment might seem irresistably dazzling and attractive, but which bring in their wake the inevitable curse of unhappiness — that is, if we do not remember that we share a larger responsibility for the welfare of others and that we are not meant to walk in this world alone.

"Yes, we have done our small part in coming tonight, and I see from this platform that there are several large canisters where many, if not all, of you have already generously contributed toward our community's food bank. But the challenge of the story you are about to hear goes far deeper than one contribution on a single night. Far better for us, and for our broken world, if we could rise to the occasion of 'honoring Christmas in our hearts and keeping it all the year.' But the pressures and demands of daily life are not so kind as to allow us that privilege. Still, I appeal to you to consider doing it, if not at least once a week, then once a month, so that whatever you do for others can become part of the love and goodness that is manifested here tonight. If we can bring Christmas into our hearts a little more, in little ways, so much better the world will be for our labors. This is my challenge to all of us tonight — that we, through our love and action, might bring the spirit of Christmas alive *at least* once a month for this coming year, and perhaps *once a week* for the next year, and who knows what might be done after that? Indeed, my job tonight is not only to give you the best reading that I possibly can, but also to express hope that my small efforts will kindle your generosity, so that upon leaving this auditorium tonight you will remember what you offered when you entered, and will gladly choose to offer once again a similar token of your love for others.

"My reputation as a reader has not been tested in many years, and so I also realize the chance that most of you are taking tonight. Nevertheless, if I meet your expectations and my words bring inward satisfaction and delight, let them say of my audience's response: 'They paid to get in, and they paid to get *out.*'"

Laughter resounded throughout the auditorium as the audience gleefully noted the speaker's intent and humor. Applause soon followed as Mr. Pennythorpe once again acknowledged the audience before sitting down in the reader's chair, closing his eyes and holding Mr. Charles Dickens' celebrated *A Christmas Carol* in his lap.

A hush settled over the audience as the lights in the auditorium were dimmed, thus allowing the stage lights to illuminate the speaker. It was apparent that Mr. Pennythorpe was centering himself, tuning himself to the marvelous story he would soon recite.

Most in the audience expected the frail and diminutive teacher to open the book before he began to recount the story, but instead he opened his eyes, surveyed his listeners, and began, "*Marley was dead, to begin with. There is no doubt about that. The register of his burial was signed by the clergy man, the clerk, the undertaker, and the chief mourner. Scrooge signed it. And Scrooge's name was good upon 'Change, for anything he chose to put his hand to.*

"*Old Marley was as dead as a door-nail.*

"*Mind! I don't mean to say that I know, of my own knowledge, what there is particularly dead about a door-nail.*"

Mr. Pennythorpe smiled as a rustle of laughter coursed through the auditorium.

"*I might have been inclined, myself, to regard a coffin-nail as the deadest piece of ironmongery in the trade. But the wisdom of our ancestors is the simile; and my unhallowed hands shall not disturb it, or the Country's done for. You will therefore permit me to repeat, emphatically, that Marley was as dead as a door-nail.*

"*Scrooge knew he was dead? Of course he did. How could it be otherwise? Scrooge and he were partners for I don't know how many years. Scrooge was his sole executor, his sole administrator, his sole assign, his sole residuary legatee, his sole friend, and sole mourner. And even Scrooge was not so dreadfully cut up by the sad event, but that he was an excellent man of business on the very day of the funeral, and solemnized it with an undoubted bargain.*

"*The mention of Marley's funeral brings me back to the point I started from. There is no doubt that Marley was dead. This must be distinctly understood, or nothing wonderful can come of this story I am going to relate.*"

Standing, Mr. Pennythorpe walked around his chair as he related Dickens's brief allusion to*Hamlet* and the need that its viewers must be convinced before the play begins that Hamlet's father has died.

"*Scrooge never painted out Old Marley's name. There it stood, years afterwards, above the warehouse door: Scrooge and Marley. The firm was known as Scrooge and Marley. Sometimes people new to the business called Scrooge Scrooge, and sometimes Marley, but he answered to both names. It was all the same to him.*

"Oh! But he was a tight-fisted hand at the grindstone, Scrooge! a squeezing, wrenching, grasping, scraping, clutching, covetous, old sinner! Hard and sharp as flint, from which no steel had ever struck out generous fire; secret, and self-contained, and solitary as an oyster. The cold within him froze his old features, nipped his pointed nose, shriveled his cheek, stiffened his gait; made his eyes red, his thin lips blue; and spoke out shrewdly in his grating voice. A frosty rime was on his head, and on his eyebrows, and his wiry chin. He carried his own low temperature always about with him; he iced his office in the dog-days; and didn't thaw it one degree at Christmas."

The gestures that Mr. Pennythorpe had used when describing Scrooge were so fluid and fluent that by the time he had finished, everyone in the auditorium was fully centered on both the character and the story, listening intently to the teller's every syllable, the magic of the story descending and beginning to work its wonders. Many students later said that the reading had been far more vivid and compelling than any of the Scrooge movies they had seen. Furthermore, Pennythorpe was able not only to change his voice to offer fresh vigor to the story's characters, but also had facial expressions and gestures that brought each one fully alive. David thought to himself that, if this is what Pennythorpe had feared would be a 'rusty' performance, certainly the magic of the story and fervor of the moment had caused the presenter to become very well oiled.

As Mr. Pennythorpe continued, David was astounded at how focused the audience had become, veritably hanging on the speaker's every word and gesture. The story had found in its teller a new and vital incarnation, and its experiences and lessons were sweeping through the minds and hearts of those who listened, igniting the collective imaginations of those now assembled, and offering up a cascade of images, words, and nuances of another time and place, yet revealing a deeper story that was still most timely and relevant.

—For truly, thought David, — in every person in this auditorium, in every person in the world, there lives an Ebenezer Scrooge, as well as a Bob Cratchit and a Belle and a Tiny Tim — representations of all manner of ways one can be a human being.

As Pennythorpe's exquisite rendering of the tale continued, the audience deepened its suspension of disbelief and saw and felt and heard the three ghosts who came to visit Scrooge. The audience saw and felt and heard the places the spirits took Scrooge as if in Scrooge's own slippers. The sheer marvel of the story continued to unfold, as eyes watered and were wiped and as occasional coughs were heard, yet nothing detracted from the vast power of these rich images as they stirred people's minds and hearts.

When Scrooge's internal resurrection came, an unmistakable and profound joy swept through the audience, kindling hearts and bringing high hopes for the character who had been reborn in love, from Scrooge's calling out to the small boy about the turkey as big as the lad himself, to Scrooge's giving many back payments toward the benefit of the indigent and needy, to his attending Christmas dinner at his nephew's home, to his teasing Bob Cratchit for arriving late the next morning. And although everyone knew how the story would turn out, it mattered not, for the glory and grace of the words themselves provided a verdant river of pictures and feelings, a tide which carried listeners along toward the joyous dénouement.

Pennythorpe paused to wipe his brow and, as he did so, he considered his audience, much in the same way he had before he began his recitation. Smiling with a mirth and joy that was immediately infectious, he lifted his arms as if giving a solemn benediction.

"*Scrooge was better than his word. He did it all, and infinitely more,*" whispered Pennythorpe, lowering his arms and stepping forward to the center of the stage, bringing himself as close to his listeners as possible. "*And to Tiny Tim, who did* NOT *die, he was a second father. He became as good a friend, as good a master, and as good a man, as the good old city knew, or any other good old city, town, or borough, in the good old world. Some people laughed to see the alteration in him, but he let them laugh, and little heeded them; for he was wise enough to know that nothing ever happened on this globe, for good, at which some people did not have their fill of laughter in the outset; and knowing that such as these would be blind anyway, he thought it quite as well that they should wrinkle up their eyes in grins, as have the malady in less attractive forms. His own heart laughed: and that was quite enough for him.*

"*He had no further intercourse with Spirits, but lived upon the Total Abstinence Principle, ever afterwards; and it was always said of him, that he knew how to keep Christmas well, if any man alive possessed the knowledge. May that be truly said of us, and all of us! And so, as Tiny Tim observed, God Bless Us, Every One!*"

A short silence followed Mr. Pennythorpe's last words, for no one wanted the tale to end, although everyone earnestly had yearned for the arrival of the dénouement and Scrooge's resurrection. In that brief silence, a sudden recognition and understanding had seized the audience, and it was the certain knowledge that a great gift had been given to all assembled, first by a genius named Charles Dickens and, second, by an incomparable teller of stories named Thatcher Pennythorpe, diminutive in physical stature but a giant in the compass of the human spirit. No thanks could possibly suffice to avow so profound an epiphany, but, in truth, no acknowledgments were ever expected or necessary. The important thing was that it had happened, and that everyone who had come was now a different and better human being for all eternity, these short few minutes fully and forever felt in the larger expanse of non-linear time.

Suddenly applause broke forth, bursting from every quarter, as Pennythorpe wiped a tear from his right eye and acknowledged the applause with a modest bow. People stood, wiping their eyes, and the thunder of hands increased and continued as the frail teacher returned to his chair and donned his top hat and frock coat, again giving an appreciative bow to his audience as he proceeded to walk demurely off stage.

The applause continued, would not stop, until the self-effacing teacher appeared from backstage, again taking a modest bow, the applause continuing until he had once again left the stage. As members of the audience prepared to leave, queues could be seen forming so that those exiting could contribute once again, and no doubt more generously, to the Community Food Bank cans, confirming Pennythorpe's witty prediction.

David was the first to reach Mr. Pennythorpe back stage, as the teacher mopped his brow and wiped his eyes. Giving David a winning grin, he nodded, whispering, "We did it."

"*You* did it," corrected David, grabbing his mentor's hand and shaking it with enthusiasm and gratitude.

"But *you* fathered the idea," retorted Pennythorpe.

"Then *we* did it," rejoiced David, feeling it a privilege to have been part of so profound a moment.

"A line of people is forming to thank you," said David, pointing to well-wishers who were waiting for Mr. Pennythorpe to exit back stage into the corridor.

"How very kind of them," he said. "Let me go thank them for coming."

"And people are really filling up the community food cans," announced David.

"Good," observed Pennythorpe. "Then they really *were* listening to me at the beginning."

A great good feeling abounded in the auditorium. Truly the Spirit of Christmas had come early to those who had attended the program.

On the way home, although Aunt Lillian, Bobby, and David spoke no words in the car, a great deal of gratitude and love was shared.

Chapter Eight
A Christmas Eve Like No Other

"David, what time did Professor Potter say he would pick us up?" called Aunt Lillian from the top of the stairwell, as she studied herself in the full-length mirror. Tugging at her rose and cream dress with her left hand, she adjusted her pearl necklace with her right hand.

"Sean said it would be around seven-fifteen. That still gives us a little time. He and Mary have to sing in the Youth Choir, and they have to rehearse at seven-thirty. The service is at eight o'clock."

"I do suppose we might just as easily have walked through the field and up the hill," sighed Aunt Lillian, adding, "It would have saved them the trouble of stopping for us."

"Yes, but they *wanted* to stop. Remember they just got that spiffy new van that seats up to fourteen passengers," called David, who was polishing his shoes. "Anyway, the path up to the church is a little uneven, especially in winter."

"That path has always been very well worn," protested Aunt Lillian as she entered the boys' bedroom, seating herself on David's bed. "And why did the Potters get such a large van?"

David grinned as he contemplated his response, finally saying, "Do you want the official story or the truth?"

"Both," replied his curious Great Aunt.

"Well, the official story is that the new van will be shared with the church's middle school youth group for some of its trips, and that's really nice of the Potters to do," explained David.

"And?" prompted Aunt Lillian.

"And what?" teased David.

"The truth?" she reminded him.

"Ah, yes! It seems that POTS has demanded a vehicle that will allow the twins to have their own separate seats."

"Maybe we should walk up the path after all," mused Aunt Lillian.

"The path is tricky after dark and difficult to navigate," said David, adding slyly, "I might fall, you know."

Looking at him fiercely, yet in full appreciation of his humor, Aunt Lillian chided, "You mean that *I* might fall." With a deep sigh, she added, "It doesn't pay to get old and rickety, especially when you feel only twenty-five inside."

"I don't want you to go breaking anything again," laughed David. "I have much too much school work with that big science report on the megafauna."

"Just order some cotton wool and pack me gently," sighed Lillian.

"I'm trying to order a Wooly Mammoth. And, besides, you're not the cotton wool type and you know it," remonstrated David.

"It's too bad that the good Mrs. Dr. Potter had to work at the emergency room tonight," observed Aunt Lillian, "but better Christmas Day off than Christmas Eve, isn't that what Sean said?"

"They're an amazing family," said David. "Bobby, did my tie fit?"

Bobby looked sheepishly out of the bathroom where he had been trying to tie one of David's ties, shaking his head in frustration.

"Here, give it to me," said David, hastening to the rescue.

A light snow had fallen that morning and Midville now resembled many of the quaint village scenes one sees depicted in greeting cards. There was no wind to speak of, and the forecast for Christmas Day even called for sunshine, a true rarity in the all-too-often overcast region of Central New York.

"I'm never gonna learn to tie a tie," lamented Bobby.

"Yes, you will," said David. "It's easy. Just watch me. You're a quick study. You'll have it in no time."

"I very much appreciate the Potters' kind invitation," said Aunt Lillian. "I haven't visited Midville's Methodist Church in years, and I understand they have a good music program."

"Sean gave me a summary of tonight's sermon," said David impishly.

"But how could he know?" wondered Aunt Lillian.

"He's a little menace of a magpie, that's why," growled Bobby.

"You've got to forgive Sean, Bobby. After all, it's Christmas," said David.

"Yeah. I can't wait to see his little magpie jaw drop when he reads my card," said Bobby.

"David, how could Sean have possibly found out what the minister is preaching about tonight?" persisted Aunt Lillian.

"Well, it's sort of a long story, but I'll give you the abbreviated version. Sean is treasurer of the Methodist Youth Fellowship. His private agenda is to get church funds for trips and parties. So he regularly goes in to see the ministers, hoping to fleece them, to get them to ante up for a skating party or a movie or some pizza."

"Do they cave in?" asked Aunt Lillian.

"Well, they do, but I think it's mainly to get rid of Sean. And he knows that. He just goes in and puts on his bright-eyed, bushy-tailed inquisitiveness and talks a mile a minute, and they sort of get dizzy and excuse themselves from their desks and leave, and then come back a little later saying they have to do this or that but that his idea is a good one and they will find the necessary funds. Sean says it works at least eight times out of ten. He visits the retired pastor one week and the real pastor the next. Each minister has some sort of discretionary fund for stuff like that."

"We must give Sean an A+ for his persistence," Aunt Lillian smiled. "But that still doesn't explain his foreknowledge of tonight's sermon."

"Well," continued David, "when the ministers excuse themselves, Sean usually walks around the office and, of course, he notices *everything*. Sometimes their sermons are lying on their desks. Sean says that the retired pastor's sermons are yellow with age, with a barely legible scrawl."

"If they ever catch him snoopin' around, *he'll* be yellow with age," quipped Bobby.

"You know Sean, though. He's like a cat. Probably still has five or six lives left," laughed David.

"He ain't gonna have that many when I'm done with him," promised Bobby. "I still owe him."

"David," inquired Aunt Lillian. "The sermon? Did Sean get to read the one the pastor wrote for Christmas Eve?"

David grinned and contemplated his response.

"Yes and no."

"What do you mean by 'yes and no'?" asked Aunt Lillian.

"Well, he *did* read it, but the pastor didn't write it," explained David. "Here, Bobby, try this tie now."

"I don't understand," said a puzzled Aunt Lillian.

"Late last summer Sean discovered that Rev. Havens buys his sermons. Isn't that a riot? I'm sure he's very good at other ministerial duties, but it seems that he subscribes to a sermon service," explained David.

"I bet that whet Sean's curiosity," observed Aunt Lillian.

"You're absolutely correct. But his mom and dad were upset when they learned that he had been poking his nose around Rev. Havens's office. So they struck a compromise. Since Sean remembered the address of the company that sells the sermons, he wrote and took out a year's subscription, for which his parents paid. Now he reads the sermon recommended for each week just to see how much Rev. Havens departs from it."

"Sounds to me like they might be sellin' some magpie pie at some future dinner if that little hoodlum's ever caught in some of his little shenanigans," said Bobby, hopefully.

The doorbell chimed.

"They're here," shouted David.

Opening the door, Sean stood there catching his breath, having bolted in from the van. "Sorry we're early, but Old Skunk head got a little panicky about having only fifteen minutes to warm up, so we need to get going right away."

"Skunk head?" asked Aunt Lillian, descending to the foyer.

"I'll explain later," said Sean, a little red-faced, adding, "But maybe you'll understand after you see her conduct the choir tonight. She's really okay. It's her husband that bugs me, but that story will take a lot longer than we've got now. Maybe you'd like to come and sit in on one of his horrible little Sunday school sessions and suffer along with the rest of us?"

"I believe David has told us a little bit about Mr. & Mrs. . . . Lytle, isn't it?"

Sean nodded with obvious self-approval.

"David also tells me that you have dubbed Mary a sheep, owing to her long curly hair, in retaliation for having called you a little hoodlum for so long."

"Not for the 'little hoodlum' slams," explained Sean, "but for all that jive about my having been a raccoon during the great canasta showdown between David and Bobby. I can't help having these circles under my eyes."

"I think I'm beginning to see," smiled Aunt Lillian as she observed to herself that Sean's circles had not dissipated, adding, "So, Mary, then, is a sheep?"

Unable to resist such an obvious cue, Sean grinned and gave a rousing, "BAAA!"

Professor Potter cheerfully honked the horn as Sean, baaing the whole way, led David, Bobby, and Aunt Lillian out to the van. Christmas greetings were shared all around as the merry travelers made their short journey to Midville's United Methodist Church.

Dropping everyone off near the front entrance, Professor Potter said he would meet the others upstairs in the sanctuary after parking the van. The twins ran off to their rehearsal while Aunt Lillian, David, and Bobby followed POTS to what were the family's usual seats, situated midway back in the right center pews. The church dated from the late nineteenth century, with a large addition having been added shortly before the first World War. Recently the lower level had been completely remodeled and an elevator had been installed in the bell tower that allowed the elderly and handicapped access to the sanctuary. Sean relished riding up and down the elevator during youth fellowship meetings, using it as a vehicle to startle and ambush the unsuspecting.

David liked the warmth exuding from the sanctuary, the bright and festal Christmas decorations, the fresh scent of pine needles from the large tree and window trimmings, the musty smell of the hymnals mixing with the scent of wax from the dozens of burning candles.

Professor Potter soon joined the entourage, seating himself at the end of the pew as he studied the bulletin for the Christmas Eve Service. Many additional worshipers were now flooding in and several stopped at the Potters' pew to wish the Professor and his family the merriest of Christmases.

"Part of being so famous," POTS whispered to Aunt Lillian. "People do it all the time, and he's such a dear about it."

"Does all the attention ever annoy him?"

"Only when he's working in his study. If you ever hear the old Bach playing on the stereo, don't dare go in," admonished POTS *sotto voce.*

"Has anyone ever broken that rule?" asked Lillian.

"Only that little dickens of a Sean, when he was younger. Now there was a handful of a lad, let me tell you, if you ask me or anyone else on the earth for that matter," sighed POTS. "He would barge in on his poor, dear father at any hour, despite all my warnings and threats."

"What did the professor do?"

"That man is a living saint, I swear," explained POTS. "He never even shooed him away the way I would have, but maybe that's what a father and son relationship is all about."

"You mentioned that Professor Potter listens mostly to the music of J. S. Bach?" inquired Aunt Lillian, with obvious approval.

"His favorite composer! And not only listens but, as you know from that wonderful night at your Advent party, he plays as well!"

"Yes," smiled Lillian, "I've not heard very many who could play Bach's music as well as he does."

"What I say," whispered POTS, "is that a genius is a genius no matter what frightful punishments life throws in the way."

"Frightful punishments?" asked Lillian, raising her right eyebrow.

"Come, now," scolded POTS, "the little rag-a-muffin has been at your house night and day these many weeks."

Lillian repressed the strongest impulse to laugh, for she had been privy to hearing Sean's considered opinion of Muriel Mullarney, whom the twins had confidentially christened as 'POTS' some years ago, an acronym meaning 'Poor Old Thing, Shame!' —If POTS only knew, thought Lillian, smiling as she took time to notice the many poinsettias that decorated the front of the sanctuary. Her eye also caught the console of a large three manual, electronic organ, which had been turned on and was ready to rip.

"I've not been in this church for many years, long before they bought this organ. At least twenty years, I should say. How do you like the organ?" asked Aunt Lillian.

"Well, you must remember I grew up in Ireland, an old country with little money. The larger churches in the cities, however, did have pipe organs. I grew up hearing what I call the real organ sound. I remember it as being a purer sound, with more clarity than you hear from one of these electronic gizmos. And I'm not saying that Mr. Gantry, our organist, doesn't make up for it in volume. Sometimes you can't even hear yourself think. You'll see that tonight, or 'hear it', I should say. It's Christmas Eve, so I expect the church will be packed. I'd wager a month's pay that Gantry's going to make that instrument really thump. Personally, I'd prefer an organ with real pipes, but they're very expensive, as you well know. Only the Episcopalians and Presbyterians could even think of affording that kind of luxury, if ever they had a mind to pay for it."

Lillian thought of the two manual, twenty rank tracker pipe organ she had enjoyed playing at the Episcopal church for so many years. POT's perceptive comments on almost everything were colored with a practical stoicism. The instrument Lillian had played at Midville's Episcopal Church was over a century old, but none the worse for wear, and had become a celebrated treasure of the church. Of course, it also meant that some Episcopalian, way back, had mustered the vision to see how such a legacy could serve future generations.

The mahogany door to the right of the organ swung open with impressive purpose as a very dapper Mr. Gantry, attired in a maroon gown, entered the sanctuary and strode deliberately to the organ console. Seating himself on the bench, much as one might mount a horse, Wayne Gantry placed his music on the music rack and proceeded to push a few stop tabs down at various locations on the instrument. Then, with singular attention, he ventured to place his left foot on the appropriate pedal and proceeded to play J. S. Bach's Christmas prelude *In Dulce Jubilo*.

Members of the congregation, who had previously been whispering, now raised their voices by a factor of two so as to be heard by one and all. Fortunately, Mr. Gantry was now much too absorbed in his music to hear what he would have called the 'small talk.'

"What's that on his shoulders?" David whispered to Aunt Lillian.

"He's wearing an academic hood for his music degree," responded Lillian.

"How do you know?" persisted David.

"That pink velvet border stands for music, and that hood is about the same size as my master's hood, but I'm not sure which school conferred the degree. The school colors appear on the interior of the hood — mine were light blue and scarlet," explained Lillian as she and David studied Mr. Gantry's academic apparel, adding, "For Christmas, though, I think I would have picked red and green."

"Can you pick the colors?" inquired David.

"No, not really. The school does that. You're sort of stuck with what you get."

"He only has orange on the inside of his hood. That's kind of a loud contrast to the burgundy gown, isn't it?" observed David.

"I wouldn't have matched them that way myself," agreed Lillian.

"He's a Syracuse University graduate," whispered Professor Potter, who had been listening with interest, now that his many well-wishers had found their own pews.

"Perhaps he teaches college music classes," mused Lillian. "I'll ask PO . . . I mean Muriel."

The inquiry having been successfully communicated, Lillian whispered back to David and Professor Potter, "Muriel remembers hearing that he teaches college music courses."

The door to the left of the organ opened once again and two young acolytes dressed like angels entered and proceeded up to the podium to begin lighting the numerous Christmas candles that decorated the front platform. As they pursued their labors, the Senior Choir, also attired in maroon, entered into the choir loft that sat above the organ console. At the same time, members of the Youth Choir, in royal blue gowns, processed through the door most recently used by the acolytes. Following the Youth Choir were the two clergy of this church. The Rev. Lindsay Beecher Havens was a tall, slender man with a full head of curly gray hair who, if his life had been different, might successfully have attained prominence as an actor. In his company walked the Rev. Dr. Julius Meachem, a rotund and jolly-looking pastor of not only considerable girth but also enormous presence, who now served as minister emeritus of Midville's Methodist congregation.

Mr. Gantry had some time ago finished his prelude and had been improvising until the choirs and clergy were seated at their respective stations. Suddenly the melody of "O Come, All Ye Faithful" could be heard in the improvisation. The organ, true to POTS's prediction, grew in brightness and volume as it thundered the final part of the hymn's refrain. The congregation was now standing, with their hymnals open, and soon robust singing welled forth and filled the highest reaches of the sanctuary.

David had never heard anything quite as glorious. He became very certain that if there was anything that Methodists could do well, it was to sing hymns with great passion. Mr. Gantry directed the sopranos in the adult choir as they sang a descant on the hymn's third verse, after which he departed from the familiar harmonization for the next several verses, finally playing an organ interlude before the last verse. By the conclusion of the hymn, it seemed as if the assembled voices and full organ had opened a door to heaven itself, with the night's Christmas sky, riven with angels' voices, calling all creation to join in singing the glorious words of Christ's birth.

The Rev. Havens stepped to the pulpit, leading the congregation in a responsive reading and then a prayer, after which he announced that, owing to a recent bequest, the church was, on this very Christmas Eve, fortunate to inaugurate its new lighting and sound system. The congregation was further apprized that the departed donor had spared no expense on having this state-of-the-art system installed and that its ability to blend sound and light would prove enormously enhancing to the congregation's worship experience.

"This new light and sound mixing system will first be utilized to dramatize the anthem that will soon be sung by our Youth Choir," concluded the enthusiastic pastor. So, on this special Eve, as we join to celebrate the coming of that little child who draws all humankind unto Himself, let us forevermore give thanks in our hearts for God's love and mercy."

After the Rev. Haven sat down, a small octet of first and second graders was escorted to the front of the church, whereupon the Sunday School Superintendent conducted them in two verses of "Away in the Manger." As these young children sang, Mr. Lytle crouched in front of them holding a portable microphone. During most services, the realtor sat in the very front pew with his arms folded and a scowl on his face so as to lend disciplinary support to his wife's efforts to marshal the Youth Choir, although Elvira Lytle and the choir sat off to the right side of the organ. Steadfastly, in his newest role, Mr. Lytle held the portable microphone like a rock, as the children's sweet and slightly dissonant notes and words rang clearly through the room, thanks to the new sound system.

After the lambs' song, all of the children of the congregation were invited by Pastor Havens to cluster about the tall Christmas tree, which stood to the left of the pulpit. Of course, the poor man was mobbed, and little room was left in front. Spotlights illuminated the area as the minister's lapel mike helped even the deafest member of the congregation to feel like a little child again. Pastor Havens's best sermons were those he prepared for children of all ages, but no one had ever had the insight to suggest that he limit his preaching to that venue. Methodists love music, and Rev. Havens's mellifluous voice had such symphonic effect on his flock that no person had ever dared to communicate the importance of brevity to this cleric, hence generations of Sunday noonday roasts had been condemned to becoming quite crisp, their disappointed owners the not unwilling victims of an articulate and sometimes overzealous cleric whose mesmerizing voice had intoned many to glory.

The Children's Sermon embraced a culinary theme and ended on a happy note, since each participant was given an oversized Christmas cookie. Rev. Haven, with his usual wit and diplomacy, observed that several dozen cookies still remained in the large box he held before him and that those cookies would be shared among the members of the Youth Choir at the end of the service, after which he promptly plopped the box on top of Mr. Gantry's organ console. Fortunately, Mr. Gantry had no music sitting beneath the box, for he had learned long ago to photocopy and bind all of his music so that he need not fumble his way through the service, changing from anthem to hymnal back to anthem and so forth.

The time had come for the Youth Choir to sing, although most of their individual and collective attention was focused on the tempting box of Christmas cookies that Rev. Haven had just placed on the top of the organ console. The congregation sat in the fullest expectation of seeing the first application of the new lighting system. Mr. Lytle, Midville's most persistent Christian realtor, was stationed front row center in his regular pew, with his arms folded and a scowl etched on his face. If public religion were to mean anything, so thought Lytle, it must be solemn; unfortunately, Lytle's efforts to be dour made his religion come off on the decidedly sour side of things. Rising abruptly, Lytle motioned vigorously for members of the Youth Choir to take their appointed places to the left of the organ console.

Mrs. Lytle, the only Skunk-head choir director in Midville, followed after her young charges and purposefully took her place in front of the eager ensemble of seventeen budding voices, although their inner eagerness now centered on their desire to devour the Christmas cookies that had been so temptingly placed on Mr. Gantry's organ console. What made matters worse was that most of these adolescents could now smell the sweet, almond and vanilla flavor wafting toward the congregation. Mrs. Lytle never used music when she conducted; memorization was first and foremost the order of the day for all of her singers. The result was, more often than not, a polished and professional offering, sometimes even more daunting than that given by the very talented Senior Choir. Smiling at her young singers, Mrs. Lytle looked at Mr. Gantry who stared in rapt attention at her through his mirror, waiting for her cue to begin the anthem. Mrs. Lytle was waiting patiently for the ushers to turn out most of the sanctuary lights, so that the remaining lights would illuminate the members of the Youth Choir.

All this had been meticulously rehearsed the previous Sunday morning, except for the actual reformatting of the lights. Mr. Lytle knelt down in front of the choir, holding his portable microphone to what he called and fancied to be their 'singing center.' Mrs. Lytle looked toward the rear of the sanctuary where the new light and sound controls had been installed. The poor ushers, however, were trying to decipher Mr. Lytle's illegible scrawl and scrambled stage directions, the very ones he had scratched onto an old envelope during the previous Sunday morning's rehearsal. It had not occurred to anyone that any rehearsal of ushers or lighting equipment was required.

What Mrs. Lytle now saw greatly aggrieved her. As she looked back at the little cubicle that now served as the electrical and sound nexus of the sanctuary, she observed that, in their confusion, the first light the ushers shut off was the one giving light to the cubicle itself. What followed was nothing less than a classic spectacle of incompetence. Lights began to flash on and off throughout the sanctuary, as if by trial and error the ushers hoped to succeed at arriving at the prescribed solution to the current lighting problem. In their considerable consternation and confusion, one of their number, and there were four who were attempting to serve, somehow managed to hit the master switch that suddenly plunged the entire sanctuary into complete darkness, except for the candles and the lights on the organ.

The resulting darkness was too much for Mr. Lytle. Lifting himself up from his kneeling position, which at his age had become increasingly difficult to maintain and uncomfortable to endure, he stormed to the back of the sanctuary to put, from his own idiosyncratic point of view, 'things right.' In his haste, he forgot that his clammy little fist clutched the live microphone most recently intended for the larger amplification of the Youth Choir. The lights from Mr. Gantry's organ console served to make Mr. Lytle's flight to the rear of the sanctuary very like the beginning of an unpleasant hobgoblin invasion from All Hallows Eve. Reaching the cubicle, Lytle poked his rude, shadowed face up into the confused faces of the four ushers who were desperately searching to find the master light switch, growling, "What da ya think you're doing?" The men looked slightly abashed as their accuser added a most uncharitable assessment of their collective situation, "Don't cha know you're ruinin' the service?"

"Shh! They'll hear you!" scolded the head usher. "We're trying to find the master switch."

"I don't care if the Lord himself hears me! Why couldn't you just follow the directions I gave you? I wrote everything out plain and simple," persisted an increasingly indignant Lytle.

"Well, maybe a hen could have read it," challenged a burly usher, giving Lytle the evil eye. "What do you think we are? Handwriting experts? I've never seen such a wretched scrawl!"

This pointed criticism was much too much for Hank Lytle, a bully who was infinitely better at dishing it out than taking it. In his defensiveness, he had mounted his highest horse, and now smirked at this unexpected challenger and jeered, "Even an idiot could run this switch box. Maybe I should bring a couple of the kids back here. They'd certainly do a finer job than any of you."

The congregation and choirs and clergy sat dumbfounded as the strains of this emerging argument flooded through the new, state-of-the-art loudspeaker system. It would have been gratifying to the installers to know that not one whisper was lost, even on the deafest of ears, and that all ears were now acutely tuned to the tenor of the rising storm, its tensions tightening at every word.

"What we do need back here is not you, but somebody with a few brains," intoned the burly usher, and everyone in the sanctuary knew that the 'you' in question was the ushers' newly discovered antagonist, who could now be heard sputtering, as the deep, authoritative voice continued, "How about that famous Professor? The one at the university. I saw him. I bet he'd know how to put these foolish lights on."

"Are you kidding?" retorted an irate Lytle, his voice now recoiling from insult and straining with anger. "All they ever know how to do is blow things up. I mean, like the atom bomb, posting everything to kingdom come and back again. I've got that little terror of a son of his in my Sunday school class and let me just clue you in: he's an entire World War all by himself."

"Quit talking and push some more of those idiot switches," ordered the shrill and desperate voice of the head usher, who was now on the verge of panic.

Lights started flashing on and off, and murmurs and half-heard oaths rolled over the new speaker system. A new voice was now heard whispering over the others, after which came Mr. Lytle's clarion question, "What do you *mean* the damn mike is on?"

A sharp and immediate metallic click was followed by a short interval of silence, after which the appropriate lights were miraculously illuminated. After another brief pause, Mr. Lytle strode purposefully to the front of the sanctuary as if nothing untoward had happened. Kneeling down, he turned the portable microphone on and dutifully held it in place as the Youth Choir sang about a little drummer boy. The tension that had filled the sanctuary dissipated in the sweet and gentle lyrics of the Youth Choir's anthem. David repressed the urge to laugh as he fancied, for the briefest moment, that he was bearing witness to a skunk directing a choir that had among its members a raccoon and a sheep.

After the anthem, the congregation then rose to recite in unison the Apostle's Creed, which was followed by Mr. Gantry playing an offertory during which time the ushers brought forth the collection plates. Then began the rite of Holy Communion.

As members of the congregation came forward to partake the Holy Eucharist, Mr. Gantry led the Senior Choir in a series of Christmas carols and anthems. When the Youth Choir was motioned forward, the Lytles joined them, one on each side, lest anyone escape. Their number perfectly filled the extent of the communion rail, and all went well as the small bits of consecrated bread were distributed by the solemn and dignified Rev. Havens and the venerable and portly Rev. Dr. Meachem. As the small communion glasses were given out, Sean felt the most curious temptation to glance at Mary as she lifted the glass to her lips.

His thought train had not been especially reverent, for he had asked himself, 'I wonder how a sheep takes communion?' Looking at Mary, who was kneeling on his left, he saw out of his peripheral vision her lifting her glass using both of her hands, which seemed quite unnecessary. This unexpected sight struck his funny bone and he suddenly felt like laughing, but instead bit his tongue, quickly attempting to suppress this devilish urge.

The rising power of Sean's focused imagination, however, had kindled in his wiry frame a kinetic energy that had to find release in some outward and visible form, but in anything except laughter. As he felt this kinetic energy flood through his being, and biting his tongue even harder, Sean snorted heavily through his nose and mouth as his body began to convulse. His irreverent shaking now fanned down each row of communicants, for Sean was kneeling near the middle. In front of him stood the aged and sometimes dubious Dr. Meachem, who had noticed Sean's aberrant movement and was now studying him with a curious gaze. Daring to open his eyes just a crack, Sean saw that which he feared most, namely the Rev. Dr. Meachem peering at him. Shutting his eyes, Sean wondered if he would ever be able to fleece Dr. Meachem for pizza money again. Sean desperately hoped that he would suddenly awake in his bed, but there was no help for him and, as he waited, his shaking increased, as did that of the entire row, including the spouses Lytle who served like bookends for the youth choir members, and hoped to quell the adolescent spectacle that raged between them.

"All rise," instructed the Rev. Dr. Meachem, who continued to study Sean with a telling gaze. "And as ye go from this place, think clearly on how our dear Lord has touched your heart this night, wondering how he may be calling you to serve Love's greater purpose, perhaps even as a member of the royal priesthood itself."

Standing when told to do so had helped Sean to cease his shaking, and when he opened his eyes, he saw the Rev. Dr. Meachem smiling at him, in fact, beaming at him, as if Sean had done some very special thing or had had some very unique experience. Returning to his choir seat, fully drenched in his own sweat, Sean offered a real prayer of thanks that he had not laughed like an idiot nor ruined the service nor, since he himself was rarely ever embarrassed, brought a frightful shame on his father, Mary, POTS, David, Bobby, or Aunt Lillian. So relieved was this wayward twin that he was unable to sing "Silent Night" or the closing hymn, "Hark! The Herald Angels Sing."

POTS made it her business to notice everything, especially about her two young charges. At first she found it curious that Sean wasn't singing "Silent Night," for he typically went after anything and everything he chose to do with gusto and passion. POTS discerned that something was different, although she wasn't quite sure what had transpired in 'the little dickens.' Noting the subtle change, her heart went out to him in a new way. So used to scolding him, she now looked at him in the warmth of Christmas love, seeing a young, if occasionally bellicose, lamb, needing her protection and guidance. There were times in the past when she had become quite sure in her own mind that only one of the twins would ever get to heaven, but now she realized that Sean would make it, too. The thought brought back ancient memories, those of her own father and his unfortunate difficulties with religion. When told that he should contribute more to his family church, he had curtly informed the priest that he would do so when he saw God coming to take all of the collected donations. The priest, of course, considered this the epitome of blasphemy and vague threats of excommunication followed. The controversy, however, drove a pithy question home, 'If we give back to God, why doesn't God get what we give back?' That was the year POTS's family had ceased attending church. She had only resumed the custom after she became engaged as a nanny in the Potter household. Images stirred in her and brought a time long past, where unloving recriminations and damnations were tossed about rather blithely at those who would not heel. Her father's rugged independence had inspired her in her own resolve never to be 'taken in.' Of course, she had had ample opportunity to practice this virtue in the face of the many onslaughts of the twins, most notably 'the little dickens.' Now as she looked at Sean, her heart went out to him even more, and she rejoiced that the love and mercy of the Infinite was such that even the likes of this Little Dickens could be assured a place in Paradise.

After the service, Aunt Lillian waited until Mr. Gantry had finished playing his postlude to congratulate him on the fine, festal music. Downstairs in the choir room, Mary called Sean a perfect idiot and he responded with a resounding 'baa' that would have earned him a good clip, had he not darted back from her right hook just in time.

Professor Potter went to fetch the van.

"What a glorious and wonderful service," exclaimed Aunt Lillian. "I'm so glad we came. Aren't you, David?"

David nodded in agreement as Sean joined their ranks.

"Mr. Gantry is certainly an excellent organist," announced Lillian, "and we just had a wonderful visit about various kinds of organs. Did you know that he very much hopes that the church might be able to replace its aging electronic organ with a real pipe organ? They've had an organ fund for years and the current instrument is showing its age. Mr. Gantry also invited me to accompany him and his wife to the next meeting of the local chapter of the American Guild of Organists. I look forward to getting involved in that organization. When I was playing at the Episcopal church, the only real communication among organists in the community came when we all shared responsibilities for the annual joint Thanksgiving service that was usually held at St. Mary's Roman Catholic Church, since it is the largest in the village."

"How did you like our church's organ?" asked Sean.

Aunt Lillian smiled as she answered, "Any instrument in the hands of a musician like Mr. Gantry would sound its very best. Still, I do hope he will be able to get that pipe organ he's after."

"Mighty loud at times," offered Bobby, wanting to let everyone know he had attended and enjoyed the service.

"Hey, let's go throw snowballs at the new van," said Sean with a mischievous twinkle in his eyes. Bobby, David, and Sean made a quick exit, leaving Aunt Lillian and POTS waiting in the church foyer for the poor Professor who would soon be ambushed in a hail of snowballs.

"You've got to watch that one," warned POTS, referring to Sean.

"A touch wild, wouldn't you say?" said Aunt Lillian sympathetically.

"Some days I would say 'really touched' and other days 'very wild'; there isn't a happy medium with that little dickens. But I can never stay mad at him for more than ten minutes. He's a real charmer, that one."

"Still, it can't be easy," confided Aunt Lillian.

"Just watch what you say," warned POTS.

"How so?" inquired Aunt Lillian.

"It's like talkin' to a human recording machine," POTS grimaced. "And I'm not saying that every word isn't one hundred percent accurate. That's the problem. It's *always* one hundred percent accurate. And he always manages to put it in a different light, if you know what I mean. Not so much that you can accuse the little dickens of breaking the truth, but more like twisting it. Ah, and what a master he is."

"I suppose that we're only hearing what he hears?" speculated Aunt Lillian.

"That child gives a whole new meaning to the word 'bellicose'— I mean, he's a warrior's warrior, with so much energy, and so few places to expend it," sighed POTS.

"You don't mean — " began Aunt Lillian.

POTS nodded vigorously, quickly saying, "Poor Mary and me. Sean needs a brother or two."

"Oh, my dear, I didn't know," exclaimed Aunt Lillian.

"It's a cross I willingly bear for the sake of the kind Professor and the good Mrs. Doctor. They are the ones I'm trying to protect, not to mention the little lamb Mary," confessed POTS.

"Is there anything I can do?" asked Aunt Lillian.

POTS considered long and hard as they waited for the van, no doubt now enduring an avalanche of snowballs.

"Well, just between you and me, it's been a little harder than usual," whispered POTS.

"Why, my dear?"

"Because David is so busy with his school project. Sean sees him as an older brother. Sean has his own friends, his own age, but David is a year older, and in some ways acts a couple of years older. Sean and his friends are always romping around, wrestling and fighting like a litter of pups. But the little dickens really needs an older brother, and David has become that. He'd do anything for David, but David has been busy with that animal report he's working on."

"Animal report?" asked Aunt Lillian.

"The big beasties that died out long ago," explained POTS.

"Oh, yes, the megafauna. Yes. He's pretty obsessed with that," agreed Aunt Lillian.

"Well, whenever he tells Sean he can't see him or play chess or something like that, it causes an intensification in the Little Dickens's energy, if you know what I mean. Usually Mary gets the brunt of it, until I get wind of it and step in," explained POTS.

"Well, perhaps I should say something to David," suggested Aunt Lillian.

POTS shook her head, saying, "I don't know what could be said to change things in a natural way. The little dickens could see through it, anyway, if you know what I mean. There's also another matter."

"What's that?" asked Aunt Lillian.

"Do you know that Bobby and David became blood brothers the night of the big blizzard?" asked POTS.

"I remember David mentioning something about it, but I didn't take it literally," said Aunt Lillian.

"Oh, I'm sure it was only two pin pricks and not knives, but it was very literal. And when Sean found out, he felt jealous of Bobby," explained POTS.

"Ah. Exclusion from blood and bond," nodded Aunt Lillian. "And from a young warrior's point of view — "

"You got my meaning," said POTS. "He's been just awful, with no let-up, but there's no addressin' it, either. That would only make matters worse."

"I appreciate your taking me into your confidence," whispered Aunt Lillian. "At least I am more aware of what is going on."

Mary appeared at the door, announcing breathlessly, "The van is here."

"Dear child, did you run here to tell us that?" asked POTS.

"No, they're throwing snowballs at each other," said Mary.

"The boys?" asked Aunt Lillian.

"And Dad," glowered Mary.

"Ah. There's still a little boy left in the Professor," agreed POTS. "Some say it's where his creativity comes from. Shall we wait here for the 'all clear' or go out and face it?"

Mary hesitated, but then decided that the two elderly ladies would bring a new sense of forbearance to the snowball war. Unfortunately, she was wrong, for POTS and Aunt Lillian were nearly hit with snowballs as they got into the van.

When the males entered the van, POTS said scornfully, "So, it's every man for himself, is it? A Merry Christmas to all and to all a good night."

On their journey home, no one thought to remark about the glorious spectacle that had erupted with the church's new sound and light system. Instead, Sean decided to give a detailed account of how Rev. Haven had veered from the purchased sermon, saying, "You know, he usually uses about eighty percent of it, but tonight he only used sixty percent. What makes it come alive is how he delivers it. I don't know how he does it; it always sounds so 'holy.'"

"I suppose the purchased sermons give him a sort of launch pad through which he can organize his ideas," suggested Aunt Lillian, hoping to put a good face on an obvious flaw.

"Maybe," agreed Sean. "But that's an awfully kind way of saying that he doesn't have many original ideas of his own. Isn't it?"

"You don't have to have any original ideas to be a minister," said David, adding, "As long as you convey some *very* original ideas about love."

"Well, I suppose it's good the poor man knows his limitations," said POTS.

"But everyone was hanging on his every word," observed Aunt Lillian.

"That's true," agreed POTS. "Obviously he's a better conveyer than originator."

"I think it's perfectly beastly that Sean has weaseled a way to receive the sermons ahead of time," said Mary.

"I'm only studying human nature," quipped Sean. "I haven't gotten to sheep, yet, but when I do, you'll be next. BAAA."

A sturdy whomp rattled the Potters' new van.

"Professor, it is very good of you to pick us up and bring us home," said Aunt Lillian. "Thank you very much."

"Very glad to. This van is going to let us do more in that way. It will also certainly be a help to some of my graduate students."

"If you ever want to go to church again with us, we'll be glad to pick you up," volunteered Mary. "Right, Daddy?"

"That's right, pumpkin," agreed Professor Potter.

"It's BAAAkin," corrected Sean.

"Sometimes I wish I had straight hair," lamented Mary.

"So do the sheep," retorted her brother.

"Children, children," scolded POTS, "it's the Lord's own birth night."

"Hey," invited Sean, looking at David and Bobby. "Come with us to the Watch Night Service. Nanny's driving. There'll be plenty of room."

"What's that?" asked David.

"It's a New Year's Eve Service for youth in the community," said Mary.

"I'd love to," said David. "How about you, Bobby?"

"Okay by me," agreed Bobby.

"Teens from a lot of the village's church groups get together for a big party," explained Mary.

"Yeah," chimed Sean, "the party's the bait, the praying is the switch, but everyone who went last year had a good time. So we're going to chance it."

"Is it okay with you if we go, Aunt Lillian?" asked David.

"Fine by me. I'll be in bed by ten o'clock, as usual."

"Count us in then," said David. "And thanks for the invitation."

"Great. Glad you're coming," said Mary.

By the time they were dropped off, David was beginning to wonder if the light spectacle had ever actually happened. He resolved to conduct a personal 'reality check' with Bobby and Aunt Lillian the next morning. Exchanging final Christmas greetings and bidding everyone goodnight, mid the strain of Sean baaing in the van, after which there followed a muffled thump, Lillian, David, and Bobby quickly retired for a well deserved night's rest. The boys wearily climbed the stairs to their bedroom and soon fell asleep to the sound of distant sleigh bells.

Chapter Nine
Christmas Shopping after Christmas

DAVID AND BOBBY AWOKE TO THE FAMILIAR SMELL of bacon and eggs and Aunt Lillian's summons, "Boys. Up and at 'em. And Merry Christmas. Santa left a number of presents."

Scrambling out of their beds, quickly brushing their teeth and washing up, David and Bobby grabbed their bathrobes and joined Aunt Lilian in the kitchen.

"I can't believe it's already nine-thirty," exclaimed David, noticing the kitchen clock as he devoured his breakfast.

"It was a late night," said Aunt Lillian. "I was tired myself."

After breakfast, dishes were postponed so that presents could be opened in the living room. David built a fire and the first package to be opened was for Her Majesty, Aunt Lillian's huge gray fluffy cat that presided over the household, usually sitting on a favorite hassock in front of the dining room window. Catnip was the Christmas offering for Her Majesty, and she feasted on the leaves in the kitchen as the other gifts were distributed.

"David and Bobby," exclaimed Aunt Lillian. "Thank you so much for this perfume. How did you know I needed some more?"

Bobby looked at David, who sheepishly said, "Well, I sort of made a recon of your bathroom."

"Very enterprising," concluded Aunt Lillian, "although I do fear this gift has set you both back a tidy sum."

Both boys blushed, flattered that their joint gift had been appreciated and well-received.

As paper was torn from packages, Bobby and David were delighted to see that their respective wardrobes were now augmented with several sweaters, pants, and pairs of socks, as well as new suits.

"Here's a last gift for each of you," said Aunt Lillian, handing each of the boys a card.

"Wow!" exclaimed Bobby, "A hundred dollar bill."

"Mine, too," said David. "Wow!"

"It seemed to me that you both could use a little 'mad' money. Do enjoy whatever you use it for. But my last gift is only an announcement. Remember the Christmas surprise I refused to tell you about?"

"I forgot all about it," said David.

"Me, too," agreed Bobby.

"Well, it's this: the three of us are going to take a trip out to the Southwest, probably during your Easter break or, at the latest, sometime next summer, although it will be pretty hot out there by then."

"Why are we going?" asked David.

"To see a different part of the world," explained Aunt Lillian. "I thought it would be fun to see the Grand Canyon—"

"Wow!" shouted David.

Bobby's mouth dropped open.

"And some other beautiful places," concluded Aunt Lillian.

"How will we get there?" asked David.

"We'll fly out to Phoenix, and then rent a car," replied Aunt Lillian.

"That's an awesome Christmas surprise, Aunt Lillian," announced David. "It'll be great."

"Never thought I'd get out of Midville," dead-panned Bobby.

Her Majesty returned from the kitchen and barely managed to jump up on her hassock, owing to the influence of the catnip. Beginning to wash herself, she suddenly fell off, much to her consternation and embarrassment as well as to the laughter of the humans present. Attempting to restore her dignity, she sauntered under the grand piano and flopped down, licking her paw as if nothing had happened.

As Bobby, David, and Aunt Lillian tidied the kitchen, David announced, "With all that has happened, Bobby and I only managed to get the perfume for you for Christmas. We told Lisa, Sean, and Mary that we would get their gifts tomorrow. Sean recommended that we visit a second hand shop that has some unbelievable stuff in it. His dad takes him there occasionally when he stops in to see the owner. Sean said both the shop and the owner are amazing."

"Well, so much for the hundred dollar bills," Aunt Lillian smiled.

"Not gonna spend that much," protested Bobby. "Especially on that little ne'er-do-well hoodlum."

"Well, don't be too cheap, either," reproved David. "Remember what Mr. Pennythorpe said about Christmas and all."

"I remember," retorted Bobby. "And my just lettin' that little beggar Sean live is a big gift all by itself."

Aunt Lillian studied Bobby for a minute, saying, "Perhaps it's time to let bygones be bygones."

"No way," protested Bobby. "Sean robbed a month off my life in the library, and I still owe him a big one for that shenanigan. He knows that, too, but he also keeps givin' me the evil eye. So we're gonna have it out some day."

"Well, you two will just have to work it out then," sighed Aunt Lillian, looking at David for support, but only getting a shrug.

"We're going to exchange gifts Wednesday morning," announced David. "POTS is going to pick up Lisa and then bring her and the twins over around ten o'clock."

* * * * *

The snow fell gently the next morning, fluttering like feathers against the already thick and irregular mattress of white that blanketed Midville. It had been nearly two weeks since the blizzard, but much of its snow remained. The boys' boots crunched against the mixture of frozen ice and snow as the morning's flurries added its fresh texture of white to building, tree, road, and snowbank alike.

"Are you sure it was on this street?" asked Bobby, as he and David strode purposefully to an unfamiliar destination.

"Sean is really good at directions," answered David. "If he said it was here, it will be here. Trust me."

"I trust *you*," retorted Bobby, "but not that little rapscale."

"Rapscallion," corrected David.

"Whatever," Bobby retorted. "You know what I mean."

"Live and let live," admonished David.

"Live and kill," concluded Bobby.

"You've got to forgive Sean his little joke," sighed David.

"It didn't take a month off *your* life," sighed Bobby.

David could see Aunt Lillian's suggestion to Bobby on Christmas Day had been a sore point. Hoping to encourage Bobby toward a more positive stance, David suggested, "Maybe you'll find something at this second hand store. It seems funny buying Christmas gifts after Christmas, but you're the one who gave me the idea with your IOU note to Sean. It sort of became IOU's all the way around. We were so busy getting ready for Mr. Pennythorpe's reading. And my science project on the megafauna is going to be a real killer. I might as well kiss the rest of this holiday goodbye."

"I never heard of no mega whatever they are," said Bobby.

"I tried to explain it to you last week, but you fell asleep snoring," chided David.

"Did not," protested Bobby.

"Next time I'll tape you," threatened David. "Anyway, the megafauna were huge mammals that once lived on this planet, and many of them died out only about ten thousand years ago. Most people have heard of the wooly mammoth, but I bet a lot haven't heard of the giant ground sloth that stood six feet tall. These mammals were monsters by today's standards, although elephants, hippos, rhinos, and giraffes are among the last surviving examples. The biggest mammal fossils ever found were from a place in Siberia and for a creature that was estimated to weigh over twenty tons. It was a kind of rhino and was named Indrincothermium."

"I'd hate to meet that sucker on a dark night," quipped Bobby.

"Probably wouldn't even notice us. If we didn't have enough sense to get out of its way, we'd be squashed like ants," said David.

"Must 've been an ancestor of Coachman," quipped Bobby. "Too bad she ain't extinct along with the rest of 'em. 'Course, there's still some pigs around."

"There really *were* giant pigs thousands of years ago," David answered.

The boys turned a corner and ventured into a small, dark alley, at the end of which was a small shop front, painted in bright blues and golds. Over the shop windows a sign, painted in bright red letters, proclaimed ASTOR'S SHOP OF JUNKEN TREASURES.

As they neared the shop door, David laughed, whispering to Bobby, "I love the pun in the name of this shop."

"What pun?" asked Bobby.

"*Junken Treasures* is a pun for 'Sunken Treasures' as well as for 'Junk & Treasures.' In other words, we can expect to find junk and treasure inside and, as the old saying goes, one man's junk is another man's treasure."

"Well, that's good," said Bobby. "I'll buy a treasure for Mary and some junk for Sean."

"Remember," warned David, "Sean said that the owner's a little creepy to look at. I'm sure he's okay, since Sean liked him. Looks can be deceiving and Sean is pretty perceptive."

Entering the store, the boys were suddenly amazed to find a room which seemed too large for the small shop front. It afforded the visitor with aisle after aisle of items from which to choose. The large variety seemed instantly overwhelming yet irresistible.

"Boy!" exclaimed David. "Sean was right. This place is *really* amazing; I mean, AMAZING! We'd better think about pooling our money."

"I haven't seen no prices yet," cautioned Bobby, skeptical of anything remotely related to Sean.

"No. That's what Sean said. There aren't any. Either you trade or you barter," said David.

The boys walked up and down several aisles, looking at a cornucopia of stuff including little wooden chests, ancient books, tarnished lamps, oddly colored marbles, ornate jewelry, and beautiful crystals.

"Coming . . ." called a frail voice from some distance beyond the large room.

"Who's that?" asked Bobby.

"The owner, I guess," said David.

"Coming . . ." repeated the voice, in an indistinguishable accent.

Suddenly, near where the counters separated in front of them, a small dwarf-like figure, supporting itself with an old walking stick, hobbled into view, smiled at David and Bobby, bowed in greeting and said, "Welcome, friends. My name is Astor. What are yours?"

"My name is David," replied David, bowing in respect to the wizened figure who now stood before them. This lumbering little man was wrinkled and bald and painfully thin, apparently once having been crippled by something, for he did not stand straight, but rather slumped to one side, relying on the carved walking stick for support. His hands were gnarled and claw-like. But what most attracted David's attention were the figure's intense gray eyes, which exuded a discerning warmth and kindness.

"Ah," smiled the curious figure, contemplating David's words, "You are much loved. That is what your name means."

Turning his attention to Bobby and looking up, in smiling expectation, the small little man inquired, "And your name?"

"Bobby," flushed Bobby.

"Ah," said the figure once again, "Bobby. A diminutive for Robert, which means you are 'bright in fame.'"

"But I ain't bright in fame," protested Bobby.

The curious little man nodded, saying decidedly, "Not yet. But you will be. Sooner than you think. Much sooner."

Bobby's eyes rolled wide as he leaned toward David and whispered, "Maybe I *will* kill Sean."

"Ah," responded the little dwarf-like man, "Sean, as in Sean Potter, son of the famous Professor Potter. He spoke of both of you. I have been awaiting your arrival."

"What does the name Sean mean?" asked David.

"Gracious of God, which he truly is. Is he not?" the figure smiled.

Before Bobby could answer, David nodded in agreement, saying, "God was certainly gracious to create Sean."

A faint trace of amusement crossed Mr. Astor's lips as he considered David's response and observed Bobby's reaction.

"Perhaps," smiled the little gnome. "Perhaps."

"This is an amazing shop," said David, hoping to change the subject.

"What have you come for?" asked Mr. Astor.

"I'm not sure," answered David. "We're looking for belated Christmas gifts for Sean and Mary and Lisa."

"Mary," pondered the mysterious Mr. Astor. "Yes. Mary means 'bitter,' although some would hold that the name actually means 'rebellious.' Lisa means 'pledged to God.' Would you like to look around or would you like me to help you?"

"Gosh, you really know them names by heart," exclaimed Bobby, his mouth dropping in wonder.

Mr. Astor closed his eyes, nodded, and answered, "A hobby."

"What gifts would you suggest for our friends?" asked David.

Mr. Astor reflected a moment, stroking the bottom of his chin with his left hand, holding fast to his walking stick with his right hand.

"Follow me," he announced.

David and Bobby walked slowly behind the gnarled dwarf as he hobbled in front of them, breathing heavily as he moved.

When Mr. Astor stopped, he pointed to a beautiful collection of swords.

"Wow!" was all David could exclaim.

Bobby, equally moved, was silent in his awe at the swords' beauty and craftsmanship.

"I don't think I can afford any of these," stammered David. "I know Sean would love one, but they are all so exquisitely made. I would even hate to ask how much you'd charge for the cheapest one of the lot."

Mr. Astor gave a faint, understanding smile, saying, "I don't always deal in exchange for money. Barter is another method that I have found most acceptable."

"But I don't own anything that could equal one of these swords," objected David.

"Perhaps not," agreed the mysterious dwarf-like figure. "But how about swapping for something like time and labor? Sometime next year, probably during the summer, I will need the reliable help, perhaps from two strong young lads like you. If you feel comfortable promising me your help in moving some of my belongings, I would feel comfortable in allowing you to pick any one of these fine swords for your friend, Sean."

David examined the swords with greater scrutiny, exclaiming, "Are those *real* jewels?"

Mr. Astor nodded.

"I can't believe that even an entire summer of traded labor would pay for that one, the one with those beautiful jewels."

"Perhaps the finest of the lot, my young friend. You have chosen well. If I can count on your help next summer, which should take no more than two or three weeks, perhaps four, I would feel satisfied with this barter. Is it a deal?"

"You've got it," said David, brimming with joy, about to extend his hand, but then suddenly remembering Mary and Lisa.

"Something wrong?" asked Mr. Astor.

"I've got two more gifts to get," he said. "Perhaps I should choose the sword last."

"But you have already chosen the sword. What will you get for the boy's sister?"

David mulled over the dilemma. If he gave a sword to Sean, what should he give to Mary? Knowing Sean's bellicose tendencies, David suddenly realized that a sword would be thrust interminably at Mary, interminably *ad nauseam*.

"Perhaps something like this?" asked Mr. Astor, taking a gasping breath as he moved to the next aisle where he pointed to a handsomely fashioned shield.

"Perfect," said David. "You really must know the twins."

"I have not yet met Mary, but let's just say that I know them in ways that most people don't, which allows me to tell you that you are giving Sean a sword of truth and Mary a shield of wisdom. They will both be affected by these gifts in ways that they will only later understand and appreciate."

"How 'bout a whoppin' big box of band-aids?" suggested Bobby, conjuring up in his mind a near worst-case scenario of the newly acquired sword and shield in action.

"Fear not. For although there may well be temptation to use these gifts, especially on the boy's part, they will be accorded merely decorative status. Still, their power is real and will not be lost," replied Mr. Astor, seeming to have garnered the full magnitude of Bobby's remark.

"Now something for Lisa, if that's not asking too much for our barter," David requested.

Mr. Astor bowed in consent and pointed to another aisle.

On a long shelf sat many small beautiful, hand-painted ornamental boxes, perfect for storing jewelry and rings. David's eye was caught by a stunningly rendered wooden box with intricate designs in turquoise and in-laid mother of pearl.

Mr. Astor noticed the movement of David's eyes and nodded his own approval, saying, "Once again, you have chosen well. This box, although it contains nothing, contains everything that your friend Lisa now needs. She will treasure it just as she treasures your friendship."

"Are you sure that I can work off what I owe you this summer?" asked David, not wanting to take advantage of Mr. Astor.

"Yes. You and Bobby can give me help that I can rely on and trust. It will only be a matter of a few weeks of work, although with some difficult moving involved."

"Are you moving somewhere else?" asked David.

"If everything works out, I hope to be able to return to my home," said Mr. Astor. "But there is much yet to do. Perhaps to seal our agreement I can offer you a small gift? Here, please accept this ring, a gift from me to you."

David stared in wonder at the gold ring that had been lifted toward him. It was intricately carved in small symbols that he did not recognize. It looked extremely ancient and very important.

"I shouldn't take this. This is more for you to wear than for me," protested David.

"Think of it as not only a gift, but also as a bond between us," smiled Mr. Astor. "This ring serves many purposes, but you may think of it as a ring of understanding and knowing."

David held the ring in his right hand. It felt strangely warm to his touch, and it also seemed to vibrate as he placed on his right fourth finger. Looking at its symbols, he asked, "Is this Egyptian?"

"It's far older. It's even older than the Sumerian culture, far older," whispered Mr. Astor confidentially. "It would be hard to explain its exact origin. But it is certainly one of the oldest rings on this planet."

"It should be in a museum, then," objected David, moving to take the ring off his finger.

Mr. Astor's hand stayed his movement, and their eyes met.

"This ring, David, is for you. It has been waiting for you. Please trust me and wear it for the sake of our friendship. It will bring you to no harm; in fact, it will protect you."

"Protect me from what?" asked David.

"Certain forces," nodded the curious little figure. "Certain forces."

Feeling it would be untoward to ask for any further clarification, and because he instinctively liked and trusted Mr. Astor, David reluctantly but gratefully accepted the ring.

"Thank you, Mr. Astor," said David. "I'm glad we're friends now."

Once again, Mr. Astor gave a deferential bow.

Then the small figure looked up at Bobby with a large smile.

"Now, Robert, who will some day be bright with fame, it's your turn. Are you seeking gifts for the same friends?"

Bobby hadn't really contemplated getting Sean a gift but, under the current circumstances, it seemed uncharitable not to do so, so he nodded in the affirmative.

"Over there," pointed the little figure, and the boys followed his labored perambulation toward a series of new counters. Reaching their destination, Mr. Astor took a leather pouch from a table and handed it to Bobby, saying, "Perhaps for the boy?"

"What is it?" asked Bobby.

"A small, leather sack in which to carry things," explained Mr. Astor.

Bobby looked at David for help.

David was already studying the small leather pouch, and nodded his head, saying, "Yes. I'm sure Sean would love that."

"Okay, I guess," agreed Bobby. "How 'bout Mary?"

"Ah, yes. Just the thing right here," replied Mr. Astor, handing Bobby a small vial.

Bobby looked wide-eyed at Mr. Astor for an explanation.

"It's perfume. Smell it. See if you think it appropriate," encouraged Mr. Astor.

Bobby opened the bottle and sniffed, saying, "Wow! I think she'd love it. What do you think, David?"

David sniffed as well, saying, "She'll love it. Maybe I should get one for Aunt Lillian, too."

Mr. Astor lifted his finger and wagged it at David, saying, "No, no, no. This is the only one of its kind. And your Aunt would not like it as much as Mary. Perfume has to fit the person."

"But how do you know it will fit?" asked David.

"I know many things," the curious figure said demurely. "Perhaps it comes from having lived a long life."

Both boys were suddenly seized with an intense desire to ask Mr. Astor his age, but they also were well aware of how rude that would be.

Before David could think of a response that would tease out the answer, Mr. Astor was handing Bobby a book, saying, "This might interest your friend Lisa."

Bobby looked at the cover, which read, *Marvelous Tales of Knights, Damsels, Romance, & Legends.*

Bobby looked at the book and glanced at David, who smiled again, astounded at Mr. Astor's uncannily apt choices, saying, "Lisa will love it. She reads romances all the time."

As if he had read Bobby's mind, the little figure in front of the two boys raised his hand, saying, "And please don't judge the value of a gift by its luster or size. Your gifts are no less than David's, just because they are smaller. It is always the *essence* of the gift that is the most important thing."

"You, Robert, will also help me to move my things sometime next year? Probably in the summer?" asked Mr. Astor.

Bobby nodded his head in agreement.

"Here, then, is a gift for you," said the gnome-like figure, extending his arm and opening his hand.

Bobby looked with expectation and gasped, for extended in Mr. Astor's hand was a shining golden key, the kind that might fit into the front door of a castle.

"It is both symbolic and real, and it will help you to open doors inside of yourself as well as outside of yourself, if you feel you can accept it."

"Beautiful," was all Bobby could say.

"Take it then and contemplate it every day," said Mr. Astor.

The boys looked at the booty they had acquired, each wondering if it would ever be possible to repay Mr. Astor in time and labor.

"Is there anything else?" inquired the shopkeeper.

David thought a moment and answered, "No. But you've been really terrific. Let me write down our address and phone number so you can call us when it's time to help you, although I'm sure we'll come back to your shop before then."

Mr. Astor looked beyond the boys, as if contemplating some future calendar written in the air, and nodded his head, smiling, saying, "Yes. You will come back, and the Potter boy will come with you."

David diligently wrote their names and telephone number. Mr. Astor took the paper and bowed to the boys.

Turning to leave, David noticed a huge glass pig sitting near the front window. Surprised that he hadn't noticed it before, if for no other reason than its inordinate size, he pointed to it, remarking, "That's *quite* the piggy bank."

"Looks just like that old dame Coachman," whispered Bobby, only to be jabbed by David's elbow.

Mr. Astor looked wistfully at the enormous glass pig, which upon closer scrutiny did indeed have an open slot on top through which coins could be dropped. Sighing, he said, "That's more my white elephant than my pig. I've been trying to give it away, but no takers."

He looked up sharply at David, searching for even a small trace of interest in David's eyes.

David in turn had been formulating a plan for this huge, glass pig, should he be able to snag it.

"I'll take it," he said with resolve.

"What?" exclaimed Bobby. "It looks *awful* heavy."

Bobby was in his practical frame of mind, because he rightly intuited that he would be the one lending most of the muscle to getting this huge glass pig home. The very thought of the enormous effort that would be involved made him anticipate his exhaustion at having done so.

"Listen, Bobby," scolded David. "I have an idea. I can say that this pig is one of those extinct megafauna, and we can have a naming contest at school. It will help me to build interest and support for my science report. I mean, I've really got to do *something* to upstage Mallory."

"Mallory," mused Mr. Astor, "an unfortunate name. It means unhappy, unlucky. From the French word *malheureux*. This boy is not too tall, is he, but certainly taller than myself? *Everyone* is taller than myself."

David caught himself from laughing out loud, for he loved the way Mr. Astor was poking fun at himself as well as at Mallory. It was a safe bet that the two had never met, and it was uncanny how Mr. Astor's insight had so fully captured Mallory's insecurities and Napoleonic propensities.

"And perhaps this Mallory is a little too serious," Mr. Astor added, giving a knowing smile.

"Yes, a little too serious," nodded David.

"You see, Mr. Astor," explained David, "Everyone is crazy about dinosaurs, but the big mammals are forgotten. And we're more closely related to them than to the dinosaurs. People could name the pig for every penny they dropped into it. Then the money could be given away, like maybe to the community food bank. Mr. Pennythorpe said we should bring Christmas into the world every day, not just one day a year? He challenged us to think of others. So this would be perfect."

Bobby stared at his newfound adversary, wondering if his back would be in one piece when he finally carried it over Aunt Lillian's threshold.

"Mr. Astor, we accept your kind offer of this huge, glass piggy bank, and we will put it to good use at school. It will help us to raise money for the community food bank."

"A most worthy plan," approved Mr. Astor.

"Okay, Bobby. I'll take all this stuff if you take the pig," announced David.

Bobby gave David a look of exasperation but went ahead and managed to pick up the huge pig, although it was awkward to lift.

Smiling as he opened the door for the boys, Mr. Astor thanked them as they left the shop.

"Come again," he invited, closing the door behind them.

"Why do I always get the heavy work?" asked Bobby, as he hefted the pig over his right shoulder and looked at David carrying the other gifts.

"Because you're the brawn," said David blithely.

Bobby was content with this explanation, although he worried that the pig might become transformed into smithereens before they reached home.

"This pig is gonna hold a whole mess of pennies," said Bobby.

"I want more than pennies," said David. "People can get one vote for one cent, but I hope they put in quarters."

"I plan to put in at least a hundred quarters," said Bobby.

"Really?" asked David in surprise.

"Yeah. And the name I'll be pickin' for this frickin' heavy pig is Gertrude," said Bobby.

"No. We can't do that," said David. "It's too *obvious.*"

"Watch me," promised Bobby as they walked home.

Chapter Ten
Gifts, A Journey, & Research Galore

THE NEXT MORNING, THE POTTER VAN PULLED UP precisely at ten o'clock. Aunt Lillian had prepared some coffee for POTS and herself as the young people exchanged gifts.

Aunt Lillian felt sudden embarrassment when she realized that she had not thought to get a gift for POTS. She silently hoped that POTS had not gotten one for her, deciding to wait and give Lisa, Sean, and Mary their candy on New Year's Eve. She caught David's eye and asked if he would please help her in the kitchen and explained her thinking.

"I don't know how we could have forgotten POTS, I mean, she's larger than life," he whispered.

"You've been listening to Sean too long," scolded Aunt Lillian. "Shame on you. Double shame."

"Now *you* sound like POTS," marveled David. "Truce?"

Aunt Lillian considered for a moment, then extended her hand, nodding in agreement, "Truce."

Returning to the living room, David and Aunt Lillian noticed that presents for the young people had been distributed.

"Sean," announced David, "Bobby and I went and met Mr. Astor yesterday. He's really awesome, and we got some great gifts at his shop. We hope you all like them."

"Dad never takes *me* with him," said Mary, giving Sean the evil eye.

"Mary, you go first," encouraged David. Opening her gift, Mary's eyes widened as she exclaimed, "What a beautiful old shield. How did you know I like medieval things?"

"We didn't. Maybe Mr. Astor did," said David. "Glad you like it."

"Lisa, you go next," said David.

Lisa eagerly opened her package and her mouth fell open when she saw the exquisite wooden box with turquoise designs and inlaid mother of pearl. All she could say was, "David, this must have cost you a fortune. You shouldn't have— "

"Lisa, it's for you. Mr. Astor said that it has everything you need. He seems to know a lot about the ins and outs of things. Isn't that right, Sean?" asked David.

"Did he read your palms?" asked Sean.

"Wow! Does he do that, too?" inquired David.

"Yeah. He's read mine and my dad's," said Sean.

Mary sighed and said, "*Some* people have all the luck."

"Why don't you ask your dad to take you, too?" David asked Mary.

"They always seem to go when I'm not around. I've complained, but all Dad says is, 'Not yet, kitten, but soon.'"

"He should say, 'Not yet, BAA sheep, but shorn," quipped Sean.

Mary gave Sean an icy stare, the kind that says unequivocally, 'If we were alone, dear heart, you would soon be dead.'

"Wow! I can't wait to go back," said David. "Do you think he would read our palms?"

Sean shrugged and gave a non-committal grunt.

Mary piped up, "If he did it for Sean, he'd probably do it for anyone."

"Mary, you are SO going to get it," protested her brother.

"What are you so grumpy about?" challenged Mary.

"None of your bee's wax," snarled Sean.

An embarrassed silence followed.

"Well," said David, hoping to bring peace to several apparently sensitive issues, "maybe all five of us can visit Mr. Astor sometime."

"Six," interposed Aunt Lillian. "I've always wanted to have my palms read."

"Seven," added POTS, "I want to hear what he says about the lot of you. I'm not sure I'd offer my hands up to him myself. Some people think things like palm reading are the work of the devil."

"I would rather think it's just another way of getting information," suggested Aunt Lillian.

"That's what my dad says," said Sean. "The holographic nature of reality, as well as all of its interlinking connections, actually validates things like palm reading."

Since no one quite understood Sean's observation, including Sean, a polite interlude of thirty seconds followed as everyone tried to grasp its meaning.

Aunt Lillian finally suggested, "Sean, what's in your package? It has a peculiar shape."

Sean picked up his gift, felt its balance, and gave a knowing look at David. The heaviness of the object also suggested its high quality. Quickly unwrapping it, Sean could only look at the beautiful sword with awe and respect. Looking over at David, and evading Bobby's eyes, he murmured, "It's more than I deserve."

"Is this a joke, David?" challenged Mary.

"What do you mean?" asked David.

"You give Sean a sword and *me* a shield. I don't think that's very funny. Do you?"

"They're only meant for decorative," countered David. "I mean, Sean isn't going to attack you with his sword."

Mary gave David a look of disdain, as if to say, 'Don't you even know my brother a *little*?'

"Don't worry, Mary," said Sean. "You're safe. And, anyway, you've got your shield in case I ever go berserk."

Mary rolled her eyes at David.

"Bobby," exclaimed Lisa, opening another package, "thanks so much for these romances. I love them. How did you know?"

"Uh," replied Bobby, "Mr. Astor knew."

"I just *love* this perfume, Bobby," said Mary, smiling in delight. "Thanks so much."

Sean had also opened his package from Bobby, and had placed the leather pouch among his other presents, averting his eyes to the floor and saying nothing.

Lisa stood up and passed out her packages to Sean, Mary, David, and Bobby, announcing, "I hope you like these."

The rustling of paper revealed four sweaters.

"Wow!" exclaimed Bobby, looking at his maroon sweater. "It's beautiful. Thanks."

Sean admired his blue sweater, saying, "Thanks, Lisa. It's great."

David held his green sweater and immediately put it on, saying, "I love it, Lisa. Did you make it?"

Lisa smiled and nodded, saying, "I'm so glad you like it."

Mary looked at her white sweater, saying, "I love it, Lisa. Thanks."

"We should move along," announced Aunt Lillian. "I'm going to be taking Bobby over to Rochester to see his dad, and we need to arrive no later than mid-afternoon. We're going to have dinner with him at the facility where he's being treated."

"Okay," said Mary. "That's easy."

She passed out small envelopes to her four friends, who found complimentary movie passes inside.

Murmurs of thanks and appreciation filled the air.

"Sean, you're last," said David.

"Okay," said Sean. "I got books for everybody. Here they are."

Again the rustling of paper was heard.

"Sean," said Lisa. "How did you know I love mysteries?"

"David told me. I hope I got the right one."

"You did. I've been wanting this one for a couple of months. Thanks."

David opened his package and was delighted to see a copy of *Walden* by Henry David Thoreau.

"Thanks, Sean. I'll really enjoy this."

"You're welcome."

All eyes turned to Bobby who was looking at Sean with resentment. A medium-sized paperback dictionary sat next to the torn wrapping paper.

Sean averted his eyes.

Not knowing what to say, the others fully felt the hurt that had just been perpetrated on Bobby, which had ignited that kind of hurt and shame that is only made worse if someone suddenly points to it.

Mary became very short with Sean and put her coat on and walked out to the van, beckoning for Lisa to follow her. POTS put her coat on, too, and, shaking her head, said, "I'm sorry, dears, but I think it best that we go now."

She, too, left for the van.

Sean had already donned his coat and was following POTS, slamming the door as he left.

"Oh, dear," sighed Aunt Lillian. "I can't believe a gift-giving party could turn so sour!"

"That was *really* mean," said David. "Sean is a crumb bum."

Bobby sat in his chair. Tears were trickling down his cheeks. He wiped them and blurted, "I know I got no huge vocabulary, but I still manage."

"You get along perfectly well," said Aunt Lillian. "And it is unfortunate that Sean is having some difficulties right now that I am *not* at liberty to discuss, but I'm afraid you have become a victim of his problems, Bobby."

David scowled, saying, "Well, if that's the way he wants it, that's the way he's going to get it."

"What do you mean?" asked Aunt Lillian.

"I don't want to see him until that Watch Night Service. Now I'm even sorry that we promised to go to it. He's been pestering me to play chess, but I've been too busy with all this research on the megafauna. I *was* thinking of making a little time, but not now. He can lump it. Just *forget* any fun or games until next year. Bobby, I'm sorry."

"Not your fault. I guess he was makin' a point," said Bobby.

"And just what was that point?" asked Aunt Lillian, feeling it better to have such feelings out on the table.

"That I'm not very smart and that I need to look up words to understand them," said Bobby.

"He's wrong about the smart part," said David.

"I agree," said Aunt Lillian, adding, "and even I have to look up occasional words."

"With me it ain't just occasional," said Bobby. "It's never. I just plough through, like a blur. I know I don't get a lot of what's being said, but I don't care. Maybe I should."

"That's entirely up to you, my dear," said Aunt Lillian. "We love you whether you look words up in the dictionary or not."

Aunt Lillian's affirmation was so gratifying that Bobby grinned and began to laugh. David joined in, as did Aunt Lillian.

"I guess I'm still your diamond in the rough," said Bobby.

"Yes. And diamonds are the world's most priceless jewels, my love," said Aunt Lillian. "Now, we had better get ready to drive over to see your father. I know you're both nervous about it, but I promised him I would talk with you about it on the way. He wrote me a short note which I will share with you once we're in the car."

Aunt Lillian and Bobby made sandwiches for their trip, as well as one for David, who had seated himself at the dining room table where he had amassed over thirty books on prehistoric life together with two huge notebooks. He was glad that he would have most of the day to himself, for he needed to concentrate on his report, now more than ever after seeing Mallory's flashy presentation.

Bobby and Aunt Lillian left for Rochester, and David plunged into his work. In his research, he had learned many fascinating things about the evolution of life on this planet. Miss Smiley was an okay teacher, too. She came off as a bit abrupt at first, with her sink-or-swim attitude, but she really only wanted to know that students would do the necessary work to pass her class. And once you established yourself as a reliable worker, she softened up and some of the genuine pleasures of learning manifested themselves. David began to understand that teachers who expect more from their students usually get it. But before he could fully engage himself in his reading and note taking, there was one very important letter that he needed to write. Seating himself before his computer, he typed in the address and his request and enclosed a check for twenty-five dollars that Aunt Lillian had written for him on Christmas Day. He hoped that his request would be honored in a timely way. He then inserted the letter and check into the previously addressed envelope and put extra postage stamps on it.

Sitting down to contemplate his imminent research, he munched on the peanut butter sandwich that Bobby had made for him, washing it down with milk. Her Majesty jumped up on a chair and nuzzled him, hoping for a treat. Deciding that a little more catnip was justified, David called her to the kitchen and sprinkled the leaves on the floor. Her Majesty immediately flung herself into her new-found mini-patch of aphrodisiac, rolling in supreme delight and cat abandon.

* * * * *

Road signs swept by as Aunt Lillian drove Bobby and herself to Rochester. Although the roads had been sanded and plowed, the tree branches were covered with snow, with small vestiges of ice clinging to road signs where the wind had been especially persistent in its fury.

"So, Bobby," said Aunt Lillian, looking over at her young passenger, "you can see from your father's letter that he's very nervous about seeing you. But I think the good news is that he's doing well, at least so far."

Bobby sat in silence, contemplating his father's letter and Aunt Lillian's words.

"I'm glad I got him a gift," said Bobby. "He may not need it, but at least it's his *favorite* shaving lotion. He sounds kind of unhappy, doesn't he?"

"I think he's beginning to look within and probably not liking a lot of what he sees. He probably thinks he's been a complete failure to you, and that weighs heavily on him, I'm sure."

"But he *hasn't* been," protested Bobby. "I still love him. I've always loved him, no matter what he did."

"He needs to know that, dear, to hear that," whispered Aunt Lillian.

Bobby wiped a tear from his cheek.

They rode on together in silence.

"Are you all right, dear?" asked Aunt Lillian.

"Yeah. I think so. I was just thinkin' about what you said, and I realize it's not just my old man who feels he's a failure," said Bobby.

A disarming truth in Bobby's insight made Aunt Lillian's spine tingle from top to bottom. Rather than saying anything, however, she merely focused her love and her listening in Bobby's direction, waiting for him to take the lead.

Bobby reached for a tissue and blew his nose, wiping his eyes.

"It's hard, isn't it," began Aunt Lillian, "when we can't control the behavior of those we love, especially if they're doing something that hurts us?"

Bobby nodded.

"I . . . I'm wonderin' if I did somethin' different — would it've worked out?" asked Bobby.

"Perhaps," began Aunt Lillian, "but I greatly doubt it. People, on some level, make basic choices. *We* can't be responsible for their choices; only they can be responsible. I can think of many a choice I wish that I had made differently as I reflect on my life, but I can't change them now. I can only ask for forgiveness."

Bobby contemplated Aunt Lillian's words and took a deeper inventory of his own feelings.

* * * * *

David was so preoccupied in his work that he started when the telephone jangled.

"Hello?"

"David, this is Sean."

An icy silence could be felt coursing through the telephone wires.

"David?"

"What is it, Sean?" came the cold and abrupt reply.

Another awkward silence.

"I was just wondering if you'd—"

"Look, Sean, I'm really busy with my report. So let's not plan to do anything until after the New Year. Okay?"

"The New Year! The vacation will be over," protested Sean.

Another awkward silence.

"Look, David—"

"Look to yourself, Sean. That was one of the *meanest* things—"

A sharp click signaled to David that Sean had hung up the receiver.

Shaking his head, David returned the telephone receiver to its cradle and resumed his research and planning.

* * * * *

Aunt Lillian's Park Avenue pulled up to the Rehabilitation Center near Rochester. It was a modern facility, with several buildings. Parking in the designated visitors area, Bobby and Aunt Lillian entered the main building.

A nurse receptionist greeted them and invited them to sign in, after which they seated themselves in the large common area near the entrance, a large room that offered a wide choice of many chairs and sofas as well as a large screen television. As they sat waiting, Aunt Lillian noticed how Bobby fidgeted with the small package he had brought for his dad.

"Miss Biggs?" inquired a friendly voice.

"Yes," replied Aunt Lillian, standing.

"And Bobby," added an attractive, middle-aged nurse with gray hair. "My name is Jane Larson, and I am the caseworker assigned to your dad, Bobby. Please come to my office."

Once seated, Nurse Larson smiled at them and said, "I'm so glad that you could come for a visit. If it had been sooner than this, it would probably have been too soon. Your dad has not had an easy time of it these last few weeks, but he *is* making progress, Bobby."

"That's good to hear," nodded Aunt Lillian.

Bobby smiled, too.

"Your father loves you very much, Bobby," continued nurse Larson.

Bobby nodded.

"I know that you've had a difficult time, which included a fair amount of physical abuse. Now that your dad's less confused, he's blaming himself for what he did, both to you and to himself. That's not an easy burden."

Bobby looked at the floor as he remembered the many altercations that had ended in multiple bruises.

"He also needs to hear that you forgive him," said nurse Larson. "But only if you truly do."

Bobby looked up into her eyes, saying, "I do. I really do."

"Good. Then why don't I escort you to his room, and we can see how things evolve. I must also tell you that he has begun to consider what will happen to him and to you after he is released from this facility. He has come up with some ideas that I think you should listen to. At present, he prefers that you remain with Miss Biggs. Your father has, essentially, decided that he needs to get away from the old patterns and pains that caused him and you so much trouble. We are helping him to investigate options that would place him in a half-way sort of setting, to protect him from returning to his drinking. He agrees that he needs such external control, at least for the next couple of years. You should also be prepared for the fact that he will seem to you to have changed physically. You will find that he has lost weight and looks older. That is not uncommon. I just wanted you both to be prepared. Finally, let me say that it has been, and continues to be, a pleasure to work with your dad, especially now that he is rediscovering his wonderful sense of humor."

"Never knew he had one," quipped Bobby. "We'd better get down there right now before he loses it."

"I see that you've inherited his wit," laughed nurse Larson, pointing the way as the others rose and began walking toward Edward Perkins' room.

The corridors reminded Bobby of hospitals he had been in, with their off-white walls and all of the nurses and their equipment. The blue carpet on the floor was the only compromise to an otherwise sterile environment.

Rounding a corner, nurse Larson knocked on a door.

"Come in," came a tentative voice.

Entering the room, Bobby was shocked to see his dad, who looked at least fifteen years older. He had also lost a lot of weight, and it seemed as if a lifetime of worry had fallen on him. His eyes were sad, revealing an uncertain man who was both vulnerable and frail. Yet none of this deterred Bobby from his mission.

"Dad!" he cried, rushing in to hug his father.

"My boy," wept Edward Perkins, hugging his son as tears streamed down his face.

Nurse Larson gestured to Aunt Lillian that she would be leaving and pointed to a chair into which Aunt Lillian quietly seated herself.

Edward Perkins finally whispered, "I'm sorry, son."

"That's okay, Dad," whispered Bobby. "I . . . I forgive you."

More tears followed from both father and son.

Finally Edward Perkins whispered, "We're being mighty rude to the kind lady, son."

Wiping his tears away, he turned to Aunt Lillian, saying, "How can I ever thank you for taking my son in?"

"How can I thank you for having such a fine son?" replied Aunt Lillian.

Edward Perkins lifted his right hand to wipe a tear from his eye and sat on the bed.

Bobby sat down beside him, comforting him.

"Let me just say that being here has given me lots of time to think," said the senior Perkins, looking at Aunt Lillian. "I know in my heart that I love my son more than my own life, but I ain't fit to be his dad. I got a problem which I need to get past, and I'm told it's gonna take me at least a couple of years."

Bobby wiped several tears from his eyes.

"Son, you deserve more than that."

"I love you Dad," said Bobby.

"I know. I love you, too. But you *still* deserve more than that. So I've got good news and bad news, I guess."

"Bad news?" asked Bobby.

"Well, that depends on whether or not the kind lady will keep puttin' up with you."

Edward Perkins looked at Aunt Lillian who nodded and smiled

"Mr. Perkins," she said, "It would be my privilege to watch out for Bobby as long as it's helpful both to you and to him."

"I'm very grateful," said the senior Perkins, looking even older than when Bobby and Aunt Lillian had first entered the room.

"Well, no bad news then, son. Only good news."

Bobby and Aunt Lillian looked at Edward Perkins expectantly.

"I have a job offer for when I get out of here," he announced, swallowing hard. "They want to hire me to go speak to others who have the same problem. They say I have a way with words. Now mind you, they're probably not talkin' about the certain words I really have a way with, but I can learn to curb my tongue. In fact, I've been tryin'. Anyway, they will give me a room here and put me on a speaker's program. I get to work with new patients. I bet you never thought that your old man would be a role model?"

Bobby grinned and nodded in agreement.

"Well, then, I guess that's settled. I sure hope that we can work a lot more visits for next year."

"It's an easy trip," said Aunt Lillian. "I'd be very glad to bring Bobby whenever it is good for you."

"When I finally earn a little dough here, I want to give it to you to help with Bobby's expenses," offered Edward Perkins.

"Thank you," said Aunt Lillian.

"Thank *you*. Would you like to see the rest of this place? They'll let me give you a fifty cent tour."

"That would be lovely," said Aunt Lillian.

As they inspected the facility, Bobby and Aunt Lillian's hearts were warmed as they watched Edward Perkins interact with both staff and fellow patients, for his sense of humor mixed with genuine compassion and interest in his fellow patients and the facility's staff, who obviously liked him.

Their tour concluded at the dining room, where Bobby remarked he never knew institutional food could be so good. His dad retorted that institutions have to be nicer to older folks than to kids, that kids are tougher and can take tougher food. Bobby said that was for sure, that the Midville Middle School cafeteria food was usually tougher than leather.

Goodbyes were said and hugs given, and Aunt Lillian and Bobby were soon on their way back to Midville. Their journey was filled with silence, but a rich silence, certain in the new knowledge that Edward Perkins had made a very important turn toward a better life for himself as well as for those he loved.

When they arrived home, Aunt Lillian and Bobby discovered that David had been so consumed with his research that he had forgotten to eat dinner. Aunt Lillian made some chicken noodle soup and bagels that were quickly devoured.

David listened with interest to Aunt Lillian's and Bobby's experiences. When asked about his own work, he could only respond, "I never realized before how complex life can be. It's absolutely amazing how life has evolved on this planet, and we're all a part of it, and we're all connected to each other. I can't really explain it, at least not yet. But I've immersed myself in all this reading, and I'm beginning to see something that I've never seen before."

Chapter Eleven
A Watch Night Worth Watching

THE MIDVILLE UNITED METHODIST CHURCH was in its thinking both cautiously progressive yet eminently practical, especially regarding its ministry to the youth of the congregation. A village Youth Rally and Watch Night Service had been planned by several churches so as to give local middle school and high school students something to do on New Year's Eve, while most of their parents greeted the New Year by attending parties. To encourage maximum attendance, a one hundred dollar credit for take-out pizza from Bottechelli's, Midville's celebrated Italian restaurant, was promised to the church bringing the most youth. Accordingly, the authorities of Midville United Methodist Church canceled Sunday school classes for the morning of the thirty-first, and strongly urged students to attend the ecumenical program that evening. Teachers were asked to drive their own classes, with additional support coming from parent volunteers.

* * * * *

'What's a Watch Night service?' David had asked Sean the previous Friday, after the twins had invited Bobby, David, and Lisa to come as guests.

'I'm not sure,' Sean had responded. 'The important thing is not the church service at eleven o'clock, which will probably just be everyone sitting around staring at each other as they watch some big clock tick in the New Year. That will be deadsville. The really neat event is the rally ahead of time. Apparently they've hired a good band to provide music, so there will be dancing, prizes, and food!"

'Ain't we sort of crashin' the party,' Bobby had asked, 'in that we ain't exactly members of your youth group?'

'A lot of the regular kids are gonna be gone on vacation, and we really want to win that pizza credit, but that's not the only reason we're inviting guests. From what Mary and I heard, it's gonna be really fun.'

'When will we leave?' David had asked.

'Meet us at the church at seven-thirty. POTS is gonna be one of the drivers.'

* * * * *

New Year's Eve, however, brought a series of intense snow squalls to the Midville area. Instead of risking life and limb by venturing out into such weather conditions that made driving hazardous, many disappointed but weary residents cuddled up in front of their fireplaces.

Even David and Bobby were late arriving at the church. The Senior Youth Group had already left in two cars and the Middle School Group sat huddled in the Potters' huge new van, waiting for Mr. Lytle to arrive. Expecting to see his late-model Lincoln Town Car careen round the corner of the church parking lot, they were all surprised to see him come chugging up in the little Volkswagen beetle that Elvira, his wife, generally drove. She was currently out of town visiting members of her family, since her husband was always too busy to be absent from his numerous rental properties.

Lytle parked the little car and leapt out into the swirling snow storm as if he were fleeing an unwanted albatross. Approaching the Potter's new van, he looked appraisingly at POTS, who sat behind the wheel of the impressive vehicle and who looked at him dubiously as she rolled down her window.

"Sorry to be late. Needed to check some of my rental properties to make sure the heat was on. Didn't dare bring the Town Car out in weather like this. That little Beetle does a lot better in the snow, just let me tell you. How many do we have here? Anyone still coming?"

"We have twelve altogether, without counting you or me," answered POTS. "The kids say that's all we'll be getting, so we can leave anytime."

"Well," suggested Mr. Lytle in his silkiest realtor's voice, "then there's no sense in taking two different vehicles. Let me ride with you, okay?"

POTS eyed her fellow chaperone. She had long observed how successful he seemed in marshaling the members of the Youth Choir, and she had dismissed the twins' many vocal complaints about his Sunday school class as exaggerated grievances against a man who had his work cut out for him. In some ways, she identified with his weekly struggles to, as he often described his penultimate function, to 'reign 'em in.'

"I'm afraid that I don't know how to get there," POTS confessed.

"Here, let me drive, then. I know a few short cuts that will get us there in no time. Apparently they count up the number of kids from each church as soon as they arrive, and then give the trophy away at nine o'clock sharp, so we'd better get moving. If there's a trophy to be won, we Methodists are going to win it. Hank Lytle to the rescue!"

POTS was gratified for Mr. Lytle's offer to drive, although she wasn't sure she should let him. Still, the wind and snow continued to rage, and she had no desire to struggle against the hostile elements. Expecting no harm would come from it, she opened the van door and let Mr. Lytle take the wheel as she proceeded to round the car and take her place in the front passenger seat.

After adjusting his seat and the van's mirrors, Lytle announced to his new passengers, "Okay. Listen up, everybody. We've got to get a move-on if we're gonna win that trophy. So hang on to your seats. We're going to take a favorite short cut of mine. I'll have us there in no time."

Two-thirds of the passengers tightened their belts as POTS looked, with growing approval, at this man who obviously knew his druthers.

With a sudden jerk they were off and running, coursing down back streets, rounding sharp corners, and dodging parked cars. The ride became quite thrilling to all after the first few anxious moments, for it was increasingly clear that Mr. Lytle knew where he was going as well as how to deal with the new vehicle. Soon all aboard fancied themselves to be on a mission larger than life, a mission to win a delectable pizza credit. Months of pizza parties passed before their eyes as rapidly as the snow blew past the van's windows. A subtle bonding crept into their common expectation, and all would have been well had Henry Hubert Lytle not inadvertently run a stop sign that stood on the corner of Eighth Avenue and Swift Street. Unfortunately, as fate would have it, one of Midville's police cars happened to be sitting by the adjacent corner of that intersection.

Henry Hubert Lytle was much too preoccupied with getting his sacred wards to the New Year's Eve Rally and Watch Night Service to realize his traffic infraction or even to notice the red and white lights that suddenly began to flash behind his vehicle.

"Mr. Lytle," called Sean, who usually noticed everything about everything and everyone. "Mr. Lytle, there's a police car behind us and its flashing its lights."

"Oh. Probably wants me to pull over so it can get by. Must be going to some accident," responded Lytle, abruptly slowing and pulling over to the right but not stopping.

Curiously, the patrol car imitated Lytle's action, and after a minute of waiting for it to pass, Mr. Lytle rolled down his window and tried to motion the squad car by, at which point a loud siren blared an unmistakable command for the van to stop, which it did promptly as a startled H. H. Lytle swerved into a snowbank.

Members of the United Methodist Church's Middle School Youth Group peered as best they could through the condensation on the van's windows as a burly figure emerged from the police car and, after adjusting his cap, lumbered toward the van.

"It looks a little like Mr. Edgerton, the head usher at church, doesn't it?" remarked one youth to the others.

Henry Hubert Lytle, having days before forgotten his untoward Christmas Eve run-in with the ushers in their attempt to read and follow his hen-scratched instructions for the youth choir anthem, quipped confidently, "Ah, a brother Chreestian, is it? Just leave this to me. You'll see. There'll be no ticket, you can take my word for it."

POTS sat in admiration of the realtor's confidence, obviously a man who knew what he was about and where he was going, all stop signs be damned.

Patrolman Edgerton stepped to the van's window and, following local protocols, requested, "Driver's license and registration, please."

"What *seems* to be the problem, Officer?" asked Lytle.

The realtor's tone and emphasis grated on patrolman Edgerton's patience and, understandably, his ire began to smolder.

"You just drove through a stop sign. There was no *seeming* about it. I clocked you at forty-nine miles an hour. If a car had been trying to traverse this intersection, you might have killed someone."

With his own culpability staring him directly in the face, Henry Hubert Lytle asked in genuine surprise, "What stop sign?"

"Step out of the car, sir," ordered the officer, "and I'll lead you over there like a seeing-eye dog and let you feel it for yourself."

In point of fact, this was not a diplomatic response, for Patrolman Edgerton's temper was now igniting into a faster burn.

Henry Hubert Lytle prided himself at never backing down from a challenge, and he unwisely chose this moment to exemplify in his words and actions that very reputation for persistence and aggression that had helped him to become a successful and wealthy realtor, although he never flaunted his money, especially when it came to making donations to charity. On the contrary, he believed that he never had quite enough money and that he would have to cut everything quite close, except his commission, if he were to be able to afford to pay his monthly bills. As he considered his situation, and the tone of the Officer's words, he suddenly saw himself paying a rather stiff traffic fine, and he felt sick to his stomach at such an unnecessary loss of resource, especially for having done practically nothing, and while on the Lord's own business at that!

"I'll just have you know that I'll not be talked to in that tone of voice by a public employee whose salary I help to pay! *Anyone* can make a mistake, especially in weather like this. I suppose *you* never made a mistake before."

Patrolman Edgerton was himself rather burly and bold, and he now took offense to what he surmised was beginning to qualify as a legitimate case of insulting an officer of the law.

"Maybe if you hadn't been going so damn fast you might have seen the stop sign before you ran it," he observed, not wanting to become distracted with red-herring accusations.

"I BEG your pardon," intoned Lytle, the jowls beneath his chin shaking in anger. "Must I remind you that there are young ears in this vehicle and that they are not accustomed to hearing such profanity. WE are on a church field trip and about the Lord's good business."

Patrolman Edgerton peered into the car and shook his head, concluding out loud, "It's a dangerous and foolish driver who would risk the lives of young people."

"As I *SAID* already," countered an indignant Mr. Lytle with exaggerated impatience as if he were addressing someone who had trouble understanding the simplest of things, "*WE* are about the Lord's business and *WE*, I add for your information, are under His protection. HE *HIMSELF* is riding with us, I'll just have you know. So *THERE* !"

"Well," concluded a grim Patrolman Edgerton as he studied Mr. Lytle's face intently, "if He *is* riding with you, He was certainly going like hell just a few minutes ago when you ran that stop sign."

Henry Hubert Lytle's face exploded into a bright crimson, as he shouted, "I WANT YOUR BADGE NUMBER, AND I WANT IT NOW!" It was obvious that for this furious realtor all lines of decency and civilized propriety had now been abrogated.

"My name is Robert Edgerton, and my badge number is 142, and you can tell the Sergeant all about it, because I'm just about to run you and your rude mouth in for insulting an officer of the law."

Suddenly realizing that he was skating very close to the brink of arrest, Henry Hubert Lytle placed his hands on his forehead and took three deep breaths.

Patrolman Edgerton didn't quite know what to make of this minor self-indulgence, whether his prospective prisoner was having the begining of a migraine headache or a major stroke.

"I'm sorry," said Henry Hubert Lytle so softly that one of the youth in the back whispered, 'What did Mr. Lytle say?'

"I said, 'I'M SORRY,'" shouted Lytle, glaring in the rearview mirror, lest any further sounds emanate from the junior quarter.

"Well, there's a right proper beginning," said Patrolman Edgerton, restraining a smile. "Let's hope that you're sorry for the right things."

A short silence followed, and Henry Hubert Lytle felt pressure building in himself to respond to the officer. In the deep recesses of his intuition, Lytle knew that the patrolman wanted him to beg forgiveness for running the stop sign and, if he did, he probably would get off with a stern warning. Still, in the deeper in the recesses of his thinking, where there was a good deal less light and a great deal more pride, H. H. Lytle felt slighted, angry, and misused. Stirring inwardly as he plumbed the shallows of his random thoughts, and looking for the most appropriate answer to the officer's snide remarks, he concluded in his most private mind that, as always, the real issue in this situation came down to money. The thought of losing even a few dollars was most appalling to Hank Lytle, and to so futile a cause as a minor traffic infraction. —You can win more with honey than vinegar, thought Lytle, swallowing his pride.

Looking directly at Patrolman Edgerton, Lytle said, "Officer, I am very sorry for running the stop sign. I didn't see it. I am afraid my mind was centered completely on getting these kids to their New Year's Eve program. If we get enough of them there on time, we Methodists will receive a year's worth of free pizza for our youth group."

Edgerton's face suddenly widened in surprise, his square jaw dropping open like a steam shovel, "Say, I know you, don't I? Your voice sure was familiar, but I didn't recognize you because of that ski hat you're wearing. You go to my church, don't you?"

"It's Hank Lytle, at your service. My wife directs the Youth Choir. I know I've seen you there, too, but I can't remember just when or where."

"My wife and I usually go to the early service," said Patrolman Edgerton. "That way, we can go out for breakfast afterwards. If you and your wife work with any of the music, you must go to the second service."

"Yes, we do. I sit up front to help her."

"Oh! Now I've got it," said patrolman Edgerton, nodding his head. "You're that little Bantam rooster who was sitting up front on Christmas Eve with that miserable frown on your face and your arms folded like this." Here the officer gave a credible impersonation of an individual who, although he has proclaimed himself to have found the one true religion, is trying very hard to keep the 'brimmin' joy' of it from touching everyone else.

"Well, my wife needs me to put a little order into that youth choir," protested the derided realtor, adding, "Where were you Christmas Eve? I don't remember seeing you anywhere."

"Oh," beamed patrolman Edgerton, "so you *don't* remember me, do you? Well, for your information, I was the usher you called an idiot when we had all that silly fuss about the new lighting system."

At this critical juncture in the conversation, Hank Lytle's smile faded as he took new stock of his situation. It was precisely at this point that he chose to commit a fatal error in his undiplomatic effort to avoid receiving a ticket. This error of judgment arrived quite naturally for him for, too, in his realty business he had early on adopted the inestimable advantage of having a most convenient memory, which means he had very little conscience, and his moral center, if it could be called that, floundered all over the place depending on which way the winds were blowing. The priority always centered on the greatest sales advantage or highest profit margin. Unlike the redoubtable patrolman Edgerton, Hank Lytle could remember the same event, or promise, or price in an infinite variety of ways.

If, at this fateful moment, Hank Lytle had looked directly into the officer's eyes, grinned and said, 'Oh, that! I never meant to call you or any one else an idiot—we're *all* idiots when it comes to running Christmas services. I should wonder why we even bother with it,' the entire situation might well have been laughed off and forgotten. Instead, Lytle determined that his situation was, in essence, one of pecuniary necessity and, rather foolishly, he vastly misjudged his mark and elected to take the lower road of creative re-construction of a past event.

"Naw! You *misheard* me. I said that only an idiot could have invented a light box as confusing as that damn thing they saddled our church with. It would have flummoxed the hell out of me if *I* had been manning it," the realtor backpedaled as he coughed up a hollow laugh and smiled weakly at the imposing patrolman, who began to consider if any truth could be found in these frail words. Lytle's mistake, however, was to forget the alert young ears sitting in the vehicle.

As soon as these words had fallen from Lytle's crooked mouth, Officer Edgerton felt a rapid surge of anger coursing up and down his spine. Many years of experience as a police officer had taught him that this sensation inevitably manifested in his backbone when someone was not being entirely sincere or truthful. Edgerton had learned long ago to act with conviction on this intuition, for it had never failed him. "What?! You *never* said that. I have a pretty good memory for what people say. You said, 'Even an idiot could run this switch box!'"

"Did NOT!" protested Lytle, for how could it be proven?

"You most certainly did say it," challenged the officer.

"Are you calling *ME* a liar?" fumed the realtor.

"I'm saying that either you have misremembered what you said, or else you're just a damn liar, trying to weasel out of what's comin' to you."

"How *DARE* you use such language in front of these innocents!"

The brisk winter air had been invading the driver's window ever since the van had been pulled over. The heater was not set at maximum and had failed to prevent a chill from settling on the van, and everyone was now beginning to shiver and shake.

David suddenly remembered the remarkable thing he had learned about Mr. Pennythorpe, Professor Potter, and Sean at the Christmas party that he and Aunt Lillian and Bobby had hosted.

—What better place to have someone with a photographic memory! He thought. —Sean could quickly settle the entire question because the portable microphone Mr. Lytle had clung to during the Christmas Eve service had allowed everyone in the church to hear all that grumbling over the new lighting system. Hoping to be of help, David announced, "Mr. Lytle, I know how we can settle this once and for all."

Both men stared quizzically at David, Lytle through his rear view mirror in frantic exasperation, the officer from the window with intense curiosity.

"And how's that, son?" asked the patrolman.

"Sean here, sitting next to me, is proven to have what's called a photographic memory. He never forgets *anything*! Trust me! And he was at the Christmas Eve service, taking it all in, like a tape recorder."

Several others in the car nodded, as did POTS, who lamented, "Aye! I've got to hand that to the little dickens. I've known him most of his life and many are the times he has pilloried me into a corner with his razor sharp recall. It's a curse, I say. He should've been an elephant."

"Well, son," said the officer, looking in admiration at Sean and extending a confident smile,"will you please set us straight?"

"He may ask to see your gun first," whispered Mary, promptly yelling, "Ow!" and responding by striking her brother with her mittens.

Hank Lytle's face turned crimson as he shouted, "No scuffling in the car! This isn't a sideshow, you know." Ironically, every other passenger in the van had just been arriving at the opposite conclusion.

"Shh!" prompted officer Edgerton. "Let the boy talk."

"Well," Sean began, decidedly relishing his new role as a fair witness in the Heinlein tradition, "let me think back to the service. Hmm. We were getting ready to sing when all the lights went out. Then Mr. Lytle ran back to the control room and asked in a sick sort of gravelly voice, 'What da ya think you're doing? Don't cha know you're ruinin' the service?' Then someone said 'Shh! They'll hear you? We're trying to find the master switch.' Then Mr. Lytle said, 'I don't care if the Lord himself hears me! Why couldn't you just follow the directions I gave you? I wrote everything out plain and simple.' Then someone said, and I think it was your voice Mr. Edgerton, 'Well, maybe a hen could have read it. What do you think we are? Handwriting experts? I've never seen such wretched chicken scratch!' Then Mr. Lytle said, 'Even an idiot could run this switch box. Maybe I should bring a couple of the kids back here. They'd certainly do a finer job than any of you.' Then Mr. Edgerton said, 'What we do need back here is somebody with a few brains' and then someone asked, 'How about that famous Professor? The one at the university. I saw him. I bet he'd know how to put these foolish lights on.' Then Mr. Lytle said, 'Are you kidding? All they ever know how to do is to blow things up. I mean, like the atom bomb, posting everything to kingdom come and back again. I've got that little terror of a son of his in my Sunday school class and let me just clue you in: he's an entire World War all by himself.' Then— Hey, that was about me!"

"Oh, SHUT THE HELL UP!" yelled Lytle, livid at having his exact words thrown back in his face.

"Well, Mr. Liar," continued the officer, "I guess we all just got your number tonight."

"This is outrageous! You're exceeding your authority! Give me the damn ticket and be done with it. I would have expected to have gotten a lot better treatment from a fellow pilgrim of the faith," growled the greatly distressed and wrongly persecuted Chreestian warming the driver's seat.

"Fellow pilgrim of the faith?" mocked the officer.

"Of the Methodist faith, you numbskull!" seethed the realtor.

"That's it, buster. I'm runnin' you in," announced the officer.

"You can't do that! I'm a member of the Official Board."

"The Official Board?"

"Yes, you nitwit. The one at our church."

"Well, just fancy that! That puts the whole situation in a much different light," continued the officer.

"It does?" asked an incredulous Lytle.

"Yes. I'm not just runnin' you in; you're under arrest, as well."

"For what?!"

"Insulting an officer of the law. You called me a numbskull and a nitwit. You need to find yourself some manners, buster. Maybe cooling off in a jail cell will help you to focus your attention on treating the law with a little more respect."

"I'll going to sue you for your back teeth!" cried Lytle.

"I'm sorry, but I don't know how that could be done, biologically speaking," mocked Officer Edgerton. "I'm just a numbskull."

"And you *are* a numbskull, you idiot!"

Patrolman Edgerton looked over to POTS, asking, "Ma'am, can you drive this vehicle?"

POTS nodded in the affirmative.

"Okay, Mr. Official Board, step out of the car and put your hands behind your back. I'm runnin' you in," ordered the officer.

"AND I'M SUING YOU FOR FALSE ARREST!" shouted Lytle.

"Officer, I need directions to the church we're going to," said a panicked POTS. "We going to the First Presbyterian Church."

"It's just down this street about four blocks on the left, Ma'am," responded Officer Edgerton. "Would you like me to escort you?"

"No, thank you. I think we'll be fine," said POTS.

Within a minute, the squad car had turned around and sped toward the Midville police station, with H. H. Lytle handcuffed in its rear seat.

When POTS tried to pull the van back on to the street, she discovered that Hank Lytle had ploughed so far into a snowbank that it would have to be physically dislodged. —No matter, thought POTS, —I've got lots of young muscles to do it. The Potters' new van was thus free of the snowbank seven minutes after POTS really started to rock it back and forth.

The Midville United Methodist Church's Middle School Youth Group arrived just in time to be counted for the attendance prize.

Unfortunately, members of the First Baptist youth group beat their number by ten.

What followed, however, was a spirited party, with music by a local and popular band, refreshments donated by a local restaurant, and dancing and games until the eleven o'clock Watch Night Service.

The service was almost as droll as Sean had predicted. What attenders did not know, however, was that a certain twelve middle school students used the service time to mindfully relive those glorious moments that had transpired in the Potters' van only several hours before.

Because Elvira Lytle, the long suffering wife of Henry Hubert Lytle, was out of town visiting family members, she was unavailable to bail her husband out of jail.

Forced to consider more expensive aids, Lytle called Horace Vanderkamp's answering service. Half an hour later, Midville's best-known attorney and counselor at law arrived at the station and was shown to Lytle's cell. After his client related to the astonished attorney all that had happened, bail was paid for the immediate release of the realtor, who upon leaving the station chose as his parting words to the Sergeant,"When I am done suing all of you, I will own this police station and every other piece of property that belongs to this lame village."

Lytle would have said more, except for the firm tug that his attorney gave him as he whisked him from the building.

* * * * *

Elsewhere in town at that precise moment, Gertrude H. Coachman, Midville Middle School's illustrious and ignoble English teacher, sat writing at her desk in the dreary chill of her parlor. Two bare lights shone, one on her desk, the other near the stairwell that she soon would ascend to retire to her bedroom for the night. It mattered not that this was New Year's Eve. To Gertrude Coachman, New Year's Eve was like any other eve.

—Damn fools, going out and spending a fortune to get plastered to their gills, thought Coachman, never having known a New Year's Eve when she had not remained at home. In the early days of her service to the Countess, she had watched the holiday festivities on television, but now that seemed ages and light years away.

"Got to save my money," chortled Coachman to herself. "My paltry retirement will be a pittance as it is. Gotta get this wreck of a house on the market before it falls down. Maybe I can dump it this spring. No maintenance to speak of in over twenty years.

"Let me see," she announced aloud to herself, "I've got eight New Year's resolutions." She studied her considerable list.

1. Eat less, exercise more.
2. Go to dinner buffets to save money on groceries.
3. When going to a buffet, don't eat all day until you get there.
4. Save $ 25.00 a week for a short trip.
5. Write more poetry.
6. Take care of yourself. Don't overdo it.
7. Form a literary guild to bring a little culture to this town.
8. Find a public place to read my poetry.

Number eight was her prized resolution for she saw herself advancing to a new level. By spring the poem she had submitted to a book company which had offered to publish any poem as long as it was accompanied with a check for $45.00, would appear in a new collection and would thus allow her to claim that she was a nationally-published poet. She would show the ingrates in this backward village who had doubted and scorned her talent, although those had been relatively few;

the sad truth, however, was that most people merely ignored her weekly poems in the Midville *Courier*.

—I'll show 'em, she thought to herself. —I'll sure as hell show 'em all. Let me see, I can use the school's paper and xerox machine and the big stapler that allows binding. I could even require it for a textbook for my advanced students. Have to pay for the heavy cover myself. But the school won't mind, all that prestige in having a member of the faculty who is a nationally-published author.

Gertrude Coachman heaved herself into her chair, snorting from the effort, and slowly lifted herself and tightened her bathrobe. The house was as cold as a tomb. Turning out the desk lamp, she advanced to the foyer and climbed the stairwell. After preparing for bed, she slipped under the cold covers, certain that her own body heat would soon warm them under the heavy comforter.

As she fell asleep, her mind raced wildly as she fantasized the pamphlet of poems that she would create and distribute at her school's expense. If she included every single poem that she had sent to the local newspaper, she would have more than two hundred to her credit.

As fate would have it, however, in the deepest ironies of its peculiar turning, Gertrude H. Coachman would not have her pamphlet of poems printed under the generous auspices of Midville Middle School. In the wee hours of her sleep, random forces in another part of the world would soon shower favor upon her, changing her life so dramatically that it would require her to walk an even more eccentric path than she had hitherto trod.

Chapter Twelve
An Unlikely Winner

DAVID LAY FAST ASLEEP, snuggled tightly under his covers. By their common preference, he and Bobby would leave a window slightly open at night to enjoy the crispness of the cold winter air.

Aunt Lillian had entered the room and stood observing both boys as they slept. Marveling that, now nearly seventy, she had been given two adolescent boys to raise, she knelt by David's bed and gently shook his shoulder.

"David? David, I'm sorry to wake you," she whispered, "but Mr. Leonard, the editor of the *Courier*, is on the telephone and is asking to speak to you. I told him you were asleep, but he said it was urgent."

David opened his eyes, blinking several times. He had heard his Aunt's words and they were just beginning to sink in. He looked at her, still a fuzzy figment in his vision, repeating, "Mr. Leonard . . . for me?"

"Yes, my dear. Can you speak with him?"

"What time is it?"

"Seven-thirty in the morning on New Year's Day, and most of the world is sleeping. I'm afraid that is not your option, at least not until you've talked with Mr. Leonard."

David sat up and got out of bed, quickly putting on his bathrobe.

"The phone is off the hook in the kitchen," said Aunt Lillian.

Stumbling downstairs as he attempted to wake up, David advanced to the kitchen with growing curiosity and quickly seized the phone receiver.

"Hello?

"David, I'm very sorry to wake you, especially on a holiday but, as you know, newspaper people never sleep. I've been working half the night getting our copy ready for tomorrow's paper, which is due to go to press in just a few minutes."

David could only say, "Uh huh," to Mr. Leonard's explanation.

"The reason I'm calling is that you are my second contact at the Middle School. Mr. Ferlinghausen is my first, but there is no answer at his telephone. So...I am calling to ask you for your opinion and for some information. Would you be willing to answer a few questions?"

"I guess so. What about?"

"Gertrude Coachman."

"What about her?" David asked with sudden interest.

"Well, you're one of the first to know what everyone's going to know tomorrow morning when the paper comes out. You might even want to print a special issue of your own paper, what was it called, something about faxing, wasn't it?"

"Yes, sir. *Bare Fax.*"

"Oh, yes. Now I remember. The title was a pun."

"Yes, sir."

"Well, David, grab a reporter's notebook and brace yourself. I have some rather earth-breaking news about Gertrude Coachman."

"Earth-breaking or earth-shaking?" asked David.

A murmur of repressed laughter could be heard at the other end.

"Let's just say it's major news for our little village," replied the Editor.

"I'll be right back, Mr. Leonard."

A short pause ensued wherein Mr. Leonard could hear David's agitated scrambling efforts to find pencil and paper.

"I'm back, sir. Go ahead."

"David, have you ever heard of the *Cornish Hen Lottery*?"

"No."

"It has an obscure origin in Cornwall, England, where an eccentric millionaire left his entire fortune to his seven cats, stipulating that after their deaths, the remaining monies would be used to establish what is now called *The Cornish Hen Lottery*. I'm not even very clear how one can enter the silly thing, perhaps over the Internet. The long and short of it, however, is that Gertrude Coachman has won this year's jackpot, amounting to a little over a million dollars, to be paid in one lump sum no later than February 1st."

"Wow!" was all David could say, his mouth dropping open.

Silence followed until Mr. Leonard asked, "David, are you there? Are you all right?"

David gulped and swallowed, "Yes, sir. I'm . . . I'm . . . I'm just shocked."

"As others will be, too," concluded the editor.

"I called Mrs. Coachman as soon as I received a copy of the telegram that arrived at her door less than an hour ago. She seemed very annoyed that I had found out about it and even more annoyed that we were going to make it headline news in tomorrow's edition. In fact, she was rather belligerent, saying something about not wanting everyone in town at her door asking for money."

"I doubt that *that* would ever happen, sir," observed David.

"Somehow, I doubt it, too, David," agreed Mr. Leonard. "Anyway, she's won the jackpot fair and square, and she gave me the understanding that she soon would tender her resignation to Mr. Ferlinghausen, effective immediately, and would no longer work for what she called 'slave wages.'"

"I guess she doesn't need to teach anymore," said David.

"Well, I would like your opinion about her, both as a teacher and as a person."

"I'm not sure I'm the right person to ask. We sort of had a major run-in a few months ago," said David.

"I'm hooked now, David. You've got to tell me about it, completely off the record, of course."

After David finished recounting his various contretemps with Gertrude Coachman, he could hear Mr. Leonard laughing heartily on the other end of the line. "Well, David," he said, "thank you for your candor. And since we're off the record, let me say I'm glad she's going to resign, because we don't need anyone like her teaching in our schools."

"Yes, sir," agreed David.

"Well, I think we will do a rather bare-bones article. I've pulled some information from the morgue that will be interesting filler."

"The morgue, sir?" asked David.

"Yes, our old files and articles. We'll even have room to print a couple of her poems."

"Again, sir?"

Mr. Leonard sighed, "Yes. I'm afraid again."

"Thank you for letting me know. I will print a special issue of *Bare Fax* and distribute it early tomorrow. It will be the biggest scoop our little paper has ever gotten."

"Perhaps the biggest one we'll ever get, too," laughed Mr. Leonard.

"Anything else, sir?"

"Oh, yes. Do you know how Gertrude Coachman prefers to have her name appear? She always has used Gertrude H. Coachman with her poems, but the lottery telegram, which is a sort of publicity release, gives her full name, which I have confirmed as accurate through our local vital statistics person, who is an old friend and owed me a favor."

"What is her middle name, sir?" asked David.

"Hortense," replied Mr. Leonard. "Do you think she would like us to run her entire name or just the initial?"

"Oh, I think just the initial, sir."

"David, thank you for your help. If you'd like to stop down here later today, I can given you a copy of the article we've written. You could cull from it for your own paper," offered Mr. Leonard.

"Sir, that would be most helpful. I'll ask my Aunt Lillian to drive me down in about an hour. How's that?"

"That's just fine. And, by the way, since we are colleagues in the field of journalism, let's keep in touch on this story. I'll share anything with you that comes my way if you do the same. Agreed?"

"Yes, sir. More than happy to."

"Good. See you soon. Goodbye."

* * * * *

After returning from getting a copy of the article Mr. Leonard had offered to share, David set to work on a special edition of *Bare Fax*. The banner gave him the most trouble because he didn't know whether he should announce that Coachman had indicated her intention to resign. That, even more than news of her winnings, would be the biggest and best news at Midville Middle School. The banners he had tried and rejected included:

**COACHMAN WINS A MILLION;
THE NEW YEAR BRINGS NEW RICHES!**

Brother Bobby had been rousted out of bed by the news and sat eagerly next to David, watching his every move and occasionally offering suggestions, including the heartfelt belief that their banner headline should read: UGLY PIG RESIGNS.

"There's no way of getting around that issue," concluded David. "I need to talk to Mr. Ferlinghausen."

David found the number and called. Mrs. Ferlinghausen answered and shortly thereafter Mr. Ferlinghausen came to the phone.

"I assume you've heard the news, David," said Mr. Ferlinghausen.

"Yes, sir," explained David. "Mr. Leonard called me."

"And I have just called him," said the Principal.

"Is that where you heard the news?"

"No, David. I heard it from the horse's mouth," said Mr. Ferlinghausen.

Something gave David the impression that Mr. Ferlinghausen had really wanted to say horse's something else. Deciding that he should cut to the chase, David asked, "Is she going to resign, sir?"

"Yes," said Mr. Ferlinghausen. "In fact, she's bringing her letter to me within the hour, and then we will go to the school, where she will clean out and remove her personal effects."

"On New Year's Day?" asked David.

"She was quite insistent that she didn't want any, what was the word she used, oh yes, 'hangers-on'— she didn't want any hangers-on around when she vacated the school," explained the Principal.

"It's good of you to help her today, sir," said David, expecting that this would be all the thanks Mr. Ferlinghausen would get.

"I agree," David. "Unexpected blessings that can come out of things like the *Cornish Hen Lotteries*."

"May I quote you, sir?" asked David.

"No, David," laughed the Principal. "This is off the record."

"Can I announce that she has resigned in tomorrow's special edition of *Bare Fax*?"

"Yes, you may do that. I need to call around today to look for a short-term substitute until we can bring someone else on board."

"I'll let you go, then, sir," said David. "Thanks for your help."

"You're welcome, David. See you tomorrow."

David replaced the phone receiver and looked at Bobby and, together, in one loud, gleeful shout, they yelled, "YES!"

Sitting down together at David's computer, the boys designed the following banner:

COACHMAN WINS LOTTERY & RESIGNS!

"No better news could come for the New Year," proclaimed Bobby. "This calls for a celebration. How much dough have you got?"

David did some mental calculation, and answered, "About fifty dollars."

"Let's take Aunt Lillian out to brunch," said Bobby.

"You're on," agreed David. "How much money do you have?"

"Fifty dollars," dead-panned Bobby.

"You've got fifty, too?" marveled David.

"No, I got *your* fifty," corrected Bobby. "Thanks, brother."

"I should have guessed," sighed David. "Let me finish this special edition. You check with Aunt Lillian to see where we can go."

"Gonna let the others know?" asked Bobby.

David thought of Lisa and the twins. Yes. They should know, but it wasn't necessary to call them immediately. David wanted to enjoy the thrill of sitting on the scoop before he broke it.

"Later," he agreed. "After brunch."

* * * * *

The next morning Lisa, Sean and Mary met David and Bobby at the faculty entrance and helped them to distribute the special edition of *Bare Fax* throughout the building before the doors opened to students. Faculty were all abuzz with the news as students entered the building. The news swept like a tidal wave from one end of the school to the other, and no one lamented the resignation of this teacher who had been both disliked and despised by students and faculty alike. The general consensus was 'thank goodness for Cornish hens and good riddance.'

As he noted the various responses among members of the school community, David realized why Coachman had insisted on clearing out the day before. For a brief moment, he pitied her, for it was painfully obvious that somewhere, even if not on a conscious level, she full well knew how much she had engendered the antipathy of others.

By lunch hour, such a general good feeling abounded throughout the building that one might have easily mistaken it for Christmas Day itself. As David joined Lisa and the twins for lunch, he gave them a knowing look as he placed his tray on the table.

Sean summed up, perhaps better than anyone else had all morning, the feeling of relief that had swept the school community, as he intoned, in the familiar notes and lyrics, "Ding, dong, the Witch is dead!"

"So it would seem," agreed David. "Or, maybe, judging from the amazing response, THE WITCH HAS FLED."

"I like that, too," said Sean, "but *dead* is even better."

"Unfortunately," corrected Lisa. "The Witch is rich."

Everyone laughed as David briefly lamented that he had not considered the possibility of WITCH IS RICH for his banner that morning.

"Yeah," agreed Sean. "And the Witch is a B-----"

"Sean," scolded Mary. "POTS has warned you about such words."

"A million isn't really that much money these days," said David.

"I wouldn't mind having it," quipped Sean. "I could buy quite the arsenal."

"And you probably would, too," said Mary.

"Better than giving it to my sister," retorted Sean.

"Well, at least we're through with old Coachman," said Lisa cheerfully.

"What a horrible indictment," agreed David sadly. "But true."

"Wonder what she'll do," wondered Mary.

"Probably write more of her ratty poetry," said David.

"How did you find out about it so soon?" asked Mary.

David explained his collegial connection with Mr. Leonard at the Midville *Courier*, to which Sean retorted, "It must be nice to have important friends in high places."

"We're going to share information, although I've promised to uphold an obligation to keep my mouth shut," David explained.

"That's exactly why *you* don't have such friends in high places," retorted Mary, looking at Sean and dodging a brotherly kick.

"*Not!*," protested Sean.

"Isn't that why Bobby calls you the Little Magpie?" challenged Mary.

"As if *he* should call anybody *anything*," sneered Sean.

"Hey!" interrupted David. "Why all the hostility?"

"Sean still can't get over Max's death, and he doesn't know who to blame," explained Mary.

"It was his drunken father," pleaded David. "Sean, let it go. Give Bobby half a chance, will you? Please?"

Sean scowled and stared angrily at the table.

Hoping to change the topic of conversation, David decided to reveal something that he had not planned to share.

"Guess what?" he announced.

"What?" asked Lisa, rolling her eyes at Mary.

"I found out what old Coachman's middle name is," said David. "Mr. Leonard asked me if I thought he should use it in the *Courier*."

"Is it Witch?" asked Mary.

"Almost," said David. "It begins with the letter H."

"Hilda," said Lisa. "As in Broom Hilda."

"Not bad," said David. "But no go."

"H," mused Mary. "How about Hell's Gate?"

"That's awful," scolded David.

"Well, what is it?" demanded Mary.

"Hortense," smirked David, suddenly feeling very smug and proud of himself. He felt an electrifying satisfaction in sharing something that only a very few people knew.

"Gosh," exclaimed Sean. "I wonder what that means."

"Bobby made me look it up last night," confided David. "He thought it must mean 'big, fat, ugly pig.'"

"Right for once," growled Sean.

"It means 'of the garden,'" said David. "It comes from the French term *Hortensia*, for the hydrangea shrub."

"It fits," concluded Sean.

"How so?" asked Lisa.

"Pigs dig up gardens all the time."

"Speaking of pigs," said David, "the huge glass one that Mr. Astor gave to Bobby and me is going to go on display later this week. I asked Mr. Ferlinghausen if I could put it next to the office and start a *Name The Megafauna* contest. A penny for each name submitted. Bobby is determined he's going to stuff the ballot box so the pig's name turns out to be Hortense."

"I love it," rejoined Sean. "I'll help."

"Hey! Hold on," scolded David, realizing that he had just made a bad mistake. "It was in confidence that I got her middle name. I don't think it would be so good to misuse it. So give me a break, okay?"

"It's got to be in the public record somewhere," challenged Sean.

"Buried, probably," said David. "Let's just let it go."

"Maybe," said Sean, tentatively, "and maybe not. Wouldn't it be funny to get a picture of it in *The Courier*. KIDS RAISE HUNDREDS THROUGH PIG HORTENSE."

"Why the pig, anyway, David?" asked Mary.

"Two reasons. First, I hope we, as a school, can raise some more money for the community food bank. Remember how Mr. Pennythorpe challenged us to try to bring Christmas into our hearts at least once a month. The second reason is much less noble: I'm trying to upstage Mallory," explained David. "He's just gone nuts on this T-Rex business, and I'm trying to drum up support for the Megafauna."

"Mallory *is* nuts," agreed Lisa.

"Comes from having four sisters," quipped Sean, dodging another kick from his sister.

"He's just desperate to get that trip," explained Mary. "Since his older sisters got it, he's got to get it, too, or he'll come out inferior to them."

"Can't be easy for him," said David sympathetically. "I mean, he's a little on the short side and everything."

"A little dictator," said Lisa. "He's always pushing people around."

"Yeah," agreed David, offering an imitation of Mallory, "Hey, Andrews. I'm ALPHA and you're BETA. Understand?"

"I wonder if Mallory is a future Mr. Dandy?" asked Lisa.

"God forbid there could ever be two of them," sighed Mary.

"But Lisa has a point," said Sean. "Same kind of authoritarian personality and all. You know, sort of Napoleanic."

"If you put Mallory, Dandy, and Coachman in a bag and shook it, you might get as much as half of one whole person out of it," said Lisa.

"That's AWFUL, Lisa," David scolded, yet laughing with the others as the bell sounded to announced lunch period was over.

Chapter Thirteen
An Assembly is Planned

On Wednesday Aunt Lillian dropped David and Bobby off at school with the enormous piggy bank donated by Mr. Astor. They set it up in the lobby with a couple of posters that urged students to suggest names by completing a ballot and making a donation. Each name counted would cost one penny. Ballots were available in the office and Mrs. Dixon would accept and make a record of the money donated. David was grateful Mr. Ferlinghausen had liked the idea. Bobby was the first to complete a ballot and give Mrs. Dixon a dollar.

"There," he said proudly, "one hundred smackerooos for old Hortense."

David regretted more than ever having opened his mouth about Coachman's middle name. What had been a juicily gleeful moment now threatened to become an embarrassment if Bobby and his friends persisted with their plan to lobby students to cast their votes for 'Hortense.' Giving Bobby a reproving glance, "That was *supposed* to have been confidential."

Bobby merely shrugged and walked away.

The high spirits of the middle school had not abated from the unreserved delight over the news of Coachman's departure and the entire day felt, again, very much as if Christmas were in the air.

Rumors had circulated that Mrs. Martin might be named to replace Coachman at the beginning of the second semester. David knew he would regret that, for he had come to enjoy the privilege of doing independent study in the library in lieu of the remedial English he would be exposed to in class. A new teacher might not be as understanding, either of his natural affinity for the language or for the reason he had been transferred to Bobby's class. —It all goes back to Coachman, he thought as he entered the classroom.

"David," announced Mrs. Martin, "I just received this note from Mr. Ferlinghausen requesting that you report immediately to his office as soon as you arrived. Better take your books with you."

"Ah, bad boy! Trouble again," teased Zeke Minturn.

"No end to your acting out," intoned Danny White.

"That certainly is a case of the pot calling the kettle black," observed Mrs. Martin dryly, adding, "At least David does his work."

"Teacher's pet, teacher's pet," others jeered in jest. As David left, he thought how ironic it was that Mrs. Martin didn't understand that Bobby's class and friends now liked and accepted him, although they sometimes showed it at times like this by giving him the proverbial business.

Mrs. Dixon was on the telephone when David arrived, and she pointed to Mr. Ferlinghausen's door, indicating that David should walk directly in. As David opened the door and entered, Mr. Ferlinghausen grinned in appreciation, saying, "David, you'll never guess what's happened."

For all of the recent news about Mrs. Coachman's winning an obscure lottery and her abrupt resignation, David doubted that he could guess what additional news might be the source of his principal's obvious joy.

"Don't have a clue, sir," was all he could say.

"Well, remember that marvelous reading you arranged for us before Christmas?"

David nodded.

"And the astounding fact that we were able to raise over a thousand dollars for the local food bank?"

David nodded again.

"Have you heard of a prominent Midville businessman named Stanley Yeats?"

This question gave David the chance to shake his head the other way, for he had never even heard of Mr. Yeats.

"Mr. Yeats, I am told," continued Mr. Ferlinghausen, "is a local businessman who watches his finances carefully and who, as the saying goes, 'cuts it very close.' In fact, no one can remember his ever having contributed more than a few dollars to any of our local charities. Well, believe it or not, Mr. Yeats has done something quite remarkable. He came to hear that marvelous Christmas Reading given by Mr. Pennythorpe. Apparently it touched Mr. Yeats's heart very much, for he has just given a nearby Education Research Institute a ten thousand dollar grant to research this kind of school program and to recommend— "

Here David's curiosity was at its peak, "Recommend what, sir?"

Mr. Ferlinghausen gave a broad smile, "Programs such as Mr. Pennythorpe's *Reading of A Christmas Carol* that," and here he looked down to read from a letter he had no doubt just received, "I quote, 'stirs the spirit, opens the heart, and unites the community.'"

David's jaw dropped open in amazement. He was as flabbergasted as Mr. Ferlinghausen. The only problem he could think of he uttered aloud, "But there aren't enough Mr. Pennythorpes to go around."

Otto Ferlinghausen gave a rich laugh as he threw his head back against his large leather chair. "There never are enough Mr. Pennythorpes to go around, David. I wish there were."

"Wow! Ten thousand dollars! What will they do with it?"

"Well, it would seem that they're spending a little of it on us," smiled Mr. Ferlinghausen, "in way of thanking us, I think. They are sending one of its administrative staff members, a Dr. William Gregory, to address a full assembly of our school community this Thursday at one o'clock."

"That's only three days away!"

"Yes. And I need your help. That's why I called you down."

"My help?" asked David.

"Yes, your help. We need to make arrangements for his coming, including the formation of a program committee. We will, of course, invite him to stay for lunch after he speaks. That is only customary and courteous."

"One of our school lunches? Are you sure? Wouldn't that be like poisoning a stranger?" asked David.

"I'll pass the word to Mrs. Oliver. She'll throw some sort of special dish together. I think we could arrange to have our welcoming committee have a private lunch in Mr. Lowery's library workroom. It has a couple of large tables. You're familiar with that room, aren't you?"

"Yes, sir. Very familiar. It would work well. It would be a quiet place to visit with Dr. Gregory."

"We'll need someone to welcome him and to show him around. I prefer that it would be the same committee that organized Mr. Pennythorpe's excellent public reading. You all worked very hard on that project and, I might add, on precious short notice, since the idea itself matured less than a week before the event. You really pulled it off. And the local food pantry was astounded to have received so generous a donation."

"What will he speak about?" asked David.

"I don't know," confessed Mr. Ferlinghausen. "I suppose anything that he chooses to share. I faxed back our acceptance of their offer immediately. I think it will be a good experience for our entire school. Here, let me read from his biography: William Gregory holds bachelor's degrees in elementary and secondary education {with an emphasis in teaching science and math}, a master's degree in the humanities, and a doctorate in education in the philosophy of education. Hmm. He earned his doctorate at the Teachers College of Columbia University, which has long been one of our nation's very best training centers for educators. He has written several books on different areas of education and has also been a featured speaker at a number of national conferences. He also now serves as a Senior Evaluator at the Calhoun Foundation for Excellence in Education. That's an impressive list of accomplishments. He's even won the prestigious Calhoun Medal. We're dealing with a heavy-duty scholar and researcher. I just hope he doesn't talk over our heads."

David nodded, asking, "How can we ensure that he doesn't?"

"Can't," sighed Ferlinghausen, "Dr. Gregory will do whatever he wants to do. You can't really dictate to a guest speaker. Still, we can prepare. So what I want you and your committee to do, David, is to plan for his visit. We can fax him any questions that you have. But, like it or not, he is coming here to address an assembly of our entire school community. I do hope he's a good speaker. Some of our students get very restless if they have to concentrate for more than a few minutes at a time."

"Let me run it by my committee. I'll see if we can have a meeting tonight."

"That would be wonderful, David. Thanks."

"I'm pretty busy researching a science presentation, so I will probably delegate most of the planning to the Potter twins. Would that be okay?"

"As long as it doesn't get too wild," nodded Mr. Ferlinghausen.

* * * * *

After dinner that night, David lit a nice warm fire for Bobby, Aunt Lillian, and himself. He kept looking at the clock, watching for Poor Old Thing to pull in the driveway with the Potters' van.

Bobby sat next to Aunt Lillian. Both were reading, Bobby squinting at a short story due the next day for English class, Aunt Lillian browsing through a travel brochure.

David saw some car lights reflect off the snow as it pulled into their driveway. He was at the front door opening it just as the twins bounded up to the threshold, clad in heavy winter jackets, mittens, and ski hats.

"We should've had the meeting at our place," quipped Sean upon entering. "It's too cold to go out."

"You can say that again," agreed Mary. "POTS had trouble getting the defroster to keep the van's windows clear. Sorry we're late. Where's Lisa."

"She couldn't make it. Something came up at home. She said she would help in any way she could, though," explained David.

"Say, what's this all about, anyway?" asked Sean, hanging his jacket and winter wraps on the coat pole.

"Mr. Ferlinghausen has appointed us to be a special committee to welcome a prominent educator who's coming to speak to our school."

"Why our school?"

"Because of the Christmas Reading we organized. It seems to have had a wonderful impact on the community, especially the challenge that Mr. Pennythorpe gave to everyone, to bring Christmas into their hearts and actions at least once a month. It's really convenient that we've got that *Name A Member of the Megafauna* contest going. All those proceeds will also go to the Midville Community Food Bank."

"It's an impressive pig," admitted Mary. "Do you think it rattled Mallory? I saw him snooping around it in the lobby this morning."

"I hope so," confessed David. "Whether it rattles him or not, at least it will help me to publicize my report. I'm doing my best to raise awareness about all these amazing mammals that are now extinct. I've been working really hard. Everyone else spouts off about dinosaurs, and that gets kind of boring. I'll be the last to present, and I want to give them a whole new respect for the megafauna. Even the huge mammals in Africa are small by comparison. I told Sean about one member of the rhino family called Indricotherium that stood over twenty feet high and weighed up to twenty tons. It lived thirty million years ago in Mongolia and was the biggest mammal ever to walk the Earth!"

"Something even bigger than Coachman," Sean grinned.

Aunt Lillian looked with mild disapproval at Sean, who sheepishly apologized, saying, "Sorry. I'm just so glad she's gone. I know that it wasn't a nice thing to say."

"But it's TRUE!" Bobby chimed.

"Why don't we let go of old grudges and let Gertrude Coachman rest in peace," suggested Aunt Lillian. "Let bygones be bygones. Anyway, I suspect you all have some planning to do."

"Not me," announced David, cheerily.

"What do you mean, 'Not me?'" asked Mary.

"I'm just too busy with my research and report. I asked Mr. Ferlinghausen if I could appoint both you & Sean as Committee Co-Chairs. He said it would be okay as long as things didn't get too wild."

"Too wild?" asked Sean innocently. "He must be confusing us with some other twins."

"Yeah, yeah, yeah," laughed Bobby.

"So, okay, maybe he's got our number," grinned Sean. "Anyway, he said not *too* wild, which means we can still be a little wild."

"I'm going to regret this, I know," David lamented, shaking his head.

"Just leave it to us," announced Sean, confidently. "What do you want us to do?"

"Well, someone named Dr. Gregory is coming to speak to the school. He's a researcher at some Institute. A local businessman who attended the Christmas program was so touched that he gave ten grand to this Institute, asking them to figure out how more programs like this could be made possible."

"We'd better clone Pennythorpe, then," suggested Sean. "He's *really* ancient. In fact, he's probably overdue. If the lights are flashing for him, I bet they're flashing so fast that he's got a touch of vertigo."

"The lights might be flashing for somebody else," said Bobby, throwing a slight frown in Sean's direction.

"You and who else?" challenged Sean.

"I suppose one could say that the lights are flashing for all of us," suggested Aunt Lillian, hoping to calm the waters.

"Twins," said David, "I'm hereby appointing you as Co-Chairs of the Program Committee that will greet and host Dr. Gregory when he comes."

"What kind of program is it going to be?" asked Mary.

"He's going to give a speech to the whole school," said David.

"About what?" asked Sean.

"I don't know," said David.

"Bo-o-ring," intoned Sean.

"That's why we need to plan for any eventuality. What if he's late? Everybody gets antsy waiting," said David.

"Yeah," agreed Sean. "It gets boring sitting there staring at each other. Why don't we have some sword play?"

"Sean is really into swords and Medieval torture," sighed Mary.

"Gosh, Mary, I wonder why?" teased her brother.

"Any serious suggestions now that we've ruled out sword play?" asked David.

"I really mean it," explained Sean. "Mr. Besio let me go down to the shop during the study hall to make a beautiful wooden sword. I could make some more, and a couple of shields, too. It could be really entertaining. It would sort of let kids relax and enjoy themselves before having to sit through a long lecture."

"I like that idea. And I'm glad you're not using the sword and shield I gave you and Mary for Christmas," observed David.

"He would if he *could*," said Mary. "But my parents made each of us hang our gifts on the wall after Sean chased me around the house with his sword. I like my shield hanging at the head of my bed. Sean mounted his sword over his bed, too."

"Yeah. I keep it in view for all who enter," explained Sean.

"Who'd want to enter a mess like that?" retorted Mary.

"I know where *everything* is," protested Sean.

"Twins! If you're going to work together, you've got to stop squabbling, or none of this is going to happen," scolded David.

"Sorry," they announced simultaneously, after which everyone broke into a peal of hearty laughter.

"So," David continued, "we need to plan for Dr. Gregory's speech. I think we should try to make it a solemn occasion so that everyone will sit up and pay a little more attention. We don't want to be impolite. Mr. Ferlinghausen is a little nervous because we've never had a speaker come to address the whole school since he's been there. So it's going to be new ground for everyone."

"I think our committee should escort him into the auditorium," said Mary. "That would be dramatic. Maybe we could have a small delegation representing different parts of our school community. We can talk with our dad, too. He'll know more about what happens when speakers come to colleges."

"Yeah. It's about time his university connections helped us," retorted Sean dryly.

"If you could please sit down and write up all of the plans, then we'll take them to Mr. Ferlinghausen for approval," suggested David.

"Okay. Why don't we play some chess before we go home?" Sean invited David.

"I'd really like to, but I've got so much work to do on this report. Maybe on the weekend. Okay?"

"Guess so."

"Why don't I make some popcorn that we can enjoy around the fire," offered Aunt Lillian.

"Soda, too," begged the twins.

"I'll take you home after our popcorn," Aunt Lillian nodded as they followed her into the kitchen to help.

Bobby looked at David, saying, "That little magpie is gonna mess up the whole shootin' match."

"No way. You'll see. The twins are very creative. I think it will all work out."

"Sometimes I'd like to make his lights flash a little faster," confided Bobby. "I still owe him a big one for what he did to me in October."

"He's been a little wilder recently. Why don't you offer to play him in canasta?"

"'Cause I'd kill him before I drew my first card," explained Bobby.

"That bad?" asked David.

Bobby nodded. "I'm not sure what it is, but he's got it in for me for some reason I ain't been able to figure out."

"And you still owe him that big one," David observed as he began to walk up the stairs to return to his research. Bring me some popcorn. Okay?"

"Yep, when it's ready," snorted Bobby.

* * * * *

Two days later the Potter twins and David sat in Mr. Ferlinghausen's office, intently watching their principal as he reviewed their proposal. "Well, this all seems very well thought out," he finally concluded.

"The twins did it all, sir," said David.

"Good work. I do have a few questions, though," said Mr. Ferlinghausen, looking at Sean.

"The sword fighting. It will be done with wooden swords and shields?"

"Yes, sir. And the five of us, friends of mine from the seventh grade, are going to practice a lot so we can actually have a routine worked out. We call ourselves the SWASHBUCKLER SWORDS."

Mr. Ferlinghausen smiled, saying, "I see. It's not just random bashing, but rather a scripted routine. That should be fine and fun. How long do you expect it will take?"

"Probably about fifteen or twenty minutes," estimated Sean.

"Good. And now, about this delegation. I don't quite understand."

"Sir," explained Mary, "That's my idea. Sort of the way the Congressmen escort the President into Congress. It would add some drama to the entrance and make it more serious. We will all be dressed up, too, and after we take our respective places on the stage, I think it will clue everybody in that they should sit up and pay attention."

"I like it," agreed Mr. Ferlinghausen. "And do you really think we should invite Doctor Gregory to wear his academic gown?"

"Our dad told us," continued Mary, "that on special college occasions professors wear their academic robes. It's part of an ancient tradition that dates back hundreds of years. Our dad has some funny outfits from his honorary degrees."

"Yes," agreed David. "On Christmas Eve Professor Potter was able to explain that the organist at the Midville United Methodist Church has a master's degree in music from Syracuse University. Because he knew that Syracuse's color is orange and the study of music is pink, he could tell where the organist got his degree from."

"Yes. I'm an old Syracuse man myself. I remember wearing a light blue hood when I received my master's degree in education," reminisced Mr. Ferlinghausen. "If Dr. Gregory is willing to do it, it will certainly dress up the proceedings. You young people are experts in the fine art of drama. And, finally, what is this about flowers?"

"We think some big vase of flowers should be in front of the podium," said Mary.

"Flowers are expensive," said Mr. Ferlinghausen doubtfully.

"Not if we get them donated," explained Mary. "I called a local florist. They said they would be glad to donate a medium size display of flowers that they would have had to discard a day or two after the event anyway. They'll even deliver them. I told them I thought we could thank them in the school's newsletter article about the program."

"That's really sharp thinking, Mary," congratulated an obviously impressed Mr. Ferlinghausen.

"Well, actually, it was David's aunt who suggested it."

"Well, no matter. You had the sense to act on it. Good work."

"Sir, would you mind calling Dr. Gregory to see if he would be willing to wear his doctor's outfit when he addresses our student body?"

"I'd be glad to. I do appreciate your good work. It will be fun to see how it all works out. Who do you plan to have on the stage behind the speaker?"

"You, of course," began Mary, "and we hope you'll introduce Dr. Gregory."

"I'd be honored to," smiled Mr. Ferlinghausen.

"Then Mr. Pennythorpe, since he gave the Christmas reading. We also plan to ask Mrs. Jones, since her classes made all the posters for the Christmas program. We made over a thousand dollars as people left. It was awesome to be able to give so much to the community food bank."

"And important, too," agreed Otto Ferlinghausen.

"We also plan to invite Mr. Dandy as the representative of the Guidance Office," continued Mary.

"There isn't anyone else, is there?" asked Sean slyly.

Mr. Ferlinghausen shook his head gravely.

"And then Kenny Lynch, president of the student council, followed by this committee, except Sean, who will be putting away all his swords and shields and getting out of his costume."

"Costume?" asked an interested Mr. Ferlinghausen.

"It *was* going to be a surprise," Sean chided David, looking at Mr. Ferlinghausen. "We've made up some really cool outfits for our sword play. It'll add to the entertainment."

"We also plan to ask Bobby Perkins to accompany the escorting delegation," continued Mary.

"Yeah. He represents the *rougher* element," said Sean sarcastically.

"And he almost belted you when you said that last night," warned David. "Seriously, Mr. Ferlinghausen, we wanted to let Bobby enjoy the spotlight in his new Christmas suit if for no other reason than to affirm how far he's progressed since last month."

"He has come a wonderfully long way, David, thanks to you and to your Aunt Lillian," Mr. Ferlinghausen smiled.

The meeting ended with everyone shaking hands all around.

*****

The next morning a seventh-grade 'runner' brought a message to David when he was in Ms. Smiley's science class, listening to Mallory rave about the life and times of some of the gigantic and monstrous Tyrannosauruses that once ruled the planet. The brief note read: *Further to our committee's deliberations yesterday afternoon, Dr. Gregory will wear his academic robes when he addresses school. Seemed impressed and pleased to be so asked.*

Chapter Fourteen
A Giant Speaks

THE DAY OF THE ASSEMBLY PROGRAM was one of anticipation and confusion. *Bare Fax* posted the news about Dr. Gregory, together with his biography. The announcement had also hinted that there might be some surprises in store for a school community that remained interested and alert. The program was scheduled for ten o'clock. The Program Committee would meet informally with Dr. Gregory and Mr. Ferlinghausen before going to the rear of the auditorium, and from there the honored speaker would be escorted to the stage by a larger delegation representing various components of the school community. English faculty had assigned their students to write summaries of Dr. Gregory's speech, hoping to assuage any outbreaks of disinterest or boredom.

The speaker arrived at the Midville Middle School office shortly after nine o'clock, thereby affording himself and the principal a little time to get acquainted. The Program Committee joined their ranks at nine-thirty, at which point David knew everything would be fine, judging from the broad smile on Otto Ferlinghausen's jolly face.

After introductions were made all around, with Dr. Gregory nodding to each student as he sat comfortably in his chair, Mary, Lisa, Bobby, and David sat down.

"Dr. Gregory was just saying how much he appreciates all the careful preparation that has gone into this morning's program," announced Mr. Ferlinghausen.

"Yes," interjected Dr. Gregory, "I am rarely so welcomed. I look forward to getting to know more about your school and, of course, to meeting the celebrated Mr. Pennythorpe."

David studied Dr. Gregory's face, which was craggy and rugged, weathered and well-tanned. He could easily pass for a robust explorer or daring adventurer, for his muscular frame and broad shoulders suggested an athlete of considerable physical prowess. His head was also quite striking for its enormous size, his wavy black hair dangling down to his shoulders. Large eyebrows accentuated his every word and gesture, hanging over perceptive and introspective eyes that radiated passion and intensity.

"Dr. Gregory asked if we've had much in the way of physical violence in our school," said Mr. Ferlinghausen, looking with a knowing smile at Bobby and David. "I explained we have a few fisticuffs every so often, but nothing on the order of knifings or shootings that happen in city schools."

"One or two would say that we have a few who are miniature world wars all by themselves," said David slyly, thinking of what Mr. Lytle had said about Sean.

"Ah, yes," smiled Dr. Gregory. "You refer to the typical adolescent male, but fortunately there are many outlets through which to sublimate those energies. We know how the hormones begin to rage at your ages. Unfortunately, violence seems to be the last, desperate alternative found in schools where there is little hope. I'm sure the same energies are found everywhere, and I sometimes wonder how village schools like this one handle their presence."

"Ah, yes. We *do* have some rather bellicose students among our ranks," confessed Otto Ferlinghausen, looking with sympathy at Mary. "But as you have observed, they do seem to find creative ways to release their energies. In fact, you'll witness a prime example in a few minutes."

"Now I'm not only curious, I'm eager to get out there," laughed Dr. Gregory. "Should we be going?"

"Yes, indeed," agreed Mr. Ferlinghausen, standing up.

When Dr. Gregory stood, David suddenly realized what he had somehow known but not realized consciously. His neck, in fact, now felt that circumspect intuition directly, for he had turned it upward to gaze upon an imposing Dr. Gregory, who towered over everyone in the office, much like a kindly giant who had dropped in for a casual visit.

"Gosh!" exclaimed Mary. "How tall *are* you?"

"Six foot, ten inches," smiled Dr. Gregory. "It makes it fairly difficult to navigate around this tiny world. I suffer from being uncommonly tall. Try sleeping in an average hotel bed or even getting into a large car. This blue suit you see is not just another one off the rack. A tailor had to make it, and it nearly cost the earth."

"Is that what you carry it in?" asked David, pointing to a large garment bag.

"Oh, my gown and hood! I was enjoying our conversation so much I almost forgot to put them on. Are you sure you really want me to wear it? I usually do so only at college functions."

Since Dr. Gregory had taken the trouble to bring it, David quickly affirmed, "Yes, sir. Please. It will help dress up the program. It will be good for our student body to see something a little different." He didn't add that the student body would no doubt be completely captivated by Dr. Gregory, if for nothing else than his astounding height, perhaps all the while unconsciously aware that if any rudeness be shown that any one of them might suffer an immediate and untoward emergency of dealing with "The Man" who would soon tower over them.

Dr. Gregory took from the garment bag an impressive gray gown that had two vertical black velvet panels near center, just where it opened. Each sleeve had three light-blue velvet bars. Donning the gown and stepping into it, Dr. Gregory threw a shield-styled hood over his head. Light blue velvet adorned the front, with the back of the hood showing again light blue with a white chevron.

Remembering his conversation with Professor Potter at the Christmas Eve Service, David asked, "Sir, what does this gown signify?"

"It shows that I am a Doctor of Education who graduated from the Teachers' College at Columbia University. These light blue bars and this light blue velvet on the front signify the field of education. Columbia's colors are represented by the light blue and white on the back of the hood."

"Thunderation!" exclaimed Bobby. "It's . . . it's . . . majestic!"

"Yes," agreed Dr. Gregory, placing a four cornered black velvet tam on his head. "I rather like it myself, especially this gold tassel."

"You look like a king or a prince," persisted Bobby. "I mean, a *real king or prince*, not just some short little ne'er-do-well tryin' to puff himself up to look like the cat's meow."

Dr. Gregory gave Bobby a studied look and smiled, saying, "I bet there's an interesting story behind your words, young man, and I look forward to hearing it."

Bobby nodded in agreement.

"We'd better go to the auditorium if we're going to see any of the preliminaries," urged an enthusiastic Otto Ferlinghausen. "We'll take the formal stairwell so we can view the proceedings from the second floor foyer."

The plan was for this elite entourage to meet the escorting delegation at the back of the auditorium, in front of the foyer's entrance. As Mr. Ferlinghausen led Dr. Gregory, Mary, Lisa, and David up the stairwell, the normal echo of this seldom-used space could hardly be heard for the laughter and hooting emanating from the auditorium itself.

As Mr. Ferlinghausen opened the door leading into the rear of the auditorium, cheers and hoots echoed from the balcony above where most of the seventh-graders sat. The spectacle on stage explained why.

Five students, all of them seventh-graders, battled each other with wooden swords and shields. The shields had been painted bright colors — orange with a black chevron, red with a white chevron, green with a yellow chevron, royal blue with a scarlet chevron, and light blue with a dark blue chevron. The swords were all painted a brilliant silver, with handles of gold. The five young warriors were obviously playing out various stratagems of attack and defense, those wounded falling to the floor, those triumphing raising their swords in victory, only then to embark upon a new scenario, this time with two against three, and so on.

The drama of the event had already reached a feverish pitch, and the student body's responses rose and fell as various players' fortunes brightened and darkened. Sean manned the orange and black shield and wore corresponding black tights and a brilliant orange jersey. Glancing at the clock on the balcony balustrade and, seeing the speaker's party now waiting in the rear, Sean signaled his cohorts.

Suddenly the action reached its highest pitch, with four of the swordsmen launching an all-out attack on Sean himself, who deftly deflected each jab and blow, finally felling the lot of them to the oceanic roars, unbridled cheers, and piercing hoots of approval from his classmates, especially from the balcony of seventh-graders sitting above the main floor.

Sean moved up next to the speaker's podium and bowed with great glee to the tumult of applause and cheering. In a sudden flash of inspiration, he reached over and plucked up four daisies from the lovely floral arrangement that sat in front of the podium and, walking over, tossed one down on each of his slain enemies. The cheers grew wilder and louder. Sean again bowed to the assembly. Suddenly one of his victims rose up and a red arm reached around from behind his neck, affording the appearance that this revived attacker had thrust a sword in Sean's back. Staggering back a little, while turning to look at his assassin, Sean toppled forward on the stage. Only the lack of any visible blood prevented watchers from worrying that a real murder had just occurred. The uncommon élan with which Sean had managed to die could only be credited to the dozens of motion pictures in which he had seen similar assassinations.

All five swordsmen were now bowing to the assembly, the hoots and applause filling the auditorium.

"I'm not going to be able to compete with that kind of entertainment," Dr. Gregory whispered to Otto Ferlinghausen.

"You don't need to," responded the principal. "Just be yourself and speak from your heart."

The strains of a trumpet fanfare now quieted the final ripples of applause. The auditorium public address system echoed with strains of a processional. David nodded to everyone to begin walking, the place of highest honor at the rear of the line accorded to the principal and the speaker.

As the delegation proceeded into the hall, a new decorum swept through the audience, as the sudden change of proceedings demanded a refreshment of focus. When students finally saw Dr. Gregory at the rear of the procession, many gasped in surprise, poked at each other, and marveled at the gentleman's enormous stature, to say nothing about the elegant gown that he wore. To many students, this speaker's advent seemed a visitation from royalty itself, perhaps from the King of the Giants. Until they could weigh the speaker on the merit of his words and wisdom, nothing could sway their minds from the drama of his lofty entrance.

The platform party was composed of the student committee, including Sean in his battle dress, on the right-hand side of the stage.

On the other side of the podium sat the speaker and representatives of the faculty, including Mr. Dandy, who represented the guidance office, and Mrs. Jones and Mr. Pennythorpe, who represented the faculty, with the latter's relatively modest gnome-like stature standing in amazing contrast to that of the uncommonly tall Dr. Gregory. Next to Mr. Pennythorpe sat Mr. Walker, the school's chief custodian, who represented non-teaching staff members.

Mr. Ferlinghausen mounted the podium, announcing in his deep baritone, "Students, faculty, and staff members, without further ado, it is my singular privilege to introduce to you our most distinguished speaker, Dr. William Gregory, of the Calhoun Foundation for Excellence in Education. I now give you Dr. Gregory."

As the speaker strode to the podium, everyone became newly amazed at the giant who stood before them. Some of the seventh-graders privately wondered if he might even be able to touch the bottom of the balcony on either side of the stage. Advancing to the microphone, which now seemed insignificantly short, Dr. Gregory lifted the gooseneck microphone toward his lips, announcing, "I am very pleased to be here. And I must make a confession."

After saying this he studied his listeners intently, and they him, waiting for his imminent revelation.

"I came here with any number of things to say to you about the current state of public education, at least as I can best discern it. But after seeing the remarkable spectacle to which we were just treated," and here a series of hoots, hoorays and cheers greeted the speaker's acknowledgment of where the hearts and passions of the students had just been, "I have concluded that nothing that I can now say will come close to competing with the entertainment we've just enjoyed. So, my friends, one and all, I confess to you that I find myself quite speechless. But I suspect that all of you, at one time or another in your lives, have enjoyed a similar lack of words."

Now a much louder wave of applause greeted the speaker, who had admirably and honestly connected with the minds and hearts of his listeners.

"So, if I may indulge your patience, I shall try to improvise. I may not be able to improvise as well as your young classmates—"

Applause rippled through the auditorium—

"But, nevertheless, I will give you my very best. Your principal wisely counseled me to be myself and to speak from my heart. And I promise you *I will*!"

Louder and even more enthusiastic cheers greeted the speaker's promise, for anything was better than a stuffy, canned speech, and for that alone the distinguished doctor had now won the hearts of his listeners.

Mr. Melvin Dandy sat on the stage with his arms crossed and a growing scowl creeping across his face, obviously miffed at the prospect of hearing a merely improvised speech. For many years, the counselor had come to trust and to rely on only the cut and dried, for he took comfort in the mundane regularity of lifeless attendance forms, student records, and the like.

Dr. Gregory again studied his audience, looking slowly from one side of auditorium to the other. No one was spared his gaze, and an expectant hush fell across the room.

"Of course, we must first acknowledge that learning is not always entertaining. In fact, it is more often very hard work. If we expect it always to be entertaining, we are sadly disappointed. I would venture to suggest, though, that learning offers enduring satisfactions to those who choose to take the time and trouble to work at it. And from such persistence comes a kind of engagement, a growing fascination about a particular subject and how it relates to the world we live in. Those who do persevere are amply rewarded in their endeavors for they ultimately arrive at a larger understanding of not only the world they live in but, perhaps even more importantly, a larger understanding of themselves. This clarity of self that learning offers is an important asset to any individual when encountering life's many confusions and challenges.

"Your good principal, Mr. Ferlinghausen, suggested that I speak to you this morning from my heart. And one thing that distresses my heart today is our traditional system of assigning grades, be they numerical or letter, to the visible results of our learning endeavors, whether we speak of tests, quizzes, compositions, or what have you. I am, personally, totally against the use of such limited symbols of accomplishment, for I believe they do more harm than good."

Cheers echoed throughout the auditorium as students embraced the speaker's vision. Mr. Ferlinghuasen's face broke into a huge grin at the thunderous applause while Mr. Dandy's scowl deepened.

"I believe we commit grave violence to learning when we reduce our evaluation of learning solely to quantitative measurements such as numerical and letter grades," continued Dr. Gregory, pausing to take a drink of water from the glass that had been placed on the lectern.

"Why does mere quantitative measurement inhibit the learning process? Because it provides the learning environment with what I call a weighted focus. That weighted focus relates to a twisting of priorities, at least in the sense that I use it. I believe learning at its best should be *learning for learning's sake*. We can never know how what we learn may prove valuable. And when one learns for the *love* of learning, an enormous difference is found in terms of that learner's energy, success, and satisfaction.

"But when we learn something just to pass a certain test, that mere practical attitude becomes counterproductive to learning for the sake of learning. Such practical considerations intrude and we are robbed of the joy of discovery. And I think I can prove my point to you."

Dr. Gregory paused to study his audience once again, noting that most eyes were wide open and fully concentrated on his every word.

"Think back to when you were in the early grades, to when you took joy in anything new and unexplored. Think back to those moments. Close your eyes. You can remember those days, I am sure of it. Picture yourself as that youngster who took great joy in new experiences and new knowledge. I know you all have had that experience. Keep your eyes closed. Take in those moments of real joy that you knew when you explored and discovered something for the first time. Now compare how that healthy and robust openness has become clouded and jaded. What happened to destroy those pristine moments of discovery?"

Here the giant speaker paused to allow his listeners to compile their respective inventories. A concentrated silence settled over the auditorium. An occasional cough was heard, but so intense was the silence that nothing diminished its power.

"My friends," whispered Dr. Gregory into the microphone in front of him, "if your experience is like most others, you will find that your natural passion for learning diminished when you were suddenly forced to learn for an extrinsic reward, such as a grade."

A number of students nodded their heads. Most students still had their eyes tightly shut.

"If this is true, please raise your hand," requested Dr. Gregory. A wave of hands lifted throughout the auditorium.

"Now," continued the speaker, "please open your eyes and look around at your fellow victims."

As students opened their eyes and noticed that most of their classmates' hands were also raised, a torrent of whispering swelled to an oceanic roar.

"Do you see the tyranny we have unwittingly allowed?" asked the speaker.

Murmurs of recognition and agreement coursed through the audience.

"Do you see how the very life blood of learning has been sapped out of the learning process?"

Many in the audience were nodding in agreement.

"And I fear this pattern has taken a far more odious turn," continued Dr. Gregory.

"What's odious?" cried an interested eighth-grader.

"It means vile, repugnant, reprehensible," answered the speaker. "And I'm glad you asked, for it is important to understand the words we use. The new pattern I speak of is the politically correct fad of requiring that schools themselves be assigned a grade, a grade which supposedly tells how good that school is. That grade is closely tied with how well students perform on mandated standardized tests. Consequently, some teachers are now spending all of their time teaching students how to pass some silly test, rather than trying to excite students' imaginations. And I speak of this ignoble process happening to students far younger than yourselves. It would seem that one way or another, we're going to make the experience of education so dry and deadly that only robots, able to recite a body of meaningless facts, will succeed in passing these new portals of so-called 'required knowledge'.

"Now I don't mean to imply that the learning of facts is bad. It is certainly essential for all students to acquire a basic, critical mass of knowledge in order to negotiate their way through the world. What I am saying is that we don't need to kill the spirit of discovery in the process. I am not optimistic about the direction of current education, which is, in my opinion, doing many of the wrong things for all of the wrong reasons. How is it possible to measure wisdom?

"Let me conclude my comments by saying that I hope and pray that all of you will determine within yourselves to keep that spark of curiosity alive, no matter how much our system of education unwittingly tries to destroy it. You are all greater than any body of facts ever compiled, and your spirits are far more resilient than you might think.

The secret is to remain open to your experiences, learning all that you can from everything that comes your way. Perhaps the most important things we can learn come not from within the subjects we study but rather from within ourselves, individuals seeking to know other individuals, groups seeking to know other groups.

"Mr. Ferlinghausen," concluded Dr. Gregory, looking over to the principal, "perhaps this would be a good time to invite questions?"

Mr. Ferlinghausen returned to the lectern and, despite his own height, looked comparatively small next to Dr. Gregory.

"Dr. Gregory has agreed to respond to questions. Please speak loudly and clearly so that all may hear. Dr. Gregory."

Half a dozen hands went up.

"Yes?" said the speaker, pointing to a young seventh-grader in the third row balcony.

"How tall are you?"

"Six feet ten inches," Dr. Gregory replied. "Yes, over here?"

An eighth-grader stood and shouted, "Down with grades!" Applause thundered throughout the auditorium as Melvin Dandy's scowl continued to deepen.

"Yes, my young friend," replied Dr. Gregory. "I, too, say 'Down with grades!' But I do not say 'Down with excellence.' It is important to remember that we are all here to learn, students and faculty alike. Perhaps the real question to ask is, 'Did I do my *best*?' And I fear that very few of us could always give an honest and unequivocal 'Yes' to that question."

The student who had shouted the slogan blushed and sat down.

"Another question?" inquired Dr. Gregory. "Yes. Over here."

Miss Smiley had stood up.

"What advances do you see happening in education today that seem to be the most promising?"

"Collaborative learning. Essentially it gets rid of the notion of the teacher as 'the expert' and centers on group learning that has proven both productive and edifying, at least in the studies I've seen. The teacher then becomes a 'guide,' and the students learn more because they are no longer considered empty vessels to be filled up with facts, but rather co-researchers who are accumulating information to share with others. Something in that process of research, reporting, writing, and speaking appears to help students to better absorb and retain what they learn. They make it more their own. There seems to be a clearer ownership of responsibility and involvement, which brings not only engagement in the learning process, but also lasting satisfaction."

"I do believe in that method," rejoined Miss Smiley. "My classes are now working on science presentations."

"Good for you," encouraged Dr. Gregory. "Do you find that this approach is more productive?"

"Yes. Both for them as well as for myself," agreed Miss Smiley.

"Very good. Other questions?"

"Behind you," shouted a young voice.

Dr. Gregory looked at the platform party and pointed to Bobby Perkins, who, following Miss Smiley's lead, stood.

"Yes, young man?" prompted Dr. Gregory.

"Are you a *real* Doctor of Education, or an *almost* Doctor of Education?"

Bobby's question prompted two responses: Dr. Gregory gave Bobby and the audience a quizzical smile, and Melvin Dandy went into a spasm of intense coughing, his face becoming beet red.

"What is an *almost* Doctor of Education?" inquired Dr. Gregory.

"Sort of a ne'er-do-well, if you catch my meaning," said Bobby. "Always puffin' himself up and sayin' he's so dedicated to workin' with students that he never finished his oration."

"You mean his 'dissertation'?" corrected Dr. Gregory.

"Yeah. That's it. Now *you're* really smart," said Bobby.

Dandy continued to sputter and cough, his face now a bright crimson.

Dr. Gregory took quick measure of the racket of coughing and easily put two and two together. Looking at Bobby, he replied, "Unless someone has successfully completed and defended a dissertation, I would say to you that it is unlikely that he is a Doctor of Education."

Bobby nodded in agreement as Dandy's coughing increased.

Looking at Dandy, Dr. Gregory added, "Such a person, therefore, would *not* have the privilege of using the title of doctor."

"Thanks," said Bobby. "I just wanted to be sure. There are some in this world who try to put on airs and lord it over the ignorant ones, hopin' to pull the wool over their eyes."

Dandy, still crimson-faced and coughing, now elected to leave the stage, ostensibly for a drink of water, although he did not return to the assembly.

Questions continued from both students and faculty, and Dr. Gregory took time with each one and even asked a few himself.

In his concluding remarks, Dr. Gregory thanked the members of the school community for the opportunity to speak. Appreciative applause filled the auditorium as the very tall and distinguished doctor was escorted from the stage and conducted back to Mr. Ferlinghausen's office.

An informal lunch followed in the library workroom, catered by the cafeteria. Miraculously, everyone survived. Mr. Pennythorpe became an amicable raconteur, telling stories of some of his funnier experiences garnered from decades of teaching. Hilarity ruled the day.

Few, if any, would ever forget the day that the majestic and forthright Giant visited the Midville Middle School.

Chapter Fifteen
A Pilgrim's Regress

ON THURSDAY MORNING, January 11, Gertrude Coachman woke even before her alarm clock sounded. Having fitfully anticipated her self-styled pilgrimage to Washington, D.C., to visit the Library of Congress and to engage in vaulted scholarship and research focused on Vachel Lindsay, her poetic mentor, she woke early to the fleeting realization that she had slept very little during the night.

—The taxi cab will be here in an hour, she thought, as she rousted herself out of bed and turned up the heat. The icy chill that had settled on the house during the night began to dissipate. Soon the aroma of coffee wafted through the house as Coachman sat devouring a box of danishes, washing the rich, sweet flavors down with bitter coffee.

Turning the heat down again, she sat patiently in her foyer, waiting for the cab to arrive. It was prompt, and she exited her stone mansion, locked the front door, and lumbered down the steps, nearly sliding onto her fanny on a patch of black ice.

"To the airport?" inquired the driver, as he loaded Coachman's suitcase into the car.

"Are you kidding? Take me to the bus station, and make it snappy. I don't want to miss my connection."

"Yes, Ma'am," was all the incredulous driver could say.

During her many-hour bus journey to the nation's capital, Coachman slept intermittently. That she had actually won a sizeable lottery still evoked in her a sense of disbelief and awe. In fact, she wouldn't believe it until she was holding the actual check in her hand, although she knew it would probably be waiting for her upon her return to Midville. Although she had long dreamed of becoming rich, she never expected to win a lottery. The best thing about the whole business, however, was that she could put that damned, unappreciating middle school behind her and not have to cross swords every day with those ignorant snot-noses who had proved such a torment to her.

Finally arriving at the Washington bus station, Coachman took a cab to the modest hotel outside the city where she had reserved a room. Its central advantage was that it was within walking distance of the Washington Metro, thereby affording her cheap and easy transportation to the Library of Congress.

—Tomorrow will be the first day of my entry into high scholarship, thought Gertrude Coachman as she fell asleep. —Perhaps I'll write a biography about the good Mr. Lindsay.

The next morning, after sleeping in past nine o'clock, Coachman decimated the hotel's modest Continental breakfast and then walked to the nearby Metro station. It was bitter cold and the wind froze her face as she walked the several blocks to the station.

By eleven she had reached her destination, and walked with reverence up the majestic steps of the Library of Congress and strode purposefully into the Main Reading Room. Going directly to the information desk, she waited her turn until the clerk, a middle-aged lady with brown hair and small glasses asked, "May I help you?"

"Yes. I'm a scholar of poetry, and I want to see the Head Librarian."

"That won't be possible, but I think Dr. Callahan might be able to speak with you. Let me call his office. What is your name?"

"Gertrude Coachman."

Five minutes later, a tall, slender gentleman in his early fifties, with gray hair and intense blue eyes, approached the information desk.

"Ms. Coachman?" inquired Dr. Callahan, studying the Coachman's rumpled attire with telling curiosity.

"Yes, Doctor. I'm Gertrude Coachman, a long-time scholar of the work of the wonderful American poet, Vachel Lindsay. I'm independently wealthy, and I think I might be writing a book about Mr. Lindsay, and I wonder if you could please lend me one of your staff members for a little while, so that I can get going?"

"How do you need our assistance?"

"I want to have all of the books about Mr. Lindsay brought to me so I can delve into my scholarship. I'm not just talkin' about a little skimming' here and there, but honest-to-goodness true, heavy-duty scholarship, if you get my drift? I've come on a mighty expensive pilgrimage to engage in my research."

"I think I can ask Mrs. Mott to help you for a little while. Please wait here. She'll be with you in few minutes," said Dr. Callahan as he gave Coachman a wry smile.

"Thank you, Doctor. Good day, Doctor."

About five minutes later a slender, sharp-featured woman in her forties, with raven-black hair, strode to the information desk. Scowling, she abruptly asked, "Where is Ms. Coachman?"

"Right here," replied Gertrude Coachman, a little taken aback by the librarian's seemingly rude stance. "Are you Mrs. Mott?"

"I am. If you will please follow me, I will bring to you all of the books that we currently have on Vachel Lindsay."

"Thank you. I hope I haven't inconvenienced you."

"Most of our visiting scholars fend for themselves," retorted Mrs. Mott, "but Dr. Callahan said that you needed some help. I shouldn't be long; we don't have very much on Mr. Lindsay."

Gertrude seated herself at a large table near the rear of the Reading Room and sat staring at the enormity of the room, waiting for Mrs.

Mott to return. About half an hour later, Mrs. Mott brought a cart with over twenty books on it and piled them on top of Coachman's table.

"When you're done with these, let me know, and I will re-shelve them."

"Thank you," muttered Coachman as Mrs. Mott stomped off.

Gertrude Coachman licked her lips and pawed through the books sitting in front of her. Although she had taken out her notebook, she wrote nothing down as she surveyed the volumes. She was feeling an empty pit in her stomach and, after about forty-five minutes, hunger won out at last. Standing up from her desk, she slammed down the last book and went to the information desk to inquire about a nearby inexpensive place to eat. Once armed with the necessary information, she shot out the library's front doors like a cannon ball looking for fodder, nearly knocking down Mrs. Mott, who was just returning from a short errand.

"Are you okay, Deborah?" asked one of Mrs. Mott's colleagues.

"Yes. But I think that I have some books to re-shelve. So much for high scholarship."

The nearby restaurant proved to be just right, for it offered a diverse menu at modest prices. Coachman picked up a newspaper that had been abandoned on one of the seats in the waiting area and followed the blonde hostess to a booth.

"Here's the menu. You're waiter will be with you shortly," said the young hostess.

"Good. I'm absolutely ravenous."

Soon a young, brown-haired waiter approached Coachman, saying, "Can I get you something to drink?"

"Coffee, young man. And make it snappy. I'm a scholar on important business over at the Library of Congress. And just so we don't waste any more time, get me a double stack of pancakes, a double order of sausage, and the biggest piece of cherry pie you can bring."

"Yes, Ma'am," said the astonished waiter.

After gorging herself on her late breakfast and early dessert while browsing through the newspaper, Coachman ordered a second piece of pie.

"Here's you check, Ma'am," announced her waiter.

"You've been pretty snappy, sweetie," said Coachman, smiling at her waiter, contemplating the size of tip she would leave. "I appreciate all the coffee you've been bringin' to me. As I said before, I've been researching up a storm. It's hard to keep your eyes open after you've read so much. By the way, I used up all of the sugar in that big bowl. Needed the energy for my work, and I've got to watch out that I don't eat any beef. It makes me sleepy."

"Do you want anything else?"

"No, sweetie. I have my heart's desire. My time is my own, now that I've won the lottery."

"Wow!" exclaimed the young waiter. "You won a lottery?"

"Yep! I'm going to be independently wealthy from now on. But I'm not gonna put on any airs, either. I don't look rich, do I?"

"No, Ma'am," confessed he waiter. "You could have fooled me."

"See, Sweetie. Never forget. No matter how high you rise, never lose the common touch."

"Yes, Ma'am," agreed the waiter, hoping that the so-called common touch would not extend to his forthcoming tip.

"May I ask how much you won, Ma'am?"

"A little over a million, son," replied Coachman, bucking in pride.

"Is that all?" exclaimed the surprised waiter.

"What do you mean, 'Is that all?'" said Coachman suspiciously.

"That's not much these days, if you know what I mean," said the waiter, adding, "I mean—it might have been, say fifty years ago."

"Now don't you get smart with me," warned Coachman, as she began to heave heavily, as if she were going to have an anxiety attack.

"Are you okay, Ma'am?" asked the waiter, alarmed at Coachman's sudden snorting.

"You just gave me a tremenjous start. I mean, I *thought* I was gonna be rich. I mean, really rich."

"Well, I don't mean to knock down what you've won. It's great that you got something. I mean, that's half a million *after* taxes, right?"

"Taxes?"

"Yes. The IRS will take at least half of it."

"You mean they haven't already?" groaned Coachman.

"Was the lottery in this country?"

"No. In England."

"Well, then, if I'm not mistaken, you're gonna have to ante up at least half of that half a million to the Feds," said the waiter.

Coachman turned pale white and her breathing became more labored.

"You can always figure that the IRS will bleed you just dry enough to keep you alive so you can pay 'em again next year," said the waiter, cynically.

"That's a pretty rotten view," Coachman reflected.

"It's always been that way. The rich people who set everything up back in Greece, or some place like that, wrote the rules so the rich would get richer and the poor would get it right in the neck. There's no gettin' ahead and no use tryin' to get ahead, no matter how hard you try."

"You've just taken ten years off my life, dearie," said an exasperated Coachman, wondering if the United Kingdom would levy a tax on her winnings.

"Well, maybe you can beat it. Some do, I think, but they're mighty rich."

"How do I beat it?"

"You should probably go visit the IRS right here in Washington," suggested the waiter.

"Good idea," agreed Coachman.

"But what about your research at the Library of Congress?"

"Screw that, dearie. I've got bigger fish to fry now. How much do I owe you?"

"With tax, the total is $ 19.39," said the waiter, looking at the slip he had placed on the table.

"Here's twenty dollars. Keep the change," announced Coachman.

"Excuse me?" said the waiter incredulously.

"I know it's a bum tip, dearie. But I can't go throwin' money around now until I fully understand my financial situation."

Bundling herself against the bitter cold temperatures and the bad news she had just received, Coachman ventured out into the winter blast, hailing a cab and ordering it to take her directly to IRS headquarters.

Arriving at the headquarters, and having been directed to an area dedicated to answering taxpayers' questions, Coachman nervously approached the section's receptionist, and announced, "Dearie, I just won a whopping lottery worth over a million, and I want to know how much I'm gonna owe the government."

"Your name?" asked the disinterested clerk.

"Gertrude Coachman."

"Take this number and have a seat. An advisor will be with you as soon as possible."

Coachman sat herself in the large waiting area, breathing heavily, as she began to envision her fortune funneling down a huge drain.

—I can't even go back to teaching, she reflected. —I've burned all my bridges there.

She suddenly laughed out loud, for no apparent reason, drawing the attention of some of those sitting nearby.

After nearly an hour, a small man with a bald head, large owl-rimmed glasses, and very pronounced black eyebrows entered the waiting area and called out, "Number 37?"

"Right here," answered Coachman, rising to her feet.

"Please come with me," invited the advisor.

Arriving at the man's office cubicle, Coachman was invited to sit in the chair facing his desk.

"I'm Mr. Morgan and you are?" he began.

"Gertrude Coachman."

"How may I help you?"

Coachman, to her surprise and embarrassment, burst into tears.

"Now, now," said Mr. Morgan, comforting her and handing her a tissue, "It can't be all that bad. Tell me what's the matter, and maybe we can help."

Coachman proceeded with a disjointed account of her lottery luck and the events preceding and following it, from which Mr. Morgan gathered that Coachman had won a foreign lottery, which would certainly be taxed. She had also resigned her job, which she hadn't cared for in any case.

"So," concluded Coachman, "Will I have to pay the government anything on my winnings, since it's a foreign lottery?"

Mr. Morgan nodded, saying, "Yes. Probably about half of it."

Coachman's eyes ballooned in size. Up until now, her worry had been no more than guarded speculation, but now that the truth had come home to roost, it did so with a vengeance.

She tried to say something, but nothing came out of her mouth when she opened it, the first such anomaly of her entire lifetime.

Mr. Morgan stared at her, waiting for her to say something, but all she could do was move her lips.

"Are you all right, Ma'am?" inquired the IRS advisor.

Coachman took a quick inventory and contemplated whether or not to feign a heart attack.

"That . . . that . . . that . . ." she began in a halting way.

"Yes? That?"

"That can't be," was all she could say.

"I assure you that this is a most accurate appraisal, Ma'am," insisted the advisor.

Coachman shook her head.

"I'm sorry, Ma'am, but you will owe the government a sizeable amount of your winnings. It may help you that you have resigned you teaching job, because that will be less income to weigh against your tax obligation."

"That can't be," said Coachman, mostly to herself.

"Can I be of any further assistance, Ma'am? I have others who are waiting," said Mr. Morgan.

"That . . . that . . . can't be," persisted Coachman.

"Ma'am, I'm going to have to ask you to return to the waiting area," announced Mr. Morgan.

Coachman sat impassively in her chair, saying again, to herself, "That can't be."

It was as if the continual denial might change the reality of her circumstance.

"Ma'am?" said Mr. Morgan more forcefully.

Coachman sat in silence.

"Ma'am," began Mr. Morgan, standing, "let me escort you back to the waiting area."

Walking to her chair and touching her arm, Mr. Morgan was shocked to hear Coachman scream, "Unhand me, you cad!"

Backing away, he went promptly to his telephone and called for security.

Within a minute, two security guards were standing next to him as he told them of his interview with this curious woman sitting in front of his desk and of her strange response to the assessment he had shared.

The security guards strode to each side of Coachman's chair, one of them announcing, as they each took her by her arms, "Ms. Coachman, you'll need to come with us for a little while."

"What?" exclaimed Coachman, as she was pulled to her feet.

"Please come with us, Ma'am," repeated one of the officers.

"You can't arrest me!" shouted Coachman. "I'm a published author!"

Five minutes later the published author was sitting in a containment room adjacent to the building's main security office.

Gertrude Coachman's previous external stance in Mr. Morgan's presence had now changed dramatically, for she seemed to be talking to the world at large. Her painfully loud tirade now involved many recriminations, mostly against the government and the Internal Revenue Service, with occasional flares of reproach against specific former students and people in general. Throughout her raging litany, she kept repeating that she, a published author, could not be treated in this fashion. Half an hour passed and, finally surmising that no one was listening, she once again burst into tears.

At a security desk outside the containment room, one of the guards whispered in a worried voice, "Larry, do you think she'll hurt herself?"

"Not that one," concluded Larry. "She's much too fond of herself for that, which I suppose is all the more the pity. Kicked me in the shins after they brought her in. Said I was nothing but a vassal to a filthy, greedy government, and that she was going to put things right in her next published work."

"Is she really a published author?" ask the first guard.

"Probably," replied his partner. "They're all a little crazy, so she fits right in there with the best of 'em."

"How are your shins?"

"Still hurting, but that's okay. She's gonna sit there for a couple more hours before I let her out."

"What if she makes a fuss?"

"Let her. We'll just ignore it."

"She's pretty hefty."

"Get the red flag out and pretend you're a matador, then. She's too full of herself to worry about us mere vassals."

"Guess you're right."

"It's all in a day's work, although she's the biggest corker we've had here in a long time."

"Guess we don't get too many published authors."

"Thank God."

Late that afternoon, when Coachman was finally escorted out of the IRS headquarters, she shouted, so that everyone in the common area could hear her, "I'm ruined for sure! Our lousy government is nothing more than a damned leech, and its gonna to take away half my winnings! I'm gonna have the police down on you and all the other blood-sucking weasels that work here."

Coachman returned to Midville on Saturday, arriving home in the wee hours of the morning. What she found when she entered her house displeased her as much as her untoward trip to Washington, but despite the misfortune that awaited her at home, she quickly saw how she might avenge the wrongs that had just been suffered on her and how she also might be able to send a local weasel packing.

Chapter Sixteen
A Sunday School Extravaganza

MIDVILLE'S MOST PROMINENT REALTOR was none other than the illustrious H. H. Lytle, or so he thought, with his initials standing for the Christian names Henry and Hubert respectively. Fortunate were all who had occasion to have dealings with so upright and scrupulous a man, or so assumed and believed a certain realtor named H. H. Lytle, whose favorite realtor was none other than the inimitable H. H. Lytle.

Neither a large nor a tall man, but rather stationed on the rigid and Napoleonic side of things, H. H. Lytle sat on his righteous roost, looking very much the preened vulture when pleased, and much more the indignant cassowary when ruffled.

A certain grandiloquence hung about his persistent loquacity, and clients often purchased his properties merely to spare themselves being talked to death. When not talking about realty, Mr. H. H. Lytle talked incessantly about what it meant to be, in his affected pronunciation, a *Chreestian.* Often mixing his private religion and business affairs together, he earnestly attempted to convey his passion for the faith in all circumstances where he felt he could instruct others to greater light. Outward sincerity he did not lack, for he had discovered early in life that he could be sincere on a moment to moment basis about anything he chose, most especially anything that would augment his bank account or status in the community. Several slogans ran regularly in the local *Courier*, such as FOR HONEST TITLE, PICK H. H. LYTLE and LYTLE PROPERTIES — INTEGRITY YOU CAN DEPEND UPON.

H. H. Lytle Realtors, Inc., offered an array of services, from house finding to house sitting. No challenge or job was too great or too small, with all comers welcome. Some of the clients who had dealt with H. H. Lytle never returned to solicit his services again, remembering too late their parents' or grandparents' injunction: 'actions speak louder than words'. Much to their later consternation and regret, they found that Lytle had secured at best only average sorts of deals and that, for all the moralizing they had received, none of it had translated into an especially scrupulous contract.

On alternate Sundays of the school year, H. H. Lytle fervently presided over the religious education of a particular band of Methodist youth who also happened to be middle school students. Lytle's pedagogical methods could be accurately compared to those techniques of Attila the Hun, except that Lytle's energies were doggedly directed toward the building up of a *Chreestian* empire, this better effort designed toward the promotion of the goodwill and fortunes of a certain local realty agency, one H. H. Lytle Realtors, Inc..

Since Elvira Lytle, the better half of H. H. Lytle, had fled north shortly after Christmas to nurse to health an ailing cousin, youth choir had been canceled on Sunday, January 7, and the middle school students at Midville's United Methodist Church had been subjected to the rants and rancor of H. H. Lytle, defender and champion of the local faith—ravings which involved the public excoriation of a local police officer who had run afoul of Lytle's failed attempt to transport the same middle school youth group to a New Year's Eve Watch Night service.

Today, Sunday, January 14, students sat waiting for their ruffled teacher, surmising that he would continue his litany of disdain from the previous week's rantings, as well as hold forth at painful length about Midville's celebrated lottery winner, Gertrude Coachman. 'Don't know,' Lytle had intoned during the previous week's class, 'whether this newly famous lady is a fellow *Chreestian* or not, but I certainly will pray that the Lord will lead her to this house of worship, should she have no other. I'll have you know that she has engaged my agency to watch her house while she's on her pilgrimage to the Library of Congress in Washington. The fact that she even used the word 'pilgrimage' to me would suggest she has some very real religious roots.'

Knowing better, however, the Gang of Four had merely rolled their eyes at each other as they sat in deeper knowledge of the personality in question. It was ironic, too, that the castigated but unnamed public law enforcement official also served as one of the trustees of the Midville United Methodist Church. The Gang of Four now waited in anticipation to see what new theme, if any, would fall from the lips of Mr. Lytle's peroration.

The door to the rectangular classroom burst open, and Henry Hubert Lytle surveyed his 'little pagans,' as he sometimes affectionately referred to them during his most important business luncheons. The zeal of his unrest burned in his eyes like a refiner's fire, even more brilliantly than it had the week before. The root of the dilemma he confronted lay in utmost paradox; he had been arrested by one of Midville's finest when escorting a band of local youth to the annual New Year's Eve Watch Night Service. That he had inadvertently run a stop sign was of no matter to the higher cause he had served on that snowy night. How could he have been wrong while working in the service of his *Chreestian* faith? The Lord surely should protect his own. That the ticketing officer was, in fact, a member of his own congregation deeply rankled him, sticking in his craw like a boulder.

When facing such paradox in the past, Mr. H. H. Lytle invariably had erred on the side of making a hasty generalization or reaching a false conclusion. This time was no different, for in his own peculiar way and in the deepest recesses of a suspicious mind, Henry Hubert Lytle had wrongly concluded that Patrolman Robert Edgerton Jameson was no true believer, but rather a dangerous atheist running amuck under false colors in the very nest of the faithful. Frequently such kinds of criticisms reveal more about the critics themselves than about those whom they criticize, but such subtlety of insight troubled not the apprehensions of this realtor who was now on a march of righteousness.

Walking purposefully to the far side of the room, lugging an enormous Bible with both hands, Mr. H. H. Lytle sat solemnly at the head of the table.

"We are here," he intoned, using the royal we as he occasionally did when making a particularly important point, "to learn about our faith as it interacts with the world, a world full of liars, cheats, and vipers. Last week we discerned, from my own bitter experience and painful *Chreestian* witness, that one among us, one of our so-called brethren, may not be what he appears to be, that is, a brother *Chreestian*. No, the one of whom I speak is anything but that. He is, instead, a viper in this innocent brood of believers. Oh, Good Lord, deliver us and protect us! I'll not mention names, but I will mention causes. Never, in my entire life, have I been as humiliated by another human being as I was on New Year's Eve. And I never *will be* as humiliated as I was on that dark and foreboding night. I begin to see that I was perhaps too polite, too restrained that night. No, my brave hearts, fear not, we are not undone by the likes of him of whom I speak. I only warn you that there is much in this world that calls itself *Chreestian* that is anything but *Chreestian*."

Here Mr. Lytle took a handkerchief from his pocket and mopped his brow, sighed, and preened himself, dusting some dandruff off his suit coat. As he did so, he lifted his nose in the air as if he could smell a bad odor in the room, glaring fiercely at everyone in the class, as if they had committed some grave atrocity.

After half a minute or so, which seemed a much longer time since mental daggers were traversing the space-time continuum, Molly Smith raised her hand and asked, "Mr. Lytle, what is our lesson for today?"

Staring at her blankly, in obvious disbelief, H. H. Lytle tapped his right ear with his hand, saying, "Beg your pardon?"

"I said, 'What is our lesson for today?'"

The plain truth was that there was no real lesson, owing to Lytle's having been so consumed and provoked by his New Year's Eve debacle. The best he could muster on this second Sunday of the New Year was a curious admixture of innuendo, intrigue, and insolence.

"You've just had your lesson for today," the defensive instructor pompously growled. "And if you want anything more, know that the Lord will provide it."

In the light of this revelation, Molly was just beginning to ask if the class could be dismissed early when, suddenly, the door crashed open with such fury and violence that all started and turned their attention to the unlikely but overwhelming presence of Gertrude Coachman, who stood in the doorway, like a bull, breathing heavily and leering with seething ire at H. H. Lytle.

The emotional temperature of the room immediately became ten degrees hotter, and Henry Hubert Lytle coughed and pulled at his collar as he studied his recently-acclaimed client. Searching for words, as well as for his voice, he blinked and coughed nervously, stammering, "Ah, my dear, dear lady, the lady who won the huge lottery . . . wel . . . wel . . . wel, I mean, welcome. I told these little ones last week about your asking me to watch your place for you while you were away on your mighty pilgrimage."

"Mighty-flighty," growled Coachman, never taking her eyes off Lytle, who continued to blink and cough and pull at his shirt collar.

Not knowing the reason for his client's ire, and not knowing quite what to say, Lytle decided to launch a trial balloon: "Always good to see a client in the Lord's house."

"STOW IT, BUSTER!" shouted Coachman, with such force that teacher and students alike cringed where they sat.

"Ah, ah, ah, I mean, ah, ah, ah, I don't—"

"I said, 'STOW IT!'" screamed a furious Coachman.

Mr. Lytle gasped and shut his mouth, all the while mopping his brow. The class was all attention at this unfolding drama.

"Watch the house, check it every day, check the heat, and no delay, my foot," continued a rancorous Coachman. "A pack of damned lies, you sniveling little weasel of a man."

Lytle sputtered and coughed, his face turning dark crimson.

Mocking the realtor's voice, she intoned pompously, "'I'll be there, never fear,' and all that hooey about being as religious as a saint. I'll have you know that I'm not the fool I look."

The Gang of Four silently contemplated Coachman's last assertion, each concluding that it was scarcely possible that anyone could be that foolish.

"Ah, dear lady, ah, ah,—"

"Don't 'Dear Lady' me, you conniving, thieving, lying, cheating hypocrite. Watch my house, my foot. A cadaver fresh out of Holmes' funeral parlor would've done a better job than you and all your empty promises."

The students sat spellbound as the curtain on this unfolding spectacle lifted higher.

"Ah, not in front of these innocents," warned Lytle, shaking his finger in mild reproof.

Coachman glared at the class, taking a rapid inventory of their number, recognizing to her mild surprise members of a certain Gang of Four with whom she had on occasion crossed swords, as well as the visage of Bobby Perkins, who also sat in their company, visiting the Sunday School for the first time.

"Looks to me as if you're running a reform school here instead of a Sunday school, with all these little infidels sittin' here," quipped Coachman as she pursed her lips. As her comment sank in, a wry smile crossed her face as she added, "And you, you call yourself a Sunday school teacher. Be better off havin' Attila the Hun, for my money, rather than the likes of you introducing these little infidels to the fine art of ripping people off."

Slights to his students Lytle easily endured; after all, they were merely middle school youth, wayward adolescents, little pagans. But to his own sterling reputation, so fragile was his ego, such criticism he could not tolerate. Gertrude Coachman's candid observations now impelled H. H. Lytle into indignant and defensive posturing, for she had unwittingly struck a significant kernel of truth in her attack.

"And just WHO do you think YOU are? You dare to enter the Lord's house and cast aspersions on His faithful chosen. I'll just have you know that *I* keep the Sabbath."

"You keep the Sabbath and anything else you can latch your little greedy hands on to, you conniving hypocrite. And don't you *dare* give me any of that holier than thou jazz," retorted Coachman. "I read in college about some Danish bigwig philosopher who wrote about the churches, and how they're all sittin' chockablock full of vipers."

Whether or not this word viper still hung in the air from Lytle's earlier discussion about the poor anonymous officer Edgerton mattered not, for Coachman's words had now effectively felled Lytle's self-righteousness.

"Oh, I've got your number, all right," retorted Lytle with a crooked little smile, as if he had seen through the rather enormous presence now intruding upon his precious classroom, "money, money, money . . .

that's *your* game. You're nothing more than a self-centered, money-greedy, sinful, hateful mortal."

"Well, if it isn't little Mr. Immortality himself speaking to all of us," chortled the Coachman in mock approval, smiling derisively.

"I demand an apology," glowered the teacher.

"For what?" asked Coachman. "The plumbers told me less than an hour ago that nobody could have been in my house for at least two days. They have ways of gauging that, you know, after all the pipes have burst and the water has run amuck and destroyed the basement, not to mention the bathrooms and the kitchen. And you're the lyin' weasel who promised to check my place every single day while I was gone, who swore that you'd make sure the heat would stay on, who said not to worry about a thing, that my place couldn't be in better hands. And then what do I find in my mailbox? A damn dunning notice from you for services *rendered*! Some services rendered."

"How was *I* to know your damn pipes would burst?" pleaded Lytle defensively.

"The weather's been freezin' cold, and the power's been on again, off again, on again all over the northeast. Seems to me even an *idiot* might put two and two together, but all you can do is stuff your stinking, measly, little dunning notices in innocent peoples' mailboxes for services never rendered," concluded the Coachman.

"But I had my *own* properties to worry about," defended the realtor, turning even a darker shade of red and sweating profusely.

"You've just bought yourself a new house, Buster, and I'm tellin' you right now it's a seller's market. I'm just gonna name my price, and you're gonna pay it, too, you miserable, lyin' weasel."

Here great credit should be given to the surprising degree of courage mustered by Realtor Lytle in the face of such an attack, for he was, physically, a rather small man, and his adversary was by comparison more than a trifle unwieldy. It was as if a shabby, little tug boat were being rammed by an enormous garbage scow. Plucking up his courage and summoning his best professional 'I'm not paying for that' voice, Lytle matter-of-factly asked, "How do you know the freezing temperatures even caused your pipes to burst? At the temperature you keep that icy tomb, it's more likely than not that your furnace ran out of fuel just because you were too cheap to fill it up for proper winter protection."

"Don't give me any of that cheapskate jazz, you conniving fool. I could buy and sell you ten times over and still have enough change to buy the Washington monument."

"Don't be too sure, woman. I've got my own resources," growled the realtor. "And I know an excellent attorney in town if it comes to that!"

"How dare you speak to me in that ugly tone and threaten me with the law!" exclaimed Coachman.

"Oh, it's okay for you, but not for me, eh? What's good for the goose is not good for the gander?" mocked the realtor.

"You should've been a preacher, with deep wisdom like that just brimmin' out of you," snorted Coachman. "When I'm finished with you, your goose will be so well done it'll be burnt."

"How dare you threaten and bully me!"

"Oh, I knew you'd puff right up like the little hen you are when I started over here. I called your office and got that foolish recording about how you'd be here in the Lord's hallowed house, where all good Christians should be. You dishonor the name, you conniving, little, no-good weasel of a man."

"You've gone too far, now, woman. I'm suing you for slander."

"Not until I've sued you for your last dime. When I'm through with you, you won't even be able to pay court costs."

"I'd not be too sure about a court verdict, if I were you."

"The plumbers will be there, and my neighbors say they never even saw you drive by the place, you lying cheat. I'm gonna move out—lock, stock and barrel—and store my stuff is some expensive warehouse, and then I'm gonna check into the Village Inn, and you're gonna pay for the storage, the room, and my meals—"

"Not your meals!" pleaded a cornered Lytle. "I'll be ruined for good if I have to pay for your meals. You can't get blood from a stone, you know. Perhaps I *could* manage the storage costs and your hotel room."

An eerie silence settled on the room as all present considered the implied insult in Lytle's last plea. As the whammy set in, the terrified realtor added, "I mean, I didn't mean, I mean, it wasn't what I meant, I mean, what you eat is your own damn business, I mean, eat as much as you want, I mean—even elephants have to eat."

"You don't *know* what you mean, you vile, little man. Make whatever slights you want about my girth, the price of my house just went up by one hundred thousand dollars!"

"One hundred thousand dollars! That's extortion! The whole damn thing isn't worth a penny more than that! And these poor innocents witnessing all of this! They'll swear to it all in court, too."

The Gang of Four now wondered if their idiosyncratic teacher would give them a new lesson in court matters, perhaps as enduring a lesson as the one he had rendered regarding obeying the law on New Year's Eve.

Mr. Lytle's face had turned crimson as he started coughing and pulling at his shirt collar. Feeling that she had now gained the final advantage, Gertrude Coachman slowly walked toward the realtor.

"No closer, no closer," warned an obviously frightened Lytle, who looked as if he wished he could crawl under the table.

Coachman proceeded down the right side of the room, moving relentlessly toward her quarry.

"A court case would hurt us both!" enjoined a trembling realtor.

"Not as much as the full page ad I'm going to take in the *Courier* that will show photographs of the destruction your measly neglect caused, not to mention a copy of your bill for bogus services."

"You . . . you . . . you wouldn't," pleaded the realtor.

"Full page," reaffirmed the Coachman. "You won't be able to sell a dog house in this town after I'm through with you."

"Thr . . . thr . . . eats. I . . .I . . . dle threats," sputtered the realtor, putting on as brave a face as possible. "After all, we had no wri...written agreement."

Gertrude Coachman caught hold of H. H. Lytle's left ear with her right hand and proceeded to place it on the huge Bible that sat on the table in front of him.

"Ouch, my ear, my ear!"

"Don't give me any of that no written agreement tripe, you sniveling, little worm. I have enough evidence on you to put you behind bars for six months, but even jails have their standards, and I wouldn't want to corrupt any of the decent folk that might be staying in them, or subject them all to your foolish blather."

"My ear!"

"Swear on this Bible that you didn't neglect my place. If you do, I'll leave you alone and walk out that door without another word."

In the lives of most people come such moments of truth; thus came one to Henry Hubert Lytle. If he swore a lie on the Good Book, the Precious Book as he so often called it, his immortal soul would be consigned to the perils of eternal damnation. If he remained silent, he would lose hundreds of thousands of dollars.

A seemingly endless interval followed. If a pin had been dropped, it would have proved as deafening as thunder. No one dared to stir, much less to breathe. Little had the class expected that the Lord would provide so instructive an addendum to teacher Lytle's lesson for the day.

"Well," shouted Coachman, "will you swear, or will you keep your silence in the face of your stinkin', cheatin' neglect?"

"Si . . . si . . . si . . ." stammered Lytle.

"What?" intoned Coachman, releasing his ear.

"Silence," gasped Lytle, breathing heavily.

"Well, then, my pretty," continued Coachman, "I will write a little document for you to sign."

Lytle's face was still bright red and he buried his head in his hands, as if he wished he might awake from this unseemly nightmare.

"I, H. H. Lytle," Coachman read aloud as she wrote, "will pay Gertrude H. Coachman, with a cashier's check from my local bank, the sum of three hundred thousand dollars for her stone mansion here in Midville at three o'clock Monday afternoon, January the twenty-second, at the village courthouse. I will also pay for her lodging and meals at Midville's Village Inn until the end of May, and further I will pay all storage costs for her furniture and personal items until further notice. Signed . . . H. H. Lytle."

Lytle groaned, not wanting to look up.

"Here's the paper, you cowardly, little man. Sign it, or I'll have the courts post you to hell and back again."

With the greatest resignation and reluctance, Henry Hubert Lytle took pen in hand and signed the document. Reading it over, he thrust it toward Coachman, and then stood up, brushing off his coat on both sides as if he had just been mugged. Adopting a remarkably debonair air, he strode toward the door and, without looking back once at his middle school charges, he walked out of the classroom.

Coachman pursed her lips, licking them as she inspected the document. Snorting as she tried to regain her own bearing, and following in Lytle's train toward the door, she crossed the threshold, turned back, glaring at the astonished infidels, and growled to the class, "Now, dearies, let *that* be a lesson to ya."

Chapter Seventeen
The Triumph of the Megafauna

On Wednesday after school David was setting up his slide presentation about the megafauna that was scheduled for the next day. Sean stopped at the door to Ms. Smiley's classroom and knocked.

"Hello, Sean," said David.

"Hi," said Sean. "How about a chess game tonight?"

"I just can't," said David. "Tomorrow's my big report, and then we're going to break the pig open on Friday to find out how much money we've raised. Mrs. Dixon will count it during the day, so they should be able to announce the total before school is dismissed."

"Yeah, sure, okay," said Sean unenthusiastically.

"Come on," scolded David. "You, Mary and Lisa have played key roles in all this. I bet we'll bring in at least four hundred dollars. I mean, even Bobby and his friends are contributing."

"Bobby, Bobby," grumped Sean. "That's all I hear any more: Bobby, Bobby."

"Now that's not true," retorted David. "And you know it."

"I just miss seeing you and playing chess," said Sean.

"Just give me another day. Okay?"

Sean considered David's request, replying, "It's always 'Just give me another day.'"

"Sean!" said David firmly, "I really need to get this set up for tomorrow. I'm sorry that we haven't had much time recently."

"You mean NO time," persisted Sean.

"Okay. NO time. I *just* don't know where the time has gone," said David, rather disingenuously.

"Into the past. Where do you think?" Sean's impatience had now graduated into a full-blown ire, and he glared angrily at David. His stinging retort was no less painful than his immediate slamming of the door, to which David could only sigh, shake his head, and hope for better days.

David rehearsed his slide program several times, making sure that he could complete the entire presentation in thirty minutes, which would leave fifteen minutes for questions.

—Tomorrow is my big day, David mused to himself, as he walked home. —I'm finally going to upstage that twerp of a Mallory.

* * * * *

Excitement reigned in Science 8 on Thursday morning, for everyone realized that the prize for the best presentation, the trip to Ontario, would be won either by Mallory or David.

No other presentation had yet equaled or surpassed Mallory's, although Jimmy Bradley had given Mallory a scare with his presentation on the pterosaur, dazzling his listeners with a passionate recounting of the evolution of winged lizards on this planet. Class members had been told that pterosaurs originated from the pseudosuchian gliding reptiles in the Triassic period, lasted 130 million years, and had died out in the great extinction that killed much of the life on earth around 65 million years ago. Some scientists considered these huge creatures to be weak fliers, having had to rely on moving air currents to keep themselves airborne. Fossils of the carrion feeder Quetzalcoatlus, perhaps the largest animal ever to fly, found in Texas and Alberta, had revealed it had a remarkable wingspan that had stretched up to 39 feet. Jimmy had presented a number of remarkable depictions from several books, but his presentation still fell short of Mallory's program of slides and intense pushing of the T-Rex. Even the amazing theory that these huge flying reptiles and the ancient megadragonfly of the period would not be able to fly today because of the decrease of oxygen in the atmosphere failed to carry the day for Jimmy.

As David entered the classroom, Mallory, who was waiting for him near the bulletin board, whispered, "Throw in the towel, Andrews. You don't have a ghost of a chance against the T-Rex. That ugly piggy bank you put up in the lobby is just another desperate gimmick to tear down the T-Rex."

"At least my pig will help the community food bank," retorted David. "All your creepy T-Rex did was take up room in the lobby and collect dust."

"T-Rex isn't a weakling Beta that dishes up food, Andrews," corrected Mallory. "T-Rex is the supreme Alpha that *takes* food."

"Pretty selfish, then, isn't it?" retorted David.

"Listen, Andrews, you'd better— " began Mallory.

"Get off your high horse Mallory and sit down. You've had your chance. Mine's today, and Ms. Smiley will decide who's done the best job," said David with justified impatience.

"Just you wait till it's time for questions," threatened Mallory as he slunk off to his seat, where he folded his arms and unfurled a scowl that could have curdled milk.

"All ready, David?" asked Ms. Smiley.

"I think so. I've coordinated the slide program with all of the comments I'm going to make, and I typed out two copies, one for you and one for me. I know it pretty well, so it won't seem as if I'm just reading it."

"Wouldn't it be nice to be able to memorize something like this?" asked Ms. Smiley.

"Yes," said David, nodding and thinking of Sean with envy.

"This is very efficient of you. I look forward to your presentation."

"Ms. Smiley," began David.

"Yes?"

"Since my presentation is the very last one, I thought it important to give a sort of closing overview about how animal life evolved on this planet before leading up to the megafauna. That's okay, isn't it?"

"I would say that it is most important. You'll help us to draw a full circle around our marking period reports," said Ms. Smiley.

"It's amazing how life has come and gone," said David, slyly baiting his teacher for one of her classic maxims.

"All life must either sink or swim, David," came the hoped for response. Ms. Smiley glanced around the classroom and added, "Everyone is finally here. Shall we begin?"

"I'm all set."

"Attention, everyone. David will now give his report on prehistoric life, with an emphasis on the megafauna," announced Ms. Smiley.

Mallory sighed and refolded his arms, shifting himself in his chair.

David turned on the slide projector and then went to the front of the classroom, holding the remote control with his left hand.

"Friends," he began, "we have heard many fine and interesting reports these last few weeks on the different kinds of prehistoric life that once inhabited this planet. It's been like looking into a never-ending cornucopia of creation, an amazing tapestry of experiment and variety."

Mallory stretched and yawned, looking around to gauge class interest. "As you know, most animals belong to the phylum Arthopoda, meaning 'joint-legged.' Early arthropods lived in the sea, but their colonization of the land began about 400 million years ago. But we're getting ahead of ourselves. Let's go back to the beginning, to approximately 1.6 billion years after the earth first formed. During this Pre-Cambrian Period, which lasted until about 570 million years ago, the first and simplest forms of life evolved in the ocean, and it took these plant forms another two billion years to change the atmosphere of our planet, through the production of oxygen, so that it would accommodate more complex life forms."

As David presented this overview, a variety of slides flashed depictions of the early earth and the emergence of living organisms.

"The increase of oxygen in the atmosphere helped to form the ozone layer, which began to absorb ultraviolet rays. New and larger cells emerged around 1.2 billion years ago. DNA was organized into chromosomes instead of just floating around in the cell-soup. The earth at that time was a very violent place, with earthquakes and volcanic eruptions. The volcanic ash in the atmosphere caused great ice masses to form across the planet, and perhaps caused the first great mass extinction of life; however, in the aftermath of the upheavals, multicellular animals arose.

"The Cambrian Period lasted from about 570 to 500 million years ago. During this period a huge variety of life appeared, and not one new phylum of life has manifested since that time. The conditions for such a proliferation of life seem to have been ideal, with much of the planet offering shallow ocean shelves, soft muds, and warm water. Sea levels kept rising and falling during this period, and many creatures emerged, only later to become extinct.

"The Cambrian Period was followed by the Ordovician and Silurian Periods, a time which saw the emergence of the first land plants as well as the first land invertebrates, which were a little like scorpions. The Devonian Period, which followed between 408 and 360 million years ago, saw new turbulence, with continents drifting and colliding. Fish evolved in greater variety and complexity, as did land plants. The new forests served as homes to the early insects."

Colorful Powerpoint images continued to capture the attention of the class.

"The Carboniferous Period followed and lasted until around 286 million years ago. This was a time when insects were everywhere. Insects are highly adaptable and can adjust their bodies for flying, jumping, swimming, walking, and running. Dragonflies in those days had wing spans of up to 27 inches. It is also interesting to note that the design of dragonflies has changed very little since those early days, suggesting that they are a resilient and successful life form.

"The Permian Period followed and lasted until about 248 million years ago. It was a time when the earlier amphibians gave way to the new reptiles, although another great extinction happened at the end of this Period. It was a time when some reptiles developed warm blood, and although most cynodonts perished with the passing of the Permian Period, a few of the small to medium-sized ones survived into the Triassic Period, with their descendants leading the way toward the evolution of the early mammals."

David continued to mesmerize his classmates with slides; even Mallory was paying attention and taking notes.

"The Triassic Period lasted from 248 until 213 million years ago. It gave rise to some of the plants that still live today, including the Gingko. Land animals were similar and could travel almost anywhere throughout the giant super continent of Pangea. The Triassic was also important because it saw the first flying animals, the pterosaur that Jimmy so enthusiastically described to us.

"The beginning of the Age of Dinosaurs, the Jurassic Period began about 213 millions ago and ended 144 million years ago, followed by the Cretaceous Period which ended abruptly with a mass extinction 65 million years ago. The Cretaceous Period is also important for the emergence of angiosperms, also called flowering plants, which formed a working alliance with insects for the distribution of pollen."

Slides of these creatures and the earth on which they lived continued to flash up for the students, dazzling them with rich colors and imaginative scenes. David continued to weave an astounding web of how life developed on planet earth.

"I won't repeat what has been said about the dinosaurs. Suffice it to say, these magnificent reptiles ruled this planet for over a hundred and forty million years. Unfortunately, the so-called terrible lizards seem to get the most attention and hype these days—"

"I beg your par— " began Mallory, his face flushing.

"Questions *later*," said David firmly. "As I was saying, the T-Rex and his compatriots get all the hype. I believe that such undue attention is a sad reflection on our society, for in our fetish to raise up such aggressive saurians, we forget the graceful and beautiful sauropods, such as Brachiosaurus and Diplodocus."

Slides of these magnificent creatures flashed on the screen, although Mallory could be heard to snort from time to time.

"The Ornmithischian, or bird-hipped, dinosaurs were perfectly designed to chew leaves, their teeth and jaws fully up to the task. There was a large variety of this family of dinosaurs, including the gazelle-like Hypsilophodon and the ever popular Stegosuarus.

"Mammal-like dinosaurs followed, called the therapids, meaning 'mammal arch'. The theriodonts most resembled mammals and some were no doubt warm blooded and even had hair.

"Some scientists believe that birds evolved from flying reptiles. The most famous early reptile-bird link is the fossil *Archaeopteryx*, considered to be one of the first known birds, resembling a small dinosaur but also displaying feathers. To date no clear ancestor has been found for the huge, flightless birds we have in the world today, such as the emu and ostrich, although there were huge predatory birds during the Paleocene era, between 65 and 54 million years ago. Diatryma, a nine-foot bird, ruled North America during these years. Its counterpart in South America ruled that continent for more years because it was inaccessible by predator mammals for a much longer period. The Madagascar elephant bird, which weighed nearly a thousand pounds, became extinct only about three hundred years ago, along with the giant moa of New Zealand, which stood over eleven feet high, and died out about a hundred years before that.

"And our own ancestors, the small shrew-like mammals that survived through the Triassic and the Jurassic Periods, led the way to become the new dominant life form on the planet. The monotremes seem to have been one of the transitional forms, for like the spiny anteater today, they could lay eggs, yet they also had many mammalian features. The duck-billed platypus is another monotreme that still survives; both of these unusual creatures are virtually living fossils, windows into our past.

"I won't mention all of the minor epochs that have occurred since the last great extinction, but the two major ones are the Tertiary Period and the Quaternary Period, which began about two million years ago. Marsupials, at one time much more prominent than today, also represent another of Nature's courageous experiments in evolution and form. As mammals evolved after the last major mass extinction, many also increased in size. Megatherium, one of the megafauna, was the largest ground sloth our world has ever seen, over 20 feet in length, and it died out only about ten thousand years ago. Glyptodon, which you see here in this slide, was a huge armadillo, literally bigger than a car."

David noticed with appreciation that his classmates seemed to be hanging on his every word, their attention riveted on the slides he had prepared.

"Mammals began to establish themselves about 57 million years ago. Bats, the only mammal that flies, first appeared about 50 million years ago. One of the most impressive and massive of the megafauna was Indricotherium, which weighed nearly 20 tons and measured 16 feet at the shoulder. It was an early form of hornless rhinoceros, and its remains have been found in Siberia.

"Giant pigs, called Entelodonts, although not closely related to modern pigs, were about the same size as today's cows. As you can see in this slide, their heads had really large cheek bones and they also had long legs, which is why some scientists suggest that they were fast runners."

David continued to give visual and oral examples of members of the megafauna, those larger-than-life mammals that dominated this planet for millions of years before the emergence of humanity. They included the great wooly mammoth, the mastodons, the cave bear of Europe, the sabertooth tiger, the giant beaver of North America, the remarkable rhinos from northern Eurasia, the North American camel, the antlered giraffe of lower Africa, among many more.

As image after image flashed by, David drove the point home again and again about how these magnificent creatures, fellow members of our own Mammalia Class of creatures, had vanished from the face of the earth, never to be seen again.

"As you all know, it is possible to visit a very special place in Ontario, Canada, where dozens of life-sized sculptures of dinosaurs and the megafauna give one a whole new perspective on the size of these creatures."

Slides from the Canadian park began to flash on the screen. Ms. Smiley opened her mouth in surprise and made some rapid notes on her grade sheet.

Astounded by David's ploy, Mallory could only growl, "Give me a break! What a wimpy . . ."

"These creatures almost come alive to the visitor with a vivid imagination. Note these dinosaurs, and now, here we are, walking under the huge legs of Indricotherium itself. Notice how small the neighboring trees seem when seen in contrast to this true giant."

David continued to show slides of the representations of extinct life forms found in the park, slides that Mr. Pennythorpe had suggested

David secure for his presentation. Having done so, David hoped it would cook Mallory's goose once and for all. And that very goose, indeed, sat in sullen attention, his mouth hanging open. As Mallory watched slide after slide of the trip, the place, that he coveted getting more than words could describe, he began to realize that his assumed victory might be receding from his grasp. Woe to Alphas and their kind.

"Although very few of the megafauna survive today," David continued, "we can still see them in Africa. I speak of the lion, tiger, leopard, elephant, rhino, hippo, and others creatures like them. In the name of progress, however, their habitats are being encroached upon and destroyed. Soon these majestic animals will also become extinct."

David noticed Ms. Smiley wiping a tear from her eye and taking out a tissue and blowing her nose. Mallory, looking around and noticing her unusual reaction, scowled even more at David and shuffled about at his desk, hoping to distract those around him.

"To help us place the age of our Earth in context, some geologists liken our planet's history to the calendar year. Extraordinary as it may seem, the dinosaurs do not appear until the middle of December, making their unexpected exit on the day after Christmas, and all of what is called human civilization and history may be found in the most recent seconds of that very last day of that calendar year.

"We are the stewards of this planet, at least for this brief moment, although very poor stewards we have been. We have arrogantly assumed that we were the sole reason for the existence of creation, raping and consuming this world's resources in the name of technology and progress."

David looked at Mallory and couldn't resist the insertion of a barb, albeit a fallacious knock.

"We have nothing to be proud of, we humans. We have been traveling this planet, pillaging everything in our path, like an army of modern-day T-Rexes, devouring *everything* in our way."

Mallory started to lunge from his desk, but was held back by Rory Winter. Rory tried to calm Mallory, as Mallory gave *sotto voce* protestations to David's indictment of the T-Rex.

"We need to learn that we share a deep interconnection with all life, in fact, with all that is, for we are all made of the very same material that originated in the first stars in this universe."

A slide of a spiral galaxy appeared on the screen.

"We must honor life and honor our deeper interconnectedness to everything that exists," continued David. "We must do so while we still can, for who knows if humanity itself will survive? The most successful creatures alive today on this planet are *not*, I repeat, *not* the mammals. Rather they are the insects, who literally rule the planet by virtue of their numbers and adaptability. Perhaps *we* are the visitors and they are the hosts. But whether or not we survive, or they survive, does not matter, for we all have all been part of this great flourishing of life on planet earth. And no one can take that away from us; I only pray that we will begin to honor the opportunities we have been given."

The last slide showed the earth as photographed from space.

David said nothing as his audience considered the photograph; after about ten seconds, he concluded by saying, "Thank you for your attention."

Applause thundered so loudly in David's ears that he took a step back. Mallory, however, sat sullenly in his seat, scowling more than ever.

Ms. Smiley had risen from her desk in the back of the room, and cleared her throat, saying, "David. What a splendid report. Thank you. You have given us all a lot to think about. Are there any questions?"

Unsurprisingly Mallory's hand shot up.

"Yes?" smiled David, wondering if Mallory would sputter in his anger.

"Andrews, you've pulled a cheap trick on all of us," began Mallory. "You don't give enough credit to the T-Rex— "

Hoping that Mallory would begin in this manner, David interrupted him, saying, "Mallory, it's time to move beyond the T-Rex. Everyone is sick and tired of hearing only about the T-Rex, how strong the T-Rex was, how tall the T-Rex was, how Alpha the T-Rex was."

Another burst of applause affirmed David's contention.

Mallory looked aghast and yelled, "Shut up!" to his classmates.

The applause abruptly stopped.

"Now look— "

"No, you look, Mallory," began David, having decided some weeks ago that the best way to have an argument with Mallory was not to have one. "If T-Rex had been such great shakes, he'd still be around today. But he couldn't even survive the mass extinction 65 million years ago. But the little mammals did, so apparently they're at least a wee bit tougher than your precious T-Rex."

More applause as Mallory's face turned deep red with fury.

"Don't get me wrong, Mallory," continued David. "T-Rex was pretty impressive, and I wouldn't have wanted to meet up with him, but he became extinct millions of years ago. Then the mammals became dominant for a short while and have been disappearing ever since. And that includes us, you know. Perhaps the insects are biding their time. Why rush us out? There will be more to eat the more we propagate ourselves."

Mallory was so furious that he stood up from his desk and walked to the front of the room, standing only a few feet from David. Glaring at the entire class, he sneered at David, beginning, "Andrews, you're really sick— "

David didn't hear anything else, because his attention was suddenly captured by a bright light, which suddenly seemed to flash above and around him. He wasn't sure if he was going to be able to remain standing, so disconcerting were these flashes of wonderful color, so he sat down at a nearby desk as Mallory raged on.

He looked at Mallory but found his eyes focusing on the screen where the famous photograph of the world still showed itself. The room lights had not been turned back on, and the flashing lights increased in their intensity. As he studied the image of the earth before him, it disappeared and he saw instead a row of beings, some humanoid, others distinctly different, standing in a line, like a horizon line, on the deep black background that had replaced the earth. David had the eerie and distinct feeling that these beings were watching him, and he suddenly heard their collective summons, 'Watch'. After this, behind their ranks, a small intense white light could be seen in the center of the screen. The light grew more and more brilliant and finally exploded. Out of it came a stream of light, which formed into galaxies and star clusters and planets. David realized that he was watching the creation of the universe. He also realized that he had always been and would always be intimately connected to all that was in the universe and all that might lie beyond.

The galaxies continued to swirl in brilliant clusters of light, dancing together and flowing apart, only to return. David saw images of life emanating from the center of the scintillating light, as it spewed all kinds of life, a seemingly infinite process of beauty and wonder, of majesty and utter uniqueness. There was an awe and beauty to everything that had ever existed, a beauty that far surpassed humanity's poor ability to comprehend, as if in one endless procession, an infinity of life forms, plant, animal, and others. David could scarcely understand marched in this procession that marched before him, each having played a singularly unique role in the dazzling tapestry of creation and light which was unfolding. Some of the entities seemed to have an existence that was not diminished by time, others emerged and disappeared, although their roles were no less important.

David now felt himself lifted out of his chair and into the screen, and as he suddenly became a part of the swirling life, a marvelous feeling of well-being infiltrated every atom of his body and renewed the energies which coursed through his psyche. Now David saw spirals of the universal light touching everything around him, including himself. Somehow he knew, in a way deeper than knowledge itself, that everything that exists draws its being from and is in some way a manifestation of the ineffable and glorious primordial light he had just seen explode into the entire universe, perhaps into an infinite number of universes and permutations. A deep sense of joy washed over him as he also unexpectedly realized that no matter what happened to him, either today, or tomorrow, or next week, or next year, or even in twenty years, or even in a hundred, that which was uniquely David would never die. Yes, form rises and falls, like the ocean tides, but spirit and light, light and spirit, never die, always remaining intimately intertwined with the primordial light from whence they derive the diversity and uniqueness of their being. And as David opened himself to the new joy that now flowed through his entire being, he also realized that what is called matter is merely an illusion. To transcend the limitations of time and space, it is thought that is real. David felt embraced by all of Creation, and now knew, deeper than knowing itself, that he and everything else, was a unique and wonderful part of a larger whole, a whole that was yet part of a larger whole, with all the wholes eventually merging into Infinite Light and Love, which could be nothing less than the Mind of God.

Gradually the bright and radiating images faded, replaced by the slide of the earth which still showed itself on the screen, and David felt himself returning to the classroom, albeit suffering a little dizziness from his journey. Mallory, however, was still on his high horse, blithering at the class, hoping to demean David's presentation in some way and thus defend his prized T-Rex.

As David returned more fully to the world of his five senses, he realized several things at once: the first was that he would never see himself or the world or others in the same way again; the second was that he knew he would be alive forever, no matter what form he might take; and the last was that he hadn't heard a single thing Mallory had said. Deciding to make a generalized, global response, hoping that it would meet any criticism that Mallory had leveled at him, he waited for Mallory to finish.

"So that's why T-Rex rules!" concluded Mallory, looking smugly at David as if to say, 'I guess you just got yours, Andrews, you little Beta shrimp.'

David surveyed the class, which was watching him with intense interest, wondering how he'd respond to Mallory. But no words would come, for David was still reorienting himself to the classroom. In a great gesture of emphasis, Mallory had taken up a ruler from the chalk board to emphasize his points. But when David did not even dispute his points, Mallory threw the pointer on the floor and stomped back to his desk, as if to say, 'I give up. How can anyone deal with such a fool?'

Mercifully, the passing bell rang at that very moment.

As the students filed out of the room, David continued to sit in his chair, totally unable to move, still trying to understand what had just happened to him. This encounter was unlike anything he had ever known. Somehow, through a miracle or a chance of fate, it was as if a door to heaven had opened and David had been admitted for the briefest of moments.

Beginning to take stock of himself, he found that he was overflowing with joy, inexplicable, wonderful, marvelous joy.

"David?" asked Ms. Smiley, shaking him. "Are you all right?"

David studied his teacher and saw a blue and green aura emanating around her head. He blinked his eyes at her.

"David? Are you all right?" she repeated.

"Yes," he said. "Do you have a class now?"

"No. It's my free period."

"May I please just sit here for a while? I need to be quiet," asked David.

"Of course, you may. I need to run a few errands. Just turn the lights off when you leave if you decide to go before I return."

"Thanks."

"You're entirely welcome. And thank you for a fascinating report. It has given me a lot to consider before I announce the winning presentation tomorrow."

"Thank you."

After Ms. Smiley left, David sat still for many minutes, enjoying the silence. He knew that he wouldn't be able to talk to anyone about his experience for a long time, for he didn't know what words he could use that could do justice to his vision. He would hold the experience within himself and ponder its meaning. Whatever it meant, or might mean, would become apparent to him eventually.

More than half an hour passed before he rose to leave. Everything around him seemed more real, more vibrant, more glorious than he had ever noticed. It was as if everything had suddenly become alive. Turning the lights out as he left, he resolved that he would ask Bobby if they could walk home in silence today. He needed silence and he needed water, for he was suddenly very thirsty. His departure for the closest water fountain couldn't have been swifter.

* * * * *

Friday morning saw the long awaited breaking of the pig. It was decided that the amount of money collected and the name of the pig would be announced simultaneously at the end of the school day. For once, students had two things to look forward to through their daily routine.

The voting and contributions had followed an ingenious system, wherein contributors would write their preferred name for the pig on an official slip of paper. Mrs. Dixon would then record the number of 'votes' cast for that name. A student preferring the name Peter would write 'Peter' on the slip, and then donate fifty cents or a dollar. Mrs. Dixon would accept the slip and money, and make a record of fifty 'votes' for the name Peter. The money collected on any given day was to be inserted into the pig the next morning as students entered and milled about the lobby.

David hoped the pig Mr. Astor had given him would serve as a enticing advertisement, and he apparently had been correct for, despite Mallory's recriminations, most students took a fancy to the pig and donated a fair portion of their lunch money and extra change to help baptize it.

Although invited to help, David had refused to have any part of the counting of names, for fear that someone would suggest that he had rigged the tally.

*****

It was appropriate that the winners of Ms. Smiley's science presentation contest be announced during David's and Mallory's period, for that was the period where the potential winners sat.

"For the first time in my thirty years of teaching," began Ms. Smiley, "two presentations were so good, so out of the ordinary for different reasons, that I have determined that a tie should be declared; therefore, I am declaring David Andrews and Mallory Evans to be this year's winners. David, your presentation was quite remarkable. It has caused me to see things in a new light. This year we are *not* going to go the Ontario dinosaur park. Instead, we are going to go to New York City, where we will visit the Bronx Zoo and the Museum of Natural History. And, yes, Mallory, there are dinosaur bones at the museum, but David's presentation was so compelling that I thought it would be much more important to see the living megafauna that still survive, for we may not have that privilege much longer. You may each select two friends to accompany you. I will make arrangements for us to go to the city by train. I will also ask at least one of your parents to accompany our group."

Mallory sat at his desk, stupefied, not knowing what to say.

David put on his best smile, contemplating how unbearable a trip to the Big Apple with Mallory and two of his buddies would be. He immediately resolved that he would invite Sean and Bobby to be his guests, and they would be sure to have a little chat with Mallory before he boarded the train, very like two T-Rexes chatting with a baby stegosaurus. Before Bobby and Sean were done with Mallory, he'd be claiming that the Statue of Liberty was way too Alpha for her own good and that everyone should draw their horns in and be a little nicer to each other. 'Live and let live' would become Mallory's new motto, or else Mallory might unexpectedly find himself part of a far different place.

The class applauded with enthusiasm and respect the work both boys had done. The consensus of opinion later was that David's report was far better than Mallory's, more like a college lecture, and that David's passion for the extinct and vanishing megafauna had worked its magic upon both students and teacher, except, of course, for Mallory, who was still stuck in his T-Rex Alpha rut. Students did credit Mallory, however, with having given an extremely intense report about the T-Rex, and that his presentation had almost sufficed for them feeling that they had actually met one.

* * * * *

Near the end of the last period, Mr. Ferlinghausen made the following announcement to the members of the school community:

"May I have your attention please? I wish to announce the results of our "Name One of the Megafauna." First, let me say that it is most gratifying to report to you that our school has raised $ 649.23 for the community food bank. Now, what you've all been waiting for: the name selected for the pig, and may I add that it had no real contenders, is Hortense."

As wild cheers, whistles, and shouts swept like a wave through the entire school, David was delighted at the amount of money raised, but he also hoped that no untoward events would transpire from his having revealed Gertrude Coachman's middle name. David made a mental note to take the photograph of the pig and results of the election to Mr. Leonard, when he, Sean, and Bobby would meet with *The Courier* editor at the Courthouse on Monday afternoon. They were intrigued to witness the Gertrude Coachman's legal and official transfer of her stone mansion to H. H. Lytle.

* * * * *

As they walked home that afternoon, Bobby Perkins was in an upbeat frame of mind.

"Well, I guess we got back at the old witch at last," said Bobby.

"I guess," said David. "But how will she know?"

"'Cause you're gonna give Mr. Leonard the photo and the name and they'll run it in Tuesday's paper," said Bobby.

"Do you think she'll even notice?" asked David.

"Are you kiddin' me?" asked Bobby. "I bet she reads every word of that paper just because it's free and 'cause she's hopin' to find one of her lousy poems."

"Well, she'll put two and two together if she sees it," said David.

"Hope so," agreed Bobby. "I'd love to see the old pig's face when she sees her picture."

"You'll see her for real on Monday," David reminded Bobby.

"Hey. Don't ruin my weekend."

Chapter Eighteen
Three to Astor

SATURDAY BROUGHT WARMER WEATHER and the beginning of a January thaw. POTS dropped Sean at David's and Bobby's promptly at 10:00 a.m. and now the three boys made for Mr. Astor's shop of Junken Treasures, slushing and sliding their way along the sidewalks.

"Hey, Davie boy," teased Bobby, "I guess we got that old dame Coachman with the name the pig contest."

"Yeah," snorted David. "I just hope she doesn't decide to sue me.

"The *Courier* lost on that deal," quipped Sean.

"Mr. Leonard told me that when I dropped off the photograph of the pig that he'll run our short announcement with the photo on Tuesday. Underneath it will say: Midville Middle School students name huge pig HORTENSE and raise $ 649.23. Proceeds donated to Midville Community Food Bank."

"What did Mr. Leonard think of the photograph?" asked Sean.

"He laughed," said David.

"See," said Bobby. "He sees the likeness, clear as day."

"He also wants our help," said David.

"Our help?" asked Sean.

"Especially *your* help, Sean," said David.

"What for?"

"To listen to an interview he will try to get from Coachman after she and Mr. Lytle close their deal on her big stone mansion. Remember, she invited those of us who were in Sunday School to go witness the transfer on Monday between 3:30 and 4:00 p.m. I thought we'd wait on the Courthouse steps and try to get her to give an interview for the paper," explained David.

"Why would the paper want an interview with *her*?" asked Sean.

"Because she won the lottery and that's real news in a dinky little town like this. The paper tried to get information on her trip to Washington but that ended up in a dead end, so they're not going to publish any of that," said David.

"What dead end?" asked Sean.

"I'm not at liberty to say. I learned my lesson about blabbing the hard way when I revealed Coachman's middle name to everyone," said David.

"So are we walking down to the Courthouse after school on Monday?" asked Sean.

"Yes. Mr. Leonard will meet us there. He's bringing a camera, but he wants you to listen to what she says, Sean, so he will be accurate should he want exact quotes," explained David.

"I'm game," said Sean. "How many times does one get to see and listen to an old witch?"

"You mean *pig*," corrected Bobby.

"Hey," exclaimed Sean. "Why not 'pig-witch'?"

Bobby started to laugh.

"What's so funny?" asked David.

"I'd only add one word that rhymes with witch," said Bobby.

Sean nodded his head in approval.

"Aunt Lillian says Coachman has to live in her own shoes and that's punishment enough," said David.

"For the shoes," quipped Sean.

"At least we raised over six hundred dollars," said David.

"The Food Bank is gonna start lookin' like that fat pig of a Coachman," said Bobby.

"I doubt it," said David. "There's always someone who can use the help, especially at this time of year."

"Do you really think he'll do it for us?" asked Sean.

"Who?" inquired Bobby.

"Mr. Astor," explained David, realizing that he had switched subjects completely. "Sean's hoping he'll agree to read our palms."

"I'm sure he will," said Sean with confidence. "He's done it for me and Dad at least three times."

"Kind of spooky, huh?" said Bobby.

Sean frowned at Bobby, saying, "Only to the faint-hearted."

"I've never had my palms read before," said David. "How about you, Bobby?"

"My hands ain't never been clean enough to read," retorted Bobby.

"Mr. Astor sure is . . . *unusual*," said David.

"I like him," said Sean. "And so does my dad. Dad said that I could trust Mr. Astor with anything or anyone."

"That's high praise, especially coming from someone like your dad," said David.

Sean nodded silently.

"Where did your dad meet Mr. Astor?" asked David.

"I don't know. I should ask," mused Sean. "Dad hasn't known Mr. Astor for very long, maybe a couple of months. He goes to the shop a couple of times a week. If it's a Saturday, he takes me along and I get to rummage through all the neat stuff. I mean, you wouldn't believe some of the stuff old Astor has stashed away."

"Do you think Mr. Astor will mind our coming?" asked David.

"Naw. At least, he's never seemed to. I think he likes to see people. I doubt if he gets many visitors. People aren't exactly knocking the doors down to look at all that junk," concluded Sean.

"I didn't see any junk," said David.

"I know. That's the funny thing. Why would he called it the *Junken Treasure* shop? The stuff's a lot better than that," Sean reflected.

"It's a pun. Junken for sunken, you know," said David.

"I know," agreed Sean. "But, even still."

"Maybe old Astor ain't even there," speculated Bobby.

"He usually is," said Sean.

"What if the door's locked?"

"It's *never* locked," announced Sean. "Didn't you know that?"

David and Bobby shook their heads and looked at Sean.

"The best thing to do is just to go in and begin to look around. Sooner or later Mr. Astor will come out to see who it is," said Sean.

"I still can't believe he didn't charge us for the gifts we got," said David. "Said he would prefer for us to work it off and to help him when he moves."

"Fine, by me," said Sean.

"Wow!" said David. "Guess we'll all be in for a moving party. How about Mary?"

"I doubt it," said Sean. "Dad's never even brought her to the shop. Astor's probably just looking for muscle."

Bobby wanted to quip *Then why'd he ask you?* but remembered Sean's prowess in judo and karate. Silence seemed the better part of valor when dealing with proven seventh grade warriors; Bobby was content to bide his time until a certain big one could be repaid.

"A lot of that stuff that he has hanging around looks really heavy," continued Sean. "We'll probably all end up with hernias, but don't worry, my mom can fix us up."

"A pretty threesome we'd be," observed David.

"Lisa and Mary would be waiting on us hand and foot," interjected Sean hopefully.

"Well, maybe on Bobby and me," said David.

"Yeah, yeah, yeah," said Sean.

"They can have their fun with Aunt Lillian today," laughed David.

The boys plodded on as their boots kicked up the slush that the warmer weather had brought. Turning at the corner that would lead them to Mr. Astor's shop, Sean stopped Bobby and David and whispered, "Whatever Mr. Astor says about any of us stays strictly between us and us only. Okay?"

Bobby and David looked at each other in wonder, and David asked Sean, "Why? Has he ever said something about you that you wouldn't want anyone else to know?"

Sean pondered the question, answering, "All that he's ever said about me has been one hundred percent true, but everyone is entitled to a little privacy. I have a soft side that most people don't see, but old Astor saw it right away and went in for the kill. I mean, it's scary how much he can see. I never gave a hoot about palm readers until he offered, and now I doubt if there's another palm reader anywhere who's half as good as he is. He rocks. I mean, he really rocks."

David and Bobby were unable to envision, despite their best efforts, any image of Mr. Astor 'rocking,' but they knew Sean reserved such a description solely for things that he found both profound and amazing. His sudden unease, however, stirred within them faint misgivings for what might await them.

The shop looked closed, although no sign was ever posted. No light could be seen within, but the boys, following Sean's lead, entered the shop unannounced. Enough sunlight entered via the front windows to give the boys an opportunity to look at Astor's so-called junk. David could only wonder all the more about the mysterious figure he and Bobby had met the day after Christmas. —There must be gypsy blood in him, thought David, thinking of Mr. Astor's apparently remarkable gift for palm reading.

"Shouldn't we make a little noise so that he'll know we're here?" David whispered to Sean, who was studying a brightly colored aluminum mobile.

"He knows," said Sean. "Trust me. He knows everything."

Sean wasn't accustomed to using such hyperbole, and his words only deepened the mystery David was pondering anew.

"Ah, my young friends have returned," came an almost inaudible gasp from behind a pair of curtains that were beginning to part. The wizened figure that appeared was the same awkward, crippled homunculus, wrinkled and bald and extremely thin, slouching to one side as he walked toward them. His carved walking stick seemed to carry him along on his challenging journey, and he paused to catch his breath as he walked.

The boys were so captivated by the way he moved toward them that they remained where they were. When Mr. Astor reached them, he looked at each one intently, his ancient gray eyes surveying their faces, saying, "Something tells me that you have not come for anything material today."

"Is it *that* obvious?" laughed Sean.

"I well remember your enthusiasm, Potter the Younger, for my small talent at reading human palms. It was only a short jump in logic to presume that you have brought your friends back for the same experience. As they say, "What's good for the goose is good for the gander."

"I'm the gander, not the goose," corrected Sean.

"As we have seen before, my young friend, there's a bit of goose and gander in all of us, is there not?"

Sean nodded, as if looking into a crystal ball.

"But why such somber faces? No one has died, at least not yet. The future is bright, so let's look to what it will tell us," continued Mr. Astor.

"Do you want us to sit down at a table or anything?" asked David.

"Thank you, David, for thinking of me. I find it as difficult to sit as to stand. Walking is even harder. So, we can have a reading here and now, if you'd like?"

David looked at the others as if to ask 'Who'll go first?'

"Why not you?" suggested Mr. Astor.

This apparent feat of mind reading threw David back apace, and he suddenly wanted to let Bobby or Sean go first.

"But Robert, I mean Bobby, or Sean could go first, instead," offered the little dwarf-like figure, his claw-like hands pointing at each boy mentioned.

"No," said David. "That's okay. I'll go first."

Opening and extending his hands, he said, "Is this okay?"

Mr. Astor nodded as he studied the lines.

Smiling, he announced, "David, you are going to live a *long* life, well over one hundred years."

"Wow!" said Sean. "Just like old Pennythorpe."

Mr. Astor didn't seem to hear Sean's allusion, and continued, "And you will marry in your late twenties. Your family will number five children. You will also have health problems when you are in your late sixties, but you will successfully put those behind you. You are a healer, David, no matter what you choose to do in life. It would not surprise me, however, if you became a physician. Have you ever thought about that profession?"

"No, sir," said David. "I haven't really thought much about any profession."

Mr. Astor suddenly looked more closely at David's palm.

"Please open your fingers wider," he whispered.

David promptly obeyed.

"Yes. Just as I thought. You have quite recently had a profound experience, something others would call a vision. It's changing you enormously; in truth, it has already changed you, although you have decided not to look at it right away. You have sort of tucked it away until you have more time to take it out and study it. Am I right?"

"You're more right than you could guess," David marveled.

Mr. Astor looked up, and searched David's eyes to know the meaning of the words he had just spoken, and finally said, "I can go deeper, if you'd like."

David thought for a moment.

"It really has to do with the beginning of everything. Doesn't it?"

Mr. Astor nodded.

"And how everything is really connected, I mean, sewn together so seamlessly that we can't even see it," continued David.

"The transcendent realities merge in many ways and on many levels," whispered Mr. Astor, adding, "It would seem that we walk through mere shadows here. Should I continue?"

David looked directly into Mr. Astor's gray eyes, asking in his mind, "Is it true that everything is actually light?"

Mr. Astor, without veering from David's gaze, nodded, saying, "Yes. It's true. But your five senses are very limited. That is why a new power is unfolding in you, so you can see light in a new way. Should I go deeper?"

Somehow this made perfect sense to David, but he also felt that he had absorbed all he could for the moment. Sean had been entirely correct in warning them as to how accurate Astor was, for the little dwarf had just read David's soul like a book. It was now time, however, to put away that which had been brought to light.

"Not now," whispered David. "Maybe another time?"

"What is time, David, beloved," smiled Mr. Astor, "but the moving image of eternity on this world?"

Looking at Bobby, who had already anticipated that he would be next and had opened his palms and lifted his hands, Mr. Astor became sad and quiet, finally saying, "Robert, bright of fame, your hands show that you have suffered greatly in this life, both physically and spiritually."

"Will I get married?" asked Bobby.

"You will die young, in another place, but you will still live here," said Mr. Astor. "I can see no marriage line until after you have been through your trial."

—I knew it, thought Bobby. —I'm gonna murder the little hoodlum and fry in the electric chair and be remembered as a hero by all who knew him.

"Do you have any questions?"

Still trying to absorb and understand the paradox he had just heard, Bobby couldn't think of anything, especially if he wasn't going to be married. All he could stammer was, "Will I pass the ninth grade?"

Mr. Astor smiled as he looked more closely at Bobby's fingers.

"Perhaps," he concluded. "It will be a near thing, however. As you say, 'Too close to call.' But you will have more than ample opportunity to prove yourself, as will your fellow class members. I see a turbulent time ahead, and you will be called to the mantle of leadership, but you also will have salutary assistance and counsel. But remember always to be sincere and to have no hidden agendas."

If Bobby had scarcely made sense of Mr. Astor's first prediction, this one left him entirely at sea.

"Whatever," was all he could say.

"And, now, my fine young friend, Potter the Younger, for," and here Mr. Astor smiled, "God *is* gracious."

Sean extended his hands, his eyes studying the wizened figure that stood before him.

"What's this I see?" inquired the little dwarf, who looked suddenly very perplexed. "Yes. But is it possible?" Mr. Astor gave a darting, almost mistrustful, glance at Bobby and then peered again at Sean's opened palms.

"Blood will pass between two of you very soon," announced Mr. Astor.

—Lord help me, thought Bobby, —I'm really gonna kill that little magpie deader than a doornail. That's why my name means 'bright of fame.' It's predictin' the frickin' electric chair, all aglow and sittin' there starin' me in the face.

"But blood also among the three of you, and soon!" announced a startled Mr. Astor. "How could this be?"

He looked intently at all of them.

—Of course, thought Bobby. —David will try to come to Sean's rescue and I'll have to hurt him before I finish off the little magpie.

Sean smiled.

—Maybe I'm going to become blood brothers with David and Bobby, Sean thought happily to himself.

David look worried, and asked, "Will it be serious?"

"I cannot tell," responded the dwarf sadly. "I can only tell that it *will* be, and sooner rather than later. I would ask that you all walk with forbearance of each other and in the Greater Light."

All three nodded their heads in assent.

"After all, I'm going to need your strong bodies to help me in my move. Soon I must go away for several months, but then I will be back, and at that time I will need your help."

Here Mr. Astor looked intently at each boy, studying their faces and looking intently into their eyes.

"And you will help," he nodded. "*All* of you. And for that I will be very grateful."

"Just let us know when," said David.

Mr. Astor bowed, saying, "I will contact the good Professor at the proper time and Potter the Younger can let you know. I'm afraid I will not be able to give much notice."

"That's okay," said David. "We'll be ready."

"Ready?" questioned the small being. "No one is ever ready. The best we can ever do is stream along with the radiance that is in all, and that is all. But that is a matter for another day."

"May we come again?" asked Sean.

"Yes and no," came the surprising response. "You may come, but I will not be here. I am leaving soon. I will contact the good Professor after I have returned and when conditions are acceptable."

"Thank you," said Sean, extending his hand to grasp Mr. Astor's claw-like hand.

"You're welcome, Potter the Younger. You're all welcome."

The boys turned and walked to the shop door. As they opened it, they heard Mr. Astor calling to them. Looking around, they saw that he was now standing next to the curtain from which he had appeared.

"Remember," he cautioned, "the blood you will shed will first be in anger, but then in friendship, or perhaps I should say in brotherhood."

"Okay," said Sean. "Whatever you say. Thanks again."

As the boys returned to Aunt Lillian's, David could only talk about the strange prediction the curious figure had made.

"Blood!" he exclaimed. "Shedding blood. I mean, I don't think so. We have friendly scuffles, and we've even survived some bitter misunderstandings, but to come to bloodshed? I just can't believe that can be true. What do you think?"

"I think that old Astor knows more than he tells," said Bobby. "And I think he's probably always right."

"His predictions for me have always been dead accurate," rejoined Sean, who had become convinced that he would, sooner rather than later, join David and Bobby's in that blood brotherhood.

"Kind of creepy the way he gives the meanin' of your name when he addresses you," said Bobby, thinking about himself strapped into a brightly illuminated electric chair and recalling the headline:

**TROUBLED TEEN MURDERS MAGPIE;
MIDVILLE REJOICES.**

"He must be of the old school," said David.

"The old, old, old school," corrected Bobby, adding, "I mean, even older than Pennythorpe, and that's gettin' up there."

"I think he's amazing," said Sean. "Just amazing."

Chapter Nineteen
Four Witnesses Observe a Press Statement

ON MONDAY AFTERNOON, as soon as school students were released for the day, David, Bobby, and Sean met in the lobby and then walked to the village Courthouse, where they would meet Mr. Leonard. A mixture of rain and snow spit down as the boys walked, and they pulled their wind breakers ever tighter against the gray weather.

Mr. Leonard was waiting on the Courthouse steps when the boys arrived, bundled up in a ski jacket and ski hat. He held a digital camera and a small note pad.

"Hello, Mr. Leonard," said David. "I would like you to meet my brother Bobby and our friend Sean Potter."

"Pleased to meet you," said Mr. Leonard as hands were shaken all around.

"Have you been here long?" asked David.

"I arrived about 2:15," said Mr. Leonard. "I brought some editing and my coffee thermos to keep me warm. Mrs. Coachman and Mr. Lytle entered the Courthouse together around 2:30. Mrs. Coachman indicated to me on the telephone last night that they were first going to go to Mr. Lytle's attorney and then would bring the papers for filing. They should be coming out any minute. She agreed to make a statement and to have her photo taken. She also warned me that there might be some unsavory youth gawking at our proceedings."

"That's us," said David cheerfully. "Guess she didn't forget that she invited us, too."

"I ain't no unsavory youth," protested Bobby. Looking furtively at David, he whispered, "What's 'unsavory'?"

David grinned, whispering in turn, "It means distasteful. Coachman doesn't like us, but she knew we'd probably show up after seeing that spectacle in Sunday school."

"When she nearly killed the teacher?" asked Bobby.

"Exactly," said David. "Now she's sold Mr. Lytle her stone mansion and they're filing the papers. He's giving her a wad of money and she's giving him a house full of broken pipes, although I suppose the broken pipes and flooding were his fault because he didn't check on the house the way he promised he would."

As the foursome stood talking, they weren't aware that Gertrude Coachman and H. H. Lytle had spotted them as their elevator door opened on to the lobby.

"My God! Leonard's on the front steps," exclaimed Lytle. "That's all we need—why is the damn Press always sticking its nose into somebody else's business?"

"I'll have you know that he's here to interview *me*," said Coachman. "Don't put on airs. Nobody gives a dang about you."

"I might have guessed you were behind this. And who's with him?" asked Lytle, squinting his eyes the better to see.

"Three ne'er-do-wells from that God-forsaken Sunday school class you browbeat every week. Don't you remember, when I paid you that little visit, I invited the whole lot of them to come watch us close the deal?" said Coachman snidely.

"You're too much, you know?" sputtered Lytle. "You're just too much. I'll be glad to finally see the back of you."

"All in good time, you vile little man," sneered Coachman. "Don't you dare ruin my moment in the sun or I'll have every lawyer in the county after your worthless hide."

"Our business is finished, you ignorant woman," Lytle corrected her.

"Not until you take me home today in my brand new Cadillac and pay for my food and lodging at the Village Inn on June 30. *Then* we are finished, and let me tell you that Village Inn bill is gonna be a whopper," snorted Coachman.

Lytle blanched at the thought of Coachman's food bill alone. His only consolation was that she could have probably gotten a lot more out of him owing to his stupidity at neglecting to check her house as he had promised. The threat of a full-page advertisement exposing his negligence would have put him out of business entirely. He'd recover, although it might take a couple of years. He'd unload the stone mansion if he could; if not, it would make an impressive realty headquarters if he could float a hundred thousand to sink into it. Some of it could even be rented.

"Now listen to me," ordered Coachman. "We're gonna go out on those steps and you're not even gonna open your damn mouth. Leonard's here to interview *me* and take *my* picture for the paper."

"You'd better not say anything about our financial arrangement," Lytle reminded his nemesis. "I have the best lawyer in the county, and that was explicitly understood in the waivers you just signed half an hour ago."

"Don't worry," retorted Coachman. "I won't ruin your precious little reputation. But if you know what's good for you, you'll button up. Let's go."

The two strode purposefully toward the Courthouse doors, emerging into the cold, wet weather.

"There they are!" announced Sean.

Mr. Leonard and the boys walked up to Coachman and Lytle.

"Mrs. Coachman," began Mr. Leonard, "Now that you've returned from Washington, would you consent to a brief interview for *The Courier*?"

"Gladly," intoned Coachman. "Glad to help the press out anytime that I can. Go ahead, but make your questions lively; it's cold out here."

"Is it true that you've just sold the old Sperling mansion?"

"Yes. Mr. Lytle here has purchased the property. He is one of the village's foremost realtors and he acceded to all of my demands—I mean, to all my requests. He now takes immediate possession of the property."

"Where will you live now?"

"I am now in residence at the Village Inn until June 30th. Between now and then I will decide where I will live and what I will do, now that I have become independently wealthy."

"What will you do with the lottery money and the money you have received for your old mansion?"

"I'm not sure yet. I'll probably invest some of it. Although if you look across the street, you will see a brand new red Cadillac that was delivered to my home this morning. Nothin' like traveling in the best. Mr. Lytle kindly consented to chauffeur me today because I am a little skittish at driving in slushy weather."

"Will you keep our little community apprized of your activities now that you've joined the jet set?" continued Mr. Leonard.

"Well, I wouldn't exactly say 'the jet set.' Let's just say I don't need to punch a time clock anymore. I'll be glad to take interviews from time to time, provided I'm in town and not traveling. In fact, owing to my long-standing relationship with *The Courier*, which has distinguished me as Midville's poet laureate, all future interviews with the press will be exclusively with *The Courier*, before any other publication. You'll always get first rights on me."

"Thank you for that courtesy," said Mr. Leonard, biting his tongue so as not to laugh. "Will you miss teaching?"

Coachman suddenly looked with condescending appraisal at Bobby, David, and Sean, and smirked, answering, "I'll miss a few of the good kids, but not the ne'er-do-well types. They're mighty hard on a lady, and they never seem to learn good manners."

"Mr. Lytle," asked Mr. Leonard, "Do you have anything to say for the record?"

Lytle gulped, and began, "Just that everyone in Midville should come to good old Hank Lytle for their — ow!"

Coachman had soundly whopped Lytle with her heavy pocketbook.

"Just so," said Mr. Leonard, hoping to forestall any hostilities. "I'm sure everyone in Midville wishes you well."

"Thank you," said Coachman. "We've got to go now. I've got a busy schedule ahead of me, beginning with a porterhouse steak at the Village Inn."

Lytle caught himself back a little, groaning at the expensive image.

"Before you go, may I please take your photograph for *The Courier*?" asked Mr. Leonard.

"Yes. Of course. Always," said Coachman, posing for Mr. Leonard.

"Thank you. That will be splendid."

"Good day, then," said Coachman as she and Lytle walked toward the crosswalk.

"Can you believe it?" said David. "She even knocked us in her interview."

"I wouldn't worry," said Mr. Leonard. "I won't quote her."

"She's quite the pig, ain't she?" said Bobby.

"She is, indeed," said Mr. Leonard, suddenly catching himself, saying, "Sorry. I'm afraid you caught me off guard. Journalists are supposed to be objective."

"Wow!" said Sean. "Look at that flashy Cadillac."

Coachman and Lytle were now getting into her new car. The foursome noted that Lytle had neglected to open the door for his passenger—so much for *Chreestian* manners.

"Why don't you get a picture of them as they pay their toll and leave the parking lot?" asked David. "Sort of, they're off and running."

"Good idea," said Mr. Leonard, adjusting his camera and waiting for the right moment.

The cherry red Cadillac had now pulled up to the toll booth, although nothing much seemed to be happening. The attendant was merely standing there, no doubt listening to Coachman complain about the parking fee.

Suddenly the car went into full reverse, nearly hitting another car parked adjacent to the toll booth, and then, roaring its engine, lunged toward the entrance of the lot. Snow obscured the sign warning drivers that vehicles should not exit via the entrance owing to sharp, pointed metal claws that would destroy an automobile's tires. As if the sign didn't even exist, the brand new Cadillac sped backwards through the entrance over the claws. A muffled popping of tires could be heard as the vehicle suddenly slowed to an awkward stop, at which point realtor Lytle was seen thrusting the driver's door open and running as fast as he could, with Coachman in hot pursuit.

"Now, I'll be," said Mr. Leonard. "I've never seen anything like that before. Have you?"

The boys all shook their heads.

"Let's go ask the attendant what happened," announced Leonard.

Approaching the attendant who was making a note on a small piece of paper, Mr. Leonard introduced himself and asked, "Can you please tell us what just happened?"

"Darnedest thing I ever saw," said the attendant. "These two drive up and start arguing about who'll pay the parking fee. You'd think one of 'em would have enough dough, with an expensive car like that."

"Did they say anything?" asked Mr. Leonard.

"Not to me. They just drove up and I said, 'That'll be a dollar fifty.' The gent who was driving looked at the dame and said, 'Well?' And she said, 'Well, what?' And he said something like, 'You don't expect *me* to pay the lousy toll, you ungrateful hag; I just paid you over three hundred thousand dollars.' That seemed to rankle the hell out of her, so she says something to him like, 'I don't have any. Cough it up, or I'll call a press conference with Leonard. He's still standing over there tryin' to take our picture.' Then I think the little man said, 'To hell with Leonard and to hell with you. I'm not paying you another red cent, woman.' And then the dame said, 'So we're just gonna sit here all day staring at each other. Time is money.' The man got real red in the face and jerked the car into reverse and then tried to drive out the entrance, right over those retractors and all. Look, there she comes now. Looks pretty exhausted from giving that little gent the chase. I'd watch out, if I were you."

Coachman approached the toll booth, breathing heavily from her failed efforts to catch a fleeing Lytle. Slowing down, she moved ponderously toward Mr. Leonard, and stood in front of him wheezing as she tried to catch her breath.

Looking at the attendant, Coachman said, "Call the police and a tow truck."

As the attendant obliged, Coachman looked at Leonard, who, of course, was all ears. She also glared at David, Bobby, and Sean, as if these three would be ne'er-do-wells had caused the whole incident.

"Do you have anything to say for the record?" asked a hopeful editor.

The surprise response nearly floored Mr. Leonard, for Coachman said, "Never you mind, Buster."

"And why's that?"

"'Cause anything I'd like to say couldn't be published, and I'm under a gag order by our realty agreement for reasons that are none of your business, so butt out buster and let me take it from here. That little vulture's lawyer is gonna hear from me and receive a bill for damages done. Now why don't you all just move along? The show's over."

And they moved along in good style, and what a show it had been.

Chapter Twenty
An Attorney is Consulted

When David and Bobby arrived home from school on Tuesday, Aunt Lillian opened the front door for them.

"Now *this* is the service we've been waiting for," teased David.

"Come here, boys. You must see something right away. I've been laughing ever since the paper came."

David and Bobby followed Aunt Lillian into the kitchen where she had left part of *The Courier* open on the table.

"Come look," she invited.

The front page of the second section carried two prominent banners and articles: one about Coachman returning from Washington and selling her house, the other about Hortense the Pig and the money the students had raised for the community food bank.

It took Bobby and David no more than a second to realize what had happened, and they both began to laugh hysterically. Whether from design or printer's error, under the banner **COACHMAN RETURNS AND SELLS HOUSE** there appeared the photograph of Hortense the Pig, while under the banner **HORTENSE THE PIG** appeared the photograph of Gertrude H. Coachman.

Heartfelt laughter is often contagious, and soon Aunt Lillian was laughing with the boys. A box of tissues was procured as the three continued to laugh, wiping their tears of mirth.

"She's probably down at the paper now pullin' old Leonard's ear," said Bobby.

"Or maybe she had a stroke if she thought she might have to donate six hundred dollars to the community food bank," said David.

"I hope she can laugh about it," said Aunt Lillian. "But the likeness—-"

"Is so accurate," David finished her sentence.

More laughter echoed around the table. David thought his sides would burst; Bobby felt a little dizzy.

"Do you think?" asked Bobby.

"Do we think what?" asked David.

"Anybody 'll notice the mistake?" dead panned Bobby.

To which David answered, "No."

Again more laughter was shared.

"I wonder if she's seen it?" said Aunt Lillian.

"Probably thought she looked mighty good," retorted Bobby, and everyone began laughing again.

*****

No mirth reigned at Gertrude Coachman's room at the Village Inn. She had picked up the paper to read during dinner and became so upset at the switch of photographs that she couldn't even finish her salad.

"Cancel that lobster," she said as she rose from the table, wiping her puffy lips. "And send up a platter of cheese and crackers with some hot tea to my room in case I'm hungry later."

"Was anything wrong with the salad?" inquired the waiter.

"Ain't the salad, laddie," said Coachman. "It's *fame*. It doesn't pay to be famous, at least not these days."

By the time she had reached her suite, Coachman had decided that almost everyone in Midville was against her. Such lucid moments had rarely struck her, and she had determined she would wage a war to get even with her detractors, beginning first and foremost with that waster of a realtor who had cost her a young fortune in new tires. Next on her list would be that idiot newspaper editor Leonard. Before she was finished with both of them, she'd own half of Midville as well as the entire newspaper itself.

The cheese and crackers arrived half an hour after she had returned to her room. Sitting at the long table in her room she snorted and licked her lips as she took and wrote notes and considered what strategies might best serve her cause.

On the 24th of January, the next morning, she called Horace Vanderkamp, H. H. Lytle's attorney, and made an appointment to see him at 11:00 a.m..

* * * * *

Later that morning Gertrude Coachman was ushered into the elegant office of Horace Vanderkamp, Esq., and greeted with an abrupt 'Hello' by a rotund balding man in a pin-stripe suit, wearing wire-rim glasses.

Taken aback by the gruff acknowledgment of her arrival, Coachman stood staring at the attorney as he shuffled papers on his desk. She heard his secretary close the door behind her, and saw him glance at her again and say briskly, "Sit down. Sit down. Up here. Don't waste my time."

This small bit of rudeness quickly got her ire up, and she flounced forward and threw herself in the mahogany chair.

"Don't break the furniture, for God's sake," scolded the attorney.

"Now see here— " began Coachman.

"No," interrupted attorney Vanderkamp. "*You* see here. I'm very busy today, and I cleared a place on my schedule so that I could listen to your complaints and then get rid of you. I assume you've come about the tires?"

"In part," said Coachman coldly, having been taken off her stride with Vanderkamp's unexpected effrontery.

"Well, my client came to me directly after the incident. Very shaken he was, with all of the stress of that particular day," began the attorney.

"Stress!" exclaimed Coachman.

"Yes. The poor man had been forced to pay three times what your house is worth just so you don't poison his reputation to the community. That's called 'threat of blackmail,' and he had no leg to stand on because he had been remiss in checking your place when you were gone."

"Got what he deserved," agreed Coachman. "And no one put a gun to his head for him to sign on the dotted line, if I recall correctly."

"No," agreed Vanderkamp. "He went quietly, against all of my protestations and counsel to the contrary."

"You can't be serious?" said an astonished Coachman.

"Yes, I am. As I see it, he was bullied into the agreement, and there are witnesses. It would have been far less expensive for him to pay for damages."

"Never offered," growled Coachman.

"Never was *allowed* to offer," corrected Vanderkamp.

"What's done is done," came Coachman's smug reply. "What I want is compensation for my ruined tires. Brand new they were."

"Forget it," said the attorney.

Gertrude Coachman's eyes widened and she leered at Horace Vanderkamp.

"You haven't got a case. It was your car and you refused to pay for its parking fee, which thereby denied you legal egress from the lot."

"Never you mind all these fancy lawyer terms like egress," warned Coachman. "I know your tricks. You spin out a lot of words that no mortal could understand and then go in for the kill."

"I thought you would know a simple word like 'egress'," retorted Horace Vanderkamp. "You *did* teach English, didn't you? Or, so said my daughter, although she never had you. She's in the eighth grade, but thank the merciful Good Lord, she didn't get you for her teacher. Believe me, your reputation has preceded you in this office."

"Lucky you," snarled Coachman. "I'm surprised the red carpet wasn't set out next to your spiffy manners."

"People sometimes get what they give," retorted Horace Vanderkamp.

"Meaning?"

"Meaning that I'm gentle with gentle people, and I'm a little rougher with self-styled bullies who don't know how much they harm others," came the unexpected response.

"Are you calling me a bully?"

"If the shoe fits, wear it, although it must be of considerable size."

"Why— "

"Why, nothing. Listen to me and look here. I have in my hands a restraining order duly signed by the Superior Court judge, ordering you to cease and desist any contact with a certain Mr. H. H. Lytle."

"Why, that measly little— "

"Furthermore, you are not to call Mr. Lytle or to make reference to him in any public statement or opinion, and you are expressly ordered to stay away from Midville's Methodist Church."

Gertrude Coachman sat in her chair in shock, for this was the last eventuality that she had expected from her mis-dealings with Lytle. Perhaps she could still salvage the cost of new tires for her new Cadillac.

"He had *no* business driving over those steel claws," protested Coachman.

"And what choice did you give him? You, the lottery winner, refusing to pay a dollar and fifty cents after he's just signed over nearly a third of million."

"He owes me for those tires," insisted Coachman.

"He owes you nothing. And if I hear that you have menaced him in any way, you will be arrested and detained for stalking. If you want to sue him, go ahead. I'd welcome it. It would be fun to see you squirm a little on the bench."

"Why, you . . . you can't talk like that," said Coachman.

"And why not?" asked the attorney.

"You're supposed to be objective," said Coachman.

"I *am* being objective," was the attorney's response.

"Forget that loser," growled Coachman. "I have bigger fish to fry. Look here."

Thrusting a newspaper page across the desk, Coachman continued, "That fool of a Leonard has gone too far this time, let me tell you."

"And to what are you referring?" asked Horace Vanderkamp.

"The photographs. The switching of photographs!"

"*I* don't see any switching here," said the attorney blandly.

"What? You viper. You're in it with them. I should have guessed, you being that little cretin's attorney. Birds of a feather and all that. You weasel. You sit there and have the audacity to tell me that you don't see the mistake they made in the photographs under the headlines?"

"Well, let me put it to you this way. *I* don't. And I doubt if very many in Midville would see what you see. For me the photos are easily interchangeable, because the subjects are so similar."

"Why you— "

"No," corrected Horace Vanderkamp. "It's Q, R, S, T, U, V, and then W, X, Y, and Z."

"I'll sue you for your back teeth," threatened Coachman. "And before I'm done, *The Courier* will be mine, too."

"I wouldn't be too sure of that," warned the attorney.

"And why not?"

"You, Madam, owing to your lottery winnings and recent fame, have become what is considered a 'public figure.' Unfortunately, public figures are not entitled to sue others for supposed instances of slander or libel. They must accept ridicule as part of their eccentric destinies. However, this little foible in the newspaper was a printer's error. The matter has been addressed."

"And how has the matter been addressed?" asked Coachman.

"The printer's assistant, who made the error, has been named the new printer's journeyman," explained Horace Vanderkamp.

"That sounds like a promotion to me," Coachman frowned.

"I hope so. It certainly has given the town a lot of good laughs," said the attorney.

"I've been made into a laughing stock," reflected Coachman.

"So it would seem," agreed Horace Vanderkamp.

"I'm not going to let you get away with this," promised Coachman, rising from her chair.

"Excellent," said Vanderkamp, also rising.

"Excellent?"

"Yes. I like a good fight, and I would love to cross swords with you in the legal arena. You haven't got a leg to stand on, and my clients will be able to chip away at some of those hundreds of thousands of dollars that you've been raking in. And I'll get a little of it myself. So, please file as soon as possible. I look forward to enjoying some of your lottery winnings."

"You are a disgrace to the legal profession. No wonder lawyers have such rotten reputations," snorted Coachman, opening the door.

"Perhaps I have helped the legal profession as much as you've helped public education," smiled Horace Vanderkamp.

"If I had the means, I'd fight you till the cows came home," retorted Coachman.

"Since your friends aren't here to help you, I would ask that you find a more suitable advocate, perhaps even an attorney to whom you will have to pay some big bucks. I could tie any suit you would bring into so many knots that you wouldn't have a moment's rest for the next ten years."

"Is that a threat?"

"No. It's a promise, and please quote me, if you don't mind," concluded Horace Vanderkamp as he closed his door.

Coachman gave an exasperated look at Vanderkamp's secretary and immediately vacated his office.

As she drove home in her new Cadillac, her visions of suing that little snake Lytle and *The Courier* melted into bitter memories. In her deepest self, she knew she would never spend any of her hard-won money on lawyers and legal fees. Most people whom she had known had been on the receiving edge of her acid tongue and sharp retorts, but she had more than met her match with Horace Vanderkamp. Coachman knew she had been bested, and she skulked home to lick her wounds, all the better to accuse the world of constant subterfuge against her and to feel sorry for herself.

Chapter Twenty-One
An Inadvertent Reprise

THAT NIGHT AN ARCTIC COLD FRONT invaded the Finger Lakes area, and students arriving at Midville Middle School Thursday morning were bundled in extra warm clothing and scarves. The large yellow brick building itself had taken on an uncharacteristic bone-cold chill, despite the vain efforts of the heating system to provide suitable warmth.

Sean Potter had just picked up his books from his locker and was beginning to proceed down to the first floor in order to buy a new lunch ticket at the office when he was abruptly stopped and pushed up against the wall by none other than Bobby Perkins. The firm physical restraint was so surprising that he stood momentarily in shock as he noticed the anger smouldering in Bobby's eyes.

"Well?" scowled Sean at Bobby's unfriendly overture.

"It ain't *well*, and you know it," countered Bobby.

"What 'ain't well'?" asked Sean.

"David's feelin's. You and your tellin' him, when he says to you that he ain't knew where the time went, and you with your damn mealy-mouth blurt out that 'into the past, where do you think?' jive."

"What are you talking about?" asked Sean, incredulously.

"Yeah. As if you don't know how much you hurt him when you snapped your little magpie mouth off the way you did yesterday."

Sean reflected for a moment, and sighed to himself.

"I was mad because he won't play chess with me anymore."

"Yeah, yeah, yeah. Thinking only of *yourself* and of nobody else."

Since his confrontation with Bobby was not lessening in its intensity, Sean decided he would call the question.

"What's *any* of this got to do with *you* anyway? You've got your *own* so-called friends. So why don't you just butt out and stay out?"

There may have been more polite ways to say 'it's none of your business,' but the back of Sean's neck was hurting from where Bobby had pushed him into something very hard, and he resented Bobby's intrusion.

"David's not only my friend," leered Bobby, "he's my *brother.*"

"Brother schmuther," challenged Sean.

"Blood brother," clarified Bobby, moving his face down closer to Sean's, daring him to take a swing.

"I'm not afraid of you. Remember how I sent you packing the day you beat David up?"

"Well, if it isn't little Mr. Karate himself," mocked Bobby, hoping Sean would take the first swing so he could smash his nose in.

Accurately intuiting Bobby's game plan, Sean yawned as if he were bored, blandly observing, "Sticks and stones . . ."

Bobby, however, jabbed Sean really hard in the chest, thundering, "Don't give me none of that 'sticks and stones' crap. You're not so tough without your little sister around to wipe your damn nose for you. I bet she's the brawn of your miserable, little outfit."

Sean's temper began to flare at this insult and Bobby began to smile, as he added, "*And* the brains."

Not wanting to get into a fight, for he was wearing the brand new beige cashmere sweater his parents had given to him for Christmas, Sean squinted and jeered, "Hey, what do you *want*, anyway?"

"For you to stop makin' poor David miserable, like a jabberin' magpie, always shootin' your mouth off, but never thinkin' about other people's feelings," demanded Bobby.

"Who died and left you boss?" challenged Sean, with a mocking grin.

"Maybe you forget who you're talkin' to," warned Bobby, the adrenalin coursing through his body as he clenched his right fist.

"Oh, I *know* all right," retorted Sean smugly. "You're the little bully who's dad killed David's dog and who owes me a big one."

This was too much for Bobby, who suddenly felt thrown out of himself. Like lightning his fist was in motion, heading right for Sean's nose.

Sean, however, was an extremely quick study, owing in part to his considerable expertise in karate. Adroitly avoiding Bobby's fist as it sailed through the space where his head been a fraction of a second earlier, Sean could feel the wind of the punch as he ducked.

As fate would ordain, Sean had been standing plumb in front of one of Midville Middle School's ancient fire alarm boxes. It was indeed this rude red device that had hurt the back of his neck when Bobby had pushed him against the wall. Hearing Bobby's fist shatter the glass in the alarm box, Sean suddenly found blood spurting all over his new sweater.

CLANG, CLANG, CLANG, CLANG, announced the first series of bells. Bobby stood dumbfounded as he pulled his bloody fist out of the red box, cupping his left hand over the blood that was flowing out, as if that alone would minimize the pain.

CLANG, CLANG, CLANG, CLANG, followed the second series of gongs after a brief pause.

At critical moments individuals often remember where they were when something unexpected or surprising happens. When the fire bells began to sound, most students and teachers were collecting in their respective home rooms, waiting for announcements to be read and classes to begin. The unlikelihood of a fire drill being conducted prior to the beginning of school, much less on what would probably be remembered as the coldest day of the year, clouded the worry of many faculty minds that there might indeed be a real fire somewhere in this vast expanse of building, and they began to urge students to evacuate quickly and quietly.

In the main office, Otto Ferlinghausen was reviewing with Mrs. Dixon the order of morning announcements. As the bells began to ring, he looked up, saying, "Call the fire department and tell them this is no drill. I hope to heaven it isn't a real fire. I'll search the building. If any reports come in, announce it to me over the PA."

Mrs. Dixon nodded, immediately complying with his instructions.

CLANG, CLANG, CLANG, CLANG, echoed the bells.

In the guidance office, Melvin Dandy had been reviewing his appointments with Mrs. Fullerton, as he blew his rather large, swollen nose from what had become the most devastating winter cold he had suffered in over a decade. His eyes kept watering mid his sporadic sneezing fits. The cold had taken root the previous Thursday and the counselor had been absent on Friday. He hadn't even wanted to return to school except that he had scheduled one or two important meetings with parents regarding their children, and one of those parents, Mrs. Weston, was a prominent and vocal member of the School Board.

CLANG, CLANG, CLANG, CLANG, sounded the bells.

"Eh? The fire bell?" said Dandy, looking up blankly in disbelief. "Has Otto lost his wits? It's at least ten below zero outside!"

"Oh, Mr. Dandy," exclaimed Mrs. Fullerton, "I'm sure he wouldn't spring a drill in this weather! It must be a false alarm, or worse still, a *real* fire. We'll be standing outside forever, everyone catching their death of colds."

CLANG, CLANG, CLANG, CLANG.

The counselor, foremost at considering the needs of himself before anything or anyone else, looked with desperate calculation at Mrs. Fullerton's thick fur coat, which hung proudly on the coat rack in the outer office. Mrs. Fullerton caught the intent of Dandy's rather obvious appraisal.

"Oh, no!" she announced, "No sir! That's my Christmas and birthday presents together and I've been waiting for it for ten years."

"But if I go outside, I'll catch *my* death of cold," remonstrated Dandy, coyly adding, "You said so yourself."

Mrs. Fullerton studied her boss, weighing in her conscience the relative chances of such an unexpected turn of fate.

"Don't look at me like that!" cried Dandy. "Help me! I need to be protected if I'm going to freeze outside for two hours!"

"But *I* need it, too, sir! It's cold out there!"

"But I need it *more*! I'm at death's door already. This will shove me over the brink."

Again Mrs. Fullerton weighed this unlikely possibility rather delicately in the balance of her decision, still coming to no clarity.

CLANG, CLANG, CLANG, CLANG continued the bells.

"Amelia," threatened a suddenly sinister and vindictive Melvin Dandy, "if I don't get that damn coat, I promise you that you'll *never* secretary in this town again!"

This stratagem threw her off her guard, of course, for it had never been a part of her job description to lend her fur coat to her boss, although it seemed almost every other duty that a secretary could perform had cascaded her way under her present boss. In short, Melvin Dandy ran mercilessly on her good will.

"Take it," she grumped with resignation. "Just don't get it dirty."

"Thanks," said a grateful counselor, as he bundled himself in the luxurious coat's welcoming warmth. "You'll *never* regret this."

In point of fact Mrs. Fullerton was already regretting it.

Melvin Dandy advanced quickly to the outer door of the larger office, the one that opened into the hallway. The bells continued to ring and he didn't want the faculty to conclude that the guidance staff was in any way asleep at the switch, although many had come to exactly that conclusion many years previous to this current exigency. Now that the counselor had gotten what he wanted, he lunged at the door handle, thrusting it open and springing into the hall, where the fire bells repeated their dire warning.

CLANG, CLANG, CLANG, CLANG.

Students were forming into several queues and, at the urging of their teachers, were now evacuating as quickly as they could. That there was no noise, save for the fire gongs and some frantic urging, did not deter Melvin Dandy from hollering at one boy who stood silently, waiting for his cue to join a line, "PIPE DOWN! AND LOOK A LITTLE LIVELY THERE!"

What students and faculty beheld in amazement was their rather eccentric guidance counselor, newly attired in a lavish fur coat much too large for his frame, causing him to look more than a little peculiar. Next to him stood what some considered to be his hopelessly flitty secretary, looking as if she had lost her best friend.

With the Dandy-Fullerton guidance show now on the move, Dandy took advantage of the students' surprise to say to Mrs. Fullerton, "That line across the cafeteria is moving quicker than this lot. FOLLOW ME!" as he grabbed her hand and raced with her across the large expanse of room, there to budge in front of an astonished but deferential seventh grader.

This rather rude sally into the orderly fire evacuation decorum proved to help the pair exit the building sooner than usual, but it also heaped blasts of arctic air on their bodies as they exited the building. Wanting to stay as close to the building as possible, the two took refuge on the top of the steps to the left of the double doors as students filed out past their chosen shelter.

CLANG, CLANG, CLANG, CLANG persisted the bells.

Students and teachers streamed through the doors, protecting themselves as best they could against the harsh cold air as they exited.

The siren of a fire truck announced the arrival of members of the fire department. As the truck drove by the building toward the office entrance, it slowed its pace since so many students were now on the snow covered sidewalks. The Assistant Fire Chief, who had encountered Melvin Dandy some weeks before when the latter was serving as acting principal during a similar false alarm, was riding in the first truck's cab, watching the evacuation as the truck arrived at the school.

The Assistant Fire Chief's attention was suddenly caught by the spectacle of Melvin Dandy standing on the school steps in an overly large fur coat, slapping himself with his arms and hands to keep warm while a poor, frail woman stood next to him shivering.

The very fact that Dandy had donned the fur coat made him an extremely mawkish sight, and the Assistant Fire Chief's appraising stare, written over a raised eyebrow and mocking grin, deeply infuriated the counselor, for the horrible silent judgment had cruelly written off the counselor as being nothing more nor less than a namby-pamby. As far as Dandy was concerned, he had been unfairly castigated by the Assistant Chief's approximating stare.

Melvin Dandy's pride seized the better control of his reason, and convinced that he and this vulgar assistant chief had some serious unfinished business, the counselor suddenly bolted into the building, even as the bells still sounded. Dandy now sought to ward off any incursion into *his* middle school by the likes of this mocking fireman. Sadly, he neglected to offer Mrs. Fullerton her own fur coat back before storming into the building.

The bells still rang throughout the building as Dandy strode toward the main office. Upon entering, he saw Bobby Perkins sitting in a chair holding his right hand over which a handkerchief had been skillfully wrapped, although bloodstains showed through. Sean Potter sat next to him speaking words of encouragement, although Sean himself was trying to blot blood flowing from two of his fingers with a tissue.

"Mrs. Dixon, call everyone back into the building," announced Otto Ferlinghausen. "The bells must be on their last cycle by now. I'm taking Bobby to the emergency room myself, and I am depending on you to keep a lid on this madhouse when I'm gone. Bobby, let's go. Sean, are you sure your fingers are okay? Do you want to come along with us just to be sure?"

"No, sir," said Sean. "The bleeding is slowing down. I'm going to get a couple of band-aids from the nurse. I cut myself trying to pull some glass out of Bobby's fist. My mom is working at the emergency room today and if she saw me, she'd have a fit. Please don't mention my name, if you can help it."

"I'm afraid you're too big a part of the story," said Mr. Ferlinghausen. "Come along Bobby." Bobby Perkins dutifully followed the principal out the door.

"Melvin! Why on earth are you wearing that ridiculous coat?" Otto asked Dandy as he escorted Bobby out the office door.

The counselor could only call after him, in the most embarrassed and feeblest of voices, "Winter cold!"

Noticing that the former acting principal had newly arrived, and in rather unusual attire, Mrs. Dixon instinctively decided not to entrust an otherwise orderly office to the counselor's whims and fancies. Looking at Sean, she instructed, "Run to each of the exits and tell everyone to come back in and go to their first period classes. Then come back here so you can explain to the poor firemen what happened."

Like a flash Sean was gone.

"Mrs. Dixon, don't spare me any bad news," announced Dandy. "I want it plain and straight. What in the devil happened?"

"Bobby Perkins took a swing at the Potter boy, who just happened to be standing in front of one of the alarm boxes."

"So?" said the counselor, not quite catching her point.

Sighing with exasperation, Mrs. Dixon added, "The Potter boy ducked."

"Oh. So *that's* what happened. Well, let me get rid of these damn firemen and we'll soon be done with all this nonsense."

Just as the counselor announced this intention, the Assistant Fire Chief reached the office and stood in silence at the doorway. Melvin Dandy had no clue that anyone else was present, much less was listening, and Mrs. Dixon's attention had now caused him to feel a little pluckier than usual, for usually no one paid much attention to him at all.

"Ah, yes!" he continued, "I wish I had that insufferable assistant fire chief in this very room. Oh, he's probably already on his way here as we speak, a large fool on a fool's errand. But don't worry; I'll get rid of him and his men before they have time to snoop around. I'll send them packing back to that little fire house where all they do is play cards and watch TV. Why, if I were the mayor, I'd give 'em hell and show 'em what real fire is. They'd all be out on their ears, burnt to a crisp."

The assistant fire chief smiled and winked at Mrs. Dixon, as he raised a not disinterested eyebrow at the counselor's innuendo.

"You wouldn't *believe* the look he just gave me when the fire truck drove by the exit where Amelia and I were standing. Why, I've never been so humiliated in all my life. It was a cruel, mocking grin that he gave me, let me just tell you."

"Do you think it might have been because of the fur coat that you're wearing, sir?" asked Mrs. Dixon, hoping to keep the counselor from inserting his foot any further into his mouth.

"Coat, my foot," chortled the counselor. "That ignominious fire chief, and I hasten to point out that he is a mere *assistant* chief, wouldn't know a fur coat from a top hot. NO, SIRREE! It's a plain and simple case of jealousy."

An incredulous Mrs. Dixon found her mouth dropping open as she asked, "Jealousy?"

"Yes. *I* am an educated person. As you know, I'm almost a doctor of education. No, that assistant fire chief is the type that is *always* jealous because deep down they know you know something they don't know that they hope you don't know that they don't know you know."

Mrs. Dixon shook her head in bafflement, feeling her mind swimming in circles as she tried to fathom the larger meaning of the counselor's words.

"For that kind of low mentality," Melvin Dandy continued, "it's all a power trip. They're just waiting and looking for a chance to find someone in the wrong, and then *watch out*! That poor devil's goose is cooked before it's over and let me just tell you, it's no treat."

Sean entered the office panting for all his running, announcing, "Everyone's gone on to first period, Mrs. Dixon. Should I go or stay?"

"I think you should stay here and explain to Assistant Fire Chief what happened," replied Mrs. Dixon.

Here Melvin Dandy turned to Sean, who had now stepped between him and Mrs. Dixon, intoning brazenly, "If you need someone here to translate for you when he finally gets his duff in here, I'll do my best, provided I'm permitted to use charades. That's all they understand."

"Sir, I think you should know—"

"Don't patronize me, Mrs. Dixon," reproved the Counselor, becoming intoxicated with his own self-importance. "I've been around here too long for that. I'm not going to let any measly little fireman bully *me*. This is *our* school, *our* building, and *they* don't belong here. WE DO! And if they insist on showing up here whenever we ring the bells, let 'em. It's no skin off our teeth. And if we please, we'll ring 'em in the morning and in the afternoon, and any time it pleases us, we'll ring 'em to the moon."

A short silence followed this sudden outburst of verse.

"Ah, you didn't know I was a poet, did you?" asked the counselor.

"I'd say more of a saucy, little namby-pamby than anything else," observed the assistant fire chief, finally breaking his silence.

"What!" exclaimed the irate counselor. "How long have you been standing there eavesdropping?"

"I came in when you were strutting about saying you would like to be the mayor. I've never heard such drivel. Talk about empty gongs signifying nothing. The bells on these walls make more sense than you do."

"I'll *not* be talked to that way in *my* school," intoned Dandy.

"So it's *your* school, is it?" smiled the assistant chief. "I thought it belonged to the students. The kids have more common sense than you do."

"For two cents I'd run for mayor just to see the back of you," sputtered the counselor.

"With all *your* blather, you could run for governor," reflected the assistant chief.

"And maybe I will . . . ah choo . . . just so I can see you canned to hell and back again," glowered the counselor.

"And quite a spectacle you would make running for governor," chortled the Assistant Fire Chief.

"And how's that?" puzzled a posturing counselor.

"You and your ridiculous fur coat. What a sorry duo!" came the embarrassing retort.

The counselor looked down at the fur coat which he had forgotten he had been wearing. Pointing dramatically at Sean, Dandy brought himself up with the largest dignity he could muster, announcing, "You are fortunate that an innocent is within earshot, or else I would let you know what you *really* are."

With these pompous words, the counselor strode from the office.

The assistant fire chief looked at Sean, saying, "You're the one, I hope, who's gonna explain to me why all this happened?"

Sean nodded, albeit sheepishly.

"You may use Mr. Ferlinghausen's office," suggested Mrs. Dixon.

And as they entered, the Assistant Chief took out his notebook and asked, "Now, son, first tell me a little more about this Mr. Dandy, isn't it? What does he do around here, and why do they keep him?"

Chapter Twenty-Two
Brothers Three

SUMMONED TO THE HOSPITAL EMERGENCY ROOM, Aunt Lillian felt it important to tell Bobby some of what POTS had shared about Sean feeling left out and forgotten. The Mrs. Dr. Potter also shared some of what had been going on at home, which was essentially that Mary's life had become a living hell.

The next evening, by prior arrangement, POTS dropped Sean off at Aunt Lillian's at 8:00. David and Bobby had invited the little magpie to come over to spend the night.

"Hello," said Sean cheerfully when he entered. "Hey, Bobby, how's your hand?"

Bobby lifted up his bandaged hand, saying, "Your mom says it will be better in a few days. It took twenty stitches to stop the bleedin'."

"Sorry about that," said Sean.

"Don't be sorry," said Bobby. "I would 've ducked, too, if I'd seen a truck like that comin' at me."

"Maybe a bicycle, certainly not a truck," began Sean. "I doubt if—"

"Boys," reproved Aunt Lillian. "This is supposed to be a time for healing, both physical and emotional. There will be no more blood-letting."

"Well, maybe just a *little* later tonight," smiled David.

Sean could feel his heart leap in his throat.

"Sean, you have become very dear to our family," announced Aunt Lillian, "and we are so glad you could come over tonight. On most

Friday nights, barring some special event, we watch a movie. Tonight's movie is the Disney classic *The Fox and the Hound.* Does that sound appealing?"

"Sure," said Sean. "Anything is fine."

"Well, you and David can put the tape in and get the cushions out while Bobby and I make popcorn and get the sodas," said Aunt Lillian.

"Great," said Sean.

As Sean and David took the tape from the video collection and inserted it in the video recorder, David said, "You know, Sean. I'll never forget all your help this last year. I'm sorry we haven't had much time recently, but I promise that I will make up for that. Why don't we plan to play some chess after the movie?"

"I'd love to," smiled Sean.

As the pillows were arranged, David also shared, "Sean, if I could ever pick a younger brother, it would be you. I really admire who you are, and I love you enough so I can even forgive you for beating me at just about every game we ever try, you little beggar."

Sean grinned at hearing this brotherly acknowledgment, saying, "Thanks. I'd love to have an older brother like you."

"I'd probably get some black eyes when we wrestled," said David.

"No. I go for areas that can't be seen. You'd only get bruises."

"Comforting," sighed David.

"Want to go?" asked Sean.

"Maybe after the movie," said David tentatively, not knowing what Aunt Lillian would say to a brotherly scuffle. Most women didn't seem to understand the way males played together, but David thought Aunt Lillian would, if any woman did.

Popcorn and soda were enjoyed by all during the movie, after which David and Aunt Lillian cleaned up. Bobby and Sean remained in the living room, rearranging the pillows.

"You know," said Bobby, "we ain't never gonna get off on the right foot till we put some stuff behind us."

"Like what?" asked Sean.

"My *dad* killed Max. *I* didn't. I loved Max," said Bobby.

Sean's eyes started to tear. He had not expected so direct an insight.

A short silence followed as Sean wiped his eyes, saying, "I loved Max, too, and I miss him."

"Me, too," said Bobby. "We all do."

"You got a bum rap. Sorry," said Sean.

"That's okay. But I *still* owe you a big one, from that day you took a month off my life with that toy derringer," warned Bobby.

"That was great, wasn't it?" said Sean.

Bobby laughed, saying, "Yes, it was. But I *still* owe you a big one."

"Okay, okay," said Sean. "I'll remember. But if you do anything, please make it a *really* big one. I don't like halfway measures."

"I'll make it my mission," said Bobby.

"Good. Be lean and mean about it," said Sean.

"Count on it," guaranteed Bobby.

* * * * *

Aunt Lillian and David emerged from the kitchen. Bobby frowned, wondering why David was wearing such a huge smile.

"Bobby and David," announced Aunt Lillian, "why don't you two take Sean up to your bedroom and wrestle a little or push each other around, the ways brothers do? I have some things to do down here and I don't want to be distracted."

"Wow!" said Sean. "You cut a mean figure to POTS, in more ways than one. She'd have a stroke. When my friends come over, she makes us go into the basement. Not much to break down there, although we've done our best."

"Last one up is a rotten egg," announced David, leading the way on the stairwell. Sean scampered after him, so Bobby arrived last.

Entering the room, he got a surprise push from David, who announced, "No rotten eggs allowed."

"I ain't no rotten egg," said Bobby pushing back.

"What are you, then?" asked David.

"What do you think?" asked Bobby.

"A damn dog," said David, laughing. "What am I?"

"A damn fox," said Bobby.

Sean looked at them both as if they had lost their senses. Soon he was laughing, as well, after they shared the history of seeing *The Fox and The Hound.*

"Maybe you look a *little* like a fox, David," observed Sean, "but I'll always think of you as Howdy Doody, fox or not."

"Would you just listen to that—" began Bobby.

"And *now* that you both mention it," continued Sean, looking closely at Bobby, "you *do* look like a damn dog."

"Bow wow," responded Bobby.

"What do foxes do?" asked David. "Anyway, if I'm a fox and Bobby's a dog, Sean's got to be something, too."

"Well, just look at the little magpie," declared Bobby.

"How about a boxer, instead, " pleaded Sean.

"Only *one* dog allowed," said Bobby, "and that's me."

"Magpie?" asked David, looking at Bobby.

"Yes," said Bobby, "A damn magpie."

"Magpie? Really?" asked Sean, looking at David.

"Well, Bobby's right. You *do* talk a lot," said David shrugging his shoulders.

"So we got a damn dog, a damn fox, and a damn magpie," announced Bobby.

"Okay, okay," agreed Sean. "I'm a damn magpie. What's it to you?"

"What's it to *you*," said David, shoving Sean on his left shoulder.

Sean dove at David and they both went scrambling on the floor, a brotherly scuffle into which Bobby quickly followed.

Aunt Lillian had to turn up her music twice to keep from hearing the thuds, crashes, scrapes, cries, and other noises attendant on the fraternal fisticuffs transpiring above her.

For their part, Sean, David, and Bobby all took turns in various permutations of classic two-on-one scenarios, until all confrontations that could be imagined had been exhausted.

Finally, the three struggled downstairs, seeing which one could be the first to get to the kitchen. Sean won, and with it came the honor of selecting which soda would be opened with the cheese twists.

Aunt Lillian joined the boys briefly for a few cheese twists before saying goodnight and retiring for the evening.

David, Bobby, and Sean cleaned up the kitchen and then went back to the bedroom. A sleeping pad had been put out on the floor for Sean prior to his arrival, and now sheets and blankets were added together with a pillow.

"Does the poor little baby have enough blankets?" teased David.

"Do you want to go?" asked Sean.

"Yes!" shouted David, shoving Sean over his own bed and against the far wall and on to the floor.

"That's it," said Sean as he lifted himself up.

"Nobody's gonna bother *my* brother," shouted Bobby as he tackled Sean again. As Sean struggled to get up again, Bobby pushed him down on the floor.

"Nobody's gonna bother *my* brother," shouted David as he tackled Bobby.

Sean realized immediately that he was in the middle of a fraternal initiation, so as soon as Bobby shoved David over, Sean shouted, "Nobody's gonna bother *my* brother!" Immediately he attacked Bobby and sent him crashing to the floor, much to the silent consternation of Aunt Lillian, who began to calculate carpenter repair bills as she tried to doze off to sleep.

Then David shoved Bobby to the floor, and Sean once again shouted, "Nobody's gonna bother *my* brother." Immediately David was tackled by Sean. Soon all three were shoving each other and sticking up for each other until all fell on the floor laughing and breathing heavily from their exhaustion.

Gasping, David said, "Bobby and I *knew* you'd catch on and you did."

"Does that mean we're brothers?" asked Sean.

"Yes, but we're not finished yet," explained David. "Bobby, get the candle."

Soon a sole candle illuminated the room, around which sat three adolescent boys, two waiting to induct the third into their sacred blood brotherhood.

David was uncommonly solemn as he took Bobby's sheath knife from its leather holder. Holding it up to the candle, David intoned, "It was during a blizzard, some weeks ago, when Bobby, bright in fame, and I, the beloved, entered into the sacred covenant of blood brotherhood. This evening, although the winds are calm and the snow sits peacefully on the ground, we return to our sacred bond in order to induct you, Sean, who is gracious of God, into our fraternity. Do you accept the invitation to brotherhood?"

"Yes," said Sean solemnly. "I do."

"Before we can continue with the merging of the blood ritual, we have a sacred covenant that blood brothers keep no secrets from one another. Do you understand?"

Sean puzzled for a moment, and then asked, "Do you mean *any* secrets, or only secrets from each other solely in terms of *our* common relationship?"

David thought hard on Sean's words, realizing that there must be something that Sean didn't feel comfortable revealing, or perhaps couldn't reveal, something that somehow bound them together. Not wanting to intrude on former covenants or promises, David said, "The latter only."

Sean breathed a sigh of relief, and nodded appreciatively to David and to Bobby, who was still trying to understand what had been said.

"I am ready to proceed," announced Sean. "I can honestly state that I have no secrets from either of you, about anything that would hinder our brotherhood."

"Good," said David.

"Do you have any from me?" asked Sean, never missing a trick.

Bobby and David looked at each other, and David nodded.

"Only this, and it is a small matter: during our blood brotherhood ritual in December, we used only a small pin to summon the blood before we mingled our blood together. In respect to your prowess as a warrior, Bobby thought that you would feel a sheath knife more appropriate and manly. We want to offer you the choice. Whichever one you choose will be the one we use. You see me holding the knife. Bobby has the pin."

Sean looked at each one quickly and asked, "Is the knife blade really sharp?"

"Yes," said Bobby.

"Seriously?" asked Sean.

Bobby and David nodded solemnly.

"Then *definitely* the knife," said Sean.

David gulped, although he was not unprepared for Sean's answer.

"Bobby, fetch the Band-aid box and hand towels," David requested.

Bobby returned quickly with the requested items.

"We will each cut our left index finger and then merge our blood together," David announced, handing the knife to Bobby, who took it and made a nick in his own finger and passed the knife on to Sean.

Sean quickly did the same.

Then David, who was feeling a little queasy inside, took the knife and made a similar cut.

The boys then allowed their blood to drip into a small dish, watching the drops as they commingled.

"One blood, one brotherhood," said David, with Bobby and Sean repeating his words.

"One brotherhood, one truth," continued David, whose words were repeated once again.

"One truth, one Light," concluded David, as Bobby and Sean repeated his words.

Moist hand towels were distributed together with Band-aids. After the boys had tended to their fingers, David looked at Bobby and Sean, saying, "Good night, my brothers. Sleep well."

They, in turn, repeated his nocturnal salutation and all then repaired to their respective beds. A rich silence, almost an other worldly fullness, descended on the bedroom as they each fell asleep.

Sean had found not one, but two brothers, brothers whom he had always wanted. His initiation had engendered in him a new loyalty and trust for David and Bobby that superseded any depth of friendship he had hitherto known. In his heart, he knew that he would respect and honor them both as his brothers until his dying day and that they would, in turn, honor him.

As Bobby fell asleep, he was surprised to discover that he was actually becoming fond of the little magpie, all of Sean's energy now seen in the new light of brotherhood that both was somehow tempered and transformed it. He also knew that he still owed the little magpie a big one, but that the little magpie had agreed and would be expecting it. Bobby would bide his time, trusting that just the right situation and opportunity would present itself.

Many feelings and images washed over David's psyche as he fell asleep. He felt closer to Sean and Bobby than he had ever felt to anyone, except his parents and Aunt Lillian. He knew beyond knowledge itself that the loyalty and trust the three had pledged to each other would withstand all of the tests that time and circumstance might bring. He also knew that he would die for either Bobby or Sean, and knew that they would do the same for him, if conditions ever required such a sacrifice.

David wondered what it was that Sean had been reluctant to share. As he considered this, an image of Mr. Astor appeared in his mind. Yes. It was probably something about the mysterious Mr. Astor. But what? No matter. If it proved to be important, it would become known in due course.

As David began to drift off to sleep, he could hear Sean and Bobby begin to snore. The labors of their sleeping didn't impair his own sleep from coming, however, but instead seemed to hasten it. The sounds of their sleep joined a golden light, which began to swirl like a glorious vortex, and then erupted like a fountain of life, spewing from its radiant harvest a golden cornucopia of life, flowering in all directions and into the past, present, and future. It almost seemed an extension of the vision David had experienced when he gave his report on the megafauna the week before. Since that moment, life had somehow seemed larger and more beautiful, mid David's certain knowing that everything that is, or ever was, or ever will be, shares an intimate connection through a common and ubiquitous light, a golden radiance from which all being springs and finds nourishment in its going. Like a Great Dance, a Sacred Wheel, a spiraling galaxy, never ceasing, always creating, ever new, yet somehow always interconnected, the Light was in its utter essence the entire fabric of reality as well as anything that might transcend the limited reality of humanity's five senses. David was now imbued with this sacred wisdom in his heart of hearts, that there is much more to existence than what this shadow world reveals, and he resolved to know as much as possible of these other realities and their many depths before his life ended. He also now knew that death is not an end, but merely a change of worlds, although he couldn't prove it to anyone else. How he would accomplish his new explorations, he had no idea, but he trusted that this inner knowing would guide him to new epiphanies and revelations. The visions he was having went far beyond his ability to comprehend. David resolved that he would not share these strange experiences until he was ready and able to articulate them.

—But how did Mr. Astor know? he wondered. It seemed strange on one level that this mysterious figure would know, but on another level it seemed entirely plausible, even quite correct. Mr. Astor said he would be away for several months. Perhaps new insights would come upon his return in the spring.

—I have *two* brothers now, thought David, feeling within himself the new recognition that had emerged from the bond they have formed in their sacred circle, as he turned over and fell asleep, completely oblivious to their snoring.

Companion Volumes to
An Opening of Heart

The Canasta Capers[1]

Haunted by a recurrent dream that echoes the moments before the tragic deaths of his parents from an accident caused by a drunken driver, David Andrews must relocate to Midville to live with his Great-Aunt Lillian Biggs.

As David grieves his loss, he struggles to find a place in his new community, albeit with the intrusion of a bully and the insensitivity of several faculty at the Midville Middle School. Several new friends come to David's rescue in his determination to find a non-violent way in which to relate to the school bully.

What others have said —

"Steven Swerdfeger has an eye for the details of everyday school rules and rituals that allows him to place his precocious hero and his "Gang of Four" in a convincing setting. Because he also has a feel for the fun that comes from the camaraderie of young people bucking the system, his central theme of a search for fairness and justice in life is rendered lightly. Swerdfeger remembers what it is like to be young and discovering adult hypocrisy for the first time, so he can increase the appeal of his young bunch when he creates richly comic grown-up nemeses for them to challenge. What is more, he knows how to ground the comedy in more muted and serious emotions: the smartest boy in town must confront problems for which there are no easy intellectual solutions, and in the end even the school bully has his own story to tell."

—Paul Howe, Philadelphia, Pennsylvania

"This is a gentle story, told with engaging warmth. Swerdfeger weaves a tale of four middle school children who deal with real life issues, from cutting in on lunch lines to tragic car accidents. Through these experiences, David Andrews learns to turn enemies into friends through compassion."

—Joseph Downing, Syracuse, New York

[1]Originally published in 1996 under the title *Thursday's Child*, and later accorded Finalist Honors in the 1997 Small Press Book Awards.

*Because They Think They Can**

This is a novel about a group of adolescents who encounter a new teacher who refuses to allow them to ignore their school work. At the prospect of failing ninth grade, the class implores classmate David Andrews, a respected advocate, to help them. Mr. Gregory sets as their task the requirement to demonstrate that they 'love learning for learning's sake.' Befuddled by this requirement, the students follow David's advice and form a Learning Club.

The Learning Club invites Mr. Gregory to be its first speaker. He talks about how students learn differently. Owing to Bobby Perkins' disquiet with fallacies, student leaders agree that it would seem most appropriate to invite a psychologist to speak next. Mr. Pennythorpe, the school's affable history teacher, recommends Dr. Clarence Baker, who proves enormously popular. Invited to return, he speaks first on the subject of hypnosis and later leads the club in an experience of guided imagery.

The class is assigned to present its rendering of *Macbeth* to the community, and more bonding results int their frantic efforts to rid themselves of stage jitters. The play is a huge success. An awards dinner follows which recognizes two faculty and the mayor and which distributes ticket proceeds between school and town libraries. Mr. Pennythorpe speaks, but suffers a heart attack before concluding his remarks. As Pennythorpe lies gravely ill, David works through his worry by organizing a welcome home party for his mentor. Cast members join in, and the elderly history teacher returns safely home to conclude his remarks. In his final comments about learning, Pennythorpe likes it to love, for 'the more we can understand, the more we can appreciate, and the more we can appreciate, the more we can love."

*The title is taken from a quotation ascribed to Pliny the Elder, who said of young athletes of his day, "They can because they think they can."

STEVEN SWERDFEGER was born in Massena, New York, on July 13, 1948. He attended local public schools, later entering the State University of New York at Oswego, where he earned his Bachelor of Arts degree in American literature. He also holds a Master of Arts degree in religious education from Princeton Theological Seminary and a Doctor of Philosophy degree in creative writing from the Union Institute & University in Cincinnati, Ohio.

His various career interests have included child care work, teaching high school English, creative writing, church music, hypnosis and guided imagery, college teaching, and publishing.

He is married to Martha Grout Swerdfeger, a physician who serves as Medical Director for the CrossRoads Clinic in Phoenix, Arizona, and who practices under her maiden name Martha M. Grout.

Lucy Swerdfeger was born in Syracuse, N.Y., on November 7, 1982. Having begun formal studies in painting at the age of six, she has studied art with Gale Simon Coleman and Michael White, among others.

Lucy will begin her studies for a B.F.A. in illustration at the Minneapolis College of Art and Design in August of 2005. Her interests include illustration and comic art.

She has kindly allowed her parents to adopt Brody, her tiger cat, while she is away at art school.

Photo credit: Courtesy of Matthew Marchisano

www.ingramcontent.com/pod-product-compliance
Lightning Source LLC
LaVergne TN
LVHW091026080826
845145LV00002B/370

* 9 7 8 1 9 3 2 8 4 2 1 0 4 *